Praise for THE MOUNTAINS WE CALL HOME

"In *The Mountains We Call Home*, Kim Michele Richardson once again displays her seamless blend of research and imagination that we expect in the best of historical fiction. Yet as I read deeper, I realized that Cussy Lovett's journey and challenges (first inside a prison, then a large city), as vivid and compelling as they are, are only part of Richardson's achievement: Her latest novel is also a marvelous reminder of how literacy and literature can heal and give hope, even freedom."

—Ron Rash, *New York Times* bestselling author of *One Foot in Eden* and *Serena*

"No one writes about gritty courageous women like Kim Michele Richardson. *The Mountains We Call Home* is an unforgettable page-turner that captures the dark beauty of Appalachia and its people of Kentucky with their stealth intelligence and covert vulnerabilities."

—Jeannette Walls, #1 *New York Times* bestselling author of *The Glass Castle*

"Brilliant storytelling. Cussy is one of the most dynamic characters in American fiction. Without Kim Michele Richardson's heartfelt, uplifting storytelling, the world would be a sadder place, indeed. I loved *The Mountains We Call Home*, which is woven so seamlessly of important themes that it has the potential for changing lives."

—William Kent Krueger, *New York Times* bestselling author of *This Tender Land* and *Ordinary Grace*

"Kim Michele Richardson brings the story of trailblazing Pack Horse librarian Cussy Mary Carter full circle in this mesmerizing tale of love, resilience, and hardscrabble determination. In the fight to survive prejudice, cruelty, and injustice, Cussy must draw upon her inner strength, the kindness of others, and the sanctuary that can be found within books. An ode to friendship, truth, and the power of the written word, this is a story readers will treasure long after the last page is turned."

—Lisa Wingate, #1 *New York Times* bestselling author of *Shelterwood*

Praise for THE BOOK WOMAN'S DAUGHTER

"For those who loved *The Book Woman of Troublesome Creek*, author Kim Michele Richardson offers another fine evocation of the often cruel conditions of rural Appalachia in the last century and a powerful portrait of the courageous women there who fought against ignorance, misogyny, and racial prejudice. Steeped in an intimate knowledge of the traditions and lore of the region and written with a loving eye to the natural beauty of the landscape, *The Book Woman's Daughter* is a brilliant and compelling narrative sure to please readers already familiar with Richardson's work and to win her a well-deserved host of additional fans."

—William Kent Krueger, *New York Times* bestselling author of *This Tender Land* and *Ordinary Grace*

"A mesmerizing and beautifully rendered Appalachian tale of strong women, bravery, and resilience, told through the eyes of a new heroine reminiscent of Harper Lee's own Scout Finch."

—Ron Rash, *New York Times* bestselling author of *One Foot in Eden* and *Serena*

"In Kim Michele Richardson's beautifully and authentically rendered *The Book Woman's Daughter*, she once again paints a stunning portrait of the raw, somber beauty of Appalachia, the strong resolve of remarkable women living in a world dominated by men, and the power of books and sisterhood to prevail in the harshest circumstances. A critical and profoundly important read for our time. Badass women at their best!"

—Sara Gruen, #1 *New York Times* bestselling author of *Water for Elephants*

"Fierce, beautiful, and inspirational, Kim Michele Richardson has created a powerful tale about brave, extraordinary heroines who are downright haunting and unforgettable."

—Abbott Kahler, *New York Times* bestselling author (as Karen Abbott) of *The Ghosts of Eden Park*

"Kim Michele Richardson's *The Book Woman's Daughter* sets us deep inside Kentucky's rugged Appalachia in the early 1950s and gives us Honey Mary-Angeline Lovett, a sixteen-year-old as fierce and brave as her mama, Cussy Mary. Their world is cruel with its prejudice, and Richardson is not afraid to peel back its ugliness and take us there. But, like the best writers in not only this generation but the ones past, Richardson gifts us readers with something extraordinary, a way back."

—Bren McClain, multi-award-winning author of *One Good Mama Bone*

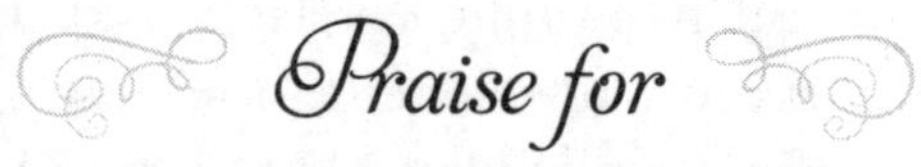

THE BOOK WOMAN OF TROUBLESOME CREEK

"What Richardson has written is a novel about the best of us. And the worst. And has done so with magnificence."

—Bren McClain, award-winning author of *One Good Mama Bone*

"Richardson's latest work is a hauntingly atmospheric love letter to the first mobile library in Kentucky and the fierce, brave Pack Horse librarians who wove their way from shack to shack dispensing literacy, hope, and—just as importantly—a compassionate human connection. Richardson's rendering of stark poverty against the ferocity of the human spirit is irresistible. Add to this the history of the unique and oppressed blue-skinned people of Kentucky, and you've got an unputdownable work that holds real cultural significance."

—Sara Gruen, #1 *New York Times* bestselling author of *Water for Elephants*

"This is Richardson's finest, as beautiful and honest as it is fierce and heart-wrenching. *The Book Woman of Troublesome Creek* explores the fascinating and unique blue-skinned people of Kentucky and the brave Pack Horse librarians. A timeless and significant tale about poverty, intolerance, and how books can bring hope and light to even the darkest pocket of history."

—Abbott Kahler, *New York Times* bestselling author (as Karen Abbott) of *The Ghosts of Eden Park*

"Emotionally resonant and unforgettable, *The Book Woman of Troublesome Creek* is a lush love letter to the redemptive power of books. It is by far my favorite Kim Michele Richardson book—and I am a huge fan. Cussy Mary is an indomitable and valiant heroine, and through her true-blue eyes, 1930s Kentucky comes to vivid and often harrowing life. Richardson's dialogue is note-perfect; Cussy Mary's voice is still ringing in my head, and the sometimes-dark story she tells highlights such gorgeous, glowing grace notes that I was often moved to hopeful tears."

—Joshilyn Jackson, *New York Times* and *USA Today* bestselling author of *The Almost Sisters*

"Kim Michele Richardson has written a fascinating novel about people almost forgotten by history: Kentucky's Pack Horse librarians and 'blue people.' The factual information alone would make this book a treasure, but with her impressive storytelling and empathy, Richardson gives us so much more."

—Ron Rash, *New York Times* bestselling author of *One Foot in Eden* and *Serena*

"A rare literary adventure that casts librarians as heroes, smart, tough women on horseback in rough terrain doing the brave and hard work of getting the right book into the right hands. Richardson has weaved an inspiring tale about the power of literature."

—Alexander Chee, author of *Edinburgh* and *The Queen of the Night*

"With a focus on the personal joy and broadened horizons that can result from access to reading material, this well-researched tale serves as a solid history lesson on 1930s Kentucky. A unique story about Appalachia and the healing power of the written word."

—*Kirkus Reviews*

"This gem of a historical from Richardson (*The Sisters of Glass Ferry*) features an indomitable heroine navigating a community steeped in racial intolerance. In 1936, nineteen-year-old Cussy Mary Carter works for the New Deal–funded Pack Horse Library Project, delivering reading material to the rural people of Kentucky... Readers will adore the memorable Cussy and appreciate Richardson's fine rendering of rural Kentucky life."

—*Publishers Weekly*

"Based on true stories from different times (the blue-skinned people of Kentucky and the WPA's Pack Horse librarians), this novel packs a lot of hot topics into one narrative. Perfect for book clubs."

—*Library Journal*

"Readers will respond to quiet Cussy's steel spine... And book groups who like to explore lesser-known aspects of American history will be fascinated."

—*Booklist*

"Richardson has penned an emotionally moving and fascinating story about the power of literacy over bigotry, hatred, and fear."

—*BookPage*

"A powerful yet heartfelt story that gives readers a privileged glimpse into an impoverished yet rigidly hierarchical society, this time by shining a light on the courageous, dedicated women who brought books and hope to those struggling to survive on its lowest rung. Strongly recommended."

—*Historical Novel Society*

Also by Kim Michele Richardson

The Book Woman's Daughter
The Book Woman of Troublesome Creek
The Sisters of Glass Ferry
GodPretty in the Tobacco Field
Liar's Bench
My Kentucky Moonlight School
Junia, The Book Mule of Troublesome Creek

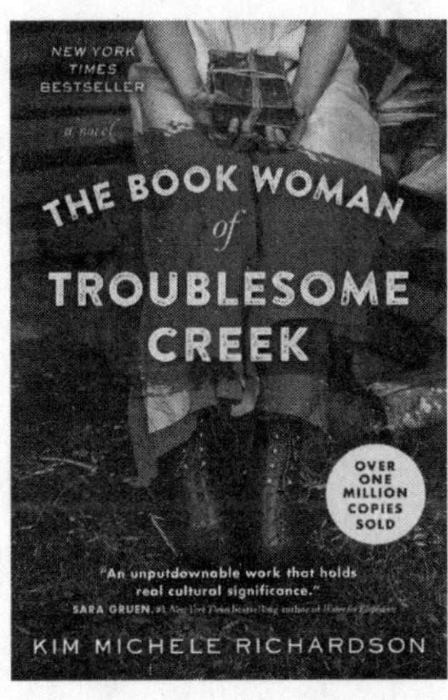

the MOUNTAINS WE CALL HOME

THE BOOK WOMAN'S LEGACY

a novel

KIM MICHELE RICHARDSON

sourcebooks landmark

Cover design by Ploy Siripant
Cover images © Mark Owen/Trevillion Images, Romanova Ekaterina/Shutterstock, alexeys/Getty Images, Lumata/Shutterstock

Published by Sourcebooks Landmark, an imprint of Sourcebooks
1935 Brookdale RD, Naperville, IL 60563-2773
(630) 961-3900
sourcebooks.com

Cataloging-in-Publication Data is on file with the Library of Congress.

Printed and bound in Canada.
FR 10 9 8 7 6 5 4 3 2 1

For Susan Schultz Gibson, a true book warrior
and protective matriarch for the people.

For book angel Dana J. Kenworthy and to the
memory of Grandma Griggs and Eula Mitcham
and all the other Kentucky meemaws—the
grannies who have carried the mantle of courage.

We shall not cease from exploration
And the end of all our exploring
Will be to arrive where we started
And know the place for the first time.

—T. S. Eliot

BOOK ONE

KENTUCKY, 1936

Somewhere among the nestled fissures and cradling dark-blue bluffs, between towns such as Hazard, Hell-fer-Sartain, Kingdom Come, and Troublesome, comes the Book Woman.

Steadfast, she rides her mule through the hollers to deliver books. Where shadow-draped days set between the hills before the blue hour dissolves into coal-dust skies and a new dawn welcomes the rare delight of a children's moon, the Book Woman pushes on.

Along winding paths of marmalade leaves, her faithful beast's steady clip-clops traverse the miles and years while the mothers of the mountains watch over their daughter, who carries the mantle of courage—loosening the stories from Kentucky's bound hands that have been rooted like the poplar and pine, forever tied to the old land.

KENTUCKY, 1953

For more than a decade, the dark hills of Thousandsticks, Kentucky, had swaddled the family, protecting them from those who would hunt their kind.

But this morning a fury swept over the small home stitched inside the pine-bathed woods crowned in March's bitter hoarfrost.

No sooner had the couple seen their daughter safely spirited away into the Cumberland Forest than the lawman descended upon the Book Woman and her husband.

The deputy reached for the woman first, and she raised a hand, trying to shield herself, dropping the pillow she carried.

He grabbed hold of the Book Woman's wrist, twisting the cobalt-blue arm up behind her back, leaving her wailing.

Her husband cursed, his bellows hulling winter bark off trees, and he snatched the official up by the collar, pulling him off his wife. Whipping out a club, the lawman pushed her aside and battered the man until he staggered and fell to the ground.

The woman cradled her injured arm and cried out for her husband as he curled himself into a ball, wrapping his arms over the pain, rocking.

The Book Woman dropped to the stiff frozen grass, hovering over her husband, pleading to the lawman, "*Please, leave us be. Please, sir, spare him.*"

Breathless, her husband struggled to rise but slumped over. Finally, he pulled himself to his knees and bowed his head to his wife's brow. "Don't you give up on us," he said hoarsely.

She brushed a kiss across his hand and pressed it to her wet cheek. He clasped it and whispered into a cardinal's quickening cheer, the cold mist escaping his breaths, "I won't ever give up."

The deputy planted a boot against her husband's shoulder and drove his heel down, breaking them apart. She watched him crumple to the ground, scattering feathers of ice and snow.

Straining, fighting to rise, the man crawled over to his wife.

"*Lie still,*" the deputy shouted.

From the nearby forest rose the fury of the Book Woman's beast, and the maddening screams of the mule's temper blistered the slumbering winter woodland.

Scolding blackbirds flew up from the trees, their blackening bursts splatted against blue skies, strangling her husband's weakened protests.

In the distance, the sheriff's automobile appeared, spraying up muddy slush. A moment later, he stepped out and motioned his deputy toward the couple's home, where the two lawmen huddled on the porch in muted conversation.

The Book Woman's gaze fell to their dirty boots planted on the worn boards atop the scattered feathers of the bed pillow and its angel crown she had been in the process of burying.

The task still lingered, its prophecy now a riddle.

She turned away to look once more at her husband before the lawman shoved her into his automobile. Swiping a palm across the fogged window, the Book Woman tried to touch it all one last time.

Soon the miles separated and the years passed, the yearning for home smoldering. Spoken of rarer as time went on but always present, the longing would not stay silenced.

Their hungers had been knitted in bone, perennial and as old as the cragged mountains of Kentucky, protected by fierce hearts that could not easily be splintered.

From time to time, amid the deafening pulleys of grinding cities, she'd close her eyes, and together they were pulled back to their wilded hearts inside the tree-thick woods. There, she'd walk alongside him on paths of knotted ivy and spring blooms, the earth's carpets trumpeting her freedom.

One

There was no undoing the crime of my pertinacious heredity.

I remained a Blue.

Imprisoned, the legacy collared with a weighted neck chain.

After spending nearly a month locked inside the infirmary, stripped of all clothing and even my necessaries, I was finally given back the penitentiary garb and assigned a permanent cot in the general population. But not before they'd taken everything.

Daily, I'd suffered the doctors' brutal, invasive examinations and their crippling drugs to rid me of the color that they felt had cursed me. That had vexed the Commonwealth.

A color that instilled fear because of a mere medical condition that me and my kin had inherited.

Since I'd arrived, my normal soft robin's-egg-blue skin remained darkened to cobalt, a telltale sign that would betray the slightest emotion—fear, anger, grief, and even an unexpected burst of happiness.

My husband, Jackson, had pressed for us to move north, far away from the hills of ol' Kaintuck. The home I loved, the puzzle I could never quite fit into. But I had refused to give up my ancestors' homestead, instead hoping one day minds would change—that one day *I* would be enough to change them.

The guard called out to me, drawing me from my troubling thoughts. "Lovett, hurry it up and grab your stuff." He jangled his keys against the metal crash gate, turning the lock.

I picked up the pillowcase with the prison belongings, my flesh sweaty and itching under the cast the medical staff had placed over the splintered bones after the lawman broke my arm during the arrest.

"Move, Lovett," the impatient guard ordered.

I followed him out of the infirmary as he led me down darkened corridors, the scents of disinfectants, disappointments, and sorrows draping the musty Kentucky institution.

While he fumbled with the lock at another massive, barred crash gate, I stared at the thin shadows shivering across a homemade calendar's bold, penciled-in dates. Someone had scrawled *April 1st 1953* across the top of a Big Chief school tablet page and taped it onto the grimy prison wall.

April.

The promise of spring had finally arrived, but the institution stayed perennially frozen in its own merciless dead winter.

We passed through more doors and by locked cages full of hemmed-in women milling about, the guard's heavy footsteps echoing atop their murmurs.

When we approached the next wing, tormented howling and weeping rivered against cemented walls. I looked ahead at the sign and shivered.

The officer stopped in front of the Forensic Ward to speak to a fellow guard, and I gripped the sack of meager belongings to my chest as the terror pummeled inside me. From the row of locked cells, a swell of guttural cries climbed from the hidden women, tearing at my very being.

I'd seen some of the women come through the infirmary. The ward was for inmates afflicted with bizarre and sometimes explosive behaviors, while others were plagued by the hysterics—and many of the torments and malaises that stumped doctors.

"Hi, Frank. The circus freaks are louder than usual. What's got 'em riled up now?" the escorting officer asked.

"Nurse is late with her nightly medication rounds, and there was another suicide," Frank said nonchalantly, picking at his teeth with a ragged fingernail. "Is that the Blue from the infirmary?"

"Yeah."

"You must be April foolin' me. Didn't get notice she'd been assigned to me."

I tugged at the collar, fear tightening my throat.

"I'm taking her to wing B, though if she doesn't stop scaring the women"—he dipped his head and scowled at me—"Warden will be sending her your way. Crazy blue witch has everyone skittish."

"I wonder if her blood's blue? Heard it wasn't like ours." Frank cocked his head at me, staring as if it would spew any minute.

It weren't. Instead, the old mountain doc had explained methemoglobinemia caused it to be a chocolate brown because there's less oxygen in me and my kin's blood.

Frank snapped his fingers. "She reminds me of that one I had in my ward a few years back…" He snapped again. "I 'member now, it was Faye. Yeah, Faye Nash—"

"The Melungeon," the other officer answered.

"The *mongrel.*" Frank snorted. "Always claiming she was white."

"Ol' Faye failed more than the one-drop rule," the corrections officer clucked. "Girl had herself a bucket of mixed-mutt blood, if not a bathtub full." He leaned in to Frank and murmured something while I backed against the wall and tried to make myself small.

The officer studied me out of the corner of his eye and whispered again to Frank.

They drew their eyes to my breasts, then dropped gazes downward. The men suddenly laughed.

I tucked my chin in tighter and stared down at my feet.

"Say, real sorry to hear about you and Ginny's loss," the guard said to Frank.

Frank shifted uncomfortably. "We'd been hoping this one

would be the one to make it, but the baby…" He rubbed his brow and turned his back to me. "Well, after losing three, it don't appear we'll ever—" His voice dipped lower.

The men talked in hushed tones until the guard suddenly barked at me. I cocked my head, trying to make out what he'd said. I was muddled in one ear, and sometimes my hearing didn't pick up words in my good one. The *muddled* came and went ever since my first husband had ruptured my eardrum. Especially when the fear pounded from my ticker and reached up beyond the lobes, drowning out everything.

I looked at him quizzically.

"Said, *follow me*."

Relieved, my legs nearly collapsing, I moved away from the weeping women inside.

Another corridor led us past the Geriatric Ward, with about a dozen inmates inside the barred wing. A graveyard of reed-thin ghosts moaned in beds while some of the elderly women were folded into tatty wheelchairs, eyes blank, weighted in agony, others with lids shut tight as if the horrors would cease if they couldn't see them. A putrid soup of feces and urine overpowered the disinfectants hovering in the halls. The guard coughed, and I buried my nose against my bag of belongings, but it weren't no match for the odor. I gagged as the smells slithered down my throat, knotting my innards.

When we turned into a dimly lit hall and passed a metal door with faded, red-blocked letters that read DEATH ROW, I stood stock-still, gawking at the sign.

"Lucky for you, that's not your stop. *Today*." He gestured ahead.

Finally, he paused in front of wing B and reached for his keys. "In here." He shoved me over the threshold into the dormitory. Voices quieted, and all eyes fell on me.

Waiting for his next order, I studied the nearly two dozen inmates and double rows of cots lining opposite walls.

"You're there," he said, stretching an arm toward the woman

lying on a mattress with her back turned. "She's the only one who didn't bellyache about your color and volunteered the empty bed beside her."

I couldn't help but wonder why. The others they'd tried to put me with claimed my disorder had given them nightmares, and after their screams awakened the dormitory wing, the corrections officer believed them and spirited me back to the infirmary.

The guard knocked the toe of his boot against the woman's metal bed frame. "Waldeen Parker, your new bedfellow's here." Then to me: "You'd do well to sleep with one eye open with this 'un, Lovett." The guard kicked her bed again. She ignored him. "Parker, she's been assigned kitchen duty. Have her there at four sharp."

When he left, I set my pillowcase on the narrow mattress, stealing peeks at the woman. I'd heard slips of prison prattles from the nurses about Waldeen Parker, the inmate in charge of the kitchen. The old woman had been in the Kentucky State Reformatory far longer than anyone could remember, serving time for shooting a man. Occasionally, she'd brought trays to the infirmary. More than once, I'd caught her staring at me with questioning eyes.

I arranged my clothes, toiletries, and the assigned Bible inside the wooden footlocker at the end of the bed.

The woman shifted her bones, keeping her face locked from my sight. "Call me Waldeen. What are ya in for, kid?"

I looked down at my cast, rubbed it alongside the stitching on the mattress, then tucked in the sheet and thin blanket. "Cussy Lovett. I'm in here for marrying."

"No crime in that unless ya killed him." Waldeen laughed.

I winced. I'd done just that to my first husband. Unlike during my second marriage, we'd stood before a yawning officiant and his suspicious-looking wife on a cold winter's eve in '36. During the ceremony, when he'd asked if anyone objected, not his woman nor the sleeping rabbit dog in the corner of his cramped kitchen, nor the field mouse scurrying behind the woodstove, nor anyone in all of Kaintuck raised a whispered protest.

Yet the objection had rang loud in my knotted throat.

Our arranged union ended as abruptly as it began when the old man, Frazier, turned dog-pecker pink while beating and raping me in our marriage bed. Then he'd collapsed, and soon a veil of spoiled bologna-gray spread across his anguished face. Doc said his ticker done broke, but it always felt more like I'd willed it to.

It was only after I married again that the sheriff forbid it.

Waldeen turned over partway to study me, her fair cheeks gaunt, hollowing with age.

A broke ticker that had done ticked its last thieving tick. I rested the unspoken truth. "For miscegenation. I'm a Blue, but the man I married isn't."

Jackson sat in a cold cell in the men's penitentiary down the road.

She swung her feet over the side of the cot, pulling herself up. "You in here for long? I'm sixty-two, a lifer, and it'll be twelve more years before I come up for parole."

"I'm thirty-six. I'll be here for eighteen months."

"Still young—and if you keep out of trouble, they could parole ya."

When I'd made my bed, I sat down on the chair at the small wooden table between our cots. A stack of books, a tin soup-can ashtray, one cigarette, and a matchbook cluttered it. An old photograph peeked out of one of the books.

Waldeen pointed to my cast. "When ya getting that off?"

"They said in about two or three weeks."

"Do you know your arithmetic?"

"I was schooled by Mama."

"Okay, I guess ya can help me with my kitchen budget. Until they saw it off, I'll assign you to light cleaning."

Lighting a cigarette, she dug inside her pillow slip and withdrew a dollar, wadding it in a tight fist. "Over here, Teresa,"

Waldeen called out to a girl busy sneaking glances over her shoulder for guards as she silently peddled a pack of Lucky Strikes. The cigarette dangled from Waldeen's lips as she waved the money. Teresa snatched up the dollar, then passed her a handful of cigarettes and a tattered matchbook advertising a near-naked lady. When a pale, green-eyed woman stopped to sell her pills, Waldeen shooed her away.

Another woman came by carrying a stack of paperback books and darted her eyes between me and Waldeen. "Hey, hon," she told the older women. "Thought I'd give you first pick and save you a trip downstairs. Just got in some *new* novels." A secret played across her wriggling brows.

Waldeen stuffed one of Teresa's cigarettes into a book on the table and handed it back to her.

"Was in a hurry, but you be sure and rip off these covers, Waldeen." The woman winked and gave her two books.

Waldeen looked around, then held up an excitement novel, *Shriek with Pleasure* by Toni Howard, and tapped the cover of a busty blond tempestuously smoking a cigarette in bed with her lover. "This looks good."

I gawked, astonished that the prison would allow such a racy read.

Mistaking my surprise for disapproval, Waldeen wrinkled her brow. "You don't like books?"

"I'm fond of the books, sure enough." I found myself relieved and also somewhat surprised she still hadn't brought up my color, grateful the talk had shifted.

"You can borrow it when I'm done." She tore off the cover. "Oh, look at this one, kid," Waldeen whispered, picking up another novel. "I've been waiting for *Kiss Me Deadly*. It's Spillane's latest." The woman blew out a lusty sigh. "Our prison librarian made parole. She's outta here in a few weeks. They're sure gonna have a hard time getting someone to replace her."

I watched the librarian pass out books, remembering my long

days on the Pack Horse librarian route in Troublesome Creek. Riding those swaddling hills with my mule, Junia.

"Well, kid"—Waldeen stubbed out her cigarette—"lights out in a few minutes. Four o'clock will get here soon enough. Better get some rest; you're gonna need it tomorrow."

Tomorrow. Measured minutes for another desperate day.

After I'd washed up in the facilities and changed into a night-shift, I climbed onto my sagging cot and pulled the threadbare blanket up over me.

Waldeen reached out, grabbed the small photograph inside her book, and held it up for me to see. The picture showed her holding a little boy who couldn't be more than two or three. Leaning in closer, I studied the photograph, not daring to pry but wondering if he was a child or grandchild. Still, there was something vaguely familiar about the boy.

I smiled when she kissed the crinkled picture and placed it in her new read to bookmark a page.

Then my mind pulled to my own child back home, wishing I had a photograph of her, worried how sixteen-year-old Honey was faring down in Troublesome Creek after we'd hidden her from the law and sent her over to stay with a family friend. *Was she safe? Would the law come after her too?*

The lights went out.

I crooked my arm under my head, the cast smelly and loosely fitted now.

How I missed my old life. Missed everyone and everything, big and small. My husband. Honey. Junia. A cry escaped my breath. The old woman settled deeper into her bed, and I pressed a palm over my mouth and swallowed Jackson's name, feeling it squeezing my breath until I thought it would shatter me.

"They all cry at first. Go ahead and let it out. The tears will nourish the courage to survive," she croaked.

Turning to the wall, I muffled my sorrows into a flat pillow as the last leaving hour seeped through curtainless, barred windows, crawling into halls, swallowing the remains of the day.

The second hand on the institutional clock ticked loudly, sweeping its time into another lonely night, another lost soul, before smothering the titters of stale conversations and desperate fevered prayers.

Restless, I turned over and my gaze fell to Waldeen's neatly stacked shadow of books.

Something from long ago stirred inside and began to take root.

I balled my palm over the frayed coverlet—unrolling, squeezing, and rolling—the comforting rhythm quieting inside.

For the first time since I'd arrived in early March, a small hope budded, and finally my restless body stilled and lids drooped as the last thoughts slipped into the quieter hours of slumber.

Two

Books: a sanctuary for my heart.

I'd found a small joy to have purpose again, though I know'd Pa would've scolded my temerity for pursuing such a notion if he were alive.

For two days, I waited to see the warden. After I finished my light chores in the kitchen, I'd ask permission from the officer on duty, and he came back with the same answer: "Warden is busy."

On the third day, a guard finally led me into Warden Sanders's office, my hands stained an ink-blue from anticipation, my mind racing with the proposal I'd rehearsed every day and now again in the long ticking moments I'd been waiting in the small alcove outside her office.

A ribbon of cigarette smoke escaped out the door as I stepped through its lingering haze into her office. I stood before the small, matronly lady seated at the large desk, my fingers laced behind my back, doing my best not to squirm under her piercing gaze.

Warden Sanders stubbed out her cigarette, her pale fingers discolored and yellowing. "You wanted to see me, Lovett?" she snapped, the annoyance flitting across her eyes, spotting her cheeks as she reached behind her and clicked the knob of an old walnut-stained Philco radio, silencing the staticky buzz of an announcer's voice. She pushed aside a four-welled glass ashtray filled with butts and twined her clenched fingers atop the desk.

"Yes, ma'am. About the prison librarian position."

She held up a piece of paper. "It says you were assigned kitchen duty. Are you trying to get an easy ride in here? Maybe thinking prison librarian would be a cakewalk?" she said harshly.

"No, ma'am. *No*. I'm keeping the kitchen books and doing whatever I'm asked until they cut my cast off."

Her mouth tightened. "Lovett, that old mountain doctor may've had some pull from the governor to get you out of my infirmary, but you're still here. And while you're still here, I'm governor *and* God. Is that clear?"

I flinched. Ol' Doc from back home had visited me in the infirmary and made a fuss, insisting I be sent to the city hospital so he could examine me himself for the prison mistreatment I'd suffered. Then he'd demanded that the penitentiary medical staff stop examining me. But I didn't realize he'd gone to the governor. "Yes, ma'am, it's clear."

"You think you can come in here without any qualifications?"

"No, Warden, I used to work—"

"Librarian is a great responsibility, with many duties involved."

The telephone on her desk buzzed and she pressed a button. A man spoke. "The director is on line two, Warden."

She lifted the black receiver and snapped, "Back to work, Lovett. And the next time you come looking for what you *think* is an easy job, I'll load you up with kitchen *and* laundry-room duties."

Her threat came to light sooner than I thought, and not because I'd gone back to the warden. It was a warning to make sure I never would, and one I'd heeded. She'd gone and saddled me with double duties.

After I checked the numbers from ordering kitchen supplies and wiped down the tables, I rushed to my next job.

Inside the laundry room, hot steam scalded my face as blinding droplets dripped from my brow. Awkwardly, I set the electric iron down, bumping it against my flesh. I blew on the stinging burn.

My casted arm was still weak and pained, its strength slow to return. And the electric machine weren't nothing like Mama's sad iron. Instead, it felt clumsy, heavy, and I struggled with the long cord while trying to keep the blistering hot plate from burning me.

"Lovett, get those officers' uniforms pressed, and stop your spuddling," the supervisor ordered.

Again, I raised the iron and tried to press a guard's white dress shirt. Suddenly, the stink of smoke drifted up, and I pulled the electric machine off the fabric. To my horror, I found a yellowish-brown scorch that looked like it might eat the cloth and disappear any second.

The supervisor snapped a wet towel across my back. The iron fell from my hand, bumping off my shin, skinning flesh. "Dammit, are you daft, too, Lovett?" She whipped out the towel again, striking my leg. "That could've been me."

I winced and gingerly touched my bloodied, burned shin. "I've never used one of these before. Only my sad iron that I'd heat atop our woodstove. No one in Troublesome had electricity and—"

"You're *troublesome*, and I've had enough of your *troublesome* work. Look what you've done to the officer's new shirt," she hissed.

I swallowed hard and slid my palm over the cloth, hiding the deed. I'd ruined the expensive, store-bought garment.

A guard strolled over. "What's going on over here, Estelle?" He looked to her and then over to me.

"Nothing, sir. Just one of the irons overheating again," she grumbled and stabbed me with a hot glare.

Bored, the officer shrugged and moved on.

Estelle snatched my good arm and whispered angrily, "Get your leg cleaned up 'fore you get blood on the fresh laundry and ruin more. Then start over there folding the sheets and prison dresses before I snitch and have your ugly ass thrown into the lockup myself."

"Yes, ma'am." I limped toward the lavatory.

"Dumb and daft," Estelle said, her words sliding through tight-tucked teeth toward the other women, but just loud enough to make sure I heard.

I stiffened, squeezed a fist, but kept moving.

Inside the washroom, I cleaned the wound and splashed water on my face, feeling the exhaustion of my double duties.

I'd been sleeping only three hours a night, and the workload had taken its toll.

That evening when I prepared for bed, a young woman with cropped auburn curls snarled as she passed by. "Keep away," she barked me back, clutching a stack of books.

"Over here, Regina," someone called out to her.

The warden had assigned her *the librarian job.*

Envy crawled across my hand, staining.

I sat on the side of my bed and watched the young woman hand out books and then pass right over me, though I held up my hand and motioned to her.

Waldeen returned from closing the kitchen. "Cussy, you best get some rest." She stubbed out her cigarette in the tin can, stretched across her bed. "I need ya in the kitchen at three tomorrow morning to break down the freezers. We got us a big delivery coming in the afternoon. Did you go over the numbers like I asked?"

"They're all good, and we're on budget."

She nodded, pleased.

I pulled back my cover and slipped into bed, continuing to study Regina while she delivered the reads. My eyes followed her as she chatted happily about the books she passed out. Then one inmate grabbed a book and ripped off the cover, tossing it onto the floor. Regina gasped, and her pale face reddened as she picked up the torn read.

Suddenly, the librarian struck the woman across the face with a book. She screeched and rubbed her jaw.

A guard yelled, "You've been warned about this. One more time, Regina Miles, and I'll write you up."

Regina held up the damaged read, offended, a protest budding on her lips. "But it's a book, dammit. *Book*. You can't go treating 'em like that," she said reverently, as if it were a Bible.

In that moment, I could see the rebellions of youth and how deeply she cared for her job, and I felt the whisper of a kindred spirit despite her cruelty.

"*One more time*," the guard repeated.

I eased out of my cot, plucked the cover from the floor, and held it up to Regina. "I can bind this for you, and it'll be as good as new."

Regina looked torn for a second, like she might accept my offer. But just as quick, her eyes turned switchblade deadly. "Bind this, Grape Stain." She raised the book and threw it at me.

I caught it in mid-air.

The guard boomed, "*Girl*, I said one more time, and I damn well meant it."

Three

One more time was all it took for Regina to be stripped of her library duties.

Daily, I debated on whether to ask the warden for the job again and risk her piling on more responsibilities. In the end, I decided sleep was more important.

Inside the kitchen, I blew on my arm, the latest burn still pained from my afternoon in laundry, worrying if I could ever properly use the heavy newfangled contraption or when my arm might fully heal and leave me less clumsy.

I'd destroyed one prison dress and three guards' shirts last week alone and had at each time suffered the supervisor's wrath. Fearful of Estelle and her devil machine, I felt my hands shake as soon as she ordered me to press the laundry. It didn't take long before I started believing that maybe I *had* gone daft.

Stupid. Idiot. Imbecile. She'd hurl the insults with such fervor that soon a few of the women in Laundry picked up on her cruelty and followed suit. And it weren't no time before the harsh words turned to vicious slaps and shoves.

It was all I could do but climb into the cot each evening to escape. But like the wild Kentucky tobacco flower that awakens only at night to sip the moon, the bloom of grief opened to pull in the pain and loneliness swallowing me.

Waldeen interrupted my thoughts as I squeezed out the kitchen mop with one hand. The supervisor stood there for a moment, studying me before pulling out a pack of Winstons from her apron. She offered me a cigarette. "Helps numb the nerves some."

I shook my head. There weren't enough tobacco in all of Kaintuck to do that.

She glanced at my new wound and sighed. "I see you're still having troubles in Laundry."

"It'll get better once my arm is healed and I can handle the bulky iron."

Waldeen reached over and grabbed a gallon can of institutional green beans. "When you get that cast off, take this and lift it every chance you get until that arm builds back its muscle." She raised it several times. "It'll take another month for it to right itself."

"Obliged, ma'am."

"You've done a good job helping me keep the books, especially with Warden breathing down my back about the budget. Not everyone can do that. For the first time in a long time, we've stayed out of the red. Most of these girls peel away the meat of the potatoes and carrots, leaving nubs. Throw away heels from the loaves of bread. Waste so much. But not you. You stretch the food and help the cook make use of everything they give us." She snorted. "It's like ya know hunger."

Starvation. I'd felt its burning in my gut too many times, the pains knocking around my cramping, empty belly. The hills had been filled with those living off nothing but mashed bean sandwiches and nettle soups, or suffering the pellagra when I rode the library route in the thirties.

"Go on, put your mop up, Cussy. Warden is waiting to see ya about monthly reports."

I stared at her, riddled by the unexpected summons.

"Go on, kid. It's not wise to keep Boss Lady waiting."

Quickly, I folded my apron and scurried out of the kitchen.

As I made my way to Warden Sanders's office, I fretted on what the laundry supervisor might have said about me. Inside her office, the warden seemed pleased, but I'd found out that moods quickly shifted behind these gloomy walls.

I squirmed under her gaze.

Warden finally cast her eyes to the papers. "Let's see, you've been working in Laundry for several weeks now. Your work has been pretty good despite your clumsiness with that cast." The last word dripped into a hiss.

"Yes, ma'am. I'm still learning the electric iron, sure enough."

She studied some notes. "Estelle says that while you work hard, you have too many mishaps and it's costing her money—*me* money."

Estelle had reported the losses.

"Yet Waldeen notes how much money you saved the kitchen. Hmm. In fact..." Warden ran her finger down the page and tapped. "The numbers are the best I've seen in years. She credits that to you."

I felt my face warm, pleased that the kitchen supervisor appreciated my work.

"Waldeen is impressed. And when Waldeen is impressed, so am I. She has vast experience with bigger numbers, given her former occupation."

I looked at her, perplexed. Waldeen didn't talk much about her life before prison.

"Did you receive a formal education, Lovett?"

"I'm book read, sure enough, and learned from my mama and the books everything I needed."

"I see," she said, airish. "It's a shame. Very few in here have education or formal training beyond fourth grade, if that."

"I handled my pa's finances and cataloged and took care of the library books just fine."

"*Library.*" The warden tapped a pen on the desk.

I held my tongue, anxious to learn why she'd sent for me. I'd found out no one ever went to the warden's office unless it involved punishment. *What could I offer her to make up for the damaged clothing?* Then I took a small step forward.

"Warden, I don't have money, but I can work the laundry debt off somehow."

She pulled away from her quietness and drew her attention back to me. "The prison purchases the clothing in bulk. Even with a discount, the garments still run about thirty-three cents each. What do you propose, Lovett?"

I glanced at the small bookshelf behind her desk filled with dusty books and tattered covers. "I'm good at binding. I can even make scrapbooks for the library to be loaned out."

"We're about to lose our small library and more because of lack of funding and our low literacy rate." She dismissed my offer with a flick of her wrist. "Now a lot of the prisons are making reading a prerequisite before an inmate can apply for parole. If I don't follow suit and make this happen, I could lose—"

She stopped herself and gave a quick shake to her head. But I know'd it meant losing her job.

I dared to speak. "I could raise the literacy rate—grow readers."

"Are you asking about the librarian position again? You were just in here." Her eyes narrowed. "You should heed warnings."

"Yes. *No, ma'am.* I wanted to help—"

"Running a library is no easy feat, Cussy Lovett. It's tedious work and not as cushy as you may think—and what I generally assign to more experienced, educated girls," she chided. "Even Regina has her high school certificate."

"I have experience, Warden," I gently pushed.

The warden rested her elbows on the desk and lightly pressed her fingertips together.

"Ma'am, I was a Pack Horse librarian for many years in Troublesome Creek under the WPA, beginning in 1935. I delivered thousands of books on my mount and grow'd lots of readers out in them hills." I paused, gauging if Warden would silence me. When she didn't, I continued, "In 1940, the Kentucky Federation of Women's Clubs gave me an award for outstanding librarian service and dedication. I believe I could do a good job for you if—"

She cocked her head, staring in disbelief, shuttering my next words. "Why, I've read several articles about the Works Progress Administration. And there was such a librarian over in War Branch—or maybe it was in Beauty—who used to visit her aunt here in Pewee Valley."

"We had lots of book women in them parts. Some were even working near the big city of Louisville."

"Sit down," she ordered, her eyes softening a little as she pointed to the chair. "Tell me more about the program."

"When outsiders came in and told us we were poor, the government set about fixin' it. Us. The women only had two options, the WPA said: Join its sewing project or deliver books."

"Yet you remained poorer from the stingy coins Roosevelt and his program courted you with."

"It was good pay, ma'am. A steady twenty-eight dollars a month for us womenfolk."

"Hmph."

For the next twenty minutes, we talked quietly. And with each passing moment, I could see something changing in the standoffish warden. That we were on equal ground, her sour face fading, opening with pleasure, friendly and welcoming, as we chatted and reminisced about our favorite reads and authors. The many families I had served back home.

"*Grow'd readers*, you say?" The warden chuckled lightly and checked her wristwatch.

I straightened. "Yes, ma'am, I did."

"We have very few readers in here. Too few. If I don't get those numbers up, my other programs will be in jeopardy. We already receive fewer funds than the men's prison. And they'd love nothing more than to strip my funds to supply more gym equipment over there for the men," Warden Sanders grumbled.

"I'd like to pay back my laundry debt and help raise your literacy rate."

She drummed her fingertips atop the desk, pondering.

"I'll work hard to keep your library, Warden." I held my breath, waiting for the stale air to collapse between us, suddenly realizing I might again be worrying for more punishment instead.

"If I assign you the job, Lovett, it would only be temporary. I have one hundred and seven inmates, and if you could get me more readers, we could possibly see about making it a permanent position."

I clasped hopeful hands onto my lap, feeling the prospect shoot up from my feet to my face.

She noted my loud talking hands take on a deeper coloring. "You've been cleared by the prison doctors, and they say you aren't infectious, correct?"

"It's a gene disorder called methemoglobinemia."

"There's still the matter of your appointment with Dr. Kennedy this summer. We'll have to take care of that."

That? What was *that* about? "He'll find that I'm fit, sure enough, Warden," I insisted despite my confusion. "In fact, when Doc gave me the drug methylene blue back in Troublesome, I looked just like you."

"If this is true, why hasn't prison medical given it to you?"

"I don't reckon they know about methemoglobinemia like my doc did. And the methylene blue drug makes me awfully ill."

She waved my words away. "No matter. The state feels you will be a lot better off after the procedure."

After the procedure? Would I have to suffer more exams? They'd sterilized me and taken enough of me. Stole my womanhood. Left the splinters of shame stitched in my womb. *What more could they possibly take?*

"I'm healthy, and once I get the cast off, I'll be more than fit." I shot her what I hoped was a favorable smile.

She looked uncertain, then opened her drawer and held up a key. "I'm desperate to keep the funding, so you'll have to do. I'll dismiss you from Laundry, but understand, I'm not releasing you from kitchen duties, Lovett. You'll be working long hours. Four a.m. till six p.m. while you're the temporary librarian. I expect you to open the library at nine a.m. and work it in between your kitchen shifts. You'll close it when you go to the kitchen…"

I listened closely as she rattled off her rules.

"The pay is nine cents a day. Which I'll put on your commissary account *after* we deduct what you owe for the damaged clothing."

Pay. I couldn't believe my luck. I would finally be able to buy stamps to write Honey.

"Still want the job?" She looked doubtful that I could handle the work, when really, I was thrilled and welcomed the long hours and the escape the job would give.

"Yes, ma'am. The Pack Horse librarians were used to hard work."

"I remember hearing such. Now, about selecting reading material, Lovett. We must be careful."

I hoped she wouldn't ask me to censor books. Anxious, I waited for her to frame my thoughts.

"You'll need to send out solicitations for reading material. The prison will provide you with a typewriter and paper."

"I did this for the project. I'll send letters right away to the Federation of Women's Club, Boy Scouts, city libraries, and the Parent-Teacher Association for donations."

She cast an approving glance my way. "Now, back to the materials you'll need to curate."

I straightened in my seat.

"Racy excitement books are not allowed. I only care about lowering our illiteracy rate, not raising more trouble into easily excitable women. Understood?"

I hid my disapproval. "I'll get started on the letters today, Warden." Bending closer, I held open my darkened palm, waiting for the key, overjoyed to be back working with books—to have purpose again.

The warden dangled the key in front of me, and I know'd she was scared to touch me. I extended my palm a little farther, desperate for this magical gift, a promised escape from Laundry and these dismal walls. "I'll work hard for you, ma'am."

Hesitant, she pinched her lips and dropped the library key into my waiting hand.

My tight shoulders slipped down from my ears, the strain of hopelessness suddenly lightened.

Four

Waldeen snatched the basket of potatoes from my hands. She set it on the steel countertop and opened the utility closet. "I can no longer ignore the complaints. It's bad enough the girls are afraid of you, Cussy, but now the guards say they don't want ya touching their food."

The words wounded me, and before I could think, I attacked with my own. "My color's not poisonous. The poison lies in their minds."

Waldeen slightly raised a brow.

I looked down at my burning hands and rattled off an apology to the supervisor.

She shrugged. "The guards insist, kid. And now that the cast is off, I'm assigning ya to regular cleanup." She pulled out a mop. "Grab the bucket and fill it. The work will build up that weak arm."

"I'll get started right away." I'd been shunned by everyone but her, called names like *blueberry* and *ink blot* and *ink stain* and *grape juice*. And I'd glimpsed the fear of most of the women when they saw me passing. Worse, the anger that would light across those distrustful eyes.

Pa'd always said there was a fire in that kind of anger, and those folks had a hard difference in them—one that would burn.

"When you're done mopping, start washing trays," Waldeen said quietly.

I looked up at the clock, worried it would be lights out before I could get my first look at the library.

Hours later, Waldeen tapped my shoulder as I finished drying a pot. "It's nearly nine o'clock. You've been cleaning since four. Go open your library."

Relieved, I untied my apron and placed it under the counter.

"Be back a half hour before dinner," she reminded.

Only *two* hours to have the library open. I raced down darkened halls and barreled toward crash gates, tapping a foot while I waited for an officer to unlock them. Once on the other side, I sped past the guard who yelled, "*Walk.*"

I tucked my head and marched briskly, slowing as I passed the noisy Forensic Ward, then stopped at Geriatrics. I was struck by how a place so quiet could be so loud—the despair was screaming across the elderly women's eyes.

I picked up my pace, putting the distance between us.

Inside the library, I was surprised to see the room weren't much bigger than the Outreach Center in Troublesome Creek, where the Pack Horse librarians had housed and logged books. Four heavily scarred bookshelves held the meager reading material, and weren't much to it at that. Torn paperbacks and a dozen hardcovers, with some missing pages and others written in. There were two shelves full of dusty encyclopedias that looked like they'd never been used, and a brand-new book still in a mailing wrapper marked several months ago. I pulled it out and placed *Charlotte's Web* onto the shelf.

At once, I went to work, cataloging all the reads. After, I sat at the small desk in the corner and typed solicitation letters on the typewriter, then locked up and rushed back to the cafeteria.

Again, I swept and mopped floors, washed down tables, and scrubbed trays, keeping one eye on the clock. I'd put up the last pot when Waldeen called out, "Hold up, Cussy."

"Waldeen?" I dried my hands, puckered from the hot dishwater, and followed her through the steel butler doors, scanning the clean kitchen, trying to figure out what I'd done wrong.

Waldeen busied herself over at the counter. "Come get it, kid." She lifted a tea towel off a tray. "You didn't eat breakfast, and now you're leaving without dinner. Second rule I have running my kitchen is, treat your girls like precious rubies and they'll return the gratitude in gold. A homemade meal of roast beef and real mashed potatoes. You won't find this coming from any of them cans of food in the pantry. Eat, kid. Enjoy."

"Sure smells good," I said, surprised by my appetite. Lately, I hadn't had one. No matter how they fixed the meals, I could still taste the metal from the canned foods they used to prepare dishes.

"I always save the best for my hardworking girls. Eat your corn pone while it's hot. And there's some fresh banana pudding that Patsy just whipped up."

I swallowed the last bite of dessert, wiped my mouth with the tail of my apron, and turned toward the cook while I savored the sweet milk and chocolate shavings she'd made it with. "Obliged. It's delicious."

"It was Meemaw's recipe," Patsy said, adjusting the hairnet over her tiny, black curls while she stood over the stove stirring a pot for supper. She glanced my way, and I thought I glimpsed a kindness in her eyes.

In the darkened hall, I fumbled with my library key and pulled on the door, only to have someone behind me open it wider. I spun around, startled to see an older man holding a ladder and wearing a tool belt around his waist. Behind him, the side exit door swung slowly shut.

"Ma'am, I'm Sullivan, from over at the men's prison. Call me Buttermilk. Warden Sanders asked me to change out the burned light bulbs overhead, offer any assistance you might need." He looked at me curiously, taking in my color, then wrestled the ladder across the threshold, swinging a leg awkwardly as he walked.

"Cussy Lovett. Nice to meet you, Buttermilk. Without any windows in here, we could sure use the light." I stood back as he carried the ladder and a toolbox inside, noting his prison overalls and the identification pinned to his bib pocket as he passed.

The man rested the ladder against a wall, then opened boxes of light bulbs and set them carefully on the table. Occasionally, I'd glance over my shoulder while arranging books on the shelves.

After a bit, he said, "As quiet as you are, I take it you didn't come by your name honestly." Buttermilk stole a peek while I snuck a last one of my own. He picked up a bulb, examining it.

"No, sir. I'm named after my great-grandpa's village over in Cussy, France. Originally sounded like *Coo see*. But somewhere along the way to the ol' Kaintuck mountains, the translation got lost and became *Cuss* with a *y*. Though I remember Pa saying more than once I'd earned the name and driven him to nothing but with my willful mind."

He chortled, his friendly eyes teasing. "I come by mine honestly, and the prison treats me to a glass every night. Cussy, France, is close to where I was shot and ended up with this dead leg." He pointed down to his foot. A metal rod ran up his work boot, disappearing under his britches. "Not far from Normandy, where I fought during the war in the airborne division at Utah Beach."

I stared at him with admiration, wondering what transgression had landed this brave soldier in prison.

"Met a nice chap over there, and we shared a hearty supper at a pub on several evenings. Smart man. Looked like you," he said casually.

"I wonder if he's related to my kin who claimed a land grant in Kaintuck in the 1800s."

"Never said." Buttermilk gestured to the table. "Let's get those bulbs changed out. *Jolie bleue Mademoiselle Coosee, la fille de la montagne.*"

I looked at him, slowly picking through his words, trying to remember the childhood French lessons Mama had taught me. Stumped, I mangled the language, and he laughed.

"Pretty blue Miss Coosee, the mountain girl," he said and then repeated it slower in French.

"*Pretty blue mountain girl. Jolie bleue fille de la montagne,*" I parroted several times. It had been a long time since I'd heard my name connected to such, and a smile budded as I couldn't help being grateful for his kind words and friendly manner.

"Warden Sanders says to let me know if you need anything else." He pulled the ladder from the wall and placed it under a busted bulb. I kept a strong hold on the rail, worrying about the wobbly ladder and his bad leg as he slowly inched up the rungs.

Beside books and bookshelves, there weren't really nothing more that I needed. I studied his ladder, remembering how the Pack Horse librarians had fastened the old wooden ones onto the Center's walls for extra shelves.

When he finished, I asked, "Would you have any old ladders the prison no longer uses? When I was a Pack Horse librarian back home, we used them for shelving."

The man rubbed his chin, thinking.

"If I could get a few, I could hang them on the walls."

"Let me see what we have over in the carpentry building. Might be able to round something up."

"I'll put them to good use."

"You'll want to wait a bit; Warden Alton has promised your warden that he'll loan some of his men to paint your library as soon as we get more volunteers."

I studied him, trying to decide whether I should ask him something else. When he looked at me questioningly, I dared. "I wonder if you might know my husband housed over there with you?"

"Who might that be, Mademoiselle Coosee?"

"Jackson Lovett."

He turned away to pack up his toolbox, rearranging the tools just so.

I prayed I hadn't overstepped.

Then: "I've met the young man. He's doing fine. I'll give him your regards and let him know his jolie woman is safe. Landed herself a fitting job. Gotta go, Coosee. Transport will be waiting. I'll be back tomorrow to install the busted wall outlet if it comes in from the hardware store. Get your ladders to you as soon as I can. Good evening, *jolie bleue Coosee, la fille de la montagne.*" He hobbled out the door.

"Pretty blue mountain girl," I said and repeated it in French, remembering librarian Mr. Taft from home once telling me, *God saved the best color for His home.* Then he'd pointed to the blue sky and back to me and said, "He must've had Himself a little left over."

For the first time since my arrival at the prison, I felt joy. I closed the door and pressed my back against it, grateful for Buttercup's news on my husband. *Jackson was okay and would find out I was too.* Finally, there would be a way to get word to him, and I wondered if I could be bold enough to ask Buttermilk to pass a note to Jackson. Somehow I'd have to try.

I typed five more letters full of pleas for books and addressed envelopes to leave with a guard. After I dusted the shelves and organized the material, I stood behind the desk, waiting for my first patron.

Waited and waited while the second hand on the institutional clock kicked into the steady, impatient taps of my feet.

Five

The last week of April brought a visitor.

"Just twenty minutes, Lovett." The guard stood close by as I sat at a table while Doc gave me the news of Loretta's death. Despite her being ninety-two, it still came as a shock. My dearest patron and friend in those hills was gone. Honey was left without a guardian.

"Since the child no longer has one, the lawyer is seeking her emancipation," Doc continued.

"Emancipation?"

Doc squeezed my hand. "Jackson has given his permission. Honey's doing well. She's back at the Carter homestead and has a reputable job with the library. So we're hoping the judge grants it."

I pinched the bridge of my nose, a headache taking hold as I tried to learn more.

"No need to worry," he chatted on. "I'm keeping an eye out for Honey, along with Devil John and others."

"Could you give her a letter from me, Doc?"

He snapped at the guard, demanding paper and pen.

The officer returned with a Big Chief writing tablet and a stubby pencil.

I looked around for a calendar.

Doc glanced at his wristwatch and then over to the locked and barred door, growing uncomfortable. "April twenty-six." His eagerness to leave rested in his shifting posture.

I didn't blame him. He wanted to rip off the collar of prison as soon as possible and hightail it far away from here.

"Five more minutes," the officer announced.

Quickly, I dated the paper, let Honey know I was well, and added a word about my new job as prison librarian.

Doc stood, patted my shoulder, and called me by nickname: "Bluet, it's sure good to see that you're better than when I saw you last. Any female troubles since they performed the"—he lowered his voice and smoothed his disheveled shirt—"surgery?"

"No, sir." I flushed but not from embarrassment, only a gnawing bitterness.

The guard stepped up to our table. "Visiting time is over."

Doc grabbed the letter and stuffed it into his shirt pocket, turning toward the door. He looked back with sympathetic eyes and said, "Take care of yourself. I'll stay on the governor about your pardon. I promise."

Two weeks went by, and book donations and reading materials began to trickle in. At the end of May, more arrived, and Buttermilk built new ladders that he put in storage until the painters could come. Each time, I'd carried a folded letter in my prison dress and tried to build up the courage to ask him to pass it for me.

At the end of the day, the note would still be in my pocket, wrinkled from my talking, damp hands as fingers fidgeted over the page. When I finally poured some starch into my bones, I asked, "Buttermilk, would you give my husband a note from me?" I lifted the crumpled paper from my dress and held it out to him.

He stared at me long and hard, then shook his head. "Mademoiselle Coosee, I'm searched each time I go back over to the men's, and if I'm caught, I wouldn't be able to come back. I would be locked in the hole for this. Tell me instead what you want me to tell your fine man, and I will get word to him."

Embarrassed for asking him to risk his freedom, I could only say, "Please tell him I miss and love him and am doing well."

"Coosee, he asks of you each time, and I tell him what words have not been spoken but I see in your heart. He knows you are well and he is loved and missed."

I'd been too bold, and I quickly thanked the gracious handyman, apologizing for my misstep.

Over the days, Buttermilk replaced shelves on several bookcases. Another morning, he brought in an old-world globe and installed an American flag on the wall. Last week, he'd built a bookcase after putting in new windowpanes inside Warden's office. As always, his work was precise and detailed.

It started to feel more like a library, and I grew fond of his visits, enjoying our conversations, with him sometimes teasing out sentences in French. Me, reminiscing about the old lessons and songs from my youth; him, regaling me with tales of medieval fortresses, abbeys, Normandy history and food, and the hint of a young French woman who'd stolen his heart but he'd regrettably left behind.

Buttermilk confided that, after the war, he'd become a prisoner of the bottle and it had made him short tempered. Drunk, he had fought a lawman and it landed him behind bars.

Today, Buttermilk taught me a few more words in French. He was working on a busted file cabinet while I organized stacks of books, when Warden Sanders stopped by unexpectedly, interrupting our light conversation in French.

"*Je vois que vous avez combattu non loin de la Normandie, Monsieur Sullivan. J'avais un frère qui a débarqué à Utah Beach,*" she said.

"You don't say, Warden. I don't recall running into a Sanders serving over there. I hope your brother has at least a few fond memories like me." Buttermilk grinned.

Warden turned to me. "My, aren't we full of surprises, *Coosee.*

A hillbilly who can speak French." She threw back her head and laughed.

"*Fille de la montagne*," I corrected, switching out the insulting word with *mountain girl*.

"*Hillbilly*," she quipped.

If she was surprised that a hillbilly like me could learn French, I was just as flabbergasted by her unpolished tongue. The word came from those who'd never been born here—never set foot in Kentucky. Instead, it had been harvested from the mirth of stick-throated foreigners in their newsprint, advertisements, and drawings.

Pa'd taught me as a child and then told me never to repeat the ugly word, not even in jest.

She raised a brow, threaded with a hint of contempt that had me stepping back. "Have you visited France, Coosee?"

"I was schooled as a child, ma'am. Though it seems I've forgotten the lessons. But, Warden, you speak as if you grew up there."

"DC," she said haughtily and turned back to Buttermilk. "Well, I don't know what we'd do without you, Mr. Sullivan." Warden clasped her hands. "The library is really shaping up nicely thanks to all your hard work. Warden Alton just needs to send the painters over here, and it will be done."

The older gentleman's face flushed, and he thanked her in French.

I watched them bandying compliments back and forth, mystified by the warden's behavior around the man.

She spun the globe and looked around. "Impressive, Mr. Sullivan." Then: "Looks like you've got everything you need for your library, Lovett." Her hand trailed down the soft fabric of the flag. "Except readers."

Readers. She'd surely see my failure and fire me.

Buttermilk cast quizzical glances between us and cleared his throat. "Warden, I still need to switch out a few more dead electrical outlets I'm waiting on to come in from the hardware store deliveryman. Can't chance a shock. I also need to get the last of the ladder shelving together and replace several rungs. And I'm almost done building the library catalog chest; just need to get those brass pulls. The painters have been running behind. Be ready for visitors soon enough, ma'am."

She glanced at her wristwatch and gestured to me. "Have Waldeen fix Mr. Sullivan a dinner tray and bring it to my office. Make sure he gets a generous helping of those apple dumplings she whipped up this morning. *And* a tall, cold glass of buttermilk," she added pleasantly enough. "Mr. Sullivan, I hope you'll join me. I'd like to discuss our latest trouble with the boiler?"

I darted my eyes between the door and calendar, still waiting for my first patron, willing a reader to step inside. Fretting the day, hour, or minute when the warden would send me back to Laundry. Worse, lose her funding, dismiss me, and shut down the library.

I'd soon found myself avoiding her whenever she'd happen into the cafeteria or inspect a wing.

Another week had gone by, and nary a soul had graced the door. I lingered by the light switch, watching the second hand slip into another lost minute on a rainy Saturday, knowing I could do a lot of things, but I couldn't stop the fear and repulsion the inmates regarded me with.

Couldn't stop the ones I needed from not needing me.

I turned off the lights and rested my head against the wall in the darkness.

Mindless, I switched the light on and off.

My moods tangled between the soft clicks, the courage laddering and descending into a rumbling rhythm.

Stepping over to the library catalog case Buttermilk had built, I admired the tiny drawers full of index cards and his fine workmanship on the beautiful oak piece.

I thought about the hundred miles I'd traveled each week to reach my patrons. The thousands of books and reading material I'd dropped onto time-worn porches over the years, and how desperate the mountainfolk had been for any printed word.

It'd been a risk in the beginning. And Pa'd fought me every step of the way.

Some back home didn't warm to the Pack Horse librarian program, and the *foolish books* and *coaxing notions* they might invite, any more than they trusted the meddling government, visiting missionaries, or predatory rich from far off.

Others greedily fed their souls with hungry bellies, reaching for hope outside the hills.

And with the violent unrest of the bloody coal mine wars, starvation, influenzas, and the Depression taking their toll on the Kentucky man, it could be downright deadly trying to grow readers in those Troublesome parts.

There had been moonshiner Devil John, a fire tower lookout, young Timmy and his mama, the Moffits, and many others.

The ones I'd won over.

Quietly, I moved over to the shelves and sat on the floor, poring over the titles, flipping through pages.

Hours later, I gathered a stack of books and index cards.

There weren't no other way.

I know'd what to do.

But I know'd it would be risky and downright dangerous if I failed.

Six

I waited by the crash gate with a laundry bag of books and a pass from the warden while the officer unlocked the door to the Geriatric Ward.

"Thirty minutes and not a second longer," the guard warned.

"Sir, Warden said I could take an hour with the women—"

He shoved three fingers in my face. "And not a second more," he growled, then grabbed my book bag and searched inside.

My eyes watered from the stench of soil and looming death. Coughing, I took a folding chair from the wall and dragged it over to a group of seven women in wheelchairs.

One woman's eyes fluttered open and then quickly shut, a small moan escaping her thin lips. Another looked empty-eyed at the big clock hanging on the wall, lost in trapped memories of yesteryear, clicking her teeth to the loud ticking of the second hand. A few more stared blankly ahead while others drooped their heads toward their laps and worried shaky, knotted hands. I set down my bag and righted my chair.

"Ladies," I said, doing my best to ignore the smell of urine and decay hovering above the circle. I blinked and wiped my watering eyes against a sleeve. "I'm the new prison librarian—your Book Woman, at your service. My name is Cussy Lovett, and I'm here to read to you today and loan out books from the prison library. Would you like that?"

Silence.

Then: "They sent her to infect us so we'd kill off quicker." An inmate pointed an accusing finger at me.

"I'm perfectly healthy, ladies. Promise, my color isn't catchin' or killin'." I rummaged through my bag and pulled out the new copy of *Charlotte's Web*, hoping some of the elderly women had come from farms and would enjoy the tale of the young girl, Fern, and her barnyard characters. Softly, I cleared my throat and began, "*Where's Papa going with that axe*—"

"We know where ol' Lila went with hers." A woman mimicked striking an axe and darted eyes to a frail inmate who glared back at her.

I noticed in the back row a younger woman slumped in her chair, murmuring with spittle collecting in the corners of her mouth. I moved toward her, but the guard blocked me and shook his head. "She won't understand any book that you could read her."

A half hour later the guard tapped my shoulder, pulling me from the story. "Time's almost up." I looked up from the page, surprised to see seven sets of attentive eyes on me.

One woman quietly said, "Grandma once saw a spider write her brother's name in its web. He died within three days."

I winced, remembering the scattered feathers of the pillow and the angel crown left behind on the porch the day the lawman took me into custody.

"My pappy said for every spider you kill, you kill an enemy," one recalled.

Another chimed in, "I 'member my granny always swore that if you have a headache, swallow a spider's web and it'll go away."

"Time to leave," the officer said. "Dinner trays will be here soon."

One woman frowned. "Not now, Officer McGee. I want her to read one more chapter."

Another had tears in her eyes.

"And just what are you blubbering about, Geraldine Clark?" one of the women asked her.

"Quiet, Bess," the guard warned.

"I once had a pet goat named Wilbur. Always stuck to my side like beggar's tick. Can we keep the loan?" Geraldine stretched out a wobbly arm.

"I'd like a book," Bess said.

"If Bess and Gerry gets one, I want one too," someone else piped up. "Ma never could afford 'em when I was growing up."

"Same, Dottie. We were so poor I had to steal scraps from the dog bowl," a reed-thin woman told the inmate beside her.

Several more chorused "I'll take a book" and "Me too."

Finally. My very *first* patrons.

I all but tumbled over to Geraldine to hand her the book, then quickly fished inside my bag for more. Still, I looked to the inmate slumped over, babbling to herself.

The woman named Dottie caught my eye and said, "That's Chaney—or what's left of her. Prison done went and gave her one of them lobotomies."

I stared, horrified for the younger woman.

"She tried to stab two inmates. They do it to all the crazy ones too." Dottie circled a finger over her temple. "Even to some of the ones who ain't"—she leaned toward me and barely whispered—"dutiful, or gets too lippy with 'em." Her old eyes warned.

Beyond Chaney, a feeble woman watched in silence.

After I wrote down everyone's names and their books on the index cards to catalog, I looked again at the women sitting alone in the back, smiled, and motioned to her.

The birdlike woman held back and refused to roll her wheelchair over to the bag of books. I walked over to her. "Ma'am, would you like a read today?" A waft of foulness lifted. She grimaced, and I could see she was in pain. "Ma'am?" I took another step and she flinched.

I hesitated, thinking I'd scared her.

Then a tear dropped, wetting her pale cheek. "The morning guard wouldn't let me relieve myself when I asked. Now I'm soiled."

The officer strolled over and wrinkled his nose. "Dammit, *not again*, Marigold," he said, the disgust souring his voice. "The nurse's aide won't be here for another two hours."

Marigold bowed her head and wept quietly.

"I've a mind to order you an ice bath." I followed as he jerked on Marigold's wheelchair, swung it around, and then pushed it across the room and into the washroom. Another hard shove and he let go, and Marigold and the wheelchair went crashing into a large metal bucket shaped like a horse trough, empty and waiting to be fed its next meal of ice and a warm body.

She moaned.

"You can just spend the afternoon alone in your own stink till the aide comes," he said.

I stepped in front, hoping he wouldn't pick up the frail woman and dump her into the trough. "Sir, since I've finished my reading for today, I can help Miss Marigold clean up."

He seemed unsure and darted his eyes between us. Then: "Be quick." He left with a disgusted breath curling into the air.

I opened one of four stalls, saw an enamel washtub, and turned on the faucets. Lifting her out of the wheelchair, I helped her over to a sink while the tub filled. Marigold gripped her corded necklace of a blackened crucifix while I slipped the cotton shift over her head. I sucked in a breath, horrified by what I saw. Her pale buttocks were pocked with oozing, angry bedsores caked in feces. "I'm sorry, I didn't mean to, I tried to hol' it…" Her apologies were warbled, soaked in shame and agony.

"We'll have you freshened up in no time, Miss Marigold. First let's wipe you down, then get you a warm soak so you'll feel better," I soothed, fighting back the bile threatening to rise. "*No time* and you'll be feeling better, and then I'll leave you with a nice read." I raised my strained words, chatted lightly, trying to distract her with book suggestions, fighting to swallow down the anger sloshing against the threatening heave in the pit of my stomach.

She clung to the basin—naked, trembling, and quietly

sobbing—while I took a soapy, wet cloth and carefully washed down her backside, bottom, and legs.

Gently, I helped her into the tub.

Again, I soaped the rag and washed down her back. "Do you have any favorite books, Miss Marigold?"

She coughed out a strangled reply, her words drowned.

When I had finished and covered her wounds with an ointment the guard had reluctantly fetched, I helped Marigold into a fresh prison gown and clean necessaries, the garments baggy and swallowing her small frame.

"Maybe we can find you a good book now," I said, wheeling her back into the common area.

I begged the guard for a few more minutes with her and then let her select from my bag. Timidly, she picked out *The Little Lame Prince and His Travelling Cloak* and handed it to me. After I read several pages, Marigold rubbed her wet lashes.

"Would you rather I read something else?"

She shook her head and said in a strained voice, "Mother read this to me when I was a little girl. It was my favorite, and she'd sewed me a magic cloak to play in."

"I'll leave it with you, Miss Marigold. It'll be just like having your own magic cloak again."

Minutes later, the guard unlocked the crash gate, and I slipped out to go on to the next wing—the one I dreaded most.

I stared at the dark-red letters on the sign hanging over the entrance to the next cell block, feeling in my bone and flesh a sense of dread.

DEATH ROW

Shortly, a guard opened the door and carefully inspected my books before escorting me down a dimly lit hall of empty cells. Ahead, a radio hummed its static, curling around the gray concrete walls of the darkened chamber.

The officer stopped at the last cell. "Sassyann, company's here." He walked over to a windowed office, cast back a glance before slipping inside. After a few seconds, he closed the sliding window and picked up the telephone, then turned his back, lost in conversation.

I peered through the bars at the prisoner resting on the mattress, her eyes shut, her face contorted in pain.

"Ma'am? Miss Sassyann, I'm the prison Book Woman, Cussy Lovett, and I've come to read to you. Would you like that?"

When she didn't move, I began reading from the book, raising my voice above the radio, peeking over the pages and past the bars.

I stopped after three pages. "Ma'am, I don't want to disturb you. Would you like it if I leave the book instead?" Sassyann didn't budge. I stepped over and set the book quietly against the bars.

Sassyann swung her legs over the cot, the scarlet-red cotton shirt and baggy britches wrinkled and stained. She turned off the brown Bakelite radio on the small table beside her. Slowly, the death-row prisoner eased herself over to the bars.

"It's right there whenever you're ready to look at it." I pointed to the book. "Unless you would like me to read a few more pages?"

Suspicious, she stared at me, then finally nodded, smoothing back her wavy brown hair.

I had almost finished with the first chapter of a tattered copy of *National Velvet* when she held up a palm. "Show me that word, girl."

I looked at her, puzzled.

"Horse." She blinked and tried to peer over the book, her glazed eyes pulling to life.

"*Horse*—oh, here it is." I tapped the page and lifted it to her.

Her eyes chewed over the words, then she pointed. "Where?"

"Right here. *Horse.* H-O-R-S-E."

"H-O-R-S-E," she repeated, slow and painful.

"Here, there's some illustrations inside." I fanned the pages and stopped at several.

"Horse." She pointed to the word on another page.

"Do you read, Sassyann?"

"My pap would never let me go to school. After my brother died, he said I needed to help on the farm."

"Would you like to learn?"

"At sixty-three? With the ol' Sparky chair waiting for me, its clock a'tickin' faster each day, it'd be a sorry waste."

I met her eyes, mooned with dark circles, wanting to give balm, offer a glimmer of hope of the outside world, a reminder that life was not always like this.

"Too damn old for that." She dismissed the thought with a hand, her pale cheeks spotting from embarrassment.

"Never too old."

"Hmph." She crossed her bony arms across her bosom.

"The elders back home attended the Moonlight Schools. Walked those paths up to their little one-room school perched atop the mountain when the moon lit the way. Learned their arithmetic and letters just fine. Some were in their eighties. I imagine a young woman like yourself can learn quick." I nodded the declaration. "Book Woman, at your service."

She looked at me with guarded eyes, as if trying to decide the possibility of such. Then she pointed. "That book reminds me of my Lu Lu. I was jus' fourteen when Mommy and Pap gave her to Casper Sipes for my dowry." Her face lit up, and then, just as quick, a storm pressed into the deepening lines mapped across it. "My Lu Lu was the only living soul that loved me. Weren't as lonely when she was around either. She tried her best to protect me from him. Till the very end."

I listened quietly. Warden had told me she hadn't had visitors in years.

Her soft brown eyes watered. "Every week, Casper would

strike me down in front of his men, then take bets on how many times I would get back up before he could lay me out cold. I was in the barn with my horse one night. Casper come home late, and when he saw I hadn't put his supper on the table, he grabbed me by the hair and started dragging me across that old dirt field. Lu Lu knocked him aside and chased him off." Sassyann's eyes filled again. "A fine horse she was for near a decade, until my ornery husband sold my beautiful girl the next day to a meat farm."

I blinked away a tear at the thought of her losing Lu Lu like that. The protective creature sounded a lot like my Junia.

"Weren't so much the weekly beatings and all my husband done to me, but when he brought home that horsemeat and demanded his supper, and I found out what he'd done, well, that bastard went down like the rabid dog he was." Sassyann sniffed.

My color deepened, and I lowered the book to my side.

"I took that horsemeat and fed him for a week. Laced his favorite shepherd's pies with rat poison, same as I did with the rhubarb pies I baked for ol' Ned, my second husband. That one always skinning my nerves, pestering me morn', noon, and night to ground the corn. Suffered a lot of beatings and…and, ya know, the other *stuff* we females ain't supposed to mention."

Stuff. The scars womenfolk carried from the misdeeds of cruel men. I looked down at my loud-talking hands, knowing my first husband was such a man. And I realized my part in his passing weren't much different from her crime of poison. I'd just been lucky enough to pray him to death, escape the witch hunt the townsfolk would've brought down on me.

Sassyann moved over to her cot. "Them killings fed me, kept me alive. The hankerings grew stronger until I couldn't help myself any more. Every time I kilt one, I felt stronger, like I was feeding, getting back pieces of me they stole."

The officer poked his head out his office door.

"I needed to protect my boys from them onery men. Hell, if Ned's meddling son hadn't contested his Last Will and pushed the prosecutor to dig up my husbands, I'd likely be working on a third." She cackled, a wheeze braiding her chortle. "It gets in the blood after all that *stuff*."

"Sassyann." The guard approached. "Stop regaling her with your vile deeds; you've hogged enough of her reading time."

"A gal can't talk without you butting in, John Pridemore." She cut him a defiant eye and turned back to me, ignoring the quiet prison guard. "Book Woman, I wouldn't mind to learn the letters to write my sons. Ain't seen nor heard from my three boys since they locked me up. I'd like to do that 'fore it's too late..." Her pause was heavy.

"You'll learn quick, Sassyann."

"Not really interested in them books. I jus' wanna write my boys. It gets a mite lonesome here. Warden gave me the radio one Christmas. It helps some. She's good to me like that. Always brings me a chocolate bar on my birthday and Mother's Day."

I was taken aback by this news. It was a side of the warden I hadn't seen. "Sassyann, I'll help you learn your letters so you can write your sons," I said, perking at the chance to ease whatever time she had left.

Hearing the declaration, she grinned, her teeth sharp-boned and browned, as she slipped back over to her skeleton mat atop the metal frame.

Hurrying down the corridor, I rounded the corner and bumped my bulky bag of books into Regina.

Before I could mumble an excuse, she raised an arm. Shielding my face, I felt the tip of a pencil push into tender flesh and break off in my palm, the blood oozing down my wrist, an explosion of piercing pain.

Seeming shocked by the color of my blood, Regina stumbled back and cursed, "Damn blue bitch, you *are* a witch." Then she lit off.

I rushed into the cafeteria, past Waldeen, toward the kitchen washroom. Inside, I scrubbed the puncture, then wrapped a frayed tea towel around my hand after peeking at the wound. It could've been worse—an eye—and I was grateful for my quick reflexes.

"Kid, you okay?" Waldeen knocked on the door.

I stepped out and around her, steadying myself beside the tall freezer. "Just a little accident. I—I was clumsy." The bloody rag dropped to the floor.

She studied me with ol' eyes that said they know'd better. I quickly turned my head to the steel-paneled freezer door and caught the reflection of my face flushed into the lie.

"Get some Mercurochrome from the medicine chest, and see that your wound is properly bandaged. Can't have ya working in the kitchen with a blood infection. And with chocolate blood, at that."

"Can I have a drop of honey to dress the wound?"

"You one of them mountain granny women who practice root witchery or sumthin'?"

"No, ma'am, but I learned about curing with the herbs and tonics."

"I'll get it for ya, kid. The men's penitentiary has beekeepers raising hives over there for both prisons. We get plenty."

When she came back with the honey, Waldeen didn't say anything for the longest time. Then she pulled out a toothbrush from her apron pocket and held it up and wagged it in front of my face.

I shrank back. The bottom had been shaved down to a dangerous point, sharpened like an ice pick.

"Cussy"—she grabbed my arm and pulled me closer—"from now on, I want ya to carry this. Understand?" She dug out Raymond Chandler's *The Little Sister* from my bag and walked over to the counter. Then Waldeen unlocked the utensil drawer and, much to my horror, took out a butcher knife and began carving out the center pages of Chandler's thick book. When she had finished making a cover of pasted pages, she tucked the homemade weapon deep inside, added a cigarette and matchbook, and closed the book.

"For the nerves. You should really try 'em; they do wonders. Hell, kid, even the doctors tout 'em in them slick magazine advertisements." Waldeen chuckled. "Ol' Santa Claus too." She held out the book.

"No, Waldeen—"

"*Go on, take it,*" she urged.

"Why would you help me?"

The supervisor didn't say anything for a bit. Instead, Waldeen took a dishrag to the kitchen and wiped down the machines, stove, and cabinets, then hung it over the sink. She pulled out a covered dish from the electric refrigerator and set it on the counter. Drying her hands on her apron, she cocked her head. "Do you know about the cathouse down in Rosebranch? The one on Saltdigger Road?" She looked around, making sure we were alone. "I ran it under an alias. WallaceAnn Deen."

"*Madam Deen?*" Why, everyone here and in states beyond had heard about the success of the infamous Rosebranch and what its notorious madam had done.

But I had a feeling I was about to hear something the rest of the country hadn't.

Seven

Waldeen nudged us back to the pantry. Inside, she stroked her neck as the wisps of cigarette smoke ghost-tailed up between us.

A guard called out from the kitchen, "Waldeen, you save me a slice of Patsy's chocolate pie?"

She stuck her head out the door. "Saved ya the biggest piece, Cap'n. Put it over there on the counter."

He grunted, and we listened until his footsteps faded and the door thudded his departure. She stubbed out her cigarette and slipped into the kitchen. I heard a drawer open and slam close.

Waldeen came back and lifted a pint of whiskey from her apron pocket, unscrewed the cap, and took herself a long pull. "If you're nice to the guards, sometimes they return the favor."

She offered me a sip, and I shyly shook my head and waited for the unspooling of her story.

"Well, about Rosebranch, kid. I had myself a working girl named Clara. I grew quite fond of her. Clara was one of my best. Lots passed through, but she was a madam's perfect whore."

I stared at her, trying to dare myself to conjure up what the *perfect whore* would be.

"But it didn't last for long, no, sir." She smoothed down her apron and sighed. "One year, I delivered her sweet baby boy into the world on a cloud-soaked June afternoon, surrounded by eight working girls as scarlet as the birthing sheets on her bed. Right there in my chandeliered bordello bedroom. It was something else." Waldeen smiled, reminiscing. "I could never have babies, but I raised little William like my own his first two years."

"The boy in your photograph."

She nodded. "That's William. He was a Blue just like you, though only on his hands and feet."

A catch climbed into my throat, thinking about Angeline and Willie Moffit, my young library patrons who'd died in the hills. I'd adopted their newborn, Honey, immediately after. Honey was also like her pa, Willie, and this William, and what my kin called blue-eyed Marys, after the two-lipped blue-and-white wildflower. Their color is only shown on those parts.

"Kid, I know the color's not a spreader. Any more than that broke arm of yours. People sure get foolish notions about things they can't understand. That's why I don't mind sharing my empty cot."

"What happened to Clara?" I asked, appreciative that Waldeen had rescued me from the bowels of the prison's infirmary.

"I always told my working girls two things: The walls of a whorehouse *never* talk, but watch for the fly parked on your headboard, and understand pen on parchment can leave a legacy of treachery."

I cocked my head, trying to make sense of her words.

"Clara was drunk on love, and the daddy refused to marry her after she birthed his child. When she caught him stepping out, the girl eventually went to the ol' tattler newspaper, *and tattle she did*. Tol' them about the *Blue* politician, Eldon, getting her pregnant after he became smitten with her. I tried to tell the foolish girl Eldon wasn't worth it."

Another Blue was out there somewhere. It'd been so long, I couldn't recall if Pa had talked about an Eldon. Though the name seemed somewhat familiar.

"Don't you know Eldon Carter had been laying his pipe all over my brothel for years? Hell, the whole county—and more pipe than Wheatly & Sons Plumbing had laid three counties wide. That horndog couldn't keep it in his pants once he'd set his sights on a pretty gal."

"*Carter?* Why, he's my kin. An uncle or great-uncle, though I've never met him," I said, astonished. The memories of Pa's stories of kin had been fading with each passing year.

"Ya don't say, Eldon's kin. From down in Troublesome Creek?"

"That's home. I worked as a Pack Horse librarian there."

"One of them Troublesome book women I heard so much about in them hills?" Waldeen studied me closer.

"Yes, ma'am. They called me a few names, but some might've called me troublesome too."

"Them smart females soldiered themselves into britches them menfolk could never fill," Waldeen continued. "One of my girls left to open a tiny brothel in those parts in '40, I believe. Weren't but three of them living atop a mountain near Paintsville, but she wrote me that they were thriving in moonshine and dough. Even had a Pack Horse librarian sneaking them books every so often."

"There was several scattered around," I said. "What happened to Uncle Eldon?" I asked, thinking I'd finally meet him one day. Even if he was a scoundrel, maybe there were cousins or other kin he might lead me to.

"It turned sideways for Clara and downwards for Eldon. Literally." The old madam grimaced. "He was a respectable, small elected official. And a highly valued client at my brothel."

Waldeen saw my disbelief and said, "Money may be green, but it don't give a whit about the color of the palm holding it."

Willie. Could William be Willie *and* the boy in Waldeen's photograph? Uncle Eldon, me, and Willie. Honey's father. *My kin.* We Blues were all knotted, *twisted tight on our branch*, Doc had told me. And I suddenly realized the woman, Clara, carried the gene and was also Honey's grandmother, and Waldeen's baby William was her pa.

Stunned, I said, "I know'd Clara's son, Willie, and her daughter-in-law, Angeline. We're all related."

It was time for Waldeen to be surprised. "I learned there's not many of you Blues, and I was hoping ya might know something when I volunteered my empty cot. My sweet boy William. What kind of man did he turn into?"

A tormented one. I'd never spoke of it to another soul after it happened. Only Jackson know'd after I had solicited him to help me give them a proper burial in their yard. I paused, not wanting to tell her how I'd found Willie hanging from the tree after he took his own life. I could still see Angeline's toppled Mother's Lard bucket he'd climbed up on to do the deed. Stunned, I had frantically snatched up the squalling newborn lying in the dirt under his swaying corpse. Grieved for the loss of my dear friend and young patron, Angeline.

I groped for the right words, shuddering from the horrors of that hot July day in '36. Finally, I said, "Willie passed after an accident, along with his wife, who died soon after childbirth. I raised their baby, Honey. She's mine now."

Waldeen's face dropped and she spoke wistfully, "If *only* Eldon had married her. The last night he called on her after the newspaper article was published, he was furious and smacked Clara around and tried to take the baby. She grabbed my gun from the bureau, and I fought her for it but lost that struggle. She shot Eldon. Died right on that birthing bed of red-satin sheets where his son drew first life."

I'd lost another kin. Saddened, I could only stare at her, the hardness of many lifetimes etched across her face.

"It broke my heart when Clara ran off with my darling William. It was the last I saw of the child. My sweet William. And when I wouldn't talk to the law, they dropped the dirt on me for the politician's murder. One of them johns of mine was a slick city attorney who ended up persuading the DA not to seek the death penalty; otherwise I'd be sitting right up there on Death Row with that ol' poisoner, Sassyann."

"*Death penalty.*"

"Lots of respectable men paid visits to my place, kid.

Businessmen, politicians, unpolished young lovers, and the souls stuck in loveless marriages. We catered to a few Bible-thumping johns, police chiefs, and honorary Kentucky Colonels. There were the stuffy old goats from the country club and wild bucks of spoon wealth from over at the university. All kinds of mighty an' powerful people came from all over the country to partake of the *special* amenities we offered at Rosebranch. And if any of 'em ever heard you'd talked, well, ya ain't gonna be jawing for long. 'Lessen it's with ol' Lucifer, himself. I buried my little black address book and protected many powerful men. Least they could do is protect me."

Heavy footfalls sounded in the cafeteria.

"Hurry, take it. The guard's a'comin'," she whispered, thrusting the book with the hidden contraband into my hands.

"I could never use it, Waldeen. My hand's fine, and I have to get to the next wing." I tried to give it back.

"In here, ya can't carry yourself too tall *or* too small. Tricky, but you'll learn the balance. Understand, Cussy?"

Not much different from outside. It felt like I'd lived most of my life as an apology. And I know'd that feeling all my life; when to rise and when to duck.

"When you feel too small and that dirt drops down, ya let this do the talkin' to stand back up." Her wise eyes warned. "Get on back to work, kid. And here, take this jar of honey for your wound."

I shoved the jar into the bottom of my bag. "I'm headed to another wing, where I'll be searched. Hold the book for me until I can tuck it inside my footlocker tonight."

I would never use the weapon, but I know'd just what to do with the big jar of honey.

In the hall, I passed the guard who had taken me out of the prison infirmary in April. He scowled, reminding me again of the horrors I was about to visit next.

Weren't nothing that could keep him from locking me in Forensics. After all, he'd already cursed me by calling me a *crazy blue witch*, and one misstep was all it would take to prove him right.

Tucking my head, I thought about Dottie, the woman in the Geriatric Ward. "*They do it to all the crazy ones, lippy ones.*"

They could experiment to erase *my crazy blueness* by performing a lobotomy on a whim. The surgery that could cause more than silencing the tongue. It could bring blindness, inflict pain and even death to the ones doctors and government had deemed the pariahs of their moral and godly society.

Terrified, I vowed to try to keep my head good 'n' tucked, lips stiff, and legs starched to toe the line. *I had to make it out of here alive. I had to make it back to protect my daughter so that these horrors would never happen to her.*

Eight

Women clutched the bars of their separate cells. Some clawed. Others wailed and spat and shrieked while tugging at thinning patches of scarecrow-ish hair as I walked through the Forensic Ward.

The guard rummaged through my bag of books, barely glancing at the titles.

"You can start your reading down at the end. Grab yourself a chair if ya need to. But if you rile them up, girl, ya ain't coming back," Officer Frank Holt warned, hardening his jaw.

The air in there felt different from inside the Geriatric Ward. Desperation, darkness, and terror wallpapered the concrete walls.

"I'm Cussy Lovett, your Book Woman," I murmured to the women. I stopped at the end in front of two locked cells and pulled out *Pale Horse, Pale Rider*, struggling to raise my voice above the loud agony and gloom crawling over the ward. One prisoner was curled up on her cot, and the other, a young woman, held a ragged cloth doll and clung quietly to the bars, her wild hazel eyes drugged and protruding.

I read the first short story, and after I'd finished *Noon Wine*, the young girl said, "*The Wonderful Wizard of Oz* is my favorite."

"It's a grand book. Who is your favorite character?"

She grinned slyly. "Scarecrow."

"Smart character for a smart young woman like you. I'm fond of Tin Man and his big heart. Maybe I can get you a copy."

She blushed and then asked, "Can I have that book?"

Stepping closer to the bars, I held it up to her outstretched hand.

Suddenly, Officer Holt sliced a muscly arm through the air, breaking our hold. The book flopped to the floor with the slam of metal, skin, and bone. The tearful girl howled and lifted a limp hand, dangled a reddening finger gingerly holding her doll.

"Emmeline, back to your cot. You, Lovett"—he stabbed an angry finger in front of my face—"ya don't give out *anything* in Forensics without permission first. Next time, I'll throw your sorry blue ass in lockup for a gawdamn week."

"You hurt Baby Mason. *Mason, Mason,*" she wailed and pressed the doll to the bars.

My mouth dried up as fear coated my tongue. Finally, I scraped out, "Yes—yes, sir. I'm sorry. I didn't know."

"Then ask! She's a gawdamn firebug," the guard said, exasperated, danger flitting across his eyes. "Done tried to kilt a bab—" He stopped abruptly, wiped a furious brow, not daring to say more. Suddenly, his eyes showed a hint of regret, a sorrow, and I remembered he'd just lost another child. "Gawdamn crazy firebug!" he spat.

At this, Emmeline sobbed loudly, as if his accusation pained her more than the physical injury.

Officer Holt picked up the book and fanned through the pages several times before tossing it inside Emmeline's cell. It bounced off her head. "Stop throwing a hissy, Emmeline, and get it 'fore I change my mind. *Git.*" He knocked his hard-toe shoe against the iron bars.

Whimpering, she rubbed her reddened forehead, then crept over to pick it up.

"You gonna read or waste time ogling into space?" The officer snapped his wrist toward the other women. "Back to work, Lovett."

I moved to the next cell and pulled out a book. I stopped when a girl in braids, looking no older than twelve in a shapeless, soil-stained dress, softly recited the next lines of "Song of Myself."

"I see you like Whitman. What's your name?" I asked and thought of Honey.

She twirled a lock of hair over a dirt-stained finger, rocking her shoulders from side to side. "Odette," she said.

"Fitting for a princess."

Odette beamed. "Mama saw *Swan Lake* in the city when she was a young girl and never forgot. Promised she was gonna take me one day."

After inspecting, Officer Holt granted me permission to pass the leather-bound volume of *Leaves of Grass*. "I can bring you more poetry books if you like, Odette," I told her.

She squealed. "Oh, yes, Book Woman, I would love that." Then her eyes took on a strange distance, rolling back into her head, and she fell onto her cot, jerking.

"*Officer*," I called out.

"Move along, Lovett." The guard shoved me over to another cell and let himself inside Odette's.

I straightened, smoothed back my hair.

A tall older woman stood from her cot and walked over to the bars as I held up a copy of *Hunter's Horn* by the Kentucky author Harriette Simpson Arnow.

"I remember that book. My auntie had a copy. And my pa was a foxhunter and farmer like Nunn Ballew." She pointed to the cover, her eyes glassy from the prison drugs. "Raised himself some fine hounds. We lived in Horse Hollow, not too far from Mrs. Arnow. Auntie traveled to Cincinnati and got her autograph one time." She lifted a lopsided grin, approving of my selection.

"One of my favorite authors."

When I finished the first chapter, I peered over to Odette's cell, puzzled, hoping the girl was okay. The guard had settled back into a chair behind his small wooden desk, reading a newspaper, seemingly indifferent to the girl's strange behavior. I recalled granny woman Emma McCain back home, treating one of the children on my book route with ginseng once when they had such a fit.

I studied her a bit more until Officer Holt shot me a disapproving look, moving me on.

When I'd look back at the guard each time to seek permission to leave a book and move on to the next prisoners, he'd stodgily nod. But I could also catch something more—a tiny wonderment and curiosity sweeping across his eyes as his rigid stance grew a bit more relaxed.

The lost women had calmed somewhat. Come home for a moment, even if briefly.

I dared to chance another peek at the guard and then back to the women, studying each hollowed face. The ghostly shells of robbed lives.

For the first time since I arrived, a deafening quiet carpeted the row of cells.

Officer Holt followed my gaze. He turned his surprised eyes back to me, feeling it too.

The tumultuous ward had shivered into a quavering charge and surrendered itself to a peaceful stillness for the printed word.

And I know'd somehow the books would heal these women.

Me.

All of us.

Nine

I visited the Geriatrics Ward a few days later. Much to my surprise, the grim room grew loud as the women raced their clacking wheelchairs toward me. Bright-eyed and eager, they surrounded me. "Read us more about Charlotte and Wilber."

"Another chapter."

"Read to us," they pleaded.

When I passed a newspaper to the officer, I could tell he was more than happy to turn his charges over to me and relax with his coffee and morning paper.

"*Charlotte's Web*," I began.

Pausing occasionally, I welcomed the women's interruptions, smiling at their memories, encouraging them to share more. A healing from the pain and suffering.

"I had an uncle named Wilbur. Did I tell ya, Book Woman?"

"Yes, I remember, Geraldine. It's a handsome name."

"My prize hen's name was Charlotte," a woman proclaimed.

"Fern's my aunt's name."

"John was the name of my first beau!"

"I always hoped to date a boy named Henry Fussy," one teased.

"Well, I wanted myself a Lurvy." A small woman crossed clawed hands across her disappearing breasts, lifting a smirk.

"Give me a good ol' Templeton any day," one spouted.

"Fitting for an old snitch," Geraldine batted back, wriggling fingers under her nose.

Guffaws and clapped laughter and smothered giggles sliced through the glum as the women named the characters, all boasting and making outlandish declarations.

Their storytelling warmed me.

Astonished, Officer McGee stood and scratched his head.

The inmates were changing into something he had never seen—human, instead of animal. Young and spirited, instead of feeble and useless.

I hoped he could see the children they were, the daughters, sisters, spouses, aunts, mothers, and grandmothers.

Many recalled childhood tales, excited to share stories of pets, budding romances, spent youth, husbands, young'uns, and lost families.

Marigold hung back in the corner despite me waving her over, her face twitching in pain.

When I packed up my reads, I asked the guard if I could dress her sores. Inside the washroom, I cleaned her wounds and smeared her backside with honey. Geraldine wheeled herself in, and when she saw what I was doing, she begged me to tend to hers, pulling up her gown and revealing ugly ulcers on her flesh.

"Mother used honey for all the ails, like her mother," she told me. "Thank you."

"Mine did too," I said, smiling. "And you'll be good as new in no time, Miss Geraldine."

"It's already feeling better." Then she quietly asked, "Does it hurt?"

"Miss Geraldine?"

"Being blue like that."

"I'm in no pain. Fit as a fiddle, sure enough, but sometimes the color can feel a bit heavy… Well, like grief. Sadness." I tapped a finger against my heart. "In here."

"I'm blue all the time," she confided, patting her own chest.

After a week, their sores were healing nicely, leaving only the train tracks of spotted scars and me begging Waldeen for more honey.

When the prison nurse was alerted to the elderly women's improved health, and I told her about the healing power of honey, she quickly ordered her aid to bring more. A few of the geriatric women were up and slowly ambling about, some insisting on using only canes, their pains lessened.

Several were interested in mending the guards' uniforms, sewing on missing buttons and hemming britches. Some even took up needlework classes the Women's Clubs provided once a week inside the prison.

I was witnessing a glimmer of light climb to the surface as they hungered for hope and found meaning in what little life they had left.

Soon, word got around about my visits to the wards, and I received an unusual request.

On a Thursday evening in late May, Warden sent word asking if I would volunteer at the men's prison for the opening of their new library.

The guard said I would be transported in the morning in a mutual exchange while several of their inmates worked on maintenance jobs here. He noted that most of the men had been instructed to visit me in the new library to get a bit of schooling.

He continued, "Warden Alton over there says the men will show their best behavior. *You* be on yours. You'll need to tidy up the library if asked, organize and shelve books, and *work diligently to spread literacy*."

"Yes, sir."

"Now, Warden Sanders says it's strictly voluntary, and if you feel that you're too busy with your own work to leave, she'll just pull in another volunteer and..."

I stood dumbstruck, hardly believing my good fortune—the chance to finally see Jackson. I could barely tamp down my excitement, nor hide my rioting hands.

"Lovett, you okay?" The corrections officer narrowed his eyes. "Can't approve this if you're sick."

"Just fine, Officer, and I'm happy to volunteer. It was a busy day and I'm ready to retire to my cot for the night," I babbled.

"Be in front of transport at six sharp."

"Six. Good evening, sir."

It was anything but.

The sun set over the prison, casting shadows. The air grew more oppressive as the clanking keys and mournful cries echoed throughout the hallways. I tossed and turned at each little noise.

It seems I had barely drifted to sleep when Waldeen shook me awake. "You're gonna miss that transport you talked about all night in your sleep unless you hoof it, kid." She chuckled.

Scrambling for my clothes in the darkness, I rushed toward the shower room.

I couldn't wait to see him, and my jittery hands fumbled with the buttons on the ugly prison dress and laces of my dull black oxfords.

Outside, dawn ignited Kentucky skies in apricot, pink, and glowing golds, heralding the new day and echoing my hopeful spirit. I couldn't help but pause to breathe in its morning's welcome.

Soon, a homesickness struck as I waited beside the automobile and looked out across the horizon. How I missed those hills back home. Longed for the forests and pine-treed canopied paths—the choral night songs of tree frogs and warblers climbing into the hymns of a fiddle, laddering a sweetness across Troublesome's coal-black evening skies.

The hunger for homecoming burned, and I carried the fevered hope, letting the fighting tears scrape across my throat, feeding me.

The guard opened the door, and I slipped inside the back seat as a plume of stale cigarette smoke, mildewed seat coverings, and other tired smells enveloped me. I fumbled for the handle to open my window, only to find the crank had been taken off.

In a moment, he rolled down his own, and we pulled out of the women's prison. I tilted forward and inhaled the grassy meadows, sweetened fresh hay, and earthy scents riding the May-morning breezes. Somewhere in the distance, dogs barked into a tractor's steady hum, and I could see cows gathering in a field. To my right, horses grazed on lush bluegrasses behind white-board fencing.

Pewee Valley was pretty country, and when the guard slowed to take a turn, I heard the familiar call of the town bird belting out its *pee-a-weee*. Passing through, I peered out at the stately buildings and fine homes with sweeping verandas along shady tree-lined avenues. The automobile slowed on Central Avenue as other drivers paused in front of us.

I gawked at one sprawling mansion with a sign in front of it.

The guard glanced at the rearview mirror, following my eyes. "I see you spotted the Beeches. That's the famous author lady's home. Wrote all them books upstairs there, and fans still come to visit to this day."

I'd read all thirteen of the Little Colonel series that Mama and Pa had bought me and then passed them down to Honey. Dreamed of visiting Annie Fellows Johnston's beloved Beeches, which inspired the books' settings. Now here I was, sitting smack-dab in front of it, eyes scanning the upstairs windows, wondering which room she'd written all her adventurous treasures in.

Behind us, a dairy truck blared its horn, and the officer jerked the automobile forward. I turned, stretching my neck until I could no longer see the big home. We passed a neatly tucked-in train depot as we crossed the tracks, and I looked back, my heart hungering for this life of oak-shaded streets and quiet.

I'd never seen such a tranquil little town. It was surely ripped straight out of Mrs. Johnston's story books and as romantic as *The Tenant of Wildfell Hall*. A place of home and longing.

The officer drove on toward LaGrange to the men's prison while I imagined the lives of all the fine folks living in even finer homes.

The towering homes and kept sidewalks became a blur, and I rubbed my fingers over the tips, tapping my thumb across each digit, peeking over my shoulder, circling, picking up speed—as I calmed myself into a steady rhythm.

In a few minutes, I turned to the countryside while my hands dipped into their rhythmic darker hues.

I lifted a palm to my face. Soon, my breaths steadied; the color faded into a pale blue.

I would finally touch him today. If only with my eyes.

Twenty minutes later, concrete-block gun towers appeared, then a single tower centered in back of what looked like the administration building. We passed by a long wall that had been quarried from stone, then turned into the prison and waited for the guard to open the gate.

Inside the building, a woman in a dark dress stood alongside a friendly corrections officer with a long stick who greeted us. My guard signed us both in under the visitor log.

"Welcome. I'm Officer Chandler," the man said to me as he gave my guard a brisk handshake. "Thank you for volunteering your library services. If you'll just step inside this office, the nurse will take your temperature and we'll be on our way." He pointed his walking stick to a door.

"Sir, I'm well," I protested.

Officer Chandler pressed his lips together.

"Lovett, do as you're told," my guard ordered.

"Won't take a minute or two," Chandler assured, his face flushed. "The warden is grateful and has received wonderful praise about your work over at the women's facility. We just, uh—"

"Inside, Lovett," my guard said, giving a hard poke to my back.

Chandler opened the door, and I slipped into a tiny room

where a nurse waited. Without a word, she picked up a glass thermometer and held it up to my mouth, her hand shaky with distrust.

I took it from her and tucked it snug under my tongue.

Minutes later, she escorted me out and nodded curtly to the guards.

"Let's get you to the library, miss. I'm sure you're eager to see it," Officer Chandler said.

I lifted a small smile. I was more than eager to see my husband.

Ten

I waited until he unlocked another door leading out to a large field. A long, circular sidewalk led us to the entrances of different buildings.

Officer Chandler walked us through, letting me peek beyond the crash gates. The dorms were well lit, with barred windows across them. As we passed more, I saw men loitering, smelled the odors of sweat, urine, cigarette smoke, and bleach rising into dead air, baking on concrete walls. I slowed my pace and cast my eyes on each face at every dorm, desperately searching for him in the clusters of inmates, even checking the Negro section as we moved along to what Chandler called the Bottoms, the dorms farthest from the administration building.

Officer Chandler stopped a man walking past us on the sidewalk. "Tuck in the shirt, Payton, and get back to your dorm and shave," he ordered. "Don't show up to chow hall unless you do."

The inmate's face flushed, and he stuffed the shirttail into his britches as he sped off. All the men were clean-shaven, with very few sloppily dressed. I looked down at my assigned striped cotton prison dress and smoothed down the collar, double-checking the buttons on the front and the laces on my dull shoes.

A few prisoners whistled catcalls as they passed us on the walkway, and their guard struck out his walking stick, quieting them. Others gasped and stared in disbelief. One remarked loudly, "I'll be damn, never seen a colored Blue'un, an' by God, now I've done seen everything."

Still, I would not lower my head, cower, or duck until I had boldly looked into all their faces—until I found him. And despite the disquiet rambling inside me, I tossed my pride and kept searching until the guard stopped at two wide metal doors.

"We'll need to cross through the gymnasium," he announced.

A gymnasium. I'd only seen pictures in magazines, and I snatched a glimpse of my guard and saw he was impressed too.

Chandler opened the door, and I stopped to gawk at the inmates playing ball on a large basketball court. A few sat on wooden bleachers and turned their attention our way. Over in the corner, two men in puffed leather gloves boxed inside a roped ring, oblivious to their visitors.

Officer Chandler paused a moment to watch the boxers, then called out, "Bob and weave, boys. Waters, you got yourself a glass jaw today? Lead right instead of using the dive. *There.* Counterpunch!"

"Are you a boxer?" my guard asked.

"Did some when I was in the Navy."

He looked admirably at Chandler.

At a table beside the ring, three inmates huddled together, two puffing on cigarettes, the smoke ghost-tailing up between them. A black licorice twist dangled from the mouth of the other man as he shook something inside a spent Dixie cup, the rattles whispering a secret.

The officer suddenly stopped behind the men, held up his palm. "Hand 'em over, fellas." One of the prisoners looked sheepishly over his shoulder, then scooped up something and passed it to him. Officer Chandler peered down at his palm, jiggling a set of dice. "Catch you gambling again, I'll write you up and you'll be going in front of Captain Coleman for disciplinary punishment," he warned. "Get on down to chow hall."

The men snatched up packs of cigarettes, the bag of Black

Twist licorice and candy bars they'd been gambling with, and scurried away.

Officer Chandler dropped the dice into my guard's hand and said, "Made from toilet paper. The men dampen a crushed-up wad of tissue and mold it until it dries rock hard."

My officer shook his head as he examined the homemade dice. "Looks real."

The guard hurried us along to another room, where men exercised and lifted weights.

Officer Chandler called out cheerfully to the men as we passed, "Keep working on that penitentiary cut, fellas."

The prisoners grinned and hollered back, "Yes, sir, Cap'n."

He whisked us down another walkway, then stopped at a wooden door with a cross above it. "Miss, our new library is in another room behind the chapel. You'll find we have it ready for your visit."

We passed through a modest chapel with rows of folding chairs facing a pulpit and a large wooden cross and painted dove on the wall behind it. Each chair held a Bible and a stiff cutout cardboard fan stapled onto a flat wooden handle with an image of Jesus praying over rock that had been printed on it. I caught whiffs of smoke, and stopped alongside the wall in front of a narrow wooden table filled with pillar candles, studying.

"Every Sunday we hold Bible study classes. The men can visit any day for private prayer or to light a candle. Would you like to light a candle, miss?"

I looked at him, perplexed.

"Light a prayer candle for yourself or a loved one?"

I could only shake my head at the notion. The Blues had been unchurched for as long as I could remember. Mama'd given me lessons, and we held church and Bible studies in our home alongside Troublesome Creek, where she taught me to love my fellow man. Still, nary a single townsfolk or God-fearing soul loved us back, nor invited us into their fold, the town churches, or chapel-dotted hollers. Instead, we'd been shunned, damned by preachers and congregations who cried out and called us heathens and immoral. And while Mama had continued my spiritual lessons in devotion, grace, and prayer, Pa taught me the gospel of those who carried their hate like a loaded rifle.

"Here we are," Officer Chandler announced and opened the library door. Gaping, I found myself stitched to the threshold. The spacious room, filled with walls of polished wooden shelves brimming with books, was brightly lit by tall, narrow windows.

Chandler moved to the side. "Welcome to our library."

I stepped over to a bookshelf, soaking up the reads, surprised that many were new. Picking up a book, I inhaled the fresh print, fanned through crisp pages.

A large wooden rack packed with magazines stood in the corner, and I spotted *Newsweek*, *Reader's Digest*, *Popular Science*, *Old Farmer's Almanac*, and even a copy of *True Detective*. Two copies of the *Lexington Herald* newspaper, along with the *Oldham Era*, had been included, and I lingered to pore over the generous reading material.

On another shelf sat a collection of poems that brought back bittersweet memories of our wedding on that brisk October day in '36.

Officer Chandler joined me. "You'll find we have a lot of good material."

I pointed to Yeats. "I have the same one in my collection at home."

"We've got plenty of poetry. Some of the men like to use the poems in their letters back home. There's even a children's section for the children visiting their fathers." He waved his arm toward the other bookshelves. "Warden Alton, along with a few trusted inmates on his library committee, selected each book. He wanted to make sure you have everything you need."

"*A library committee*." To think, we were struggling to get readers over at the women's prison. I couldn't imagine having a whole committee of inmates who would rally for a library.

"Volunteers handpicked by the warden himself," he replied.

"It's a fine selection of reads, sir. One of the best I've seen."

"I'll let the warden know. There's a new blackboard for your use, and they delivered the chairs and two big tables in the middle—and the smaller round one over there—just yesterday."

I circled the heavy rectangular table with twelve folding chairs neatly tucked under its wooden lip and admired the new furniture. At the head of another one someone had placed several primers, writing tablets, a stack of books, new magazines, and a leather chair at the end. Fresh sheets of notepaper and sharpened pencils were in the middle beside a pile of new envelopes.

"Warden wanted you to have comfortable seating." Officer Chandler hurried over and pulled out the chair for me. I sank down into the rich leather, astonished that the men's prison had received such generous funding, while at the women's we barely scraped by, begged for castoffs and even torn books and ladder-made shelves.

"The men will be here shortly, and you'll have about forty-five minutes with each group. We have several hundred. You'll at least be able to see a good many today. Help those who are needing to learn how to read. Some may want you to write letters. Now, if anyone acts up, is disrespectful, just send them back to their dorm. Today you are acting as our librarian, and Warden has put you in charge. He wants the library to be a sanctuary. Treated as sacred as our chapel."

"Yes, sir."

"Okay then. We'll get you a breakfast tray from the officer's hall directly and let you get settled." He looked over at my guard. "We'll see that you get one as well, Officer."

"Obliged," I said quietly, trying to take in every inch of this fine library, marveling over the scent of fresh paint, polished woodwork and ink-soaked books, and the newness of it all. Jackson loved books as much as I did, and I know'd he wouldn't miss the opening of this one.

My mind turned to our reunion. When I found I couldn't keep my eyes off the door, I busied myself and looked over the materials on the table, straightening the papers until I got the piles just so.

Weren't long before footsteps sounded in the chapel. I glanced back up, hopeful for Jackson, only to be disappointed. An older gentleman whistled softly as he rolled in the breakfast-tray cart.

Eleven

A prisoner collected the dirty breakfast dishes, and the first group of twenty-four men filed in and took their seats around both tables while guards sat in chairs beside the door, chatting quietly.

I held out hope that Jackson would be in the next group or the one after. Standing, I said, "Good morning, gentlemen." My nerves suddenly landed in my belly.

I gave the group a small, friendly smile. Studied the faces of each, finding some were seeking a salvation beyond these prison walls. The books would give them the chance to make parole. At this, I squared my shoulders. "Book Woman Cussy Lovett, at your service, gentlemen."

One older man stood. "Why are you blue-colored, gal, and why ain't ya teachin' coloreds down there in the Bottoms instead of us?" He hitched a thumb toward the door. "'Cause if it's catching, I'm fixin' to hightail it outta here. Don't care *what* extra privileges Warden Alton bribes us with to come to Library—"

"Sit down," Officer Chandler commanded.

Reluctantly, the man plopped back into his seat while another grumbled, "Rather be on the yard exercising. If I wanted to learnt the lessons, I would've gone to school for 'em."

Another inmate replied, "Johnny Stubs, anybody who'd cut off their own trigger finger to get out of the draft is dumber than a broom handle, and that cowpea brain of yours could use some eddicating."

Johnny shot his fellow inmates a toothless grin and proudly lifted his middle digit in a vulgar salute. More of those salutes and salacious remarks circled the table. A few sheepish inmates shook their heads, guffawing, wiping the tears from their slap-happy mirth. Giddy for the brief interruption to escape their humdrum lives.

I walked over to the blackboard, picked up a piece of chalk, and wrote METHEMOGLOBINEMIA across in big letters.

I turned to the loud one. "Sir, I have a genetic disorder called methemoglobinemia." I tapped the letters on the board and sounded it out twice and extra slow, watching the men try to lick at the big word.

"Ain't no one, *not one living soul*, ought'a be saddled with a disorder that takes a fat-talking, two-dollared word. *No, sir.* It's just quare, it is. Try an' chew that one, it'll eat the hairs right off your tongue." The inmate whistled.

I smiled at that. "My doctor calls it Met H—and my color is not catching, gentlemen. It simply means my blood isn't getting the same amount of oxygen as yours."

"Don't give a whit 'bout what ya have or don't have, ma'am," a younger man piped. "I'm here to learn my letters so I can write my girl, Becky, over in Bee Lick and get outta here with my reading certificate for parole. Been missing her kisses mightily," he said in earnest, leaning over to snatch up a pencil and sheet of paper from the table.

Several men hooted, and with that, we began our first lesson.

One of many, each beginning with the word I'd written on the blackboard to put the men at ease.

I selected books for those who could read and settled them at the table. One group wanted to write letters, so I passed out stationery, asking if anyone needed my help before going on to others.

After helping several, I glanced around to see if he'd arrived.

In another group, an inmate rose and went over to the shelves and brought back three children's books. "Ma'am, I grew up on Devil's Jump over in McCreary County."

"That's fine country, sir."

"I ain't up for parole anytime soon. But I want to learn these books so I can read to my lil'uns when they visit." He handed me new copies of *The Adventures of Grandfather Frog, The Painted Garden,* and *The Wonderful Wizard of Oz.*

I ran my fingers over the title of *The Wonderful Wizard of Oz*, wishing I had one for Emmeline in Forensics. "Wonderful choices, sir."

"Tommy is four, and my oldest, Ben Junior, is going on seven. Used to tuck them in with a bedtime story I'd concoct each night. Figured, well, maybe if I could read one of them books on visiting day, I could make it up to them."

"Let's see about getting you started. We can read over there where it's quieter." I nudged him toward the smaller table. Seated, I opened *The Adventures of Grandfather Frog*. "Would you like to read it together?"

He nodded his head. And ever so slow, word by word, and in unison, we began the first story, "Billy Mink Finds Little Joe Otter."

When we were through, I peered up at the clock, daydreaming about what it would be like to finally have Jackson arrive. I imagined him asking for a book, maybe pretending to need my help.

Thinking I should prepare for his visit, I hurried over to the shelf and plucked up the Yeats collection.

Twelve

In another group, a young man who looked not much older than my sixteen-year-old daughter approached me, carrying paper, pencil, and a book of poetry. He had thick, stylish hair and a handsome face marred by a cut across his cheek and a fresh bruise to his eye. A cast ran the length of his arm down to his elbow. He stood hesitant in front of the table, darting his eyes around the room to everyone but me.

"May I help you?" I asked, concerned he was frightened of my color. Wondering if I should repeat what I'd told new groups when they'd arrived.

The man's cheeks rosied, and his lips tucked in and disappeared behind a woeful face as he clutched the book to his chest.

"I'm Cussy Lovett. What's your name?" I coaxed gently.

"They call me Daniel, ma'am."

"Would you like help reading or writing a letter, Daniel? Please, sit down." I pushed the Yeats collection to the side.

He slid into a chair and scooted it close to mine, the spirit of fresh shaving cream lifting between us. Daniel looked all around again, then leaned in and whispered in the smallest of voices, leaving me straining for his words, "I need a little help." He raised his cast. "I'm schooled, but I want to write a letter back home to Lodiburg." He crowded even closer and, in a hushed, frightened voice, said, "Send a poem to someone I love." Daniel blushed and slid a fresh sheet of notepaper over to me. He opened the book to an envelope he'd used as a bookmark and placed a finger on the poem "On Marriage," by Kahlil Gibran. "This one right here, ma'am."

I picked up my pencil and began writing as he recited low:

"To my one and only love: 'Give your hearts, but not into each other's keeping. For only the hand of Life can contain your hearts.'"

When the young man paused, choking on his words, I noticed his shoulders quake.

His words made me ache for my own love somewhere inside this very prison. I pressed down on my lips and looked away, my eyes landing on the poetry book I would share with Jackson.

Daniel bowed his head and apologized for the interruption before whispering the next passages.

"'And stand together yet not too near together: For the pillars of the temple stand apart, And the oak tree and the cypress grow not in each other's shadow.'"

Then the young man closed his blurred eyes along with the book and murmured, "*Wait for me. I need you, Arthur. Write back—*"

I raised the pencil and did my best to swallow the surprise.

"I—I didn't mean, I—" The tips of his ears reddened. Daniel looked over his slumped shoulders and then moved in closer to the lip of the table. "Sorry, ma'am, I—" He swallowed.

I never know'd a man in love with another one. The preacher man would have marked a stain on these folks and driven them out. And the only book I'd read that dared to broach such was *Nightwood*.

But suddenly, I realized Daniel's plight weren't much different from mine. Only the man's peculiarity and his public-proclaimed stain were hidden, unlike mine.

I noted his fresh bruises and cast, knowing he'd probably been punished long enough for loving who he couldn't. Saddened for the young man, I gazed down at my shadow-soaked hands washed in indigo blue.

Forever, me and my kin had suffered our own peculiarity—an *affliction*, ol' preacher man had declared, and sought to rid me of it. I shuddered remembering all the others him and his congregation had tried to cast the devils out of in the '30s: the seven-year-old Melungeon girl who suffered fits, a young albino boy with pink eyes, and the triplet babies he'd insisted were spawned by Satan's seeds. Those who were unchurched and others with odd markings that didn't have a name. The one young woman who'd been violently raped by a circuit peddler, who'd brutally battered her face and tore off an ear, scarring her for life. And when she visited the granny woman for a tonic to rid herself of his evil root, the preacher and his flock publicly marked her, damned her to eternal hell, driving the woman deeper into the dark hills.

Over the years, many had been drowned during Frazier's frenzied baptismals in the cold waters of Troublesome Creek.

Daniel's face knotted with pain and anguish. He lowered his head to the table, scrubbed his damp eyes with a hard palm, and said, quietly, "Didn't mean for it to slip out like that. But sometimes the hurt's so bad, I can't hold it all inside."

I scanned the room, then looked over my shoulder. Some of the men practiced their letters on the blackboard; others looked at magazines and books and lingered over by bookshelves while the guards bent their heads in friendly conversation.

Beside me, Yeats sat waiting for Jackson. I leaned down closer to Daniel and confided, "I know'd how hard it is wanting to love someone others declare you can't." Then, to ease his discomfort: "It's a fine letter, Daniel. How would you like it signed?"

Hesitant, he searched my face.

I didn't know a lick about Daniel's matters of the heart, but I know'd mine, and I lifted what I hoped was a kind smile.

"Ma'am—" He rubbed knuckles over his mouth, struggling with words.

Lowering my head to the letter, I averted any indication of prying eyes, waited, and, when seconds had passed, gently coughed.

"Ma'am, uh"—he wiped his brow—"we love each other."

I nodded, dipped my chin, and hovered my pencil over the page, waiting for his closing salutation.

"Just *Love, Daniel Presland*," he barely breathed, sliding the envelope over to me.

I smoothed down the paper and penned *Love, Daniel Presland*. "It's a fine Scottish name, Mr. Presland." Neatly, I lined up the sides, creased and folded the letter twice, and addressed the envelope before passing it back to him.

Blushing, he pulled out a stamp, licked and pressed it on the envelope, and gave it back. "Can you mail it for me?"

Quickly, I stuffed it into my dress pocket. If caught, I would tell them the patron had left the room and forgot the letter. And as librarian, I felt obligated to mail it.

I watched the young man head toward the door, thinking about how folks argued that prison reform saves some but destroys others, and I shuddered at the thought of what it might do to young Daniel.

Another man came over and asked for help selecting a mystery book.

When I found one I thought he might like, he thanked me and checked it out.

I looked up at the clock. *Where was Jackson?*

Thirteen

Hours passed, and new groups came and went, but still no Jackson.

I could only nibble at my dinner. From the other table, Officer Chandler looked over at my tray. "Can I have Cook fix you something else, Book Woman? He's the officers' chef and the best of all our inmates. After he arrived, we found out he used to serve under the chef at Miller's Cafeteria, and then at the fine Colonnade in downtown Louisville. It wouldn't be any trouble to have Cook whip up something else, if you like."

He'd been kind ever since I arrived, even let me use the guard's lavatory when I needed while he waited outside the door.

"No, sir. Still a lil full from that fine breakfast I had at six thirty," I lied, feeling even more nauseous. Anxious to finally see Jackson.

Throughout the afternoon, I'd helped the men learn their letters and read to them from the primer, urged some to write beginner words on the blackboard if they were able.

When the room quieted and some of the men had settled into their own reads while others lingered near the bookshelves, I stepped over to the window. Officer Chandler followed and pointed to the vast fields. "Over twenty-seven hundred acres, and a thousand of them used to plant vegetables."

"It's like a whole town."

"You can see we even have a cemetery, named after its first occupant, chicken thief Henry 'Chicken' Montgomery," he commented. "I'll be over there by the door if you need me." The officer excused himself.

I'd learned about it from the women's prison. The graveyard was for inmates who had no family, and thought to be aptly named because prisoners know'd that even the orneriest feared above all dying alone in their own eternal embrace inside a forgotten potter's field that would never so much as see the shade of visiting loved ones, nor the beauty of a silk death-anniversary petal.

Some whispered that the dismal graveyard also held the infants of the female inmates who'd come in pregnant and lost their babies shortly after. Squinting, I made out the rise of a small, fresh mound toward the back, then turned abruptly to the table.

I busied myself helping two men work on the alphabet, grateful for the new spelling primers the library had bought.

A hearty supper of cornmeal-dusted frog legs, stewed tomatoes, leather britches, and peach pie arrived late afternoon. I appreciated the frosted bottle of Coca-Cola they'd included on my tray and immediately took a sip, and another bigger one, the raw sweetness lighting a tingle as it slid down my throat.

It was a greedy gulp, and I dipped my chin to swipe away the memories of long sweetenin' from home. It seemed to ease my nervous belly. I rubbed the thick green bottle, the droplets of ice disappearing under my thumb.

It was something else, seeing such a fine spread, and I couldn't get over how the officers had a real chef from a fancy restaurant to feed them like this. The frog legs were tender, and the leather britches had been seasoned perfectly with ham hock and salt pork. Still, my appetite escaped, and I played with the well-prepared dishes with my fork, swallowing tiny pieces of food that didn't agree with me. When I couldn't force another bite, I set down a half-eaten piece of fried corn bread and passed the tray back to the prisoner who'd delivered it. "It was tasty, sir, but I reckon I'm still stuffed from the last tray."

An inmate went around the room opening windows, letting in fresh, sun-soaked breezes. The burst of the afternoon's energy lulled while my older guard, Sam, dozed off in a chair. Officer Chandler sat beside him, reading the newspaper in between sips of coffee.

I picked up books from the tables and took them over to the shelves. An officer poked his head into the room and peered around. Officer Chandler went up to him. "Help you, Captain?"

"I see you've had a busy day in here, Chandler."

"Yes, sir. It's been a successful one."

The captain looked past him. "Where's that Lovett inmate, the fellow who's all into the books? I thought he'd be up here by now." He strained his neck, searching.

A tremble took hold of my hands. *Jackson.* Surely he'd be here any minute.

The men walked out into the hall, and the conversation was lost.

With each new group, I had watched and silently willed Jackson to appear. It was 4:55, a final class to go, and I held my breath as, one by one, the men filed in.

When the last inmate passed through the door, I quickly turned to the chalkboard and looked down at the grief painting my hands, suddenly pierced by cold shards tunneling inside, the hunger of missing him unbearable.

Don't cry, don't cry, I silently commanded, blinking away the single disobedient tear.

Fourteen

A shadow-draped moodiness pleated itself across the women's prison and mud-swept grounds while librarian duties kept me busy the rest of May and into the rain-soaked month after.

The library had been left in disarray, still waiting for its fresh coat of paint. While I had been over at the men's prison, Warden Alton had sent over his volunteers to drop off supplies. Paint buckets, brushes, and a ladder rested in a corner, and shelves had been pulled out from the walls, leaving it hard for me to maneuver around.

Kitchen duty, along with visiting the Death Row, Forensic, and Geriatric wards, took up most of my time, though I welcomed each hard-ticking second. Still, Sundays were the worst. With no friends or family visiting, and despite the clutter, I sought solace inside the library, selecting reads for the next visit with my patrons.

Though far from friendly, the guards stopped putting time limits on my visits to the wards and even encouraged me to stay longer. Officer Holt had softened somewhat and no longer made me ask permission before loaning a book to his inmates. And whenever I arrived to find some of the loudest women glued quietly to their books, he would marvel and remark quietly to another guard, and more than once, "Them books are better than anything them quack doctors have been doping 'em with."

One week, I dropped in to find Officer Holt training a new guard. The unseasoned corrections officer held up a hand. "Back to your dorm, Grape Girl. Ain't got no business here," he said, barking me away.

Ignoring him, Officer Holt strode over to the crash gate. "She's Cussy Lovett, our Book Woman, Officer Brown." He fumbled with the keys.

"Books from this—*this inkblot*?" Brown sneered and crossed his arms. "That's the last thing these harebrained females need. Can't give 'em foolish notions that could cause more trouble for us. It's too dangerous."

Office Holt unlocked the crash gate. "The books are necessary," he said firmly.

"Books ain't nothing but hogwash. Waste of a smart fella's time." Brown flattened his lips.

Undaunted, Officer Holt swung open the gate.

"Them books and that blue devil's gonna cause us nothing but trouble," Brown hounded. "Mark my word, sir. My daddy said it's downright dangerous having women read anything but the Bible or *The American Women's Almanac*, much less putting thorny notions into these bone-brained…*witless females*," the new corrections officer spat.

"It's necessary," Officer Holt snipped.

Grateful, I lifted my chin two-man tall as I slipped past the guards and over to the caged women.

Brown started to protest again, but Officer Holt held up a shushing hand and roared, "*Necessary*."

And for the first time in a long time, and even fewer times before than I could recollect, *I* felt necessary.

Inside Death Row, I sat on the concrete floor outside of Sassyann's cell, the dank air sheeting us. We'd just finished reading *Man's Search for Meaning*. I thought Viktor Frankl's life inside a Nazi prison camp would give her meaning and purpose during her difficult time. Offer her some comfort and hope.

Today, she was sullen when I handed her new notepaper. "I'd druther you read *What Katy Did* again."

Despite Sassyann's lack of interest in the books, she was fond of the ol' tale about the children living in Ohio. "I'll bring it back next time. Let's work on your writing some more," I pressed lightly.

She sat beside me with her knees drawn, balancing the Bible for a writing surface to pen her letter. The guard had been letting Sassyann out of her cell while she learned. Sometimes when I read her books, he'd glance down from time to time from his glass-windowed box. Soon, he began opening his office door to listen to the stories too.

I watched while Sassyann worked earnestly on the letter to her sons. Twice, she had thrown the pencil down, pushed aside the spelling primer, and wadded up the paper, tossing it across the hall.

Smoothing out the wrinkled page, I studied what was causing the fuss. "It's okay. Try again, you almost have it. You just need to change the *U* to an *O* here." I handed her another clean sheet and retrieved her pencil.

"It's useless. All this work to learnt my letters, an' they ain't never gonna come visit or write back. Ain't never gonna love me an' sure as Sam-hell ain't never gonna forgive me. I don't know why I bother with them good-for-nothing boys not caring about their ma. Not nary a word in a decade, an' here I did it all to protect them. Too stupid an' too long in the tooth to be learnt anyway." She pouted.

I hugged my knees to my chest and mused on something Mama'd taught me long ago about how everyone has sense; it was just learning how to use it. Finally, I said, "I know'd they'd love to hear from their mama. I'd give anything to hear from mine."

"Miss mine too. Miss my sweet boys." Her words breezed out in a rasp. She looked down at her ragged fingertips, rubbing a thumb across them, sighing. "But I don't know what to say after all them lost years. I fear my sweet boys done turned into strangers."

"It's not too late, Sassyann. Just three words: *I love you.* My mama always said, 'Regret comes fast and forgiveness is lost when the simplest words from the heart stay absent.'" I held out the pencil.

She took it, snapped her paper, and smoothed it down on the book, steadying. The corners of her mouth worked feverishly as she dated the top of the page and printed her salutation, then studied on the words. Again and again, she paused and looked up at me, scowling, tempted to rip up the page.

I coaxed her along, correcting a few misspelled words, but mostly she was determined to write it herself.

"Let's add a silent *E* to the end here." I pointed at her page. "It's spelled P-L-E-A-S-E. And bury has a *U*—"

She snatched the page away.

I pressed my lips together, hoping she wouldn't tear it up.

When Sassyann finished almost an hour later, she handed it to me, a measure of peace umbrellaing her wearisome frame.

June '53

Deer ~~Suns~~ Sons,

Its yur Ma Sassyann Sipes. I lernt to read an writ so I culd writ you. I miss you. Sum days I git reel skeered I wont ever see my boys agin. Please come see me. I love you. If I don't see you agin ~~bary~~ bury me in Pap Tates simatary next to Momma Delthea an Sister an Bruther.

Yur lovin Ma Sassyann Sipes
nmate 22407
Ky State Womins ~~Prisun~~ Prison
Pewe Vally Ky

Looking up, I opened my mouth to suggest corrections but clamped it shut when I met her prideful, shiny eyes.

Fifteen

Moods shifted when, in late June, the sun finally broke through.

Standing in front of the warden, I waited for her to address me.

"Warden Alton has asked for your library services again. I don't like piling more on my best workers. We have so few as it stands…but I hope you're up for the task."

I could hardly believe my good fortune—another chance to see Jackson—and I squawked out a *yes*.

"I also need his men to replace some leaky pipes. There's your library as well."

"Yes, ma'am. I'm hoping it will be painted soon. It's been a mess since they delivered the painting supplies."

"That's my fault, unfortunately. The damn boiler broke down again. I had to pull them from the library and send them downstairs to repair it. But now we have the director over Corrections visiting soon. I must have everything in order."

When I arrived back to my wing, I found Regina bent over my wooden locker, snooping around my cot.

"You'll not find cigarettes or any hooch here. Waldeen keeps everything locked up." I checked over my belongings, straightened the coverlet on my bed where she'd raised the mat. "And the only thing you'll get from me is books, Regina."

"Go to hell," she snipped.

"Stay away," I warned, bumping her aside as I knelt and inspected the lock.

She cursed and scurried off.

Again, I suffered a long, restless night, working myself into a tizzy, spending most of my time in the washroom with a cool rag to my face.

Waldeen poked her head inside and marched back out into the dorm. When she came back, she shoved a pint of whiskey into my hand. "Ya ain't gonna be in no shape to see your man if ya don't calm yourself down. The guards see ya like this, they'll send ya up to the infirmary. Your blue's done climbed out of its shadow and tipped into an iron gray."

I grabbed the bottle and took a big gulp. It hit my scratchy throat and scorched sliding down. My belly gurgled, and I clamped a hand over my mouth.

"Take another," Waldeen pressed.

I waved her away as the liquor threatened to come back up.

We pulled up to the rock wall in front of the administration building, the crowing of cocks greeting the dawn, awakening the quiet dew-covered fields.

Inside the men's prison, Officer Chandler stopped us at the nurse's door. After she took my temperature, I was released back into his custody.

Again, I studied every face, searching for Jackson.

When my guard, Sam, paused in the gym to watch the men boxing, Officer Chandler said, "Why don't you stay. Enjoy yourself a break. I'll send a breakfast tray down and have the guard bring you up to the library whenever you're ready. Shoot yourself a game of pool in the officers' lounge, if you like. I can take care of Book Woman." He slapped his back.

Sam jumped at the chance, more than happy to escape his boring duty.

After brief introductions to the groups, we settled into the lessons. The men drifted around tables and lingered over at the bookshelves. I helped several write letters back home, but still no Jackson.

An inmate came over carrying a newspaper. "Miss Book Lady..." He thrust it into my hands. "Wonder if you can read me this. Does that say *pole-lee-o*? Overheard Officer Chandler saying the article was about it. I, er, seemed to have lost my glasses again," he said, his hands flying over flat shirt pockets, patting as if searching for missing spectacles.

I'd heard the excuse by more than a few on my Pack Horse librarian route over the years. *The prided.* Those who were too embarrassed to admit they'd never learned their letters, the ones too proud to ask for the help. I know'd too well the unshakable dignity stiffening the bones of my people.

"My pleasure, sir. Have a seat."

He settled into the chair, and I snapped the paper and read out loud the headline:

SALK'S CLINICAL TRIALS ON POLIO VACCINES PROMISING!

> Jonas Salk, scientist and doctor, announced his clinical trials' success after he used vaccinations on monkeys, numerous children crippled by polio, volunteers at mental institutions, and prisoners who received the vaccines. Salk went on CBS Radio to report his studies and...

When I finished, the man said, "That's good news I've been a'waitin' on. I'd volunteer *any* day for his trials. Lost my little girl Nettie Jane to polio. Bud, my eldest, was left crippled by it. Me and my woman are anxious for a vaccine for us and our other four children. Could you write my missus and let her know about Salk's latest studies? She don't have money to spend on a newspaper or the stationery."

"Yes, sir. Let me get some notepaper and an envelope, and we'll send this hopeful news to your wife right away."

Smiling, I watched him walk away, then drew my eyes to the door. *Jackson, I'm here. Here*, I begged silently for his arrival.

Daniel arrived at three, and I was relieved to see him. "Ma'am." He leaned over my shoulder and whispered, "Did you post my letter?"

"I mailed it the next morning," I said, pausing to shelve a book. I'd made sure that Waldeen had sent it out with her weekly grocery invoices.

Daniel had new bruises and a cut across his mouth. His arm still sported the cast.

My heart ached for the young boy—the tortures he must be suffering while guards turned a blind eye.

He handed back the poetry book from our last visit. "Thank you, ma'am," he said quietly and walked over to the guard before I could inquire about him further.

"Officer Chandler, has the mail come in yet?"

The guard looked at his watch. "They'll be making the rounds soon enough." He dismissed Daniel.

Another prisoner wandered into the library, and Daniel turned and accidently bumped into him. The inmate jabbed Daniel sharply with his elbow. The young man bowed over and pressed an arm to his side, the pain spreading across his face.

Furious, I stepped up to the unruly prisoner and snapped, "Rude behavior is not allowed in the library. I'll have to ask you to leave, sir."

"And just who the hell do you think you are, blue fly?" The small muscled inmate bristled and took a step toward me, flexing his hand.

"Librarian Cussy Lovett. Leave, sir." I stared into his hardening eyes. "*Now.*" The command tightened in my throat and squeezed out. "*Leave.*" Immediately, Chandler appeared beside us.

The man looked back to Daniel and once more to me before turning to the guard. "You trying to jest me, Cap'n? Over that fairy boy?" A cruel laugh escaped his curled lips.

Chandler scowled. "You heard our Book Woman. Back to your dorm, Carl Honeycutt."

"The punk bumped me first, and this circus freak is falsely accusing me—"

"Pack your shit; you're going to the hole!" Officer Chandler boomed.

"C'mon, Cap'n, ya know Warden's new rule. I won't be able to have my parole hearing until I learn to read," he attempted to coax.

The officer's jaw tightened.

"*Please.* My woman's been real sick, and I tol' you the baby is due in two months. Please, Cap'n, I'm jus' trying to get it done to make it back home and help my family."

Officer Chandler wouldn't budge.

"Cap, it was jus' a knee-jerk reaction. Parole'll flop me again if I can't get the reading classes signed off on my papers."

I fidgeted with my collar. "Officer, Mr. Honeycutt can stay—"

"*Hole.*" Chandler brushed past him.

Cursing, the inmate stormed out.

I stole a glance at Daniel and recognized his terror, then worried what the brutish inmate might do to him, regretting I'd interfered and possibly put the young man more in harm's way—and now ruined Honeycutt's chances to see his ill wife and new baby.

Daniel wouldn't meet my eyes and ducked out of the library. In my rush to defend him, I'd been reckless with his safety. I slipped back into my seat at the small table, the guilt needling my flesh.

Minutes later, a prisoner brought in supper trays, but I politely declined, my nerves clawing across my belly. Instead, I checked books in and out for the men, answered questions, and wrote another letter for an inmate.

When there was a lull in my duties, I went over to the window and stared out at the sweeping grounds. My eyes were drawn to Chicken Hill, pained that babies were eternally resting there, never to have loved ones kneel over their prison graves or leave blooms.

Dismayed, I turned away and sat down next to a man struggling with his book. "Sir, can I help you with your reading today?"

Anytime footsteps sounded out in the hall, a fresh hope would rise. Still, no sign of Jackson.

When the last hour came to a close, I shoved the Yeats collection back onto the shelf and joined the guard waiting out in the hall, my despair deepening.

Sixteen

Outside, the sun beat down as I followed Sam back to our automobile. In the back seat, I turned my sweaty face toward the driver's open window when we passed the rock fencing along the men's prison. Soon, farms and cornfields appeared in the distance. Cows cooled themselves in ponds while horses turned to their run-in sheds for shade.

In a few minutes, the dusty two-lane road merged into one soldiered by tall warted trunks of crowning oaks. A collie barked and gave chase to the rumbling automobile, and I became more miserable as the distance between us grew wider.

How I missed him. I'd spent my whole life waiting for someone like Jackson. That one soul who'd been searching for that someone like *me.*

I pressed fingers to the corners of my eyelids, quelling the tears. *Just to see a loving face that I know'd loved me would be a balm for the aching loneliness of prison life.*

The guard eased the automobile into the curving necklace of tire-rutted roads. Ahead, the women's gun tower appeared, and I trembled, feeling the despair press down. When he stopped to check in at our gate, I stared out the window in disbelief as we drove through.

He wore faded-tan britches and a white T-shirt that I know'd the prison had issued. His face looked gaunt, his damp curls tousled, and he'd lost some weight, but it was him all the same. *Jackson.*

Directly, I darted my eyes to the rearview mirror. Sam's gaze dropped to the windshield, and I quietly pressed a palm against my window.

To my husband.

Lightly pressing again and again. Silently screaming to Jackson, willing his eyes to lock with mine.

I gulped back shaky breaths to silence my loud pleas.

I'm here.

Here, Jackson.

Just one glimpse would be like holding you again and carry me home.

Please look, Jackson.

Please.

But Jackson didn't see me as he and another prisoner carried ladders and paint cans toward an official white van, where a guard stood watch beside it. The men began loading the vehicle with their supplies.

Jackson opened the van door and abruptly paused and looked over his shoulder toward my automobile. His eyes narrowed and slowly filled with surprise, then tenderness.

I raised my trembling hand higher on the hot pane and pressed in close, collecting this memory of him.

Us.

Home.

The moment was a gift I would magpie away into the deepest core of my being.

I crowded in closer to the window.

Jackson's gaze held mine. Then sorrow shadowed his face when their guard pointed him and the other prisoner into the van.

"Looks like Warden Alton finally sent over his volunteers to paint the library," Sam remarked. "Let's hurry and git you inside, Lovett. Been a long day for ol' Sam here. My missus'll be waiting with my slippers and a stiff bourbon."

Sam pulled into the employee lot, searching for an empty parking spot as I watched the other vehicle pass by, gaining speed. Taking my husband back to his prison. Me back to mine. The moment passing with our lives in its iron-fisted grip.

My palm slid down the window as I realized he'd volunteered like myself, but hoping to see *me*.

Seventeen

Pounding heat and rain returned the last days of June, paralyzing the prison.

Waldeen caught me by the sleeve as I hung the mop in the utility closet and reached for my bag of books. "The warden just sent for ya. And she seemed a mite agitated."

Agitated. *It seemed everyone was.* The soupy, festering air was wrapped in molasses and barely crawling inside the penitentiary. Even the wind carried a cry when offering up a stingy breeze.

Many of the women soaked their sheets in cold water and draped themselves to escape the heat and foulness, but it still felt like we were trapped under wet woolen blankets. Some slept on the cool concrete floors, their heads swathed in dampened towels. But despite the temporary remedies and having all the windows open behind curtains of water-sopped bedsheets, a stubborn anger gripped the prison.

I rubbed my painful arm. The unrelenting weather rioted against my newly knit bones, aggravating the tender joints and nerves whenever I mopped the cafeteria floors.

"Scuttlebutt is, Warden is still griping about funding again. But luckily, our budget's not in her crosshairs." Waldeen lifted the tail of her apron and wiped the dampness off her brow.

I still didn't have any library visitors, but a few of the girls in my wing had been requesting books. Slowly, more had followed.

But would a handful be enough? Or would she fire me because I hadn't lived up to her expectations?

"I'll take your books. Ya better hurry, kid." Waldeen grabbed the bag.

As I stepped out of the cafeteria, I bumped into Regina. She shoved me, and my shoulder hit the wall.

"Wonder if book witches bruise blue," she said and hurried by.

I brushed off the injury and swiftly made my way to Warden's office, almost colliding with a corrections officer. "Slow down. Walk with your eyes open, Lovett. And dammit, step lightly; you sound louder than a parade of elephants," he scolded.

A guard came into the warden's tiny waiting room some forty minutes later. "Go on in, she'll see you now."

I smoothed down the wrinkles on my dress, tugged at the damp collar and clinging bodice, the sweltering heat a weighted misery as I cracked open the door. "Ma'am, you wanted to see me?"

"Come in. Sit," the warden replied crisply, and I took the chair in front of her desk, once more hiding my shadow-darkened hands inside the folds of my skirts.

"I have several reports we need to address." She lifted a stack of papers and squared them with several taps to her desk, then thumbed through the pages.

Breaths of wild honeysuckled winds pushed through the open window, blousing the drab green curtains. In the distance, thunder rolled across a crow's graveled cries as the promise of another summer rainstorm lightly perfumed the dark-paneled office.

Drawn to the lazy hum of the oscillating fan perched to the side of her desk, I tilted my head to the whirls, feeling its miserly breeze on my flesh.

Selecting a typewritten page from the stack in front of her,

Warden lassoed me back. "Okay. Let's start with Officer Holt's report." She studied her papers. "With Odette in Forensics."

"Ma'am, she likes the poetry books, sure enough."

"Her seizures have all but ceased."

Seizures? "That's what it was. Odette had one when I first met her."

"Clark came in over a year ago and shortly after began having these fits. The books are the only change in her life, and some of the doctors believe they may have somehow eased her disturbed mind."

I bobbed my head, proud my work was meeting her approval.

She picked up another page and skimmed it. "It appears Odette is finally communicating with the prison psychiatrist. Like most in her ward, the girl had been housed over at the old Central State Hospital asylum and always violently refused to speak, and even struck the guards and medical staff. It's no wonder they've discussed performing a lobotomy to keep her docile and obedient." She talked freely. "The director believes these type of surgeries have been a blessing to our prisons, thanks to Moniz. Now it looks like the books may offer something new for the doctors to muse over."

I shifted uncomfortably, thinking of Chaney in Geriatrics. I'd read about the Nobel Prize winner and heard plenty of tales in here about Kaintuck's horrid lunatic asylum, the torturous experiments and surgeries doctors used on afflicted folks they'd shackle in manacles. The drilling into brains, ice-water baths, forced shock treatments, and more.

"Officer Holt said he can't believe the change in his ward. Nor can the guards in Geriatrics," she went on. "The elderly inmates have greatly benefited from your library service, the nurse reports. Our former librarians would never step foot anywhere near those wards. But"—she raised a pointed finger toward me—"I should've known a Pack Horse librarian would."

"Thank you, Warden. I'm mighty grateful for the job."

"*Indeed*. Now"—she cleared her throat—"about the library. How many visitors have you had?"

"Visitors?" I asked, suddenly struck with the horror that she was finally going to dismiss me.

"Your patrons."

I couldn't meet her eyes. "None, ma'am, except for the weekly needlepoint club."

She picked up a slip of paper, set it in front of her, and wrote something down.

"That's about to change."

Would she make more demands I couldn't meet?

"There's also this report from Death Row," she said. "He notes she's been asking for stamps, anticipating writing her first letter when she finally graduates from your lessons. Thank you for working with her."

"Sassyann wrote her first letter and did a fine job, ma'am."

"Oh, which reminds me." She pushed two envelopes to the edge of her desk. "A letter from your lawyer and one from your daughter."

I snatched up the opened mail, looking at it like it was gold. It was my first letter from Honey.

"Take this note." She reached over her desk and dropped the paper close to the edge, still cautious about touching me.

"You'll need to bring those numbers up. But I'm releasing you from kitchen duty, though Waldeen has requested you continue keeping her books and help with the budget." Again, she paused to study the paper. "Therefore, I've decided to grant it."

Released. I glanced down at the note that declared it.

"Starting tomorrow morning, you'll be assigned as our new full-time prison librarian."

I cocked my good ear, not fully soaking up the words. "*Full-time librarian, ma'am?*"

"Indeed. We'll bring some of the less-disturbed women from the Geriatric and Forensic wards down to you. You begin work at seven a.m. sharp and close nightly at six p.m., Monday through Friday, except for religious holidays. Saturdays, you'll keep the library open till three p.m., and Sundays will be your day off. You do still want the job, Lovett?"

I nodded, hardly believing what I'd just heard.

"For your work, I'll continue to compensate you and will raise your state pay to eleven cents a day."

My debt from Laundry would be paid off soon. I was thrilled that I would be able to afford stamps to write Honey and that I wouldn't have to borrow from Waldeen again.

I'd seen my daughter once, and only briefly, back when they had me locked up in the infirmary. I had been drugged and could barely recall any of it, except for Honey screaming at the guards.

She'd not been allowed back since.

Warden Sanders said, "You'll continue your visits to the other wings, Death Row, and also set a schedule for those who need to learn to read and write in the library. *Your library*, Cussy Lovett."

My library. Mine. I was overjoyed by the unexpected gift.

It didn't matter none where the reading materials were housed—whether in a boarded-up woodland chapel that had seen too many rains, a small room in the back of an even-smaller post office, or inside these dank prison walls.

I jumped up, unable to control my excitement, the burst of gratitude. "Much obliged, Warden Sanders."

She studied me carefully before speaking. "Remember, no excitement books. It just riles the women—and, well, it'd be a temptation. Be mindful to use extra caution on selecting books for Forensics. No books like *Mrs. Dalloway*, or such that could poison the mind and lead to self-harm. We must not forget the long-ago *Werther fever* and how it incited the impressionable and less-educated to commit suicide and other tragic deeds."

I'd heard about *The Sorrows of Young Werther* and other similar books folks fussed and gossiped about, but still, I couldn't hide the disappointment on my face.

Warden knitted her brows. "Why, it would be like putting

Sassyann in charge of the kitchen," she said, her tone wry. "Those type of reads not only poison but can cause more damage to unhealthy minds and morally pollute our fine correctional facility."

I looked down at the floor.

"Warden Alton had asked if he could borrow you again. At least once a week in exchange for the men's extra maintenance services that we are desperately in need of. He had hoped you would be willing to train one of his inmates for a librarian position too."

To have another chance to see my husband would mean everything.

"Ma'am, I'd be happy to help the warden." I had to clear my throat to add, "Pleased to do *your* bidding."

"I will probably send you back over in late August. Perhaps things will settle down over there. I wouldn't want to risk anything happening here."

Settle down? I wondered what she meant but dared not question her.

"Warden Alton was grateful for your visits. He had his men pack up a crate of books for our library." I followed her gaze to a cumbersome box sitting in the corner on the floor. "Take a look. I think you'll be pleased. As librarian, you will of course get first dibs." She picked up her pen and made some notes on the papers.

I knelt to examine the wooden crate and saw it was one that had come off the rails long ago to be delivered to us Pack Horse librarians. After the shipped books were unpacked from trains, many of the crates would be donated to businesses and factories across the state. Others had recirculated when they were rescued from barns and vacant buildings. Once, I spotted several in a large feedstore in Tennessee that had been reused for grain bins, and another as an umbrella stand outside a funeral parlor in Kentucky. Seeing this one brought back fond memories.

The old crate cross-stitched with nicks and cracks had a black-painted address on its planks made out to the *Pack Horse*

Librarians in Knox County, KY. from a library in *Cleveland, OH.* Grinning, I lingered on the lid. Book Women Eddie Black and Jincey Miller would've likely unpacked this very one.

I recalled a young woman from up in Winchester. Agnes Griggs had driven a truck to our center one day to donate books. She'd also left us a pretty woven picnic basket filled with homemade treats from her kitchen. I'd unpacked the book crate and inhaled oak, citrus, and ink, marveling over the distance Agnes had ridden to get books to us, thinking of Janlyn Weintraub in Louisville doing the very same.

I closed my eyes and rubbed my hands over the address, calling up my route and home.

How many crates of used, donated books had I trudged into the Troublesome Creek Center from the train depot and unloaded and cataloged?

I raised the splintered oak lid and caught a strong whiff of apples that must have once been stored inside. It now held a lot of classics and some older reads, along with poetry books and newer novels I'd never heard of.

Looking over my shoulder, I stole a glance at the warden. She had her head bent toward her paperwork as the fan's breezes tousled the chestnut curls she'd styled into a poodle-cut hairdo like the ones I'd seen movie stars wear in magazines.

I ran a palm down my own dull, unkempt hair and turned back to the crate.

One by one, I pulled out the books. Then I saw it.

A copy of the present Jackson had given to me on our wedding day: the collection of Yeats poems from over at the men's library that I had toted around while waiting for Jackson to appear.

I turned it over, inspecting carefully.

Breathless, I ran my fingers across the buckram and beveled edges, lightly tracing the title on the worn leather label. Again, I peered over my shoulder.

Carefully, I opened the book to the title page.

His penciled-in inscription read:

I won't ever give up.

—Jackson

The very last words he'd said to me on the day we were arrested.

I flipped through the pages until I found our poem.

Pulling the book closer, I mouthed the last verse.

"'*To an isle in the water. With her I would fly.*'"

Jackson had written beneath the final stanza:

My Dear Bride,

Don't you give up on us either.

The words blurred as I pressed my palm to my mouth, comforted by the warmth of Jackson's spirit.

Warden called out from her desk, "Find yourself a good one?"

I closed the book. Turning around, I masked my face with a sheepish grin and held up the poems.

Warden said, "I never could pass up a Yeats collection." She leaned her head toward the window as she quoted his work in a reverent voice:

"'I think all happiness depends on the energy to assume the mask of some other life, on a re-birth as something not oneself.'" Then she finished with a wistful sigh, "From *Per Amica Silentia Lunae.*"

Warden turned to stare at me, pleased, and I gawked back, surprised by the quote she'd chosen. For a second, I feared the woman might take the collection away, but she just nodded an approval and said, "You may keep it," and turned back to her work.

Clutching the only book I wanted, I tilted my head toward the window, waiting to be properly excused, my thoughts lingering on Jackson's inscription. *Jackson*—I pressed the book to my chest—*I won't give up. I promise.*

Outside, the wind picked up, skittering its buzz across the boughs of singing leaves, fluttering the tired drapes. Content, grateful for my book, I inhaled the sweet breaths of an approaching rain, and my mind drifted again to his words.

In a moment, a bright-red cardinal caught my eye when it landed on the tree branch. It flew away after a crow perched on the branch above it, then another a second later. Yet a third crow joined them and brought back the old nursery rhyme Mama taught me long ago:

> *"One for sorrow,*
> *Two for mirth*
> *Three for a funeral—"*

Warden Sanders banged a drawer shut, pulling me away from the silly superstition.

She continued, "One more thing, Lovett: If you need the handyman, write up an order and send it to my office instead of putting it in the inbox to the men's prison. Unfortunately, the prisoners over there will not be available to fulfill our requests for an unforeseen time. Hopefully in August, it will all pass." Warden exhaled loudly.

Pass? Her words confused me.

"Ma'am, uh, they sure had themselves a lot of good books over there. I don't mind volunteering to go back...if it can help you out."

"I fear that will be a while." She tossed the pen onto her stack of papers and pulled out a desk drawer, digging inside until she snatched up an envelope. "The prison is on lockdown due to the rapid spread of fevers, and all their men are in isolation because of the polio outbreak. Buttermilk Sullivan's contracted it, and they don't know if the poor soul will make it. They've lost five men already."

"*Polio*," I barely breathed, horrified for the kind maintenance man. *Did Jackson have it? Was he even alive?*

"Poor Mr. Sullivan." She kissed her teeth, tsking. "Well, I believe we covered everything today. And now you've been given a *rebirth*. Well done, Prison Book Woman. I'll see the crate is delivered to your library in the morning." She turned her attention back to the pile of papers and dismissed me.

With the news that my husband could be suffering—or worse—I felt the life leave me, the coldness cloaking, twisting and knotting as I reached out a hand wildly and latched on to the warden's desk for support.

"Lovett? *Lovett*." She shot up and stepped back. "Are you sick?"

Quickly I righted my spine and pressed the book to my chest. "I apologize for the alarm, Warden. I'm just a little weak-kneed from skipping breakfast, and it's, uh, well, my—" I looked down and mumbled *monthly*, then turned toward the door before she could see the lie in my eyes and the color bruising my face.

"Strawberries in season again. Well, I don't miss *that*." I heard the snap of paper and her sliding chuckle.

That. "Ma'am?" I looked back at her.

She frowned.

"That! Your…whatever your kind calls it," Warden said, flicking her wrist. "*That. That.* Straw. Ber. Ries." She clamped her teeth, loudly annunciating the word.

"That," I repeated stupidly, the word pummeling and taking root, to land uneasy in the pit of my belly.

Eighteen

Waldeen shoved the bowl of bright-red berries closer to me.

Wrinkling my nose, I pushed it aside and clutched the letter from Honey I'd been reading.

The lawyer sent news of the judge's order declaring Honey had won her emancipation, and I was thrilled for her. My daughter had asked permission to see a boy. It warmed my heart that she would even bother to ask, since the state now considered her an adult and free of her parents' control.

"A picnic with a boy," I repeated to the old madam.

"Read it to me again, kid," the older woman urged, hungry for any news outside the cheerless walls.

I tapped the envelope to my chest, savoring the rare letter from home. Pressing my thumb across the three-cent stamp, I peered closer at the details of the 4H postage. Studied the drawing of the smart-dressed smiling girl and boy and the rolling hills in the distance, imagining the same for Honey.

I chewed over the words, rereading.

June '53

Dear Mama,

I received your letter. I'm sleeping and eating well enough. I've been working a lot but I still love delivering books with Junia. There's 19 families on my route with more signing up each week. Oh, how they hanker for their new books!

It makes me happy to know ~~your~~ you're working with the books and growing patrons again. Is Papa well?? I never heard back from him after we talked on the telephone. But I'm seeing Francis now since he gave his permission when we talked.

I'm taking good care of the cabin and critters. Devil John came over two weeks ago and helped me shore up Junia's stall after the rains took out the left side. The creek spilled out of its banks, almost to the corn! The weather finally cleared last Sunday and Francis asked me out on a picnic near the forks of Troublesome Creek.

But it was a ~~disater~~ Disaster!

Junia! She ruined everything! She is the most ~~onery~~ Ornery creature in all of Kentucky!! She kicked Francis's bowl of his Mama's prized banana pudding clean into the creek. Then when I tried to give Francis a sandwich, she took her big ugly teeth and tugged hard on his hair. If that wasn't embarrassing enough, Junia plopped her stinky butt smack down between us on his clean picnic blanket and wouldn't budge. When poor Francis tried to shine up to her, the wicked beast stood and peed on his polished boots! I scolded her but she sassed me right back and went running off. By the time we caught up with her, the ants had invaded our picnic!

Junia is so ill-tempered around Francis he's decided to take me to a ~~resturaut~~ restaurant for our next date. I fear she will never warm to him, Mama. Please let me know how Papa won her over.

I have a long route tomorrow and must close for now. I love you and can't wait to see you again. Write back soon!

Your loving daughter,
Honey Mary-Angeline Lovett

> P.S. Junia still misses you terrible and searches for you everywhere. Sometimes the ol' girl stops at the clearing of the boarded-up chapel. She whimpers and just makes an awful racket bawling for you. I offer her oat cookies—but no help there. Then I started toting Pennie to the outpost with us on Tuesdays. The sweet cat seems to calm her now.

"Smart kid, and that's a sure-footed beast she has there for her route," Waldeen said.

"Thank you for watching over our Honey, sweet Junia," I whispered, aching to return my daughter to the days of childhood filled with daisy chains, water-worn skipping stones, and the fairy paths of our breathing forest.

Cherishing the news, I pressed a kiss onto her signature.

My first letter from Honey, and holding the actual paper was like holding a hug from her—a homecoming that lit joy in my heart. I folded the treasure carefully and placed it inside my pocket to store in my footlocker later.

"Sweet William's daughter all grown up," Waldeen reminisced, then sniffled, smoothed back her hair, and swiped a dishrag across the clean counter.

I reached for the kitchen ledger, flipping the pages, scanning the budget. "Let me check this one more time for you."

"Eat up, kid," Waldeen said. "We're celebrating your good news. Not everyone can become prison librarian." She rested her elbows on the long metal counter in front of me, propping her chin up on both hands, folds of skin plumbed into pleated stenches of spent lard, five-day-old cooked meats, soured milk, and stale cigarette smoke hovering between us.

"Your favorite. I froze some back in the spring and found 'em while I was cleaning out the freezer." Waldeen smacked at her apron and then shoved the dish of strawberries and cream closer as I pushed the new kitchen budget toward her. "Eat," she ordered. "You've been looking a bit peaked."

Suddenly, shadows circled my brain. My belly gurgled a warning, and a slight dizziness swept over me. I blinked and looked away and then stared down at the bowl, trying to murmur my gratitude. The words fizzled down, then rose, ballooning in my throat. Gagging, I jumped up and ran to the washroom to relieve myself.

When I'd finished, I opened the door. Waldeen stood there, blocking me with a hand on her hip. She took a deep drag off her cigarette, then blew it out, sending me reeling back to the toilet.

Heaving again, I grabbed the bowl as the old woman swept up my hair and held it and soothed words above me. "Get it out. That's it, kid. You're fine. *Fine.*"

Swiping a fist across my mouth, I raised my head and stood.

Waldeen was quiet for a moment. Then: "How long ya been knocked up, kid?"

At the sink, I splashed cool water on my cheeks and forehead and met her worried eyes. My embarrassment spread and set me afire, coloring every inch, and I grabbed a tea towel to blot dry my damp face.

"A few months, by the way I tell it," Waldeen said quietly.

"No, it's impossible," I bit. "I was sterilized here in early March." But still I turned over the thought. Wondered what it would be like having Jackson's baby.

"No. *No*, Cussy. You were drugged clean out of your head. They couldn't sterilize ya until they *stabilized* ya," Waldeen corrected. "And Dr. Kennedy's the only one who performs abortions and sterilizes. He's assigned in western and southern Kentucky until late summer and then makes his way here. I know because I've logged his visits for years. He requests special dishes when he comes."

The nausea rose with Waldeen's uncertainty. *Sterilize. Stabilize.* The words tangled across my mind, bumping into the fear.

I had little recollection of my time in the infirmary. But I'd told my doc they had done it. That was when he arranged for me to be transported to the city hospital. But Doc didn't perform a personal exam. He'd only checked my vitals and ordered rest while he fought with prison medical to stop testing me.

Growing more confused, I could only wag my head. Then: "I recall a while back Warden saying, *There's still the matter of your appointment with Dr. Kennedy this summer. We'll have to take care of that.*" I thought harder. "I didn't understand then. But she was talking about the sterilization?"

Waldeen scowled. "Lying, sorry bastards."

"I came in early March, right after—" I pressed a hand to my belly and slid down the wall, dumbfounded.

"When was your last monthly, kid?" She hovered over me.

"I—I'm not sure if I had one in the infirmary, but..." I ticked off the numbers, visiting the months and days since I'd arrived. "I haven't had one. *Not one*, Waldeen. I must be childing. Sure enough, and what Mama and the elders back home had called it," I said, dumbfounded. "Finally, the baby we've been waiting for."

Still, Waldeen looked at me carefully, as if worried about something more.

"Do ya know when you might have conceived?"

I felt my face warm.

"The first day a woman comes in, they do a pregnancy test, Cussy. Do ya remember this?"

"I don't recall. They did a lot of things. Took samples of my urine, skin, and blood, but—"

"When did ya last play hide the wienie, kid?"

Mortified by the probing, I cupped a hand over my face and thought back to that night. We'd laid in each other's arms, both afraid it would be our last time, and made love. He'd talked about wanting a baby and then awakened me at dawn only to take me one final time.

"The morning before they imprisoned us," I whispered.

"As a madam who had herself a passel of girls and an even bigger passel of female troubles, I can assure *you* it would've been too early for that rabbit to die. It takes weeks after a female conceives to show up in a bunny. Dumb rabbit would've been more likely to hightail it off the table and die of a broken neck than keel over from your pee. But still, four months is too long to not have your monthly."

"The morning sickness has been churning inside a lot, but I just thought my nerves were skint. It'd be closer to fourteen weeks."

"Well, kid, you've been stung by a serpent, as my grandma would say. Seen it too many times, and with more than a few of my working girls."

My mind pored over it all.

Waldeen smiled, but it never jumped up into her troubling gaze. "Kid, if you're pregnant, they won't let ya keep—"

"*Childing*," I whispered, a wonderment and more joy surging. "They can't sterilize me now. I need to write Jackson right away. Please lend me a stamp. I'll be getting mine soon and will pay you back."

Waldeen shook her head. "It's too dangerous. You don't want *anyone* finding this out right now. They'll abort it, sure enough."

"Jackson will get word to the attorneys and Doc. They can help."

Waldeen tsked.

"They're going to do an abortion and sterilize me if I wait," I said, a truth stitched into my moan. "One stamp, Waldeen."

She grabbed my shoulders. "Kid, it's risky."

"It's risky if I don't. I can't take a chance of losing the babe. I have to find a way to protect the baby *now*. They'll not care how far I'm along. I need to plan for the baby's safety this very minute."

"It'd be suicide for ya." She poked my belly, then studied me closely. "This sickness could mean other things, Cussy. Lots of women won't bleed when they've got the nerves scratching at them. You've been through a lot."

"*Please*, Waldeen. You can mail the letter out with your weekly invoices. No one will know." I rubbed my cold, damp hands down my prison dress. "Have you heard any word on the polio outbreak at the men's prison?"

"It's bad over there. The guards were jawing about it this morning in the canteen, but I didn't hear of any more deaths mentioned."

It was a small comfort. If anyone could help, it would be Jackson. "Lend me the stamp before it's too late. No one will know." I held out a hand, a shake taking hold.

Scowling, she dropped her arms and went over to a drawer and dug out a sheet of paper and stamped envelope. "Kid, if ya ain't careful, you're gonna write yourself right into the bowels of hell."

On Sunday, I sat in the library, savoring the words I'd written to Jackson, then finally drew and colored a bluet damselfly for my signature.

Something only he and Doc would connect to me.

And the one the ol' mountain doc had proclaimed upon my arrival into the world. "*A fit girl who could turn as blue as the familiar bluet damselfly skimming the Kentucky creek beds*," he'd said, then promptly bastardized me *Bluet*.

Giddy, drunk on the thought of passing Jackson the news, I placed the letter in the envelope with the return address of the ol' Carter homestead. I'd mail it Monday morning with Waldeen's invoices.

I grabbed some books and headed toward the wards. Hummed one of Mama's old French lullabies she used to sing to me. "One day, I will sing them to you, little one." I walked lightly down the corridor and twirled around the darkened corner.

When I nearly ran into Officer Holt, he surprised me with a slight smile, not bothering to scold my silliness.

Nineteen

After visiting Geriatrics on Monday morning, I made my way back to the wing to mail the letter. I froze at the entry when I glimpsed her kneeling over my locker.

"*No.*" I pushed Regina aside. "Get away from my things!"

She whipped out an accusing finger with one hand, rattling Jackson's letter in the other. "Hell, I hope you rot in it. You and your blue bastard can go straight to hell!" Regina shoved me against the wall.

She'd picked the lock on the wooden footlocker, and all my belongings had been strewn across the cot. Flushed, I caught a glimpse of my necessaries, book, and bits of scattered paper and tossed toiletries.

My hands shook as I stretched them out to her and pleaded, "Please give my mail back, Regina. I don't want trouble."

The cruelty danced on her youthful face, bled from a blackened heart. The girl weren't nothing but a seed spreader. Miserable with life, sowing misery across the paths of others.

"*Please, Regina.* Give me back my letter." I tried to snatch it from her hand but missed. "It's not yours."

"I imagine Warden will have a helluva lot to say about that." She poked my belly. "That kid you're carrying belongs to them, not you."

Gritting my teeth, I fought to tamp down the ugliness that threatened to spew. "Regina, just hand it over."

A small group silently gathered around us.

One woman said, "Dammit, Regina, mind your own business and give her back the letter. I hope she puts a curse on your mean ass."

Another grumbled, "Best do what she says, Gina, 'fore you get us all in trouble."

"*My darling Jackson,*" Regina recited to the women, mocking, wriggling the letter in front of my face before whipping it away, "*I'm thrilled to tell you I am with child.*" She smirked. "*I love you—*"

I smacked a fist against my thigh. "Give it back, or—"

"Or what? What?" Regina snapped the page across my face, leaving a papercut down my cheek. "Or *what*, Grape Girl?" She pushed me down onto the cot she'd littered with my belongings.

Then, out of the corner of my eye, I saw it and blinked.

Blinked again and popped my eyes.

Stunned, I ran a palm over the torn bits of paper, my fingers sifting through it all.

My daughter's letter.

Regina had shred it into pieces. Robbed me of Honey's sweet news and love. *Home.* I picked up a scrap and pressed it to my trembling lips, the heartbreak almost bowing me over.

Grabbing the book, I stood, a slow, blinding fury churning, birthing a murderess heart.

I opened the cover of *The Little Sister*, locked deadly eyes with Regina, and tore out the homemade weapon inside.

A ripple of gasps rose into the stale institutional air.

"*No,*" someone cried out.

Something whorled inside me, scraped across my tongue, and escaped in a guttural war cry. I lunged at the girl, ripping off the sleeve of her dress.

Regina's jaw slackened, and she took a step back.

I raised Waldeen's sharpened toothbrush again.

Rough hands latched on to me, throwing me across the floor.

"Both of you to the hole!" the guard bellowed.

Grim, the warden lifted the envelope from her desk, then let it float down onto her stack of papers while the guard led Regina away.

A quake took hold of my body, and I could feel the fear whooshing in my ears.

"Is it true?" Her eyes dropped to my belly.

My words were hollowed out in shallow breaths.

"Answer me. Is. It. True?"

I could barely manage a nod.

She placed the letter to the side and said, "I've sent for the physician to abort it."

"I want to keep my babe."

Her mouth twitched. "There are no *wants* in here, Lovett."

I slammed a fist down onto her desk. "*No.*"

Warden pushed the buzzer on the telephone, and a guard appeared. "Take her to solitary." Her busied hands flew over paperwork, picking up speed, shuffling, organizing papers that were already neatly stacked.

I wriggled out of his grasp and leaped over to her side, falling to praying knees. "I beg you, ma'am. Please don't kill my baby." I reached for her hand and latched on.

She snatched it away and swiped the palm down her side, then pulled a handkerchief from her skirt. "Don't you dare touch me, Lovett. Mind you, if you think this procedure is bad, there's another surgery that can keep you obedient and calm."

"I won't cause any trouble. I have to keep my—"

Scrubbing the handkerchief across her hands, the warden shrilled, "*Take her.*"

"Please, *please*. My baby."

She stepped back. "You're dismissed."

"*Murderer, murderer,*" I spat.

Warden turned to the window.

The guard grabbed hold of me.

"*Wait. Please, ma'am, please, I'll do anything. Tell me what to do. Please—*"

In isolation, I sat on the floor, worrying light rubs over my belly. Time slowed and I startled when I finally saw the tray slot open. Then I heard her.

"Kid, it's me."

I crawled over to the door, rested my ear against the cold metal. "Waldeen?"

"Ya sure got yourself in a mess."

"Please help me."

There was a long pause.

"Waldeen?"

"There's nothing I can do. Here's your supper."

"Are they going to give me a lobotomy?"

"Warden's riled. But you're still valuable to her. Keeping the kitchen ledgers and your library work is the only things saving ya. I think she's more concerned about getting rid of the babe. Preventing a scandal."

"Can you get word to someone for me?"

She exhaled loudly.

"To my doc. Doc Thomas in Troublesome Creek. Tell him they're going to give me an abortion and sterilize me. Maybe even a lobotomy. Please write and ask him to help."

"I'll try, kid, *if* ya promise you'll eat."

I took the tray and bit into the cold bologna sandwich.

"All of it." Waldeen slipped her palm inside the slot, groping for mine. "They miss ya, kid. Miss their *Book Woman.*" She gave my hand a squeeze before slipping away.

I suddenly realized I missed them more. They had given me so much light. Marigold, Geraldine, young Odette, Emmeline, and Sassyann—the women locked in cells darker than my isolated one. With an aching heart, I finished the meal and tried to steel my courage.

The next morning, I paced the cramped hole, pausing when I heard footsteps. At times, my mind played tricks on me, the darkness sliding in darker thoughts.

When the slot finally opened, I held my breath, hoping it was Waldeen.

"Breakfast, Lovett."

I grabbed the tray and waited. A women whispered, "She got word to your friend. Telephoned him yesterday morning."

Then she was gone.

For a minute, I sat on the cot, flabbergasted. That Waldeen would use her one weekly telephone privilege on me filled me with gratitude and hope.

Hope. *Would he come? Could Doc get me moved to the city hospital again, where the babe would be safe?*

I stirred the bowl of oats and then set down the spoon and picked at the cold toast, staring at the door.

I had to believe Doc would get the pardon he'd been working on.

Twenty

The fourth day in isolation passed, and still no word.

No Doc.

When Waldeen showed up with dinner, I thanked her several times for her generosity.

"Did he come, Waldeen?"

"Didn't really see him, but I overheard some scuttlebutt that they sent him packing before he even made it into the administration building."

I slumped against the door. "Did Doc say anything else on the telephone?"

She hesitated a few seconds. "He was somewhat confused and insisted you'd already had the procedure. I tried to tell him it was a lie to keep him off Warden's back. He said to tell ya he's still working on your pardon."

"I have to believe he won't give up."

"Listen, kid, don't count on it. I didn't want to give ya false hope. I've had plenty of politicians slide between my satin bedsheets, and know they ain't gonna go out on a limb to help someone who can't help them. To him, your backwoods doctor is just one notch above a granny woman. If that. And if this ol' gov does grant one for ya, they'll label him soft on crime. If he denies it, well, he'll get caught up in the civil rights mess that's been brewing."

"But…"

"It's a no-win for the gov either way. Nice as he may seem on the surface, you'll not get nothing but penniless promises from money-eyed, climbing politicians."

"How much longer do you think they'll keep me here?"

"I'm not sure." She lowered her voice more, causing me to strain to hear. "But you've caused quite a ruckus. Forensics and Geriatrics are protesting your lockup and done went on a hunger strike. Sassyann too. They've had to send two in Geriatrics to the hospital. Mind ya, as much as it's eased my kitchen duties, the place is in an uproar. Warden is still livid. Guards have been grumbling that even they want the Book Woman back."

"Hunger strike?"

"It appears bravery has risen up from them books of yours. I'll see ya at supper, kid. Eat for the little bean."

She moved on to the next locked cage. "You eat up today. Every bit, young lady," she coaxed the woman in the cell close to mine. "The deed's been done, and I know that temper of yours comes from a lifetime of hurting. But ya must learn to keep it in check or face more misery in here." The madam's words were wise and understanding. "I won't have ya wallowing. Come on, get on up outta that cot and get your dinner."

Directly, the tray slot banged shut.

I listened to Waldeen's footsteps fade and the crash gate clang behind her.

A voice drifted outside the cell, and I opened the slot and pressed my ear to it.

"They took mine too," she called out dryly.

"Regina?" I switched to my good ear. She'd been here the whole time, and without saying a word.

"Took 'em. That Georgia prison took my two perfect baby girls with all their nubs. Counted each of 'em after they dropped the babies in that cold hospital bowl. I was transferred here a week after they killed my twins." She coughed back a sob. "I was well into my sixth month, and they made sure I'd never have another. Left me barren. Do that to a lot of the poorer ones coming in. Especially ones that ain't got no family around."

"I… I'm sorry." But the sympathy was weak-boned. I was about to lose mine because of her.

"I was only seventeen, just out of high school when my man up and robbed a store. Didn't even know he was going to do it till he got back into the truck. There'd been a scuffle, and he shot the store owner. The law arrested me, too, and said I was in cahoots. But I'd never kilt no one and never dreamed he would!"

I pulled my knees to my chest and rested my head.

"When I read your letters, I went mad. You have yourself a decent man, a good daughter, and a baby growing inside you—and *now* my job. I'm gonna be in here until they wheel me over to Geriatrics. That librarian job was what I needed to get out of myself."

I struggled between anger and sadness, not saying anything.

Regina coughed, and I had to strain to hear her next words. Then she kicked what sounded like her shoe against the door and moaned. "The position took my mind off the pain—the misery of this hell." Her voice cracked under the weight of so much loss. "Hope ya get that pardon. I mean it. Too late for me. But I hope you and the baby make it outta here." She choked back what sounded like another sob.

Regina was gone the next morning.

But I awakened surprised to find someone had checked in on me but didn't latch the lock. When I heard guards speaking, I scrambled over to eavesdrop.

"Dammit… Driving me clear out of my mind," Officer Holt said, palming his hand down over his mouth and clean-shaven chin. "Thought maybe I could get her to write down the names of some of their favorite books and have one of the girls she's been schooling try and read to them. Hell, anything to get 'em back to the quiet the Book Woman always brought. The guards in Geriatrics are complaining too. Even the nurses held a meeting with Warden and insisted she be released back to her duties for everyone's sake."

"Are they still hell-bent on keeping up the strike?" the other officer asked.

"Yeah. Another one was sent to the infirmary just this morning. And if Warden doesn't do something soon to restore order, the newsmen are gonna get hold of it, and there'll be hell for everyone to pay."

"You ain't heard? Newsmen with cameras were camped out all over the grounds of the men's prison yesterday," he told Holt.

Holt shook his head. "It was my day off. Did they have another polio death?"

I felt my hands shake and curled them to my side.

"No, but they have more of 'em in wheelchairs, I was told. They're saying some will be crippled for life…if they make it." He paused and looked around to make sure they were alone. I ducked my head inside, hoping he hadn't seen me. *Could one of the men be Jackson? Buttermilk?*

Cautious, I peeked back out when he began talking again. "They had themselves a helluva fiasco going on." The guard sidled up closer to Holt. He lowered his voice, but not low enough that I couldn't hear the concrete walls echo the shocking news that came next.

"One of them young bucks done went and got himself a *Dear John* letter. Only this time it was addressed to a *Dear Janie*, and he went berserk."

Officer Holt rolled his eyes with an eagerness to be done with the gossip. "Well, I need to get back to the wing. If I can just give this to the Book Woman, I'll—"

But the guard was just as keen to continue. "Lieutenant said the boy was so aggrieved, he got hold of a razor and tried to cut his damn dick off. His dick! Crazy kid. Found him hanging from his top bunk."

In unison, both guards shifted their stance, smoothed down the fronts of their uniform britches, lingering protective hands over their crotches. "If that ain't bad enough, next month he would've served out."

Officer Holt stepped back, seemingly shocked, before inquiring, "Did they say if he was a local?"

"Don't rightly know. Name was Danny, or maybe it was Daniel." He pondered. "Daniel Prescott. No, Presland—that's it. Doing time for performing lewd homosexual acts in public. Heard he dared to give a Frenchie kiss with another feller, and right in plain view of children at a local park. They're burying that poor demented soul in Chicken Hill tomorrow."

My hand flew up to my mouth, and I moaned. *Daniel, dead. Oh, not sweet Daniel, dear God.*

The men looked over at me, and Officer Holt hurried toward my door.

I slammed it shut.

Officer Holt called from outside, "Cussy Lovett, I need your help with a list. *Book Woman*?" He opened my cell door. "Odette's been having the fits again, and I need a book for her—"

"Not now. I'm ill." I clung to the basin and flung a shooing arm behind me, waving him away. "Ill!"

I heard him back out, then the clack of the lock.

Cradling my belly, I crawled over to the mat and curled up in a ball like a young'un again on her mama's lap, silently weeping for healing hugs, my fists grieving a dark blue. Begging for mercy for Daniel, my unborn babe, Jackson, and all of us locked in misery.

Outside the cell, murmurs rose from the guards and dropped in a steady rhythm of conversation.

I squeezed my eyes shut, the despair burying me like coal sludge. And I know'd they wouldn't be done until they stole all of me. Buried every inch of me. *How much more could I take? How many of us in here were one step away from walking Daniel's path?*

For three days, Officer Holt stopped by to request my help.

And for two of those days, I stared up at the barred postage-size window that I couldn't reach.

Then I thought I felt the tiniest of flutters. *Could it be the babe?* Surely not, but I became frightened. So much so, I turned over and traced invisible words onto the concrete wall. Again and again, I gave breath to our promise.

His promise.

My promise.

They'd already beat me down once, and I'd be damned if I let them again. "I won't give up. I promise," I said to Jackson.

I smothered a last wheezing cry into the thin mat, then swept my wet face across its scratchy threads and drew a ragged breath.

Kneeling beside the door, I opened the tray slot and called out, "*Guard?*"

In a few minutes, I heard the keys clink against the lock.

"Tell Officer Holt to get Odette the *Complete Poems of Robert Frost*. It's a blue book sitting in a stack on the table in my library."

I spent another long night in solitary.

When the guards changed shifts in the predawn hours, I heard the outgoing officer's latest gossip. The women in the two striking wards and Sassyann had not eaten for a week. Marigold had passed, and the newspaper reporters had finally come swooping and a'snooping, demanding their sensationalism while battering truths. "Looks like everyone's gonna have to work the Fourth, unless Warden can get this mess ironed out."

I wept for Marigold and, finally exhausted, dozed off, only to be awakened by breath-stealing nightmares of the old woman. Her twinged face and shaky hands were outstretched as her ghostly wheelchair rolled toward me. Then a red cloak descended over us both, leaving me to bolt upright, gasping for air.

Close to dinnertime, I heard keys clanging and then the startling click of the lock.

Sitting on the cot, I squared my shoulders and smoothed down my mouse nest of hair.

Warden Sanders stood on the threshold, holding a small stack of novels. "The library service is bigger than both of us. Get up, Lovett, and get back to work." She dropped the books onto the floor and tossed an open letter atop them.

I snatched up the envelope from Honey and clasped it to my chest. It was like having a part of her back with me again.

June '53

Dear Mama,

I received your latest letter from Doc. I'm glad to hear you are fit and pleased to write that I am well too. How is Papa? He still hasn't answered my letters.

I'm working in town every other week now. Miss Foster's been short on staff because several of the librarians have been taking their vacations. She also said with more roads being built, folks are eager to come and visit.

I don't really mind—though I do miss my patrons. There's still a lot of families who can't make it to town and are hankering for their Book Woman again. But Junia has gotten more difficult lately and sometimes refuses to walk the paths. She won't budge, Mama. It doesn't matter if I scold her or ask her sweetly or bribe her with the oat cookies, the stubborn beast screams and gallops us back to her stall. I was a little worried.

Mr. Mabry is our new ~~ferrier~~ farrier. He offered to come out and inspect her feet. But the old girl was so ornery. It was almost impossible for him to check. She fussed awful and kicked and nipped. After wrestling with her, he tied her up and was able to give her feet a cider bath. He mentioned her swayback and said Junia's ol bones may be suffering from the ~~Artharitus~~ Arthritis. He suggested I mix a tincture of white willow bark tea and feed a little to her daily. She seems a little spryer and content now.

We've had a lot of storms since I wrote you, but everything's ok. I am tending to the cabin and critters just fine.

Francis is working this weekend but my friend Pearl has Saturday off from the fire lookout. She's driving us over to the Moonlite Drive-In ~~Theater~~ Theatre in Booneville. I'm so excited! It's a double feature! I can't wait to see Singing in the Rain. Pearl said it was grand when she saw it at the movie house but she's been hankering to see it on the big outdoor screen. The other movie is The Day the Earth Stood Still.

I have so much more to write, but I must close for now and will send you another letter tomorrow. My dinner break is nearly over and I can't keep Miss Foster and the patrons waiting.

I love you. Write back soon!

Your loving daughter,
Honey Mary-Angeline Lovett

The crash door clanged shut behind the warden as I reread Honey's letter. With a lighter spirit, I gathered up the books and brushed past the guard. Honey was doing well, experiencing the thrills of being a teen. *Free.*

Waldeen had said I was still valuable to the warden, and that day, for the first time, I'd felt it. The officers thought so too.

I needed to work twice as hard to help the guards in the other wings. If Warden thought she couldn't do without me and the guards insisted they wouldn't, she'd surely trade off and let me keep the baby. I would write my patrons back home, Devil John and Martha Hannah, and ask them to care for the child until I was released.

I stopped inside the library, then headed straight to Sassyann and my waiting patrons in Forensics and Geriatrics.

Twenty-One

Independence Day came and went with a tiny spark of celebration but nary a smidge of freedom for the women. The hunger strike had taken its toll on most, and the prison lazed in the baked heat of another holiday heartbreak for those missing home.

A bit of cheer arrived the night before when the cook, Patsy, snuck in a surprise for the inmates. She had squirreled away a bag of oranges, slices of bread, sugar cubes, a tomato, and a can of fruit cocktail to make a large batch of prison hooch to share with some in our wing. Waldeen paid no mind to her cook when she grabbed a large pickle crock from the back of the pantry.

Amid the soft, shushing giggles and guzzles, the pie-eyed women enjoyed their early-holiday festivity long into the night while guards turned a blind eye.

I spent the Fourth cleaning the library, where I was surprised by Regina. She'd slipped in behind me as I stooped over to shelve books.

Wary, I glanced up at her, then turned my attention back to the task. "There's new novels on the table." I straightened and hitched my thumb toward a stack of books.

"I've just come from the warden's office. She wants to see you." A small smile creased her childlike face.

I narrowed my eyes. *What had the girl done now? Had her words in lockup been a guise?*

"Cussy, I just want to—"

I shoved another book onto the shelf, the smack sealing the silence between us.

She had rained misery down on me. And her cruel deeds were going to be the demise of my babe. *What more could she do?* I flicked my hands down my dress and left her staring after me.

The warden rarely came in on Saturday, much less a holiday, so it had to be bad.

My first thoughts pulled to Jackson. He'd been on my mind since the solitary confinement. He had somehow called to me in my deepest despair, freed me from my tormented thoughts and destruction. *Were they legally bound to tell me if my husband was sick, or worse?* Waldeen had said that without an official marriage license, it was doubtful.

Waiting outside the warden's office door, I heard weeping erupt, then cries landing into loud sobs. Pressing a hand to my tightening chest, I stood up.

The door opened, and Sassyann walked out in shackles followed by a guard, her tearstained face bone-white and paling against Death Row's assigned red garb.

When Sassyann brushed past, she touched my hand, and I gripped back. "My boys finally came. Thank you." The guard stepped between us, breaking off what I feared would be her last comfort of human touch.

"I'll see you now, Cussy Lovett." The warden opened and shut her palm, beckoning me to hurry inside.

I looked back at Sassyann, watched her head hang defeated, feeling something horrible was happening. *Had her boys forgiven her or damned her to hell?*

My mind ticked over the books I'd read to her. Fretted if there had been one that might have offended the warden, a book I'd let slip in—

"Hurry in, Lovett. I've got a lot of work to tend to on my day off—a holiday, at that. I'm eager to get back to the comforts of my easy chair with a good book and a cool drink."

Irritation plastered Warden's face, and I stood in front of her, worrying my hands until she curtly gave a nod, silently ordering me to be seated.

She thumped her stack of papers.

Alarmed, I jumped.

"Ma'am," I dared speak, "is something wrong?"

"*Everything*," she breathed wearily and cocked her head to the window, a hardness cutting her face.

I was drawn to the papers on her desk, and that's when I saw it. Saw Sassyann's damnation. The official execution warrant signed by the governor.

"Warden…?" The unfinished question lodged in my throat.

She caught me staring at the document and nodded. "You can take Sipes off your library visits. She's being transported down to Eddyville, where they will carry out the signed warrant." Her eyes were troubled. Distant.

The grim prison known as the Castle on the Cumberland, where they executed Kentucky inmates with ol' Sparky. Sickened, I gripped my hand, the one she'd held just seconds ago. Silently, I begged for her mercy.

Warden pushed the death warrant aside and said quietly, "I'm grateful for your work with her. Because of this, she was finally able to visit with her sons. Even a sinner like her deserves a last wish. Thank God they didn't strip her of that." I strained and had to read the next word on Warden's lips, which she uttered under her breath: "*Bastards*."

She cast her eyes to the paperwork, and her voice wavered before she cleared her throat. "Now, we have other problems to address, and they concern *you*."

I waited, and when she didn't speak, I said, "Warden, if I've done something wrong, please let me know. I'd like a chance to fix it."

"No fixing this," she mumbled, scattering papers. Then she

picked up a letter and snapped it in front of me. "You've been granted an eight-day furlough, Miss Cussy Lovett."

I could feel my eyes widening in disbelief, and I gripped the chair.

"It seems Warden Alton attended the mayor's weekly luncheon in Louisville and spoke about your work with the Pack Horse librarian project and your current prison work. The mayor was impressed. He called the state director over Corrections and requested you be given a community furlough. You've been assigned to help with the Louisville Western Colored Branch's latest outreach program. You'll be leaving tomorrow morning."

My color rose hot on my skin. How could I leave with Jackson so close? I'd miss the chance of seeing him. "Warden, I've had eight more women sign into the library and—"

"*Damn you,* Alton, for stealing my librarian," she blurted. "My money's not for *your men's* prison. You were scheduled for your procedures next week. Now I'll have to try and reschedule with Dr. Kennedy."

I leaned in closer. "Ma'am, I've been wanting to talk to you about this. Please don't—" The plea broke in my throat. "I can work more hours. Just let me keep the babe. I'll—"

"I must follow the rules, Lovett. Sterilizing and abortion are simple operations that will benefit you in the long run. It's for the best." Her thin smile betrayed the declaration.

"Please, ma'am. Don't do this." I stood and took a step toward her.

Warden flinched, souring her mouth.

"*Please.*" I fought to compose my mounting panic.

She raised her palms. "It's out of my hands. The medical committee ordered your sterilization after consulting with the board in March. They decided you don't have the capacity to rear children. It will reduce the threat to society and—"

"Could you please contact my doctor back home?"

Her mouth contorted, the bother set plain in her narrowing

eyes. "That old mountain doctor has been a prickly thorn in my side."

I fought to hold my tongue.

"He's been calling every day, insisting on examining you again. Worrying the governor for a pardon. But now he's interfering with my prison. It's been ordered that only prison medical will see you."

"But if you—"

"Enough, Lovett!"

I swallowed my last words, fearing she'd throw me in solitary again, or worse, schedule a lobotomy.

"The ink has dried. Matter of fact, I sealed that envelope. Now, I told that backwoods quack, again, you'd *already* undergone the procedure to keep him off my back. I knew he would be trouble. And he has now been stripped of his medical privileges in this prison. *My prison,*" she screeched as she pounded her fist on the desk, causing the immediate appearance of a guard.

I tried to step back, but he grabbed my wrist, twisted.

Dropping to my knees, I gritted my teeth.

Warden winced. "Leave her!" She shooed the officer away. "Now, let's finish this up, Lovett."

I eased back into the chair, rubbing my wrist.

Warden pressed down the bodice of her white blouse. When her next words came, she barely spoke above a whisper. So much so that I had to scoot my chair closer.

"As you can see, it's been a difficult day." She nodded toward Sassyann's death warrant. "I was one of the lucky ones. In DC, I'd suffered years from a man's drunken fits. He would beat me senseless... Thank God the bottle was his poison. His demise. Or I'd be right where Sassyann is sitting now."

I would have never guessed a fine business lady like herself had lived a troubled life like Sassyann. Me. And it stole my breath as I realized there were probably countless others being tormented at this very minute.

She shook her head slightly and snatched up the furlough

paper, seemingly embarrassed about sharing a snippet of her past. Then her next words came brisk: "I thought of denying this furlough, and I could in a snap. But it could be good for the prison. Show off your skills we've adopted, and maybe it'll get us more funding."

I lowered my eyes.

"You'll *not* mention your…your *delicate condition* outside these walls. I won't have our gracious hosts saddled with worry or have them uncomfortable in your presence. They are pillars of the community, in their seventies, and don't need wagging tongues fretting about their *unusual* visitor. Not a word. Understood?"

All I could think about was she had lied to Doc. He couldn't undo what she said had already been done to me. I could only hold out hope that a pardon would come soon.

She softened somewhat. "This will be a good opportunity for both of us. And considered good time earned. I'll see that time is deducted from your sentence. It will be more than generous compensation for your work."

I perked, studying on just how *much* time would be cut from my sentence.

Warden began reciting a long list of rules I was to follow: "You'll be housed with Reverend Claxton and his wife, Mrs. Claxton, the Negro librarian who runs the city library branch. You are expected to assist Mrs. Claxton and do whatever she and Reverend ask of you. You will obey their rules. You will *not* be permitted to go anywhere unless accompanied by Reverend or Mrs. Claxton. You will consider yourself under house arrest while in their care and at the library. Rules will be strictly enforced and observed. You…"

Resigned, I let my mind ruminate on this new opportunity to visit the big city for the first time. I'd heard about the first Carnegie Library there for the Negro folks and seen newspaper photographs long ago.

Warden went on, "After giving it much thought, I'm assigning

Regina Miles to take over in your absence. She'll be assisting the patrons in Forensics and Geriatrics—"

"Ma'am," I interrupted, suddenly alarmed, "I can make up my work when I get back. Won't be no problem to catch up my readers in those wings."

The women were so fragile, I feared Regina might upset them, lose her temper and hurt someone.

"You *will* require some assistance upon your return and after your surgery. The prison director is on my back to immediately implement a reading and writing course that all inmates will be required to attend before they're granted a parole hearing. We need someone to keep the library going. Despite Miles's occasional irascible moods, she has a great fondness for the books, and I'm hoping they'll keep her out of trouble—and *hoping* you two will work well together when you get back." Her commanding eyes pierced mine. "I'll need her trained properly. After all, she would be the perfect choice for librarian *after* you are paroled."

I tucked in my hands, the misery of working with the girl igniting them.

"Now, again, I must warn you to be on your best behavior with the Claxtons. Step out of line, and the consequences will be severe. Downright dire. I cannot afford any more scandals associated with myself or my prison. Is this clear?"

The warden stared at me, waiting for my reply. When none came, she warned, "There *are* ways to correct the strong-willed and other undesirable traits of headstrong females." She reached in her drawer and pulled out a letter. "From home. You may take it with you."

Twenty-Two

In the dark hallway, the girl picked up speed when she saw me, and I couldn't escape.

Regina caught up and pushed something into my hand.

I jerked my palm back, expecting something horrible. Instead, I found a flowered bookmark she'd stitched in needlepoint. It had been carefully fashioned with blue yarns that the Kentucky Federation of Women's Clubs had donated. "I thought you might be able to use it where you're going." She timidly reached for me, and I stepped back. "Cussy, I'll take good care of your patrons while you're gone next week. I'll really need you to teach me to be the best librarian. One that Warden will keep long after you're released. Can you forgive me? *Please.*"

Seeing her desperate like that broke something in me. I thought about Mama and Pa, and I was suddenly swept away with anguish and regret. How could I have attacked her—*anyone*—after I'd been attacked all my life? My folks would be so ashamed. Their lifelong burdens had been greater, and they'd carried them with a grace that made me suddenly feel small.

Her chin quivered while she waited.

The young girl's love of the job and the quietude she sought from her riotous heart suddenly stole mine. Regina grabbed my hand, and I took her cold palm and gently squeezed a forgiveness until she released it with a quaking sob and sped off.

A little after four a.m., I stepped out of the shower stall. Waldeen met me with a bulging pillow slip in one hand and a cigarette dangling out of the other, the lengthened ash threatening to drop onto the concrete floor. "Thanks for working on those kitchen ledgers for me last night. I thought I'd help ya pack. Slipped that fancy poetry book of Yeats you keep so close. Nobody will be the wiser."

I tucked the towel tighter around me and inspected inside. Along with two prison dresses, a night slip, my necessaries, and institutional toiletries, I saw Jackson's book and Honey's letters.

For the longest time, she stood looking at me, the damp air crawling from the shower stall, glowing on her flesh.

I searched her eyes. "Obliged. I've got to go straighten the library and tell the other wings I'll be gone a week. See you next Sunday."

"Kid, some advice: Don't come back."

"She's giving me good time. And a pardon could come any day."

"Your time will have run out. Don't count on that mountain doc, and 'specially no politician."

"He can help." But I began to doubt everything despite Doc assuring me he would keep trying.

Waldeen glanced at my belly. "Mind ya, them's jus' penniless words," she warned and thrust the pillow sack into my arms.

Then she was gone, leaving me flustered.

I stopped by the wards and then made my way down to the library to wait for the guard to drive me to the city.

In the quiet room I pulled out Honey's latest letter, grateful the child was writing despite enjoying her independence and courtship with Francis.

June '53

Dear Mama,

How is Papa? He still hasn't answered my letters. I've sent him four!

Last week I bought a light brown mule from a muleskinner over in Hardshell to carry me to town. I've paid Devil John and his sons to come over and build a stall.

Always contrary, Junia snubbed the young mule. I named her Willa. The ol apostle seems to prefer lazing with Pennie most days. I always find them together with the cat curled up on her back.

A few days ago Junia ran off, and Mr. Taft found her wandering your old book route. He gave chase and finally caught up with her at the boarded-up chapel where you used to house the books. Mr. Taft said Junia fussed and kicked all the way home. Then he helped me fix the broken latch on her stall. I picked off the briars on her coat, then brushed her and tried to soothe her. When I was fixin' to put her up for the night she refused. Thank goodness, Mr. Taft was there to help!

Francis took me to a church picnic in Hazard and we had a blast! He won me a teddy bear, and we visited the Mother Goose house. A real home shaped like a goose!

Mama, after we got home, he asked me to go steady and be his girl. He gave me a sweetheart ring. It's the prettiest gold ring with a small puffy heart in the middle and a tiny heart on each side of the band!! Since you gave me permission to see Francis, I wanted you and Papa to know I accepted and am going steady with him.

I think I'm in love with him, Mama, because coal miner Bonnie Powell says if you can still feel his kisses

> days later it's love. And oh how my dang feet betray me whenever he's around! They get so tangled that I make a clumsy fool of myself. It's so awkward, even Junia nickers at me like she's laughing. My friend Pearl says it's <u>Truly True Love</u>, and even Devil John and Martha Hannah approve of Francis.
>
> Mama, were you the same with Papa? When did you first know it was true love? I miss you and wish you were here! I have so many questions, but I must close for now and clean the stalls.
>
> I love you. Write back soon!
>
> Your loving daughter,
> Honey Mary-Angeline Lovett

I closed my eyes, grateful she was safe and happy but a lil saddened too. Then I lingered over the news of Junia, struck with the memory of when I first got her. She'd been my meager inheritance from my first marriage in '36. That, and a few dollars, loose change, and a blackened spittoon from the devil bastard who'd tried to kill me on my marriage bed.

The mule's coat had been sticky with blood and matted, her flesh riddled with open wounds. But despite Pa balking at the notion of me keeping her, I wouldn't leave her to die tied to Frazier's tree. I'd stood out in the snowy yard, shivering, bruised, and bloodied. I had taken one look at the broken beast and saw she had the will to live, like me. Had some fight still left in her. And there was something in her big brown eyes that said we could do it together.

It had taken a month to nurse the critter back to health. Another stretch to keep her from kicking and biting me. And not Pa, nor any man, could get close, lest the ol' girl sneak out a leg and side-kick, or stretch her long neck to nip their flesh. But despite her ill temper and distrust with the menfolk, Junia was surprisingly gentle and agreeable with the young'uns and women on our book route.

I worried a finger over my mouth, hoping the mule's arthritis had eased so she could enjoy her retirement.

Then I reread the last paragraphs about Honey's beau, poring over the feelings I couldn't rightly explain. Junia's grief was troubling enough. But the news of going steady was a surprise.

Honey would be seventeen this month. Just a mere ten years older than age seven. I worried the next letter would bring news of an engagement.

Sam, my transport guard, poked his head inside the library. "Let's git to Louisville. Sooner I git there, the quicker I can be back."

BOOK TWO

For last year's words belong to last year's language. And next year's words await another voice. And to make an end is to make a beginning.

—T. S. Eliot

Twenty-Three

I stepped out into the sunshine and steadied my nerves, closing my eyes to feel the heat on my face, the scents of lavender and lemongrass and surrounding farmlands inviting.

Sam nudged me to the back of the automobile. Behind the steering wheel, he rattled keys, then reached for the ignition. "The drive to the city shouldn't take long. If I hurry, I'll be back in time for my slippers, a sip of Old Crow, and my missus's fine Sunday supper," he said, talking to fill the silence between us, and more to himself.

I inhaled the stingy breezes coming from his window on the hot July day and studied on what lay ahead.

Sam's prattle drifted and soon dissolved as I let my thoughts wander.

We rode along the bumpy road until it opened wider into a smoother two-lane, the thrum of the big tires soothing. I turned to stare out at the farmlands and painted clapboards guarding rows of corn. Horses and cows grazed in pastures bordered by white fencing for miles.

Weren't long before I could see the big city in the far distance, the tops of buildings budding in the sky as we got closer.

Soon, the streets became fatter and crawled with automobiles, trucks, and buses.

There were so many rose-brick buildings pinched in, it was hard to see where one began or ended.

Sam turned on the radio, and the announcer reported the latest news about the polio deaths, prices of grain, before moving on to the weather. The station played several songs. Minutes later, the newsman broke in to confirm Sassyann's upcoming execution, telling the listeners, "The Black Widow's execution is scheduled July seventh at 6:01 a.m."

Just two days from now.

Excited, he went on to say it would be the first execution of a woman in Kentucky in more than one hundred years. Sam mumbled a curse and switched off the radio, leaving me grateful for the silence.

Saddened, I leaned my head against the window, hoping our lessons had been a respite.

The Sunday city flagged its welcome, the rumbling of distant horn blasts and tired pumping factories preparing for the next week ahead. A slumbering buzz crawled across the waiting pavements.

I reckoned even cities got the Lord's Day off.

Sam mumbled something about missing a street sign, cursed the city streets, then turned us around and headed in a different direction, taking a sharp right onto a side street, followed by more confusing turns and grumblings.

A small headache grabbed hold, and I stretched my neck toward the front windshield, taking in glimpses of the big town, bustling folks, and passing automobiles.

At a stoplight, I stared out at a church. Fancy cityfolk wearing hats and store-bought dresses and suits idled on church steps, their smiles and nods whispering gossipy news and invites.

Soon, Sam slowed down on East Washington Street. It was dotted with a row of neatly lined, narrow brick homes with striking-green patches of grass protected by wrought-iron fencing. A dozen or so years ago, I'd read about these shotgun houses, their history mirrored to New Orleans. They looked prettier than the photographs that had accompanied the article.

It was said the homes got their name because you could fire a shotgun clean from the front door and it would go clear out the back entry, with nary a lamp or saltshaker disturbed. But it noted some of the shotguns were also built with their front doors purposely hitched and not aligned with the other doors in the house to scare away the bad spirits hankering to slip in.

Sam parked between two black automobiles.

I walked up the small steps with him close on my heels.

The guard reached over my shoulder and knocked loudly on the door.

The older Negro couple who opened the door seemed somewhat surprised by our visit. And I worried what the warden had told them about me.

Sam took a step closer. They stared at me for an uncomfortable moment, until I feared they would shriek, turn me back over to the officer, and slam the door in my face.

They were a handsome couple and still had on their fine church clothes. Mrs. Claxton's hair was neatly coiffed in short, tight peppered curls flecked with gray, and her husband wore a trimmed beard in white that didn't match his dark, cropped hair.

I braved what I hoped was a friendly smile.

Finally, the reverend said, "Cussy Lovett, huh?" He raised a brow.

"Yes, sir. Cussy Lovett, Book Woman, at your service." I hugged the pillow sack of possessions closer to my chest. "I can do just about anything concerning the books, sir, ma'am. Bind, scrapbook, and grow readers." I shifted the pillow to my hip and tried not to squirm.

The guard cleared his throat. "Well, if there's anything else you need, just telephone the prison. Warden said she'll check in with you daily at the library, Mrs. Claxton. I'll be back next Sunday afternoon about two."

Reverend Claxton opened the door in a wider welcome and said, "Strange name for a young lady. And it better not be because of a bitter tongue, or I'll be taking my Effie's pine tar soap to scrub out any devil sass in your mouth." His face spread into a friendly tease.

Mrs. Claxton laughed and patted his arm. "Don't scare away the chile, Jed."

"Her papers are all here." Sam passed them over my shoulder and bid the couple a good day, eager for his bourbon and supper.

Reverend raised a finger. "Mind ya, my wife's soap is a lot stronger than any buttermilk lavender. Miss Cussy Lovett, pine tar will strip the hairy demons right off any wicked tongue."

I nodded, knowing it would do just that from the homemade soaps Mama used to make. Somehow it was comforting. There was a familiarity with these folks, and I was suddenly curious and looking forward to the furlough.

With that, Mrs. Claxton said, "Come in, fellow Book Woman. We've been expecting you."

Grateful for the warm welcome, I stepped inside on worn puncheon floorboards, noting the scattered hook rugs and clutching the small pillowcase of my belongings as I glimpsed the furnishings of my first city home. A Bible sat on the seat of a corner walnut hall tree holding a gentleman's fedora like the ones I'd seen in magazines. Several umbrellas with carved wooden handles rested in its attached wrought-iron circle. A large bookcase covered one wall brimming with books.

"Have a seat on the Chesterfield," the reverend said as the couple sat down in matching wingback chairs across from me.

I sank down on a worn, velvety crimson sofa and scooted next to its fat arm, feeling small, waiting for the bark of orders.

Mrs. Claxton lifted the lid off a pretty glass candy dish and offered me a piece of Chicken Bones. Jackson was fond of the little nuggets toasted in coconut and filled with honeycombed peanut butter, always insisting he stop at the general store near the Tennessee and Kentucky state line.

I thanked her and dropped it into my sack for later.

"Where's home, chile?" Mrs. Claxton inquired.

When I answered *Troublesome Creek,* surprise lifted in her

eyes. "Reverend and I are from Pike County. Around Fishtrap. Do you know it? We moved to Louisville in 1905. Isn't that so, Jedidiah?"

That was the familiarity I'd picked up on. "Never been to Fishtrap. But Pike County sure is a place of beauty. Your home's something else, too, ma'am." I brushed my palm across the deep-buttoned armrest, felt the soft teeth of velvet tickle my hand.

"A far cry from those Kentucky hills we're rooted to." Mrs. Claxton smiled, her eyes kind and friendly.

They were hillfolk, and for the first time since this morn', I felt my spine ease itself out of the day's uncertainty, the soft tug of stiff shoulders relaxing.

Then Reverend Claxton lifted a cold pipe from an ashtray, placed the tail in his mouth but never lit it. "We were told you were healthy?"

"Yes, sir." I willed myself to remain calm. Stop the rise of color that would leave him doubting or, worse, fearful. Their home was lovely, quiet, and I was suddenly grateful for the short respite away from prison walls. It would be good for the baby. Me. "I'm healthy, sir."

He considered this, and I could tell he wanted to know just *how healthy*.

"It's only a color, Reverend. It's not catching," I said quietly, hoping to ease any discomfort they might be feeling—to escape the sudden worry crawling back over me.

Suddenly, his face spread into a widening grin as he reached over to pick up his *Louisville Times* newspaper. "Now, wouldn't that be something if a feller *could* catch color. Imagine it would be quite a different world walking in all them shoes." He wagged his head at the thought. "Effie will show you to our indoor facilities, where you can clean up before Sunday dinner."

I followed her through the middle room. Their bedroom was spacious, and the bed snugged a papered floral wall with side tables holding electric lamps flanking it. A pretty chenille bedspread rested atop the mattress, tucked around fat pillows.

On the opposite wall, a fireplace fixed with a fancy bronze summer cover of an etching of a lady in a flowing gown surrounded by garlands waited for colder weather. The mantel held a photograph of the Claxtons holding a little girl, another of a married couple, and one of a young woman. A dark wooden armoire covered most of the wall next to their bed.

"That's my daughter, Vesta. She married and moved way out to California but visits occasionally." Mrs. Claxton beamed. "And this one here is my niece, Susan." She lifted the photograph and showed it to me. The smiling woman wore a nurse's uniform. "Her parents live down in Fishtrap, and the chile has always been like a second daughter to me. When Susan came to Louisville for her nursing studies, she stayed with us. We used to have us a Murphy bed in the living room where the bookcases are now."

I could see the strong resemblance. "She's a lovely woman and looks just like you, ma'am."

"Susan comes over every Sunday when she's not working at the hospital. She's the nursing director," Mrs. Claxton said proudly and brushed her sleeve over the glass and placed the frame back on the mantel. "They sure keep her hopping, but the next two Sundays, she's off, and you'll get to meet her."

She moved over to the chest of drawers. "Don't reckon you will with the weather being so hot, but there's some quilts in the bottom if you get a chill."

My gaze landed on the ornate hand-carved box with a glass lid atop the heavy piece of furniture. Inside, two death crowns rested on a sky-blue velvet lining. Mrs. Claxton pointed. "Those angel crowns were passed down to me and are from Mother and Grandma's pillows."

I pressed my lips together. Time would only reveal the prophecy of mine in Thousandsticks. For now, I was alive despite the demise of my freedom. *But what about tomorrow? My husband and daughter? The babe?*

"No doubt the angels took them straight to heaven." She patted the box.

I was surprised. Not about the death crowns, as my kin called them, but that a reverend's wife would take to such superstition.

As if hearing my thoughts, Mrs. Claxton said, "I believe He sends messages of comfort to those left behind." She ran a gnarled finger alongside the framework.

She was hillfolk, and I know'd our people would proudly display the crowns discovered in homes after a loved one had passed. It was believed if you found a hard lump of the feathers knitted in the shape of a halo inside the deceased's pillow, an angel had greeted the loved one upon death and spirited them to heaven.

Most claimed if you found double crowns inside, it took two angels to carry the person to heaven. Others believed that discovering the wreath of feathers for some less-deserving folks meant their sins had been forgiven.

Still, some held the notion that if you found the knotted halo inside a living person's pillow, death was near.

I'd checked Mama's pillow immediately after, only to find nothing. But then two weeks before Pa passed, I was changing his pillow slip and felt a lump inside and ripped it open. My hands had trembled as I inspected the perfectly formed wreath. Frightened, I'd burned the crown, pillow, and its tick down by the creek, then examined his new one daily until the night of the mine accident.

I'd kept the latest one of Pa's locked in my trunk after his passing.

I fidgeted with my pillow stuffed with the prison belongings.

As if sensing my unease, Mrs. Claxton said, "Where are my manners. Let's get you unpacked and freshened up before dinner, Cussy."

Relieved, I followed her as she moved us into the kitchen. A pot of greens simmered atop the stove, and a shiny griddle and jar of hog fat rested beside it.

Clean white cupboards hung on the wall. A Maytag wringer washer on wheels shouldered a fat stove beside a bowlegged standing icebox. I gawked at the machine's wizardry and then turned to the rose-patterned dishes. They were placed neatly on an inviting large table circled by four wooden chairs, awaiting lazy talks that come after a satisfying meal.

How I missed those with Jackson. Lingering in the kitchen with each other, making easy talk about the land, the critters, and the latest news he'd bring home from town before the daily chores swept us back to the drudgery of work.

Mrs. Claxton motioned me to the right, where a narrow door was recessed into a wall, and said, "We've had plumbing for years now. You can freshen up in there." She reached for my sack. "I'll just put this on the sleeping porch. Susan should be here any minute."

I hurried inside, wondering what the nurse would think of me—fretted if Susan would try to pry and poke at me like all the doctors and nurses had done over the years.

Twenty-Four

A lady closer to my age rose from the kitchen chair and extended her hand. "I'm Susan. Nice to meet you, Cussy. I was just telling Aunt Effie I've never been to Troublesome, nor met another like you in my nursing career."

I dared not touch her hand and risk offending her. Instead, I offered a smile and mumbled a *pleased to meet you.*

Mrs. Claxton said, "Have a seat, Cussy. Susan's very interested in medicine and knows more than most of those biggety-britched doctors she works alongside."

The nurse's eyes were gentle, and I was pulled to her kind face like Mrs. Claxton's. "It's called methemoglobinemia, ma'am."

"Please call me Susan," she insisted.

Curious, she asked about my doctor's diagnosis of methemoglobinemia and the drug methylene blue, which makes me turn white.

"We've never seen this deep of coloring at the hospital," she said, wanting to hear more. "In all my twelve years of nursing, it has escaped us here in the city."

Hesitant, I slowly told her about Pa and my other kinfolk who had it. How my great-grandpa had come over from France to claim a land deed in the early 1880s.

"And you say he was a Blue like you but married a Kentucky woman who was white, and that they had the same genes…and no ailments." She paused to marvel at the wonder, and I appreciated her thoughtfulness on the matter.

"None. We're fit. Strong enough when left alone."

Mrs. Claxton and Susan bobbed their heads in unison.

Susan said, "It's an interesting disorder to have. Downright fascinating, Cussy. Thank you. I've seen the methylene blue drug used for heart patients and for cyanide poisoning and other lung ailments—for those coming in looking slightly blue—but never knew your coloring could also be congenital methemoglobinemia. But again, I've never once seen a patient with your coloring."

"The drug does terrible things to me. Headaches and nausea something fierce."

"And I'm guessing that's why you remain blue." She jumped up. "Oh, Aunt Effie, let me get those serving dishes down from the cupboard for you."

"Now, chile, you run yourself ragged over there at General Hospital; you just sit and enjoy your Sunday dinner and visit with our guest." Mrs. Claxton caught my eye. In a flash I saw I was only a guest. Not an inmate and nothing more.

After a meal of catfish, wilted greens, slaw, and blackberry cobbler, I helped the women wash the dishes, then set about to mop her kitchen floor, slipping back into my routine of prison work. As I knelt, Mrs. Claxton took the rag from my hand, pulled me up, and said quietly, "We didn't bring you here to wear you out." She placed a hand on my shoulder.

At this, the busy day rubbed at my nerves, and I felt the sting of unshed tears. It had been a long time since I'd received a heartfelt welcome from strangers—an eternity since I'd felt I belonged somewhere. I ached for the hillwomen back home. Ol' Loretta, my sassy elderly patron, had been such a blessing to me and got me through my toughest times. Mrs. Claxton reminded me of her.

I mumbled an apology for taking over her kitchen.

Susan kissed her aunt's cheek. "I have a four a.m. shift, Auntie, so I need to get home to bed. Cussy, I hope to see you next week." She squeezed my arm and left me gawping, unable to voice a proper goodbye. She weren't scared nor scarred by my color none. Didn't feel the need to inspect me, poke, or pry.

"That reminds me, Susan, Cussy's leaving next Sunday, so come a bit earlier for dinner and you can see her off." Mrs. Claxton walked her to the door and returned to the kitchen, where she chatted about Susan's hospital duties and busy schedule. By the time we'd stacked the last dish back into the cupboards, it was growing late. Satisfied that everything was in order, she led me to the back of the house. "Since we only have the one bedroom, I try to make the sleeping porch comfortable for guests and my daughter when she visits. Do you have children, Cussy?"

"I have a girl who's a teen. Her name's Honey."

"Sweet name, and if she's as polite as her mama, I bet she honors it."

"Yes, ma'am. I'm sure proud of her; she's taken over my old Pack Horse librarian route, delivering books in Troublesome's hills."

"A young librarian with an important job," Mrs. Claxton said admiringly. "We had some hardworking Pack Horse librarians here in Jefferson County near the Jefferson Memorial Forest and other outskirts of our city. But that's been years now. I do remember two of those librarians who still send Christmas cards—an Arlene Sahraie; the other, Letty Garza. They visited us at Western and made quite the impression on my librarians."

While she chatted, I followed her into the airy screened-in porch, an overhead fan cooling the room, licking at my skin. She pulled down a rattan shade and jerked it up again. "Use the blinds if you need more privacy or the rain blows; sometimes city summers are unpredictable like that." A narrow iron bed was tucked to the side closest to the door. Several blouses, dark navy skirts, and black stockings had been draped over the footboard.

On the pillowcase was a carefully folded nightgown and light robe. I picked it up, brushed the silky cotton across my cheek, examined the delicate trimmed lace on the arms and neckline. "It's sure beautiful."

"That old thing. Why, it should be in my rag bin. Hope it all fits." She was pleased, and the comforts and care she'd tendered warmed me.

"When I spoke with your warden, I asked about your size. Another of my nieces ran these over yesterday. Comfortable summer skirts. So you can just pack up that dress"—she pointed to me—"and any you brought along. You're our librarian now, not a prisoner." The woman held up the linen skirt, pushed it against mine, studying, cocking her head from side to side. The hem rested at mid-calf and had been carefully pressed.

"Looks like it'll fit right fine, if not a bit snug." She looked up at me, and for a second I glimpsed something strange, then she washed it away and began humming, studying the skirt again.

Did this wise ol' woman somehow guess I was carrying? Ol' Loretta know'd everything, it seemed, and most times before I did. Maybe Mrs. Claxton also had the gift of grannying in her Kentucky bones. "I'll take good care of the clothing, ma'am." I took the skirt and blushed, grateful.

"You should be fine here," she commented, her eyes scanning the porch.

"It's perfect." To finally be outside in the fresh air brought a comfort like no other.

An oscillating motor fan rested on a low table beside the bed, swirling the occasional breeze while an electric hand-painted hurricane lamp perched beside it. I admired the fancy pink roses and green leaves painted on the lamp's glass.

"It was Mother's favorite," Mrs. Claxton noted. "She loved to sit by it and write her poetry. She always yearned to be published one day."

"My Honey loves the poetry, too, ma'am."

Two wicker chairs were arranged on the opposite side with a small table holding a six-welled glass ashtray between them. She smoothed down the soft feed-sack quilt on the bed. "Mother made this for me when I got married."

I bent over and admired the tight stitching. "It's a fine quilt." It reminded me of the sugar-sack quilts Loretta sewed back home.

"You should sleep comfortable enough. I just pulled the linens from the clothesline after church services." She looked around and pressed down the bodice on her pale-violet dress, as if trying to remember everything. "If you can't sleep, you can help yourself to a book in the parlor."

"I'd like that."

Turning toward the yard, I peered out, soaking up the summer breeze. My newfound freedom. It was as electrifying as the city lights buzzing under the streetlamps around me. I itched to toss off my clunky shoes and drab prison garb and run circles around her yard in my assigned prison slip.

But I didn't dare.

The grass was neatly trimmed, and a blond-and-white pup lounged under a tree. Geraniums, fist-size zinnias, and showy pink ladies circled a concrete birdbath, while several blue snowball bushes and climbing roses hugged the iron fence around the yard. A long clothesline ran along one side, an empty basket at the bottom of one pole forgotten.

"That's Daisy under the Kentucky coffee tree."

"I've never seen a dog like her."

"She's what they call a Welsh Corgi. Nine years ago, Vesta gave me the pup for Christmas. Now, when we first moved here, I planted the tree in memory of my great-grandmother Eliza, who was part Shawnee. A reminder to keep the dead who breathed life into us living." The librarian called for her dog, and it stretched and ambled to the door, its stubby legs lightly making their way. "I don't like her barking after dark and disturbing the neighbors. The old girl sleeps over in the corner. You won't know she's there." Mrs. Claxton pointed to Daisy's rug.

I looked out at the cluster of homes surrounding the Claxtons'.

Heard the rumbles of automobile engines and horns. The laddering voices of nearby folks and children at play. Weren't no way Daisy could possibly be louder than that. Back home, you could hear a leaf fall, and I worried if this city would let a person sleep.

"Thank you for the delicious supper and fine furnishings, Mrs. Claxton."

"I'll let Reverend know. The men caught the fish in the Ohio River early this morn' before church services." I could see she was itching to talk more. Then: "If you're up to it, I'd like to have a few more words with you about your library duties before you retire for the evening."

"Yes, ma'am."

"We can sit over here." She moved to the wicker chairs. "You'll be working in the children's room with me. Most attend the nearby school and read well."

For the next few minutes, we talked about favorite children's books, the conversation peeling off the day's nerves. And I could see it righted hers also.

"One of my biggest concerns is getting the parents to read. We need more of my kind who can read and write. If we can just get them to learn, they could contribute more to the community. Vote."

"Maybe I can help, ma'am." An idea latched hold, and I turned it over in my mind.

"Now, wouldn't that be something of a miracle." She stood. "You'll be compensated forty-five cents a day. I'm afraid it's all the library has in the budget currently."

"Ma'am, a few stamps to write my daughter would be payment enough if you can spare them." I dared not write to Jackson after what had happened, and what awaited me back in the prison.

"We can do both. Get some rest."

When she left, I slipped out into the yard under the coffee tree. Lifted my face to the sprays of leaflets heavy with leathery reddish pods, inhaling the earthy scent of the yard.

Freedom.

Unlike the prison's countryside, the city was soaked with a mixture of haze, smoke-belching engines, busy life, and the spent energies of a busier day. The sun was setting, and around me I could see the glow of towering streetlamps.

I trailed my fingers over a pod and looked below. The thick grass was covered in coffee tree seeds, and I plucked one up.

Tearing apart a leathery shell, I jiggled a couple of the brown seeds in my hand. Maybe Mrs. Claxton would let me borrow a needle and thread so I could make Honey a necklace for her birthday.

I stood still, wrapped in the city rhythm, watching soft, golden lamps come to life behind shade-pulled windows, the hawkish cries and clatters of the city falling and fading like a mewling babe fussing against sleep.

Back inside, I washed up, then returned to the sleeping porch. Content, I peeled off my heavy shoes and slipped into Mrs. Claxton's gown, eased down onto the bed, and closed my eyes, cocooned in safe shelter for the moment.

Daisy jumped onto the bottom of the bed, sniffed my ankle, and rested her chin there. Shortly, the lil dog snugged up alongside me and lay her head on my belly.

Suddenly, I felt a weak flutter. Daisy jerked her head up, noticing it too. She peered down, tilting her face from side to side.

In awe, I pulled up the cotton gown and stared at the naked flesh on my belly, the babe stealing my heart.

Gently, Daisy poked and sniffed me, then flattened her chin atop my small, rounding belly.

I smiled, thinking of Junia. How the sweet beast always sponged up my worries.

Daisy looked up at me with big, doleful eyes. I ran my hands over her head, ruffling her furry face. She released her own sputtered worries in a long, bumpy sigh.

The baby was safe.

I needed to rest to keep us safe.

I sank deeper into the comfortable mattress, my breaths easy and relaxed for the first time in a long time. From the kitchen, I could hear the rise and fall of the Claxtons' voices, reminding me of my parents and their nightly kitchen-table conversations, which would soothe and lull me to sleep when I was young.

Outside, the lilt of child-song carried down streets as tired mothers corralled their young'uns under starless city skies. Somewhere, the ribboned trill of a cricket protested, pulling me home toward the piney woods of Troublesome.

Wriggling my toes, I stretched under the scent of oily city breezes skittering across the washed cotton linens under my chin, a gentle nod culling my worries.

Weren't long before the city noises cobbled across the final lullaby of a child's laughter, lifting memories of Honey. Daisy's snores climbed into the whirs of a tottering fan, and the fat, deep hours of sleep came calling.

Twenty-Five

Monday morning found Daisy sharing my pillow, whistling snores against the back of my head.

I carefully untangled a paw from my hair and moved her away as I sat up, trying to adjust to my new surroundings.

Mrs. Claxton cracked open the door. When she saw Daisy on the bed, she chided, "Law, I don't know what's gotten into her. She won't have a thing to do with any of my guests, and now look at her, cozying in your bed. Daisy. *Daisy*, get your hairy bottom down. *Now.* You have the rug over there. Stop being a pest."

"Ma'am, I don't mind. She's good company."

Daisy slunk off the covers and back over to her rug. She peered up at me and thumped her tail, an elvish grin stretching across her snaggletoothed mouth.

"Breakfast is almost ready," Mrs. Claxton invited. "I thought I'd let you sleep in on your first day."

It was going on six thirty, and I couldn't recall the last time I'd slept past four a.m. Feeling lazy, I guiltily hurried to dress.

At eight thirty, Mrs. Claxton brought in three bottles of milk and two loaves of bread left by the dairy and bread trucks before we headed for the library. "He forgot to take the empties again," she said.

I stood at the front door, inspecting the empty glass bottles she'd left behind. I'd read about it many times, that you could get such riches delivered directly to city doors, but seeing it actually happen on Mrs. Claxton's porch was a wonderment that left me dumbfounded.

In the hot days of summer, the milk would be curdled and bread moldy before they ever found my cabin door in Troublesome Creek or our home in Thousandsticks. I scooped up her newspaper and followed her back inside.

"We'll walk to the library today," Mrs. Claxton said as she grabbed a brown sack and her shiny, bulky pocketbook, then stepped outside. "It's only a little over two miles, and the fresh air will do us both good."

Several times, I gawked at the folks bustling to and fro on the sidewalks in their business suits and stylish dresses. Boxy city buses whizzed past, crowded in between the blaring horns of black automobiles with their sloped tails and sleek, long-nosed bonnets sporting polished ornaments.

Mrs. Claxton led us west on East Washington, stopping to call out each street name. "Cussy, we're going to slip onto Hancock and then over to Main. Then down Liberty and over to Ninth Street, where we'll jump over to Tenth. Remember, the library's address is on South Tenth Street—604 South Tenth, to be exact. Okay? I want you to learn the way in case I'm not here or you get lost."

I turned the directions over in my mind, stopping to look up at the street sign at each crossing. "All those names. Never seen so many streets in my life, Mrs. Claxton. Why, it's a wonder anyone ever makes it anywhere in this big maze."

When I stepped down off the curb, she yanked me back just as an automobile blasted its horn and whizzed past.

"Chile, *always* look up and down the street for vehicles before crossing. You almost gave me a heart attack." She pressed a hand to her chest.

The July heat and fuel mingled with smoking factories, businesses, and people scurrying with the energy of panther bees twitching for their next meal. More than once, I stopped to stare up at the tall brick buildings soldiered above us. Many times, I jumped at a blaring horn.

Ahead, two policemen escorted an unkempt man wearing tattered britches and a dirty shirt toward their official automobile. I looked at Mrs. Claxton, questioning his crime.

"A vagrant."

"Because he's poor, ma'am?"

"It's a crime to be poor here, chile."

There had been many such living through the Depression, and not just in Kaintuck but across the country. My patrons, like the small schoolboy Henry, who'd starved and perished along with his whole family. It struck me that the law would've had to jail all of Troublesome, and I shook my head at the idea of being shackled in ball and chains because of being hungry, poor.

We came to a giant yard full of children, and I paused at the iron fence to watch. "A playground just for young'uns," I whispered in awe and pressed a palm to my belly, wishing such a place for the babe, worrying if my child would even have the chance to take a first breath.

"That's our public park and playground. During the summers, it fills up early."

"Only read about these in the newspapers. Weren't nothing like it for the young'uns in Troublesome."

"Yes, but we did have the forests and creeks," she reminded.

The girls wore store-bought summer dresses, ruffled anklet socks poking out of patent leather shoes, and skipped past boys in short trousers and shirts. Several stood on the ladder of a tall slide, waiting for a turn to speed down the slick metal ride. A group of boys shot marbles on a square patch of concrete. Still others climbed on connected iron bars, crawled across, swung, and dangled upside down. Laughter rang out, and I turned toward the swings. A boy and girl swung in harmony as they drove their legs, trying to climb faster and faster to the sky.

The swing set's poles lifted terrifyingly off the ground, and the young'uns shrieked happily and pumped their lil limbs harder.

Behind us, a horn honked.

Mrs. Claxton waved to the people in the automobile before turning back to me.

"You sure know a lot of folks, ma'am."

"We're all close down here in this small part of the city."

After they'd passed, the librarian said, "This must be your first time in Louisville. I was the same way when we arrived from Fishtrap. Only now the horse and buggies are long gone, replaced by noisy motor cars and more people."

"I've only been to Lexington and Knoxville. But everyone pointed and gawked at me. Here, they don't even notice," I said, astonished.

"A good thing. And you're in for a treat. If you think this is busy, wait till you see our bustling Walnut Street." She looked over the playground approvingly and moved us along.

Again, I paused and pulled to the rumbles of tires shuddering under my feet. I looked down at the concrete.

"That's the siren call of our business district, Walnut Street," she teased and stamped a foot. "But we'll need to save that for later and take the shortcuts."

We waited at a stoplight, and I noticed a big blue steel box on the corner that had the word LETTERS on it. I tried to recall if I'd ever seen it before in any pictures, but couldn't remember.

Mrs. Claxton saw me staring and asked, "Are these in Troublesome yet?"

"Ain't heard of any getting installed."

"They're on street corners all over Louisville. It's where you mail your letters." She stepped off the sidewalk, ready to cross.

I looked back over my shoulder several times at the spectacle, wondering what Postmaster Bill back home would think about having them all over the hills, studying on how he would keep the raccoons and other critters from nesting in them.

Thirty minutes later we stopped in front of the stately library, the Western Colored Branch. It was a massive square building with handsome stone masonry and decorative columns of brick between large windows.

Inside the double doors, I read the sign above two other doors: *Knowledge Is Power.*

"Here we are," she announced proudly. "Over there to the left, Cussy, is the newspaper alcove, my office, and the children's room."

"It's a beautiful library." I crossed to a shelf that held a silver trophy.

"Now that"—she pointed—"is from Kentucky's first Negro poet, Joseph Cotter. He used to have an annual storytelling contest for the young people. After he passed, we continued the tradition."

"Right nice tradition, ma'am."

"Over here we've got our magazine area, a study room, and the adult room. Behind is our staff kitchen." We walked into the room, and she placed her sack inside the icebox.

"I could never imagine a library as grand as this one. And one with its own kitchen," I said quietly, mesmerized by all the finery the city held, knowing that most cabins back home could fit inside this kitchen.

She went on as we returned to the large room, "The high school children have the Douglas Debate Club room back here." I followed as she led us through yet another door. It was spacious and warmly furnished with walnut floors and wall panels.

She motioned me over to a stand that held a copy of a book under its glass dome.

"This was the very first book checked out of our library in 1908," she said proudly.

"It's something else." I peered at the gold letters stamped across the red book, *Up from Slavery: An Autobiography by Booker T. Washington.* Over fifty years old, and it was still in near-perfect condition.

Mrs. Claxton crossed to more shelves. "We have an extensive collection of Negro works."

"So many books, ma'am."

"The students debate important issues like women's rights, the influence of women and how they've contributed more to the world than men, and whether Lincoln was a greater American than Washington. We also train them to speak in public. It can get mighty lively in here during the school year," she said, raising a brow as she closed the door.

An older Negro gentleman came up to us and tipped his hat to me. "Ma'am, 'scuse me. Mrs. Claxton, sorry to interrupt, but the paper's late again."

"I'll call on Steven at once, Mr. Wilson." When he left, Mrs. Claxton said, "Our paperboy is having some problems at home. We'll need to check in on him. Let's see, what else? Oh, we currently have 12,978 registered as borrowers. You just met Mr. Wilson. He's one of our oldest patrons and has been with us since the Carnegie Library fully opened."

"Almost thirteen thousand?"

"We stay busy acquiring the latest for the community."

"When we'd receive donated books from the cities for the Pack Horse project, they sent a lot of Bibles. So many that I thought cityfolk had given up on Jesus."

She chortled and clamped a hand over her mouth. "Chile, do *not* let Jedidiah hear this."

A young woman in a long stylish skirt like mine and a delicate buttoned-up blouse called out from behind the big entry desk, "You just missed Mrs. Wells. She dropped off these writing tablets for the debate room."

Mrs. Claxton announced, "Cussy, this is Lillian Carver, our front desk librarian. Lillian, Cussy Lovett is our visiting librarian for the week."

Then she leaned in to me and barely whispered, "They don't know your business, Cussy. Not even my niece Susan has been told. I suggest we keep it that way. Tamp any gossip before it starts."

I couldn't help but wonder what Mrs. Claxton would say if she know'd all of it. "Yes, ma'am," I said, my face warming, ashamed that the librarian wouldn't risk others knowing she had an inmate working for her. Still, I appreciated the ol' woman's wisdom and was relieved to escape any gossip such news would bring.

Lillian came around from her desk and said, "Nice to meet you, Miss Cussy," never once showing repulsion or fear at my color, only a shy smile that lifted to slate-blue eyes. She left to help a patron.

"You've been officially welcomed to the Louisville Western Free Public Library. Let's get your name tag in my office and get ourselves started," Mrs. Claxton said.

Minutes later, she pinned the honorable title onto my blouse.

I pressed my fingers over it, suddenly proud, in awe of being able to work in a public city library. A Carnegie one, at that. I thought about my friend Queenie from back home. She'd left Troublesome for work at the Free Library of Philadelphia. I could see what all the fuss was about in her letters. Picture her big-city library up there. She'd been writing for years, asking me to visit. I missed hearing from her, wondered if she found out I'd been in prison.

"Now, Cussy, about our patrons: It's the parents we're more concerned with, as I told you. A lot of them labor during the day and don't have much reading or writing skills, if any. We need this to change if the Negroes are to have equal rights. Many still can't vote because they're required to pass literacy tests or be able to write their name. I want to right this for all the people in this community, black and white alike." She nodded firmly. "I know you must've had the same problem with your people in Troublesome. Maybe even at the library you're at now?"

"I'm getting ready to help with almost the same dilemma." I moved closer to her and lowered my voice. "Inmates can't go before the parole board unless they can read and write." Then I thought about my dear Loretta, the elderly seamstress in

Troublesome and the special school she attended, but only when the moon was fat. Working with Sassyann on her letters. "I have a suggestion, ma'am."

I began to tell her about our Moonlight Schools back home. How, years ago, the founder, Cora Wilson Stewart, taught the hillfolk to read and write during moonlit nights when the adult students could safely walk the mountain paths to the one-room schoolhouses after their daily work chores were finished.

Her eyes rounded. "I read about this educator long, long ago."

"Mrs. Stewart founded the schools in 1911. She taught thousands to read and write, Mrs. Claxton. Postmasters, sheriffs, coal miners, farmers—anyone hankering for the books. There were married couples, soldiers, and even folks in their eighties that many thought were not teachable, and that you couldn't teach an ol' dog new tricks."

She snorted. "Nonsense, I learn something every day. Going to keep doing so till my head's buried under the last blade of grass."

"Lots of soldiers signed up before heading off to the war. They found out that writing letters home was the only way to let folks hear from them. And their kin wanted to be able to answer the letters, so they signed up too."

"I had heard the schools were successful but didn't realize the extent."

"Mrs. Stewart used beginner tablets of blotted papers and inserted the alphabet in one-half so her Moonlighters could learn their letters and etch their names. Weren't long before the students could write without tracing and copy script from a newspaper or book."

"This is exactly what we need!" She smacked a palm down onto the table.

"It helped a lot of Kentucky men stand up to the big lumber and coal companies."

"My brother was a mule for the King Coal companies and died under their rule," she said. Suddenly, she sprang up, spry as a young'un. "Law, chile, this is a grand idea. Why, I could have Miss Wells at the elementary get me the tablets, pencils, and tracing paper."

"We could hold classes every evening, Mrs. Claxton."

"Maybe my late-afternoon librarians could watch over their children in the reading room while we teach the parents."

"We can solicit volunteer teachers like Mrs. Stewart did. And I could make up some fliers for your board and then distribute them around the neighborhoods, letting the parents know about the evening classes."

Our conversation rose easily as we talked over and around, lifting each other's ideas, jotting down our notes.

After an hour of discussion, she summoned her staff for a meeting, the excitement rising in her voice.

Weren't long before eight of her librarians were gathered in the debate room. All looked to be in their thirties and forties, and very professional and serious. Nary a one complained about being called in to donate their services, a testament to their fondness for the older librarian and their own dedication to patrons.

"Lillian," she called out, "see how much typewriter ink and pencils we have in the supply room. We may need to send the janitor over to the print shop on Walnut."

Minutes later, she sent us packing into quiet meeting rooms, where we typed up fliers for the adult writing classes for the next three hours.

When I took a break, I spotted Mrs. Claxton in her office, furious fingers flying over the typewriter keys.

In the afternoon, Mrs. Claxton sent Lillian and another librarian over to the business district to ask shopkeepers to tape fliers on their windows.

Weren't long before the librarian had stacks of leaflets on her desk. While I waited for her to count the fliers, the telephone rang.

"Louisville Western Branch Library." Her eyes narrowed. Then she covered the receiver and whispered, "Close the door."

"Yes, Warden, I'm still here. She's working right now and doing quite well." Mrs. Claxton shot me a smile.

I set the fliers on the table.

"Yes, she's been a tremendous help in such a short time. I wish I had more like her... Uh-huh. I can understand why you want her back."

My heart skipped. *Had the warden changed her mind? Was the doctor waiting for me at the prison?* Maybe she had sent someone and they were already on the way.

"I'll make sure to stay in touch, and I'll have her packed and ready for the officer Sunday at two. Yes, ma'am. Thank you, I'll speak with you tomorrow." The librarian hung up the telephone.

"Come on, chile, let's grab these fliers and get going."

Relieved, I gathered up the papers and followed her outside.

She nudged me over to the end of the building and placed a small brown hand on the cornerstone inscribed:

LOUISVILLE ^ FREE^ PUBLIC ^ LIBRARY
^COLORED ^ BRANCH

^ ERECTED ^A^D ^ 1907

"The Carnegie library was the nation's first full-service library built for coloreds and staffed by coloreds. To power the people. Five years ago, we changed that to *all* the people. Began hiring whites too. Today we need to go and find the ones who've been forgotten and get them book-read to vote." She patted the rough, sun-bleached stone.

While the July sun beat down in the late afternoon, we made our way around the neighborhood, knocking on doors.

Mrs. Claxton fanned herself. "It's going to be another hot

week. I fear we're going to be wearing the weather." She wiped the tiny droplets above her mouth, and I did the same, the air draping us like wet wool.

We walked past businesses until she came to a block of homes. "Let's start here," she said.

Some were doubtful when the librarian told them they could learn to read and write, and vote come next election. She pushed hard and said to one suspicious woman, "Now, Patty, we're growing voters, and your own sons can read and write just fine. But until they come of age, we need you and all the parents to vote for them. For us. Our people. Our rights."

Patty's eyes disappeared into her big, airish face as she wagged her head.

"Come to the class tomorrow, Patty," Mrs. Claxton wheedled. "We have ourselves the first library in the nation operated fully by Negroes and built just for us. We need to honor this gift by learning to read and write. And once you can do that, you can vote. Wouldn't you like a say on who your next mayor is? Our president?"

"What about her? That disfigurement she's got—it could be catching or sumthin'." She pointed at me.

The embarrassment lifted and heated my ears.

"No," Mrs. Claxton huffed. "She's *different,* and not too unlike us or the thousands out there who are not like those who rule us. *Law*, Patty, just come to the class. For the children." she softened her voice, touched the woman's sleeve. "Our community."

"Yes, ma'am, stop by," I chimed. "Please tell everyone to come tomorrow evening."

Patty glared at me, the anger cinched in her brow.

"Reckon there's a lot who have disfigurements, Miss Patty. Some that don't have a name or color," I said, lifting a stubborn chin.

Mrs. Claxton tugged on my sleeve, and I stepped back from the woman's chilly gaze.

"Hmph, don't need any negative Nellys. We need voters!"

she declared a few minutes later on the sidewalk, hooking her arm in mine.

Overhead, a crow squawked her truth from a utility pole and took flight, rolling out its bickering caws.

Twenty-Six

I knocked on the door of a cream-colored clapboard, the home neat and tidy. When no one answered, I rolled the flier and stuffed it between the doorjamb and knob.

Mrs. Claxton had me leave several inside the cast-iron mailboxes on porches. "A neighbor or schoolchild can read it to them," she said.

We stopped on the sidewalk at another house. It was a two-story, a lot bigger than most, and the curtains were drawn. But when I reached for the latch on the ornate gate, Mrs. Claxton grabbed my arm.

"Ma'am, is something wrong? Are you all right, Mrs. Claxton?"

The woman stepped closer to me and whispered, "I'm not sure we should stop here."

Puzzled, I glanced up at the home.

Her voice dropped lower, and I had to press my good ear closer to her mouth.

"Miss Johnna's brothel," she barely whispered. "A house of ill repute."

I wondered what Mrs. Claxton would think about Waldeen.

"We had us one in Troublesome," I remarked. "Stitched high in the hills. There was a young librarian who started working with the Pack Horse project right before I left. The girl weren't but fifteen. The brothel was in her assigned territory, but the supervisor ordered her not to put the occupants on her route."

"What happened?"

"The child did the opposite."

Mrs. Claxton cackled, and I laughed with her.

"Those women up in the cathouse ended up being the library's biggest donors—funding lots of reading programs around Troublesome and the new library. Downright generous folks." I glanced up at the bright-red double doors.

"I'm not sure the reverend would approve." She pursed her lips.

"More voters, ma'am. Maybe even future congregants for his church," I said slyly, curious to see what a brothel looked like.

Mrs. Claxton hitched her bulky pocketbook up over her shoulder. "Well, I guess whores should vote too," she grumbled, crooking her arm around mine as we opened the handsome arched gate and took the wide steps together.

The door creaked open, and a silk-clad matronly woman puffing on a long, gold cigarette holder appeared. She pointed her hand. "Why, Effie Claxton, I don't recall the circus being in town. Are you bringing me a runaway?" She peered down at me and then tilted her head upward, inhaling another draw of the tobacco. "My customers would sure 'nough be interested in enjoying her pleasures." Her bronzed cheekbones lifted when she smiled as she whipped back her long, red wig.

A blush warmed my face.

"Johnna, this is Mrs. Lovett, our new librarian!" Mrs. Claxton announced. "We're here to speak with your girls about our new library program."

"Ladies, we have visitors," Johnna called over her shoulder. She opened her double doors wider. We gaped at the young womenfolk who were scantily dressed, looking like paper doll cutouts in the Frederick's of Hollywood Christmas mail-order catalog I'd received once by mistake.

Jackson had brought our mail home from town only to find out the postmaster in Thousandsticks had included it.

I tried not to stare at Johnna's working girls, but I'd never seen such gussied-up women, decked out in sparkles as grand as a starry sky, other than the peeks I'd stole before tossing out the forbidden, naughty catalog before Honey could find it.

Seven dolled-up girls crowded inside the threshold, wearing racy red lipstick and painted nails, their brassiere-covered bosoms pointed to heaven, bodies squeezed inside shimmery-laced lingerie, black fishnet hosiery, and stiletto heels adorned with silky-feathered pom-poms.

One brown girl reached out to touch my hand, and a white one dared to do the same. More hands glided over my arm, and two of the bravest touched my cheek and chin. "She's gonna steal my johns," another said, sullen, her pale face rosied with rouge, heavy blue eyeshadow painted atop lids that popped her eyes.

A tall woman reached over and touched my arm, trailing coal-colored fingers across my flesh. "Oh, Johnna, whose room are you putting her in? I'll take her. I like girls too."

Mrs. Claxton swatted away their curious hands. "Ladies, this is Cussy Lovett, our new—"

At that, the young women giggled, and a blond licked my name across her tongue. "*Cussy*. Miss Johnna don't allow no cussing." A spark of mischief danced across her eyes.

Inside, a telephone rang, and Johnna excused herself.

Mrs. Claxton scowled. "She's our new librarian, ladies, and we're here to invite you to an important program we're having tomorrow evening that will teach you to read and write. *Vote*."

Several of the girls didn't seem interested and slipped back into the house. Two remained.

"Ain't heard from my people in years. It sure would be grand to talk with Mama," a girl piped.

"If I could read, it'd be my ticket out of here," a young one leaned over and whispered to me and Mrs. Claxton.

"Classes start at six tomorrow night," I told her.

Johnna came back to the door. "Now, girls, our evening hours are the busiest, and I can't have you losing me money."

"Johnna, most of my johns slip away from their offices during the lunch hour," the one who wanted to get away said.

"I don't know, Frankie." The madam mulled it over.

"Please, Miss Johnna. I'll come straight back after classes and work till the last customer leaves," Frankie begged.

"Johnna, I want to write my family and read some of them racy books you have on your bedstand," the other said. "I'll work double shifts too."

Miss Johnna laughed, but the old librarian remained stoic in her stance. "Okay, Frankie and Otilia, but if I see my wallet thinning, the classes stop." The madam nodded to Mrs. Claxton.

Fevered chatter rose among the young women as we told them about the evening classes.

"I hope we meet some cute fellers," Otilia remarked while turning to leave. Giggles erupted from inside while Mrs. Claxton scowled as the door clicked closed.

We moved on to others who weren't so keen on welcoming the idea. At some of the homes, we were met with folded arms, the people wary of our invitation. Still, we urged them to at least try a class. "Our fine city needs your vote," Mrs. Claxton would push.

When we approached a smaller home, Mrs. Claxton leaned over and said quietly, "Mr. Kipple Culbreath. He's a bachelor and likes tending to his flower garden out back."

I latched the gate behind us and brushed past a pastel-pink rosebush, the delicate blooms heady and sweet as I passed.

The door slowly creaked open, and the older colored man squinted his eyes and stared at us curiously.

"Kipple, we're here to invite you to our free library classes that will teach you to read and write so you can vote," the librarian announced.

"Read books?" he inquired, rubbing his chin. "Why, Effie Claxton, you know'd I can't even write my name. How am I supposed to up and do that, and at my age?" He laughed and shook his head.

"Yes, I know you can't, but your sister was a smart reader.

And she used to spend every weekend at our library. She would be proud if you honored her by trying. We need every vote we can get."

"Sir, Mr. Culbreath, I'm the new librarian. Cussy Lovett."

"Call me Kip," he said.

"Sure would be wonderful if you could come tomorrow night. We can teach you."

"Kip, why don't you talk with Miss Cussy a minute. I'm going to check out those pretty zinnias in your backyard. Mrs. Lyons told me hers are the prettiest blooms she's ever grown from the seeds you gave her."

Kip beamed at that, then lowered himself onto the stoop. I sat down with him and told him about the success of the Moonlight Schools, about the tales of pirates, big-city doings, and small-town secrets he could find in those books. "I think you would really like *The Great Gatsby*, sir," I said, standing after talking with him for almost thirty minutes.

He reached out his arm to me.

I flinched. First Susan had touched me friendly-like, and now Kip. It was hard getting used to it.

But suddenly I realized Kipple Culbreath weren't seeing me. An escape from loneliness had just opened wider windows.

"From Louisville, you say, Miss Cussy? Right here in the city." His brown weathered face opened in surprise. Then Kip extended his arm farther, waiting, and I helped him up, his bones stiff and creaking.

"Yes, sir, the character Daisy Buchanan was a flapper here in your city, sure enough, like Mr. Fitzgerald wrote."

He scratched his chin. "Sylvia's gone now, but I 'member her always chattering about the library books like they were friends. She was 'specially fond of one Kentucky author named Irvin Cobb. His books made her laugh, and she loved reading me a few pages from time to time."

"A fine author. Come tomorrow, so you'll be able to vote *and* meet new friends, sir."

"Friends." His eyes lit up. "I always thought I had no business at the library since I can't read."

"It's your library, sir. It belongs to everyone."

"Fitzgerald, you say? Will the library have a copy?"

"I don't know, but I'll find out for you."

"Would you like to see my garden? Let me get you a cold cola? I'll just go inside a minute. Wait here and I'll open that tin of butter cookies Sylvia sent two years ago. I have a picture of her just inside I want to show ya," he said, stalling for more time. The gentleman gripped the wrought-iron hand railing and took the steps slow and measured. "Be right back." He winced as he tried to move faster. "I guess Effie's still in the back looking at my flowers."

Kip returned with the photograph of his sister and two soda bottles, passing one Coca-Cola to me. He forgot the cookies and wanted to go back inside, but I declined.

"You have a nice talk with Kipple?" Mrs. Claxton asked as we made our way down the street. "I had a conversation over the fence with his neighbor. Seemed interested in the classes but made no promises."

"He's a nice gentleman." I looked back over my shoulder and saw him watching us, glimpsed a mixture of longing and loneliness in his eyes.

Twenty-Seven

Mrs. Claxton opened the gate at the next house, a small, unkempt clapboard. A windowpane had been cracked and another boarded up. She leaned closer to my ear. "This is Elizabeth Hall's place." She frowned. "Her husband is a drunkard."

A young bone-white woman opened the door, a baby boy hitched to her hip, a toddler hiding slightly behind her skirts. Her skin had been bruised, and her brow bore an ugly scar knitted across it.

"Ma'am," I said, "I'm librarian Cussy Lovett, and I would like to invite you to the library tomorrow night at six. We've started a free program to teach adults to read and write, so they can vote and have other freedoms."

"A reading and writing program?" she said in disbelief. "I'm long-toothed—nineteen, past the schoolgirl age and getting longer in the teeth every minute."

"Age don't matter. Mr. Culbreath plans to attend, and he's eighty." I smiled.

"Always a pleasure to see you, Lizbeth. We sure would be pleased to have you and the babies join us. Tandy will be watching the children in the reading room while the grown-ups learn the lessons," Mrs. Claxton pushed.

Lizbeth stole a glance to the librarian. "Mrs. Claxton, nice to see you again. Freedom is something I ain't had for a long time. Since I was maybe knee-high."

The woman looked behind her, then stepped out onto the stoop, quietly closing the door as the toddler clung to her skirts, sneaking peeks up at us. "My man is…napping. I don't want to disturb him."

I had an uneasy feeling by the look of her fresh bruises, her man was likely pie-faced and passed out.

Mrs. Claxton laid a hand on her shoulder and whispered, "Come learn, chile. There's a whole lot of freedom in that. Help yourself and others in our neighborhoods by voting."

"Not sure any book's gonna free me." Defeated, Lizbeth stared past the rooftops and blinked her misty eyes.

"Please come, Miss Lizbeth," I pleaded.

She sniffed and wiped her nose with the back of her hand, hitching her babe closer to her chest.

From behind the door, Mr. Hall called out for her, cursing and slurring his words. Then something crashed inside, and she jumped and turned toward the door.

Frightened, the children looked back at the home and then at their mama as their eyes welled. The toddler at her side blubbered *Mommy* and covered his crotch. I looked down. He'd wet his pants.

Lizbeth winced. "Shh, shh, we have to be quiet. Be brave lil men for Mama." She jiggled the child on her hip and squeezed the toddler's hand in warning. "Thank you, ladies. I better get back in 'fore he tears up the house and takes a belt to me."

"Do it for you and the children," the librarian urged.

When we left, I said, "Can the law protect her from him?"

The librarian shook her head. "Chile, those stuff-coats in Frankfort, all over these United States, make laws to protect the powerful, not the common man, and especially not womenfolk. It's 1953; you would think it would've changed by now!" she spat.

"But won't the police—"

"If the policeman arrives and sees she's bloodied and bruised, their hands are tied by the lawmakers in Frankfort. They can only offer to take her downtown, ask her if she'd like to swear out a warrant. If that. Now they *ain't* going to be caring about women, especially a poor one. Unless her man is bothering *them*. And if by some miracle she has him locked up, well, he'll be out lickety-split—and back home waiting for her with a razor strap and harder fist. Men protect a man's property first and foremost."

At the next home, Mrs. Claxton paused on the sidewalk. "This is our paperboy, Steven's, place." She walked up the crumbling concrete steps and banged the brass doorknocker.

A rusted blue bicycle with a flattened tire rested to the side of the stoop.

The door swung open, and a tall, young colored man widened his eyes when he saw us. A litany of apologies spewed as he grabbed a shirt off the chair and slipped it on. "Mrs. Claxton, please don't report me. Daddy was sick, and Mama took another bad spell. I aim to deliver them papers as soon as my sister gets back from the washateria." He stepped outside and I glimpsed an old man slumped in a wheelchair and a frail-looking woman asleep on a narrow iron bed behind him.

"It's fine, Steven. Why don't you shut the door and come on down to the yard so we can talk while your parents rest." Concerned, Steven closed the door and followed her out into the yard.

"You got a busted tire, I see." She turned toward his bicycle.

"People forget to sweep up their broken glass. Some streets are worse than others, but it's so dark when I deliver papers in the morning I can hardly dodge all of 'em. Costing me a pretty penny too."

"Stop by the library, and I'll have maintenance repair it."

"Thank you, Mrs. Claxton. Is there anything else? I should be getting back in there."

"How old are you now, chile?" Mrs. Claxton asked.

"I turn twenty in three months."

"And have you signed your sister up for the school year yet? Carole must be, what, nine now?"

He scratched his brow. "Ain't been no time for schooling, ma'am. I need her home to help so I can work and pay the bills. I'm hoping one day to hire on at Belknap Hardware and Manufacturing, soon as I can fill out their paperwork. With decent pay, I could pay for help to come in for Mama and Daddy."

"Paperwork," Mrs. Claxton remarked. "And exactly what I want to talk to you about." She handed him one of the fliers. He stared blankly at it and gave it back, peering over her shoulder. "Ya know I don't read, Mrs. Claxton. Oh, there's Carole now. Where ya been? Git on up here, girl." He gestured to her. "Hurry it up."

Carole shuffled slowly down the sidewalk with two stuffed pillowcases clutched in front of her.

"Carole," he hollered, "what's took you so long? You should've been home almost two hours ago, girl. I need to deliver these papers before I lose my job." Steven grabbed a sack and opened it, digging inside. "The clothes are wet. You done went and spent the laundry coins for the dryer on candy *again*? Dammit, Carole."

The little girl's big brown eyes watered. "I was hungry, Steven—"

"Ain't my fault you wouldn't eat the Cream of Wheat I fixed you this morning," he shouted.

"Mommy always made it with milk." She stuck out her lip. "I can't stand it with water."

Steven swatted her on the bottom. "We can't afford milk, girl. And we sure as hell can't afford sweets. Git on inside, and hang them wet clothes up 'fore I take a belt to you."

Squalling for her mama, Carole dropped the other sack of laundry and ran into the house, slamming the door behind her.

Mrs. Claxton sighed. "Steven, we're holding classes tomorrow evening at six to teach adults to read and write. We need more young voters. It would be good if you could come, chile."

"It's useless." He waved his arm toward the house, then picked up the bags of laundry.

"I can send one of the volunteer ladies from the church to help out this week," Mrs. Claxton offered.

I stepped forward. "Steven, I'm Cussy Lovett, a librarian too. If you can get better pay, you *could* hire that help to come in to tend to your ailing folks."

"Too damn saddled with bigger troubles." He bounded up the steps.

Mrs. Claxton called out, "I'll send someone by just in case you change your mind."

Twenty-Eight

By the time we arrived back at the Claxton home that evening, we were both spent.

After baths, Mrs. Claxton fried ham steaks while I set the table.

When Reverend finished his meal, he leaned back in his chair and stared at his wife a long time, something stirring under his clenching jawbone.

"Can I get you more meat, sir?" I half rose from my chair. But his stern brow pulled me back into my seat.

"Effie, Gregory Davis said he saw you over on Ninth?"

Mrs. Claxton swallowed the food and slowly wiped her mouth with a napkin. "Just visiting our neighbors to invite them to a special program that Cussy is leading." She glanced at me. "Ain't that right?"

"Yes, Reverend. We're holding night classes to teach adults to read and write. Grow readers so they can vote."

"Does this night schooling include harlots?" Reverend snipped.

She dropped her napkin. "Jedidiah Claxton, we need everyone's vote!"

"I won't have my woman associating with the likes of floozies."

I pushed away from the table and began clearing the dishes.

"Cussy, I'll see to 'em. Why don't you take some food to

Daisy and retire to the sleeping porch. We have a big day tomorrow." Mrs. Claxton stood abruptly and scraped ham, gravy, and bread onto a saucer and passed it to me.

"Yes, ma'am. Good evening, Reverend."

In the backyard, I fed Daisy, then found a stick and played fetch with her, trying to stay out of earshot from the open windows and harsh climbing whispers.

Hussy.

Bible.

Scarlet.

God.

Then *Heathen.*

The word left me thunderstruck. Daisy raised her head and then trotted over and nudged my hand with her wet nose. I knelt and patted her.

The dog must've sensed my anguish, because she stepped on my knee and licked my cheek.

Long ago, when I had attended the Fourth of July celebration in Troublesome, I'd suffered the accusation when I asked to join the women's sewing club and brought them a scripture cake.

The women had called me a *spectacle*, a *heathen*, and more, damning me.

I flinched as the hot shame rose again, a feeling that was always there, like the coal dust that always found its way back into our home no matter how many times I'd swept it out.

Would this baby live long enough to feel it too?

Inside, Reverend Claxton's words climbed over his wife's.

I hurried back inside, bristling.

The Claxtons suddenly quieted as I entered the kitchen.

"Sir, about the women on Ninth Street. They want to learn—"

He shook his head and waved me away. "Don't ya fuss at me, Cussy," he warned.

"Jedidiah Charles Claxton!" Mrs. Claxton glared at him.

I stepped closer to the sullen man and said quietly, "I recall from my mama's studies that God's chosen people trusted Rahab, and God rewarded her."

He drew his brows together while a scolding writhed across his tongue.

A ghost of a smile twitched at the corners of Mrs. Claxton's mouth. "Well, now, I believe our Cussy is right about that, Jed. If God gave her equal rights the same as His chosen people, I reckon you should apply the lesson with these women and do the same."

The reverend grunted as if he'd learned long ago that he didn't have to win every argument with his wife.

"Now, Jed, I want you to make an announcement at your church meeting tomorrow morning and tell the deacons and your Bible study groups about the classes."

He was getting ready to hold up a shushing hand when she said, "We have to get our people to vote if there's going to be change."

Reverend said, "I'll let 'em know, Effie. And I'll telephone the other pastors and ask them to announce it at their services first thing tomorrow morning."

"It's settled." Mrs. Claxton lifted her chin. "Now, help me get these dishes, Jed. I've got to whip up some dinners for you for the next four nights. Cussy and I will be teaching late."

"At least stop by the church to collect Bibles for the *ladies'* first reading lesson," he said, bringing the dirty plates over to the sink.

"I promise." Mrs. Claxton patted his arm before walking me back to the sleeping porch.

"Cussy, we'll need to leave for the library at seven sharp..." She paused at the doorway when Daisy scooted across the porch on her belly, wagging her tail, her bullet-shaped body inching closer. Mrs. Claxton started to protest when Daisy jumped onto the bed.

I scratched the dog's chin. "It's fine, ma'am."

"Well, I can always put her in the washroom if she's pestering.

Daisy, no. Said *no*." The woman bent over and shook a crooked finger at the wiggling pup.

Daisy lowered her chin to the quilt, wagging her tail as I sank down beside her.

"You're spoiling her, chile."

I rubbed her ears, thinking of Junia, worrying how she was faring with her ol' bones and grief troubling her. "Good night, ma'am."

"The pup sure likes you. My daddy always said, *You can be fooled by fancy shoes and big-footed words, but you can reckon the integrity of one's character by the way they treat the creatures.* Appears Daisy knows that too."

Daisy perked at her name, then stretched and wriggled onto my lap, her tail slapping furiously against my legs as she buried her nose between my arm and belly, winning her spot with a satisfied snort.

Mrs. Claxton lightly tsked her disapproval. "Good night, Cussy, sleep well. I was told you can grow readers, and I aim to squeeze every drop of that blue magic outta you."

Twenty-Nine

From the stoop, I collected Tuesday's newspaper as the night sky dissolved behind pillows of pink-lavender clouds and a crested golden crown.

Under the Claxtons' porch light, I dropped my gaze to the paper, eager to search for the latest news about the polio outbreak at Jackson's prison. Instead, the July seventh headline screamed "The Notorious Black Widow Sassyann Sipes to Be Executed Today."

Unable to look away, I read the article and winced at a shocking photograph. It showed another electrocution that happened in 1928, of a New York woman named Ruth Snyder. Though such had been forbidden, the newspaper reported the photographer had secretly strapped a camera to his ankle and shot the ghastly scene during the electrocution, shocking the country.

The woman's arms and legs were bound by leather straps, her face and eyes hidden beneath a leather mask. Underneath the slightly blurred photograph, an article explained the history of the electric chair, noting Thomas Edison and a dentist had killed countless animals while testing the invention.

I couldn't help imagining Ruth's writhing body and wheezing breaths and tasted the bile rising and knocking at my throat. Unable to help myself, I turned back to the morbid photograph, witnessing the woman suspended between heaven and earth.

Horrified, I examined the picture of Sassyann closely, studying the photograph they had used.

Sassyann was clad in her scarlet-red prison clothing, her small frame shackled, gripped by brutish law officials as she was escorted down a long, darkened hall lined with newsmen. I stared into her blank eyes and know'd that as far as she was concerned, they couldn't torture her anymore—they'd already killed her long ago.

Again, I choked, fighting against my stomach's rebellion.

I looked to the skies, knowing there was a good chance they'd kill me along with the babe if they could. I wondered, if I started walking now, how long it would take to lose myself in this big city.

Somewhere nearby an automobile door slammed, and then came the roar of a motor, awakening the natters of nested birds. Startled, I spun around. The taillights of a distant vehicle disappeared. The yellow glow of the city's lamplights grew faint as dawn summoned the morning. The street was quiet except for a striped tabby's loud yowling as it made its way across neighbors' yards, demanding its morning meal. I stepped off the stoop and looked up and down the street, tempted to run.

The door opened. "Good, I see the paper's early today," Reverend said, poking his head out.

I thrust it into the ol' man's hands, ducked past his wiry frame, and escaped to the washroom to dry my eyes.

When I came out, I asked if I could help with breakfast or set the table. But I was shooed away. The couple had their heads together, resting their arms on the counter, intent on listening to the morning newscast gossip on their wooden radio.

Mrs. Claxton adjusted the knob as the static licked at the speaker's voice. She barely whispered, "Not now, chile, the governor's giving an important news report."

I walked toward the sleeping porch, then stopped cold.

Hearing the governor say *Sassyann*, I moved closer to the couple, the politician's shocking news sweeping across the kitchen.

"So, gentlemen, I can only ask of myself," the governor boomed above the static, "can a mere mortal be more righteous than God? Can even the strongest of men be purer than his Maker?"

The radio quieted except for the sound of newspapermen as they scribbled down his biblical quote, the shifting of paper rattling above the scissoring air.

"Who here is more righteous than Him?" the governor continued. "If I dare try to execute the wretched woman again, her spirit will rise up against me."

A harsh breath scraped over my tongue.

The Claxtons crowded in closer.

There was a long pause, then a reporter piped up, his voice riding the airwaves clear. "There's been a string of botched electrocutions across the country in the last decade. In '46, the Louisiana teenager Willie Francis survived the electric chair only to be electrocuted again the following year. My question is this, sir: Since Sassyann Sipes survived the electric chair, and if there will be no second electrical execution for her, will the state consider seeking a hanging instead—"

"God turned her away and Satan wouldn't have her!" the governor proclaimed.

"*Governor, over here. Governor,*" the men rang out, their pleas rising above the rustling papers and buzzing whispers.

"Why, it's nothing short of a real honest-to-God miracle," a newsman shouted above the others.

More static had us all pinched head-to-head before we heard the governor's words again.

"Gentlemen, I'll take one last question. You, Mr. Hagar, from the Owensboro *Messenger.*"

I cocked my ear, trying to make out his question wallowing under the squawks of chorusing crows, the newsmen hungering for more.

Reverend grumbled and fiddled with the dial as his wife smacked her fist against the counter.

"*Time.*"

"*Seconds.*"

"*Precise*—"

A quarrel of words fizzled into the governor's final choppy statement: "…immediately…hospitalized…chair malfunctioned at approximately twenty-four sec—execution was—"

I leaned in closer.

More broken questions rose, and the newsmen's urgent inquiries collided and dipped under the crackling static.

"Thank you for coming, gentlemen; that's all I have for you at this time. I'll update you on her medical prognosis as soon I learn more from the doctors."

"*Sinner,*" Reverend Claxton muttered, shaking his head, slowly pushing away from the counter.

"Warrior," Mrs. Claxton said softly, silencing the radio with a click.

Thirty

We set out for the library at seven, the chorus of the city striking under the dawn's pull chain of speedy vehicles, horns, and a budding busyness.

As we approached the building, Mrs. Claxton asked, "Did you know her? Miss Sipes?"

"Yes, ma'am. I taught her to write."

"Did she really do those men in?"

I turned my head to an empty playground. "She had a difficult life with her husband. *Husbands.* A lot like Lizbeth Hall is having now, I reckon." I raised a hand to my ear, lightly touched, remembering how Frazier had beat me senseless through the long night until dawn, and until he keeled over from my fevered prayers. "She was trying to protect herself and her sons, ma'am."

"Seen a lot of that difficulty with some of our other womenfolk around here. And no matter, it ain't right to try and kill someone three times. Poor children having to suffer a mother's burial more than once."

"Three, ma'am?"

"I imagine her men tried first, and prison life was the state's second attempt. Now today makes three. And yet she lives. Though like a limp rotting vegetable."

My hands darkened as I grieved for Sassyann locked away in the prison infirmary. She would be tortured with brutal exams by medical staff needing to poke and pry every inch of flesh to learn how she had survived the electric chair. Damned as a peculiar. And for the grievance, they would both fear and try to persecute this unknown. Maybe even lobotomize Sassyann to try to bring her back before likely executing her again. She would surely die a hundred deaths before she rested eternal under the blood-soaked Kentucky grounds.

"I'll add her to our prayer circle," Mrs. Claxton said.

"Prayer circle, ma'am?"

"Reverend's congregation knows the power of prayer. I've seen it move mountains. And I'm a mountain woman. I know."

"Mrs. Claxton, did the prison tell you what my crime was?" I studied her, trying to decide if I dared to be bold and tell her more.

She stopped on the library steps and whispered, "Only that you had library training and were not violent. Is there something else I should know, chile?"

"I was jailed for violating miscegenation laws because I married a white man. And he was sent to prison too," I blurted, unable to keep it in any longer.

"Law, chile. I didn't know." She shook her head. "They wouldn't give out any information other than what I was told. I'm sorry. *Law.* There ought to be rules against those high 'n mighty men making such ugly laws. Downright sinful!"

"I've been worried about my husband, Jackson. There's a polio outbreak in the men's prison."

"Last year was sure a bad one for it. I lost six patrons. Yet people don't seem to be paying any mind to the epidemic *this* year." She kissed her teeth. "We'll keep an eye on the newspapers and an ear glued to the broadcasts for more about the prison." She shot me a sympathetic smile.

I wanted to tell her about the baby, my fears, but two teen girls slipped up behind us, carrying armloads of books and sporting colorful swing skirts and loafers with shiny new pennies, their laughter skittling up the steps, caramel-blond ponytails rising in rhythm.

"Morning, Mrs. Claxton," the girls called out in passing.

"Morn', Becky and Sandra. My, aren't you young ladies up early," she replied.

"It's nickel day at Fontaine Ferry!" One teen turned back and smiled. "Mama said we had to return the books that are due before we can go."

"Enjoy your day at the amusement park, and be careful on that old deviled roller-coaster ride," the librarian called after them, huffing as she took another step.

I tapped her shoulder. "Ma'am, could you add me?"

She stopped. "Done did, Cussy. Added you to the prayer circle at Sunday service the day you landed here. And I'll be sure to add your Jackson and Honey too."

Inside, Lillian rushed over to meet us, her black pumps snapping across the buffed floors. "Come look what came in this morning, Mrs. Claxton."

We followed her down the hall.

Stacks of tablets and tracing papers awaited us inside the big meeting room.

I hurried over to the table. "There's hundreds. With these, they'll learn fast."

"Only if they come." Mrs. Claxton turned to her librarian. "Lillian, I need you to run over to Reverend's church and collect a few Bibles off his pews."

At noon, Warden called and checked in with Mrs. Claxton. The librarian brushed her off, excited for our big night.

I lingered among the rows of books, savoring the charm of the library. Just a mere four days to get the program going. The time would go quick, and then I would be sent back to the horrors that awaited me.

Thirty-One

Tuesday evening, we huddled together at the door, waiting with anxious hearts.

At 6:00 p.m., two of Johnna's women, Otilia and Frankie, filed in, both looking like living dolls that belonged on a toy store's shelf rather than a library one.

Soon, an older man strolled in, followed closely by a woman. We seated them at the long table and passed out tracing paper and pencils. Several librarians helped, and we wrote down each name, instructing the excited new patrons to trace the letters and then practice on a sheet of paper. When I glanced up a few minutes later, I saw Patty standing at the threshold.

She hugged a spent pocketbook close to her chest. When Patty saw Johnna's girls, she hurried over to us.

"Effie Claxton," she said, "what's the meaning of you drawing us into a meeting full of harlots? Did you hire her"—she scowled toward me—"to bring this sordid idea and filthy heathens into our community building? Shameful. I expected better from you. I will have you both fired for promoting indecency in our public library."

"Now, Patty, everyone has a right to use the library." Mrs. Claxton pulled her aside. "The mayor approves. Just have a seat, and you'll enjoy your free public library even more after tonight."

I went over to stand by Mrs. Claxton. "Please stay, Miss Patty."

Her eyes flashed, a crawl of anger lit across, and for a second I thought she would strike me or lash out with her vinegar tongue. Mrs. Claxton stepped in between us, and Patty turned in a huff and stormed out, nearly knocking over a hesitant Steven in the doorway.

Mrs. Claxton leaned into my ear. "You'll find darkness in all kinds, chile. The devil's fiery licks don't pick and choose."

Out of the corner of my eye, I could see Steven searching the room.

When one of Johnna's girls saw the paperboy, she rushed over. "Come sit by me, Steven." Otilia grabbed his arm.

The young man scratched his head and shyly grinned.

Mrs. Claxton gently removed the girl's hand off Steven. "Take your seat, chile. We're here for different lessons tonight."

"Why, I'm here to learn *all* the lessons, Mrs. Claxton," Otilia teased, swinging her shapely bottom back into the chair.

Frankie piped up, "I'm here to get my ticket out of this damn town."

"Cussy, take Steven over to the other table and get him started," the librarian said.

Eight patrons showed up for the classes, including Kipple Culbreath.

Excitement, claps, and cheers lifted in the room as they cried out their accomplishments.

An elderly woman with a cane, holding a wrinkled envelope, walked over to me. "My name's Ardell Winters." She thrust a letter into my hand. "My husband passed last December. He used to read to me. For me." Her brown face twisted in pain. "My granddaughter done wrote me and I can't..." Ardell's words slipped into a whisper and I leaned closer. "Can you read it to me, librarian?"

I took the envelope, noting that the postmark from Indiana had been dated almost six months ago. Carefully, I opened it and read the neatly written script. It was news of the birth of Ardell's first great-grandson.

Ardell grabbed my wrist. "Read that part again about the boy—slow."

"'He's healthy and weighed seven pounds, eight ounces. We named him Clyde Arde Russell after you and Pawpaw. We hope you can visit soon. Your loving granddaughter, Cela.'"

I passed the letter back to her, and she tilted her head upward. "Imagine that, *Clyde Arde Russell*," Ardell whispered. "You hear that, Clyde? Lordy, our great-grandson. You watch over him, hear now? I learnt to write my name tonight, now I'm gonna write yours."

"It's a handsome, strong name, Miss Ardell," I warmed. "Let's find you a seat and get started."

Kip tugged on my sleeve as I passed. "Show me where that Daisy flapper book is." He flapped his bony arms teasingly.

"Ah, *The Great Gatsby*."

"Want to make sure I know where it is once I can read."

"I'll get it for you after lessons, sir. Let's seat you next to Miss Ardell. I think you'll work nice together."

Later, I glanced over at the elderly couple. Ardell held up her letter to him, boasting of her good news. Kip pulled out his sister's photograph, and they bent their heads in conversation.

I'd hoped Lizbeth Hall would come. It had been a little disappointing to see, but only a handful showed up, and I saw the other librarians' eyes thought so too. And I couldn't help but worry I'd let everyone down. Especially Mrs. Claxton.

Back on the sleeping porch, I crawled into bed next to a waiting Daisy, unable to quiet my thoughts about Sassyann, fretting what her fate would be. *Had her sons been in the room to bear witness to the botched execution?*

I turned to my own fate. *Would the governor let her live out her life peaceably or fold under the pressure of citizens demanding another execution…?* I shuddered, feeling trapped.

Thirty-Two

Sassyann's fiery face hovered over mine, her arms reaching out, the flames and sparks shooting from her hands and head, licking at me, her cries folding into my strangled screams. Behind her, Warden Sanders appeared and shot out a damning finger. The heat warming my flesh, the clanging of prison crash gates ringing in my ears.

Suddenly, I was being shaken, rocked, and I fluttered open my eyes, gasping for air. Mrs. Claxton bent over me, and Daisy's hot doggy breath hit my face as she stood beside me on the pillow.

"Chile, chile, wake up. It's just a nightmare. Sit up, Cussy." She shook my shoulders again, raising me up from my pillow. "Law, you're drenched in sweat."

The reverend stood behind her with worry lit across his eyes.

"I'll go get her a cup of warm milk and a cool rag, Effie," he said and shuffled into the kitchen.

"Get her a fresh gown from my drawer," she called after him.

Mrs. Claxton sank down onto the bed and tucked my tangled hair behind my ears. "Only a nightmare, chile. You're safe now." She rubbed my back, calming me with soothing words.

Soon, the comfort pulled me back to home, into my mama's protective embrace.

It was one o'clock when I finally fell back asleep.

The nightmare lingered as we walked into the library Wednesday morning.

Shortly after we arrived, the warden called Mrs. Claxton again.

When the librarian hung up, she said, "That woman's sure anxious to get you back. Hmph. She even had the gall to ask if you could return Friday."

My breath hitched.

"Done told her the mayor said I could keep you till Sunday. And I planned on using every minute of it. *And* not to come for you until *after* we've attended church services and laid out our early Sunday supper."

"I'm appreciative of your generosity, ma'am."

"Come on, chile, we have more work to do. There's a few who've asked to come to class at noon. They work at night. One is Otilia—she said Johnna gave her permission—and the others are public servants. There's a policeman needing to refine his writing and reading skills and a fireman itching to climb rank."

Irene, an older woman who'd been in class the night before, was waiting. Dark circles bloomed under her soft hazel eyes.

"Miss, I was here last night. 'Member? Can ya read this letter for me? It's from my daughter. I had nine children, but they all grow'd up and scattered far out west, except for my Rachel. She went to Detroit and got herself schooled proper-like. But sometimes, I have to wait a week to find a neighbor to read her letter to me. That's why I'm back early today. I need to learn *now*," she insisted.

I could see the letters were her only sustenance in life. We went over the words, and I worked with her until noon.

After class, I ate my sandwich with Mrs. Claxton inside the library kitchen. "Irene is determined to read," she said.

"Irene's got the *stubborn* starching her bones, and I believe she will in no time. Right quick study, too, ma'am. She insists on coming back tonight."

"And to think, those old stuff-coats sitting on fancy boards believed you couldn't teach an old dog new tricks." Mrs. Claxton huffed.

"Not the Moonlight lady Cora Wilson Stewart."

"Not my librarians," she said proudly.

I grinned between bites, suddenly having a hearty appetite. The morning sickness seemed to be fading, and I finished my sandwich and accepted the bowl of blackberry cobbler she pushed across the table.

After dinner, I settled a sandy-haired policeman, two muscly firemen, and Otilia at a table. But the girl grew leery sitting next to the lawman and puffed up.

"Miss Cussy," she hissed in my ear, "I can't be sitting by no copper. I'm going over to the other table."

It weren't no time when I caught Otilia peeking over, curious of their lessons.

The men were quiet and polite, and after an hour, Otilia plopped herself down in between them. She even shared her spelling tips with the policeman. Pleased, I circled the table, bending over each one as they used the paper to trace new words. Then we sounded out the ones I'd written on the blackboard. After two hours, Otilia and the policeman were working shoulder to shoulder, the girl intent on sharing reading tips.

I could tell she was eager to learn and even prouder she had bested him by being a quick study.

Wednesday night drew eighty-two patrons, and we were speechless as the crowd piled inside.

I whispered to Mrs. Claxton, "Ma'am, it's just like the night when Cora opened her first Moonlight School in Kaintuck. They only expected a handful. But on that first night, twelve hundred mountainfolk climbed out of those hills to walk those crooked paths to attend their first nightly lessons in a one-room schoolhouse!"

Mrs. Claxton shook her head, astonished, as they kept pouring in.

That night, many mentioned they'd heard the news from their

ministers and pastors, and I was grateful that Reverend had contacted the churches. Others had come across it from businesses and neighbors.

Mrs. Claxton called all the librarians back in to work. We carried up chairs and tables from the basement, borrowing from other areas and stuffing the rooms, halls, wherever we could fit patrons best.

The librarian contacted Mrs. Wells for more writing tablets and tracing paper, and the principal did not hesitate to bring them. The woman even insisted on staying to help.

Once we seated everyone, I introduced myself while the other librarians passed around the tracing papers.

Mrs. Claxton's face glowed as I went over to the blackboard and wrote the letters of the alphabet.

I would miss the ol' librarian, with her gentle eyes and welcoming spirit.

Thirty-Three

As we were getting ready for work the next morning, Susan stopped by after her hospital shift, excited to share news.

"Hello, Uncle, Aunt Effie. I can't stay but wanted to see Cussy before I went to bed." Her white uniform bore the blood-specked stains and creases of a long night shift.

Mrs. Claxton jumped up. "You've got a tear on the pocket of your uniform again, chile. Let me sew that up for you real quick."

"It's fine, Auntie. I have the one you repaired last month." She pecked her aunt's cheek.

Susan looked to me. "Cussy, I had a chance to study more about your diagnosis. We had a forty-eight-year-old male patient admitted Tuesday who was the same color as you."

I felt my eyes widen. "Like me?"

"Exactly your color and having the methemoglobinemia. But unlike you, his disorder was caused by drinking well water that held too much nitrates. So his was acquired and not congenital like yours."

"Chile, I don't understand a word of this medical gobbledygook. Speak *our* language," Mrs. Claxton said.

I wrinkled my brow, trying to get the gist of it all.

"He's a farmer on the outskirts of town, and we tested his blood. And because of you, I was able to treat him. We gave him oxygen and a blood transfusion, but when he didn't show improvement and his color had not returned to normal, I urged the doctor to try an IV of your methylene blue. He healed quickly. We discharged the patient the next morning!"

Susan was so pleased with herself she suddenly grabbed me in a hug.

I blushed. "You cured him," I said, awed by this smart nurse.

"Yes, chile," Mrs. Claxton told her. "Fine work. That is some good news, Cussy. She wouldn't have saved him if you hadn't come to Louisville."

"It's true, Cussy," Susan said, smiling. "Medicine is changing quickly, and every day we learn more."

"Can I get you some breakfast, chile?" Mrs. Claxton asked her niece.

"Love to stay, Auntie, but I've got to get some rest before my next shift." She grabbed a biscuit and a sausage patty off the top of the stove. "This week has already been a month-of-Mondays-long."

I couldn't understand about the nitrates in his well water and why his blue was only temporary and could be cured completely, or why the methylene blue had made me sick but healed him. I started to ask when Susan squeezed my shoulder. "Got to run. See you Sunday, Cussy."

While Mrs. Claxton and I walked to the library, I studied more on why there was no permanent fix for my woes.

Inside the librarian's office, I wrung my blazed-blue hands as she answered another of Warden's daily telephone calls.

Sunday was coming quick, her prying calls a reminder.

That evening, when a hundred more patrons showed up, Mrs. Claxton telephoned school principals and pleaded with them to call teachers in to volunteer. Within the hour, they arrived, eager to donate their evenings to the cause.

Barking orders, the ol' librarian passed out name tags, fussed over seating, and finally quieted the crowd. I wandered between the students and hallways and other rooms, stopping to check their practice papers and offer help.

Later, when I walked into the ladies' facilities and saw a group huddled on the floor with a young teacher instructing them, I warmed, knowing they'd sure enough be standing in voter lines come Election Day.

Still, I searched new faces, hoping to see Lizbeth.

The patrons came in droves—from dark alleyways, busy streets, quiet neighborhoods, businesses, and more. We welcomed couples carrying babes, others toting canes, and two in wheelchairs who had to be carried up the Carnegie Library's steps.

We seated grandparents, factory men, street cleaners, policemen, and other girls from houses like Miss Johnna's. Lillian's eyes nearly popped when she welcomed an ol' white Baptist minister and he seated himself next to a woman from a brothel.

The minister confided in Mrs. Claxton. "Jedidiah phoned and suggested I stop in. For years I've had to rely on someone else to read the Bible to me before I practiced my sermons. I was awfully humiliated when I told my congregation that for years Peter was a fine fisherman and Paul was an *oyster man*. Found out after the sermon Paul was indeed *austere* and not an oyster man."

Like the Moonlight lady back home, Mrs. Claxton turned no one away.

Mrs. Claxton insisted I use her office to take a quick supper break since the library kitchen was being used for teaching the patrons.

Alone at her desk, I ate a sandwich she'd brought from home while I flipped through the newspaper, searching for any word on polio or the men's prison. There was a small article that reported some prisoners in Indiana and Kentucky had been selected for Salk's trials and would be inoculated. I prayed it was Jackson's prison. Again, I read through the news, looking to see if there were any new deaths reported but found none. Exhaling, I folded the paper and placed it beside the telephone.

My eyes rested on the black receiver. I reached for it, then curled my fist, pulling away.

It was useless. The inmates at the men's prison had telephone privileges like the women's once a week, but only when they had a telephone number to call.

How I wished I could hear his voice, find out if he was safe. Tell him where I was. Worried, I placed half the sandwich back into the sack and tossed it in the trash can.

I drummed my fingers on the desk, then sat back down in Mrs. Claxton's comfortable chair and boldly reached for the receiver again.

The operator answered. My hands shook, and I jumped up and twisted the long telephone cord, slowly winding it around my body. "Troublesome Creek, ma'am? Doc, please. Doctor Thomas, ma'am."

She dialed the number, and I stared at the door, listening to the loud vibrating rings. Seconds passed when the operator came back on the line. "There's no answer, ma'am. Would you like me to try—"

Footsteps fell near the door. The knob turned slowly, and I slammed down the receiver, my breaths sliding into a rattled thud.

"There you are, Miss Cussy," Lillian said, looking at me curiously and then over to the telephone. "I'm sorry if I interrupted, but Mrs. Claxton asked me to find you. The newspapermen are here looking for you."

"Newspaper?"

Thirty-Four

The reporters crowded around Mrs. Claxton as I peeked out of her office despite the librarian urging me to join her. The newspaper had been alerted of the success of the evening classes and had come calling. Camera bulbs lit up as they snapped pictures of Mrs. Claxton and some of the students and took notes. After about an hour they packed up their equipment, and I slipped back into classes.

"I wish you would've joined us, Cussy," Mrs. Claxton said.

"I don't want my photograph in the paper for everyone in Louisville and who knows where else to gawk at my peculiarity. I best get back to our patrons, ma'am."

Understanding, she nodded.

I stood beside one middle-aged man as he declared, "It's damn time I escape that shaming mark." He waved the paper. "Here's my signature written fully. And I done wrote it on my fence and carved it onto my elm. No, sir, ain't never gonna have to make a shamed mark again!" His eyes shone.

We all congratulated him.

The students were intoxicated, giddy to learn.

A man who'd said he just turned eighty-six the day before crowed, "I'd give up fifty years of my life if I could just read."

On Friday, I searched the crowd for Lizbeth. It was my last night, and I worried the woman had come to great harm.

When she showed up thirty minutes later, I saw the truths in her blackened eyes. The young mother wore a sling made from a yellow-stained bedsheet on her left arm. The room quieted, and the elders shook their heads, dismayed by her appearance.

Mrs. Claxton and the children's librarian took charge of her two little ones and swept them off toward the children's reading room.

"I'm ready to get my freedom now," Lizbeth announced to me and the class, a fiery determination flickering across her eyes.

Steven brushed past me and hurried to clear a spot for her. The young mother called out and motioned for me. "Miss Cussy, I need to get started on the lessons right away 'fore he wakes up and comes looking for me."

Mrs. Claxton's hand landed on my shoulder. "You can get started on Steven and Lizbeth's lessons, and I'll work with Ardell and Kipple."

Thirty minutes later Lizbeth had learned to write her name and her children's. Within three hours, she was sounding out simple words from the newsprint and copying them down.

As we closed the lessons, Irene came up to me with another letter. "I see you have news from your daughter, Miss Irene. Would you like for me to read it for you?" I held out my hand and saw the seal had been broken on the envelope.

Proud, she pulled herself up and shook her head *no*. "I got tired of having to wait on my neighbors, so after school the first night, I went out and bought myself a speller at the five-and-dime. I wanted to read Rachel's letter with my own eyes and write back with my own hands. Don't need no help, ma'am. I can read and write plenty good myself. And I'm getting better each day!"

"Miss Irene, I'm mighty pleased for you."

"I stayed up till midnight every night, sometimes not stopping until dawn! Here, sit with me, Book Woman. I'll show ya." The old woman folded herself into a chair and yanked one out for me. She slowly read me her daughter's latest letter. Then Irene pulled out stationery and a pen from her pocketbook, along with a small *Common School Speller First Book*. She lowered her head to the page and wrote her first letter back to her daughter while I hovered near and helped with the spelling, praising her work, nudging her on.

When she was through, she handed it to me to inspect, then dug in her pocketbook and pulled out another piece of stationery.

I read her letter and was surprised to see her wobbly penmanship and simple grammar had spelled every word correctly. She'd crossed every *t* and dotted each *i*.

"My first letter is to Rachel, but my second letter is a *thank-you* to—" She pointed the tip of her pen at me.

Grateful, I read it. And I saw the pride shining in Irene's eyes.

Ardell and Kip walked past me, clutching their canes. He held her arm as they took careful steps. "Miss Ardell," he said and cleared his throat once and then again, "my vehicle's just outside. Uh, wondered if maybe you would like to join me for, uh, for coffee at Shirley's Diner?"

"Why, Mr. Kipple Culbreath, maybe you'd like to join *me*. I have an old bottle of scotch at home waiting. Something special I've been saving."

I glimpsed Kip's surprise and the twinkle in Ardell's mischievous eyes.

Lizbeth gathered her notes, and two patrons immediately flanked her side. I caught one of the men's words as they passed by me. "We're going to walk you and the children home tonight, Miss Lizbeth. Have ourselves a good talkin' to with that cowardly husband of yours. And we're gonna be letting him know that if we have to come back, it won't be for another talk."

Walking between the men, Lizbeth stopped and took her babies from the children's librarian, then held her head high as she passed through the library doors, something bold and courageous awakening in the young woman.

After most of the patrons left, I helped straighten chairs and wipe down tables, then waited for Mrs. Claxton over by a bookshelf.

I studied some of the titles. There were a lot of books written by Negroes, and I couldn't get over how large the collection was. I pulled out *Rosemary and Pansies*, by the Kentucky poet Effie Waller Smith. Honey had the same copy, and I pressed a hand over the ribbed green cloth on the cover, admiring the gold-stamped title and floral decorations.

I read through the verses and stopped at the last poem, "Good Night," overcome with grief for home.

Dear earth, I am going away to-night
From your long-loved hills and your meadows bright;
I know I should miss you when I am dead
If a better world came not in your stead.

For the sweet, long days in your woodlands spent,
And your starry dusks, I shall not lament;
For greater than all the wonders you show,
O earth, is the secret I soon shall know...

Steven slipped up beside me. He had his sister at his side, sucking on a taffy stick.

"Hello, Steven. Did you forget something?" I smiled at his sister missing one of her milk teeth, still in awe that the young'uns in the city were only a little bit curious of my color. Not bothered at all.

Once, on the library route back home, my face had spooked a young child picking berries. "Don't look at her," his mother had warned, then shielded the young'un, pulling him off the path. But not before I'd seen the wild-eyed fright on the child's face that would cast me as the blame for his coming nightmares.

Steven's smile was infectious. "No, ma'am, I just wanted to let you know that after our lessons, I applied to Belknap Hardware and Manufacturing this morning. I start work in a week. And if I can write and read, work on them lessons you gave me, the boss man said I could earn an extra five cents on the hour. A whopping five cents."

Mrs. Claxton came up behind him and placed a hand on his shoulder. "Did I hear something about a job?"

He grinned and bobbed his head. "I was just telling Miss Cussy I start in a week at Belknap."

"Well, look'a there." She patted his shoulder. "I just grow'd myself another voter. Congratulations, chile!"

"Aim to be first in that line, ma'am." He grabbed his sister's hand and said goodbye.

Mrs. Claxton said, "Looks like we got us enough volunteers to make this a yearly summer program. The teachers have pledged to donate their time. Come on, Cussy. You've done enough. The girls can finish up here and close. It's our day off tomorrow, and I've got a special treat for you. A surprise." Her face lit up.

My last hours of freedom. Still, I would not treat her gracious spirit callously, spoil the surprise by brooding. The least I could do was return it.

I was determined that she would see my gratitude, watch me enjoy every minute of freedom I had left.

Thirty-Five

Friday night I sat cross-legged on the bed with Daisy in my lap, stringing a necklace for Honey with the coffee tree seeds. Beyond the door, I could hear the couple rustling around in the kitchen as the radio station rolled out the big band tunes, the mix of horn instruments muffled, trying to wiggle and escape through cracks.

One of them turned up the volume. The announcer said it was by a lady named Ella Fitzgerald longing to visit the city again—a dreamy song called "Louisville, K-Y."

I paused to listen, the melodies reminding me of Pa playing his worn fiddle on hot summer nights while Mama sang along on the porch.

A few minutes earlier, Mrs. Claxton had given me some of Reverend's fishing line, then held up a finger. "How old will Honey be on her birthday?"

"Seventeen, ma'am."

"You don't say, *seventeen.* Such a trying age. Hmm. Might have something special to add to it, if you don't mind."

She came back with a tiny crystal dish of loose pearls. "I've never gotten around to having these restrung." Her smile splintered and disappeared as she eased herself down on the bed. "When Mother gave me the necklace at seventeen, she said, *Seventeen's the age of sorrow for a passing childhood tethered to the chaos and joyous uncertainty of a dawning adulthood.*"

She placed a pearl in my hand.

I lingered on her mama's words. "It's lovely wisdom for a young'un. I'll pass it on to my daughter."

"Mother wanted to be a poet like Effie Waller back home. I'll leave you a stamped envelope on the hall tree. Sleep well." Her bones creaked as she walked toward the door.

"Obliged, ma'am. Honey will cherish this."

I strung the seeds with the pearl in the middle, then kissed it and placed it gently onto the nightstand atop the Yeats collection Jackson had signed.

When we'd left for work this morning, Mrs. Claxton had stacked the week's newspapers on the sleeping porch and asked if I'd like to read them before she tossed them out. It had been such a hectic week with late nights, I was eager to catch up on the news, read the latest about the polio outbreak.

Picking up Wednesday's newspaper, I combed through the pages again like I did at the library, and noted the story headings, mindful that Jackson always proclaimed the real gems were at the end. Pausing at a small article in the back, I read the governor was now reconsidering a new death warrant for Sassyann.

I flicked to the next page, scanning until the end. No articles on the men's prison.

When I picked up the following day's paper, I saw another piece about Sassyann. The governor was hedging on his decision, suggesting a new death warrant might be handed down in September despite her vegetative state. I prayed that the man's superstition would prevail. But his earlier argument where he feared Sassyann's spirit would rise up against him was weakening.

I stuffed the newspaper down into the small trash can beside my bed, pulled up the quilt, and cuddled closer to a sighing Daisy.

Fluffing the feather pillow, I froze when I felt a small lump inside, the memory of finding my crown coming forth again. Then the fright jolted my senses, and I grabbed the pillow and stuffed it under the cushion on the wicker chair farthest from my bed.

In the murkiest hour before dawn, I awoke to another nightmare as a storm blew past the city, the lightning skittering down the Ohio River. This time, Pa fought off prison doctors who were strapping me onto the Claxtons' kitchen table. I bolted upward with a scream locked in my throat.

Fumbling for the lamp, I found the switch. Daisy burrowed beside me, a string of rippled snores escaping. Out in the yard, crickets serenaded their mates.

I pulled on Mrs. Claxton's robe and stood by the screen door and looked out, the glow of streetlamps haloing the sleeping homes. Stepping out into the yard, I felt the wet grass cool my feet and a soft breeze lick at my hair.

In just one night, I would be sleeping on a prison cot, and I shuddered from the sickening realization that my time had come.

Looking to the porch, I spied my clothes inside and drew my eyes back to the rooftops.

I could feel Louisville slipping off its dizzying drunk-lit hours, stretching itself into a moment of restive slumber before it roared to life once more to grind harder.

This was a big city.

One of easily forgotten folks.

I fought between a life the babe could have and the death that was written just as sure as the crown found in the pillow.

"*Don't ya go and look back now,*" Waldeen had said.

I toyed with my thoughts. There was always Queenie in Philadelphia. My old friend would help. But with no money for a rail or bus ticket, I wouldn't get far. I could be jailed as a vagrant… if they didn't shoot me first for being an escaped convict.

Rubbing my forehead, I pored over other ideas.

Mrs. Claxton had been so kind. She would be in a heap of trouble, maybe even lose her job. The law would likely accuse her of helping a criminal escape her custody and throw the woman in jail. I would never forgive myself, and I inhaled sharply at the vision of the librarian imprisoned like the inmates in the Geriatric Ward.

My heart sank as the truth settled over me. I was at the mercy of officials.

Suddenly, Mrs. Claxton screeched.

Turning to the house, I called out, "Mrs. Claxton?"

"*Cussy*," her voice spilled out the open windows and into the yard. "Come quick, chile!"

Thirty-Six

I rushed inside while Daisy chased me into the kitchen, tangling our legs, nearly tripping us, our breaths mingling into worrisome gasps.

"What is it, Mrs. Claxton?" Daisy circled us and panted, her grin carrying the weight of the scare, the fright tinged white around her bulging eyes. "Is everything okay? Do you need an ambulance—?"

"You sure read a mess of books, but we don't have ambulances here in Louisville," she chided. "The police come in station wagons to transport the sick and wounded. This is something more."

I studied her bright eyes, puzzled on what more it could be. "Do you have pains, ma'am, and need to see a doc? Where's Reverend Claxton? I'll go fetch him for you." I shook my head, riddled that a big city like this didn't have proper transport for those struck ill.

She picked up the morning newspaper off the table, then flipped the pages to a story with a photograph of her in front of the library at the top. The librarian tapped twice. "I couldn't be better."

"*Ma'am.*" I smacked the counter. "You nearly knocked the color off my skin."

"Here, chile, just read this. Jed, *Jed,* get back in here." She poked her head around the corner into their bedroom. "*Jedidiah.* Hurry now and run to the store and buy more papers." She scrambled around the kitchen for her pocketbook, digging for change. "Cussy, we must send papers back home. *Jedidiah. Jedidiah Claxton, hurry up before they're all sold out.*"

"Woman, you done sent me out once before sunrise. Not a soul stirring," her husband complained, carrying his shoes across her spotless linoleum floor. "Nary a church mouse could be found scuttling around those dark streets." He pulled out a chair and plopped down.

"Hidelman's will be opening in ten minutes." She scattered coins onto the table, counting.

"They spell my name right, Effie?" he asked, tying a shoelace.

"They did indeed, as a matter of fact. And used it again for *mine,*" she said, a bother pinched on her lips.

"You got enough change there for me to send one to Brother back home?" Reverend stuffed his other sockless foot inside a shoe. "We need to send one to our daughter. And maybe—"

"Won't Vesta be surprised. Oh, I can't wait to show Susan." Mrs. Claxton clapped her hands and then spilled more money from her coin purse.

I sat down and picked up the Saturday morning paper with Daisy's head resting on my bare feet. Reaching under the table, I tickled her ears while reading the article, her breaths finally sliding into peaceful sighs after she was rudely awakened.

MOUNTAIN WOMEN TEACHING LITERACY AT LOUISVILLE WESTERN LIBRARY

With the aid of state educator, president, and first woman of Kentucky Education Association Cora Wilson Stewart's successful doctrine for teaching illiterates of Kentucky, California, New York, Massachusetts, Maryland, Texas, and dozens of other states to read and write, Louisville's own seventy-one-

> year-old librarian director Mrs. Jedidiah Claxton, wife of Reverend Jedidiah Charles Claxton, previously of Fishtrap, KY, along with Mrs. Jackson Lovett, a former Pack Horse librarian of Troublesome Creek, KY, and numerous volunteers, taught 219 illiterates living in the city of Louisville's West End to write their signatures and begin a reading program in a span of four days. "It was also a joint effort between the mayor's office, my staff, and local educators to offer accelerated reading classes to register more Negro voters," Mrs. Claxton explained, thanking the mayor and crediting the success to the selfless contributions of her staff, area teachers, and the resolve of her newest library patrons. The free literacy classes will continue nightly M–F and will run from 6:00 to 9:30 p.m. at the Louisville Western Branch Library, 604 South Tenth Street.

"It's a fine article, Mrs. Claxton, and a real pretty photograph of you. More will hear and join the program."

Reverend pecked her cheek as he headed out.

"Would've loved it if they'd photographed both of us," she said. "But I'm going to fix that. Tomorrow after church, Jed promised to get out his Kodak and take a picture of us out on the library steps. I'll hang it in there next to the clipping."

I'd never had someone photograph me, or any of my kin, and I mused over the thought but again fretted the ridicule and shame it might bring down on me.

"I'll get a nice frame for it," she went on. "The patrons will see it first thing when they walk into those welcoming doors."

I folded the paper neatly on the table and studied on my married name they'd used. Jackson would be proud, but my hand fell to my belly, and sadness marred the joyful moment.

Mrs. Claxton chatted on as the screen door announced Reverend's departure. "It's because of the wonderful job you've done for us."

"Ma'am, you worked harder than all of us. It's a fine program you have."

She flicked her wrist. "Oh, I wish I had a dozen librarians just like you. Matter of fact, I put in a telephone call late yesterday to the prison. The warden had already left, but I asked if I could keep you at least another week. The officer on duty promised Warden Sanders would return my call early evening, by five at the latest. So I'll have to be over at the library after our day out. There's a good chance, given all your hard work and the success of the reading program."

Warden Sanders. Just the mention of her name shaded my flesh. "That sure would be nice. Much obliged to you for extending your hospitality."

But Warden would be itching to have me back now more than ever after reading the article—back to raise her funding. Even more, eager to abort my child.

"Something nice right about now would be if you got yourself dressed. It's Saturday, our day off. Time I treated you to Walnut Street so you can spend some of that money you earned. Jed and the boys will have gone fishing later, and that means the ladies go shopping."

She placed a five-dollar bill, three-quarters, and four green three-cent Mount Rushmore stamps in front of me.

I picked up the bill, scattered the stamps and coins. "That's a lot, ma'am." Though I already know'd I'd be sending the money back home to Honey.

"You grew us voters for this fine city, and I aim to tell the mayor and ask him to write a letter on your behalf to the governor!"

"Governor," I whispered. *Just maybe it would bring a quick pardon, with praise coming from the big-city mayor.*

"Let me go get you a change purse for that." She slipped into her bedroom and rummaged through the dresser drawers. When she came back, she handed me a red leather coin purse.

"Take this, chile. I haven't used it in years."

I thanked her and opened the kissing lock and placed the folded bill, coins, and stamps inside. Opened and closed again, staring at the contents.

My life's possessions. My worth in this world.

Still, her offer to finally visit Walnut Street could not soften my nagging doubts that a pardon wouldn't come quick enough to save the baby. I wanted to tell her about the child, the abortion, and sterilization that I was facing. Boldly, I tasted the words and then wetted my lips. "Mrs. Claxton, I need to—"

"Hurry and get dressed. I'll have a light breakfast ready for us in a few minutes. We have a busy day in store."

Her cheerful words had me swallowing mine. I would not wallow and ruin her festive mood.

She set plates down on the table, thumped a heavy cast-iron skillet onto the stove. "Now, let's see. I need to pick up Reverend's church suit at the tailor's and purchase a few items at the drugstore. Oh, I sweet-talked Jed, and he gave us some spending money to dine. That reminds me, don't let me forget to cash my paycheck."

As she talked, a small headache budded, and irritable thoughts pushed up: *Sweet-talked*. I wondered exactly whose paycheck it really was. But I tucked my biting words under the fat flesh of lip, silencing my quarrelsome tongue. "Is there a post office nearby where I can mail Honey's letter, ma'am?"

"The mailman's already collected today's posts from our box. But there's a letter box along the way like the one you saw on Monday. They pick up all day long. If we're going to be dining at the Old Walnut Street Chili Parlor today, we should be leaving soon."

After a plate of egg toast, I hurried to dress while the librarian began cutting out the article from a stack of papers Reverend brought in. Sitting on the bed, I bent and tied my shoes, suddenly feeling a light rippling. The baby had moved again, and Daisy poked my side and cocked her head to my belly.

I kissed the tip of her head and closed my eyes, praying that with Mrs. Claxton's help, it would all work out.

When I walked back into the kitchen, she handed me the news clipping. I folded it carefully into the stamped envelope she gave me, along with a letter, Honey's birthday necklace, and the five-dollar bill. When Mrs. Claxton spied this, she smiled. "Maybe you can call her from Walnut Street."

"She doesn't have telephone service." I held the envelope to my chest. "But she'll appreciate this. It's been a while since I had the means to send her something."

I stuffed the change purse inside my skirt pocket. Mrs. Claxton grabbed her large pocketbook and handed me two Bibles. "We'll drop these back off at the church after our luncheon." She pulled two scarves off the hall tree. "Fashionable, and it'll keep you cooler." She hummed as she adjusted a summery green-checkered scarf around my neck and tied it in a pretty bow, then wrapped a silky yellow fabric around her own.

"Hmm." Mrs. Claxton raised a finger, then dared to take out a tube of lipstick from her purse, lift my chin, and dot my lips. She smacked her mouth, and I parroted her. I had never worn lipstick in my life, and I peered into the mirror, stunned.

"Fresh as a flower," she declared. There was a whispered buzz, a churning energy in her words, and I fidgeted with my skirt and scarf, growing anxious, lifting a palm to my belly.

Leaning our heads together, we looked into the hall tree's beveled mirror. The fabric livened my white blouse and brought out the color in my eyes. The light-pink lipstick softened my blue face.

She turned to me and pressed her hands over my bow, straightening. "Fancy as any of them big starlets in the magazines. Now, let's go shopping and have us a nice day out. You've earned it."

My face warmed. She reminded me so much of ol' Loretta.

"Hear now, don't you be tearing up on me, chile."

We passed through the city streets, the librarian pointing out stores, businesses, and factories. With each block taken, I could hear the grind of Walnut Street call louder, the drums of the business district lifting. She paused occasionally to remind me of street names.

"Now, no one need know, especially the law. But if you stay, you'll be running errands occasionally."

Stay. It gave me more hope. "I'd like that." I felt a smile bloom on my lips as I tried to imagine it.

"Jed and I are also going to sit down tonight and write the governor," she proclaimed again. "With a letter from the mayor and us, it will surely persuade him. I need you here."

We walked on, me dreaming of what a longer visit or a quick pardon would bring.

When we stopped at one of the blue boxes on the corner, I looked up at her.

"Go ahead. Mail your letter here." She opened the latch and let it drop with a bang, startling me.

"Postmaster Bill at the post office sees to our letters. Could we visit the postmaster here?" I clutched Honey's bulging envelope close to my chest and looked at the mailbox suspiciously, dared to touch the handle.

Mrs. Claxton pulled the latch open and waited.

When I didn't move, she snatched the envelope from my hands, slid it into the slot, and dropped it with a bang.

I stepped forward and jerked open the latch, digging my hand inside.

It had disappeared. "Ma'am, please get it back for me. Now," I pleaded. "I can't leave Honey's letter and her money and present in this big ugly box. Why, a squirrel or critter could easily get inside and carry it off! Get it back for me."

"Chile—"

"*No*." I dropped the handle and opened it again, and once more, then lowered my head, searched inside the darkened hole, prying my fingers and hand around again.

Pounding a blue-blackening fist on the box, I slammed the handle up and down several times. When I reached for the pull again, Mrs. Claxton chuckled lightly and snatched me away. "Now I promise you, it's safe and as good as in your girl's hands." She lightly thumped the box. "Old West Walnut Street is the next block over and waiting."

Thirty-Seven

Mrs. Claxton stopped dead in her tracks on West Walnut Street. Her jaw went slack, and she pointed at two men and a woman standing in front of a building that touted a sign that said Record Shop.

"Ma'am, is everything okay? Let's rest over there on the bench. You look ill."

"That's Cab Calloway," she squealed. "That one with the trimmed mustache and slicked-back hairdo wearing the fancy cobs. See him next to the short man? Cab's got the woman on his arm."

"Who, ma'am? Cobs?"

"Sunglasses, chile. And none other than the famous Hi-De-Ho-Man. The one in the Minnie the Moocher, Betty Boop cartoon. *Will wonders never cease.* The movie-star singer, and right here on Old Walnut Street in the living flesh!"

Mrs. Claxton latched on to my arm and started pulling me. "Hurry, Cussy, I've been dying to meet him for decades, but Jed would never allow it. Oh, how I loved 'The Honeydripper' and 'The Jumpin' Jive.' He can scat like nobody's business. His music sure is somethin' else. He's an author, too, you know? Vesta sent me his book for my birthday. *Cab Calloway's Hepster's Dictionary.* Language of jive!"

It was the first time I'd seen a hint of her bygone youth, and I rushed to keep up with her, the two Bibles plastered against my chest as we weaved in and out of foot traffic.

Once, I stopped to gawk at a group of passing women who wore fine clothing. Many sported dresses with tight bodices, cinched waists, and full skirts of cheerful colors and designs. "All these ladies look like colorful butterflies flitting about, Mrs. Claxton. Butterflies sippin' sweet, exotic nectar," I remarked.

The men were dapper in their business suits and fashionable hats. Besides in magazines, I had never seen so many folks in expensive clothing. In front of big buildings, Negroes and whites stopped to chat with each other, talk weather, business, and the order of the day. I stretched my neck toward one building called the Top Hat Club. Horns sounded, and automobiles slowed as drivers shouted out greetings to passerby.

Shop bells jingled and lured the cheer of ringing cash registers.

Walnut Street had hypnotized me with its energy, and I stood gaping, enchanted and swept up with the wonderment of it all.

I hooded a hand over my eyes and looked up and down the street, gazing at the handsome buildings that kissed sunny skies as folks bustled under shaded concrete lips and sloped awnings.

Breaths of savory cooking and baking bread drifted out of swinging doors and open windows, swirled around, teasing and inviting. My belly grumbled, and I wiped drool from my mouth, tasting the tempting spices, smoked meats, and cinnamon-sugared treats.

"Hurry, Cussy." She rushed back and grabbed my arm again.

"Never seen so many wonders on one street, ma'am. Why, this street goes on like the coal rails back home." I crooked my neck and looked back, absorbing it all.

"Mr. Calloway. *Mr. Calloway*," Mrs. Claxton called out, breathless, rushing us toward the handsome man and the woman and the other man who accompanied him. "My, he's looking sharp as a tack," she stopped to whisper into my ear while straightening her scarf.

Dressed in an expensive-looking suit, he lifted his sunglasses and dipped his brown fedora. I glimpsed the black satin band and flat side ribbon that was attached.

The woman next to him looked like she'd just stepped out of a movie picture. Her black hair was styled in the latest fashion, and she wore a soft green satin dress that was sleek and fitted to her shapely figure, with a bodice pinched into a puffy silk flower that lifted to her chin.

She fiddled with a clip-on earring, a cluster of matching rhinestones, and waited when Mr. Calloway stopped and smiled broadly while the other man held a briefcase.

"He's one hep cat. Uh-huh, a real dicty if there ever was," Mrs. Claxton whispered again into my ear.

Her words were puzzling.

"Mr. Calloway, *sir*, may I please trouble you for an autograph?" She could barely catch her breath.

"Ma'am?" I had never seen so much fussing, and alarm pricked at my brow. Worried her ticker would stop dead and lose its last tock for a man stripped clear off the magazine pages of movie star royalty.

Mr. Calloway nodded a *yes* and pulled a gold pen from his breast pocket.

The librarian dropped my arm and dug into her pocketbook. "Let me get something for you to write on, sir. Hold on. I— Now where is my—" Exasperated, she rummaged through it again, then patted her chest as if something would magically appear.

Suddenly, she looked at me and pried one of the Bibles out of my hand.

"Mrs. Claxton! Ma'am, please—" I searched around the sidewalk for paper, anything that could be signed other than Reverend's Bible. "Let me find something else."

To everyone's surprise, she flipped to the title page and shoved it in front of him, the book jumping in her shaky hand.

Mr. Calloway studied her a few seconds, and then the star dazzled her with a blinding smile as he took the Bible and set his pen to paper.

"If you'll just make it out to Effie Claxton, sir—no, make that

Effie Ruth Claxton," she said, hovering over him and the page, spelling out her name, twice, slow and measured, and then once more to be certain. *"E-f-f-i-e…"*

When he closed the book and handed it back to her, he motioned to the man next to him, who pulled out a small record from his briefcase. Cab scribbled his name over the red label and gave it to the awestruck librarian.

"'The Calloway Boogie.' *Law.* Thank you, Mr. Calloway!" She clutched the Bible and record to her chest.

When he winked, she looked like she would faint from sheer excitement, and I grabbed her arm.

Tipping his hat, the famous man walked briskly with his friends down Walnut Street and disappeared into a tall building with a large fancy sign that read STRAND THEATRE.

The librarian stared after him, youthful and dreamy-lipped.

When Mrs. Claxton finally opened the Bible, her face lit up.

She tilted the script toward me.

Effie Ruth Claxton,

You Rascal, You.
  Mama, I Want to Make Rhythm.

—Cab Calloway

"Look'a here, Cussy. 'Rascal' and 'Rhythm' are two of his songs. And he's done gave them to me." She swooned and did a half twirl, arms flailing to ground herself.

I fidgeted with my other Bible, shifted, and reached for her again, worried what Reverend Claxton might say, fretting again she might be putting a strain on her heart with all this excitement. "Ma'am, please sit—"

"Don't you go getting fussy Cussy on me," she admonished.

I dropped her arm, surprised by her feisty spirit.

"Now, not a word to Mr. Claxton. I do love Cab's music."

She tucked the Bible and record carefully into her large pocketbook, hooked her arm into mine, and rolled out a wobbly, zig-zagging verse from Cab's song, lifting it above the scorching July streets:

"Mama, I wanna make rhythm
Just wanna go zoozi-zah-zah-zoozi
Ooh-cah-dee-doodle-oodle-aah-doo.
Just wanna go wookee-ah-kay-a-kaya-kaya
Yag-a-yag-a-yag-a-yag you."

~

A heady aroma of vanilla, cigars, and cologne greeted us inside the Badger Drug Co., which advertised Venida hair nets, Dan'l Boone cigars, guaranteed rubber goods, and expert prescription work.

Lightly humming Cab's tunes, Mrs. Claxton looked over toiletries, then inspected the rack of nail polish, finally settling on one advertised as RATTLE-MY-RACY-RED-TALKIN-TATTLE. Above, an advertisement showed a lady with her slip hiked up, just enough to reveal the scarlet necessaries she wore.

The librarian held the polish in front of me, a playfulness in her eyes, the scars of the Depression stamped across mine. I hid my raggedy nails behind my skirt.

She picked up a round flower-covered box of Dorothy Perkins Lilac Dusting Powder, opened the lid, and sniffed, then held it up to my nose.

"Smells real pretty, just like the flowers."

"Mm-mm, sure wish I was wearing this when I met Cab."

I studied the woman, worrying what would come next, curious at the amount of money spent on such frivolity. Two other women nearby were selecting expensive store goods as well.

"Cussy, pick you out a little something to make you feel pretty. My treat."

"Much obliged, but I couldn't. How do these cityfolk afford such? Never seen so many expensive things." I glanced down at my ugly black prison shoes and thought about Honey wearing my worn riding boots.

"I'm a mountain woman, too, but let me show you something, chile." The librarian walked me over to the newspaper rack and pulled up a paper, flipping to the last pages. She ran her finger down advertisements for job employment. Turned page after page stuffed full of businesses begging for workers.

I know'd many could find good jobs in cities but never thought about it much. I couldn't recall ever looking at any city newspaper's job postings.

"Now, chile, back home in our hills, there is no opportunity for work unless you're working for King Coal and fattening his pocket with the meager company script he pays you to shop in *his* businesses, pay rent to live in *his* coal camps."

"So many advertisements. I'd read of such, and Louisville is sure enough big, but I never imagined one city needed so much help."

I took the newspaper and peered down the list. Column after column, jobs appeared for plumbers, electricians, painters, police and firemen, cooks, clerks, factory workers, and more.

"The pay is generous too," I said, awed, turning back through the pages, hoping to check on the polio outbreak.

But she just grinned and reached for the paper. "Come on, I'm going to buy you a tube of lipstick."

"Just another minute, ma'am." I pulled it away.

"I checked, chile. There's no news of the polio in the paper this morning. Let's enjoy this sunny day off work and forget our worries." She folded the paper neatly and dropped it on the stack.

My eyes soaked up all the advertisements in the cosmetic aisle. Mrs. Claxton read one and said, "Helena Rubenstein's will be perfect on you." She snatched up the black-and-gold tube that was on sale for eighty-five cents.

I'd never heard of this Miss Rubenstein, but the advertisement said Helena promised Bed of Roses was good for "Suntanned or Untanned. An ecstatic new color blooms rosy gold... Honey sweet on your lips." The glamorous woman rested her head on a bed of orangish-red roses and wore diamond earring hoops while a hummingbird hovered above her.

The librarian said, "My daddy always said his girls should have a few things that make them feel pretty. He'd always work a few extra shifts each month to make sure we did."

I pulled off the top and twisted the stick up and down, admiring the gift. "It's sure fancy. Thank you, Mrs. Claxton." I wondered what Jackson would think of me wearing cosmetics. Questioned just how ecstatic it might make one feel.

We walked down another aisle filled with bandages, antiseptics, cough syrups, and headache powders. She pulled a small bottle of smelling salts off the shelf and held it up to me. "Sure could've used this earlier when I met Cab. I didn't know whether I was going to wet myself or faint." She chuckled, and I laughed with her, my mood culling the worries.

While Mrs. Claxton paid for her purchases, I studied a ballpoint vending machine that touted pens for ten cents. I itched to feed a coin inside the slot just to watch the display spin around and drop the fancy retractable pen into my hand.

After paying for the purchases, she handed me the lipstick and moved us next door to Davis Brothers' candy store. At a penny-candy shelf, the librarian selected licorice laces, a package of Mallo Cups, and Teaberry gum.

Then she led us over to the soda fountain. "Let's take a seat and have us a cool drink and rest after our busy morning." She signaled to the man behind the counter wearing a papery hat and ordered an icy cold Coke for me and an orange soda for herself. I pulled out a quarter, but she pushed it away and shoved a dime and nickel toward him, paying for our drinks and his tip. While she relaxed on the red stool, Mrs. Claxton dug out her record and Bible. She ran her fingertips over Cab's inscription, sighing.

"Sure was friendly of the movie star to give you his autograph like that."

"Wasn't it ever. I can't wait to show the girls at the library. They won't believe it!"

"Do you think you'll ever get to hear him sing in person?"

"Reverend would never allow it. He feels this type of music tempts young people. I'll just have to be content listening to him on my old radio." She shot me a crooked smile.

"Tempts?"

"He thinks music that doesn't praise or lift up God could cause harm."

It was odd. "Ma'am, I never thought about God only liking one kind of music. One kind of birdsong." From the look on Mrs. Claxton's face, I know'd she hadn't either.

I fished out the lipstick from my coin purse.

She said, "Do they allow it in prison?"

"It'll likely be confiscated." I twisted it and dabbed more onto my lips, savoring how silky it made them feel.

She took out her own and swept it across her mouth.

When we finished our colas, Mrs. Claxton offered me a stick of her gum. I was curious but shook my head. She had been generous enough giving me pay, stamps, lipstick, and now the fountain drink.

We walked past the businesses, stopping occasionally to talk about the window dressings, poke a finger at the latest advertisements and displays.

Inside the crowded Chili Parlor, Mrs. Claxton led us to the serving counter, where we waited in line for someone to help with our chili. A radio played on a shelf. Newsmen talked about the rising price of gasoline, reporting it was a record-high twenty-eight cents, and noted an upcoming church picnic. They went on to talk about Stalin and the Communist Party and a Russian historian denouncing something called *hero worship*.

I turned my attention to the diners in the room, soaking it all up.

Hearing her name, I cocked my ear when the radiomen mention Sassyann, telling the listeners her execution was still being debated, and the governor was in talks with his staff. Then they moved on to chat about grain prices and polio, its rise and Salk's latest efforts for a cure.

Mrs. Claxton turned to me and noted my deepening color. "Chile, you're looking a little peaked."

"I'm worried about Jackson."

She patted my arm. "I'll try to find out if there's a list since I'll be talking with the mayor on Monday."

Grateful, I thanked her.

When the young waiter asked what he could get us, we selected the toppings we wanted in our chili. I followed Mrs. Claxton's lead, and the man behind the counter filled my bowl with a generous portion of spaghetti, a steamy, fat tamale, and a ladle of chili juice, all of it topped with a big heaping of shredded cheese. "Michael, I'll be needing you to pack up a container of chili for the reverend, and some of that sliced cow tongue he loves so much. Put an extra courting apple in there, chile."

Michael said, "Sure thing, Mrs. Claxton. Nice article about you today. I'll bring it over to you shortly."

We sat at a red-checkered-cloth table, the conversations rising cheerfully around us, Mrs. Claxton's one of the most lively. It seemed she know'd every person coming in. Many congratulated her on the article. More than once, she'd whisper to a friend, giggle, and open her pocketbook and offer them a sneak peek of the treasures from Cab.

I stared down at the big bowl of chili and scooped up a tiny spoonful and tasted it with the tip of my tongue. I tempted a bigger bite. How odd looking, but it was delicious.

"I see you like our citified chili," Mrs. Claxton noted, pleased.

"These cooks sure know'd how to make different victuals than back home." I wiped my oily mouth with the napkin. "It's ugly but tastes mighty pleasing, ma'am. Thank you for dinner." And I gobbled down the rest of it.

"We'll just head down Sixth Street to the Mammoth Life & Accident Insurance Company, where the tailor's shop is. Come on, chile," she said.

After a few blocks, the librarian stopped. "There it is." She pointed to a brown six-story building rising among the smaller storefronts. "Next to the Lyric Theatre. See it, Cussy?"

Squinting, I stared up at the large sign.

Outside the shop, Mrs. Claxton greeted a small boy sitting on the sidewalk with a cut-up cardboard box and crayons, drawing. A tin of buttons rested at his feet.

"It's a right pretty drawing, young man." I stooped over and studied the child's art, marveling that it was so detailed for his age.

"It's a statue, ma'am!" Grinning, he jumped up and held open the door.

"And a fine one." I smiled.

"This is the Hamilton boy, Ed, but we all call him Lil Biff," Mrs. Claxton said. "Thank you, Lil Biff. Won't be long now." Mrs. Claxton patted his shoulder. "Two months and you'll start first grade. You come visit me at the library for reading hour and homework help."

We stepped inside the Mammoth Life building to a sign that read YOUR VALET SHOP and were greeted by another standing advertisement that touted thirty-five-cent hair cuts and twenty-five-cent shaves.

Scents of shampoo, menthol, woodsy soaps, and musky potions greeted us. Catchy music floated around as a radio announcer broke in after a song: "Yes, sir, the weather's been a scorcher here in the city. That was Perry Como letting us know it's 'Watermelon Weather,' so get out and enjoy the *sweetheart-kissing season*," he teased. "Next up is—"

I was surprised to see a barbershop and, more so, a female

Negro hovering over a man in a barber's chair. The attractive woman turned and raised her scissors.

"A woman barber," I whispered.

"Effie!" the barber screamed. "I read the newspaper, and we're all so proud of you getting our people ready to sign up to vote." She slipped off the man's neck duster and hurried over to us.

"A fine thing you done, Mrs. Claxton." The customer in the chair stood and turned to the mirror behind him, fingers combing through his cut, lifting a forest of stylish black curls.

I could see beyond the room where young'uns bent over stoops of throned chairs shining the shoes of men in suits, sneaking glances at us. One businessman with a newspaper looked up and waved. "Reading it right now, Mrs. Claxton," he commented. "Good piece."

She murmured her thanks. "Amy," she said to the woman barber, "this is Mrs. Lovett, my borrowed librarian. It was her idea."

"Where you from, honey?" Amy asked, lifting a lock of my hair, peering closely and up and down, but not a whisper of revulsion in her brown-jeweled eyes.

My skin flushed, a warm blue hue lifting to my ears.

"We're practically neighbors. Not far from Fishtrap. Troublesome Creek," Mrs. Claxton piped.

"Amy Hamilton. A pleasure to meet you." She tipped her head slightly, her hair perfectly coiffed like in a beauty advertisement. "I hope you're going to be with us awhile, Mrs. Lovett."

"Yes, ma'am. I hope to stay longer."

"We're going to do everything we can to keep her, Amy."

Amy called out to a customer waiting for a cut and escorted him to her chair. A woman from the back appeared, a tape measure hanging from her neck, her apron pockets full of scissors and pieces of fabric. "Hello, Effie. Fine article."

"Patience, this is Cussy. She's been a great help setting up the literacy program. Cussy, this is our seamstress, Patience."

"Nice to meet you, ma'am," I said.

"We could use more people like you to get voters registered," Patience said. "If more don't vote, they'll elect some white-haired stuff-coats to bring in urban renewal to *urban remove* us. We're not careful, all these blocks of businesses that our grand-paps built in the 1800s will be gone. Destroyed."

I looked around at the comfortable shop, turned to the glass windows, the outside passersby and traffic, and couldn't imagine why anyone would want to destroy something that was alive and thriving, the bustling stores, diners, theaters, and businesses that were brimming with customers.

"Ain't I right, Effie?"

Mrs. Claxton bobbed her head. "You are indeed, chile. Our Old West Walnut Street is as grand as the French Quarter down there in Nawlins. Just today, I met the Hi-De-Ho-Man, none other than Cab Calloway," she gushed, and handed me the bags from the Chili Parlor and Drug Store. "He was looking togged to the bricks!"

Patience's eyes rounded. "He's always dressed to the nines in them movie magazines. You talk to him?"

"Did more than talk—right, Cussy?"

"She sure did." I got caught up in her happiness. "Nice fella, and handsome too." Smiling, I stepped back to let her share the news.

The librarian opened her pocketbook, and when she passed the record and Bible to the seamstress, they both squealed and broke down giggling like two young'uns.

Again, I glanced over at Amy and then to Patience, both dressed in stylish men's britches with white, tall, collared button smocks and high heels.

I tucked one of my ugly prison shoes behind the other, wanting to join in, but then I was reminded of the Fourth of July—the disastrous meeting with Troublesome's sewing circle. I dared not risk it with these fine ladies. Still, I couldn't help but grin as the two grew more excited.

"Heard he might be in town promoting his newest record,"

Patience said, passing the keepsakes back to Mrs. Claxton. "What you wouldn't give to trim *that* mustache, huh, Amy?" she called out to the barber. More outbursts of titters swept the building. "Lord, Effie Claxton, you may need to sew yourself a fancy dancing dress and beg Jed to take you to Cab's show next time he comes to the Strand Theatre. *And* don't you know"—she wagged a telling finger—"Myrtle Withers stopped by just yesterday and said she's got new fabrics in over at her dress shop." She poked Mrs. Claxton's rib lightly with her elbow, teasing. "Something red and soft, satiny would do. Maybe some snazzy red heels."

"Jed would surely have himself a hissy and declare I'd been lured by the devil's siren," Mrs. Claxton said, and they broke into more laughter.

Their easy banter reminded me of Queenie and myself when we worked the library project. How we'd sneak off our routes to meet and enjoy a dinner sack together, our easy conversations, big talk, hopes, and bigger dreams and titters, rising into the balsam-sweetened woods, lost to the hard Kaintuck hills and ol' stubborn men's harder thoughts.

"Speaking of dresses, there's two more I need to alter before we close." Patience bid us a good day and disappeared into the back.

A man walked out from beyond the shoeshine area. "Patience said you were out here, Mrs. Claxton. I tried to telephone the church and library, but neither of you were there." He took a few steps toward us. "See Lil Biff out there?" He looked over her shoulder.

"Good afternoon, Mr. Hamilton. I keep nagging Jed about getting a telephone for the house one day, but he's not fond of having to share a party line. Especially when he's giving spiritual counsel to someone in his fold." Turning, she pointed to the door. "Lil Biff's outside drawing, being a good boy. He sure is getting big. I think the lil feller will surely be an artist one day. I do hope when he starts school this year, we'll see more of him at the library. We have some mighty fine after-school programs."

"Amy will be signing him up. Uh, about the reverend. Real sorry, but his suit won't be ready until close to closing time." His rising brow worried her response.

Mrs. Claxton looked at her wristwatch and frowned. "Hmm. I can't wait until five thirty. I need to go to the bank and then have to be back at the library in time for a business call."

"I can wait and bring it home for you, Mrs. Claxton," I offered. "I'll just browse through some of the shops."

"Mrs. Claxton, I'm sorry if I've caused you any inconvenience," Mr. Hamilton said with apologetic eyes.

"It's fine, sir. Reverend won't need it till tomorrow." She studied me. "Cussy, are you sure you remember the way home?"

I rattled off the directions and then once again. She tapped her cheek, trying to decide.

"I can send one of our boys to accompany her," Mr. Hamilton offered, calling a young boy to his side. "But it will have to be five thirty, when we close."

"Thank you, but I wouldn't hear of taking your workers after their long day," the librarian replied, cupping the child's face and smiling down at the young feller.

"I'll find our address, ma'am, and have the suit home by supper."

"Okay then, Cussy, you take special care, watch all your street signs, and we'll see you after you pick up the suit. Thank you, Mr. Hamilton. Now, I best get to the bank."

Mrs. Claxton collected the bags and second Bible from me, and I walked her outside.

Leaning in close, she said, "Chile, I sure hate to leave you, but I have to deposit this check, and if I don't get back in time for"—she dropped her voice and I strained to hear—"Warden Sanders's important call, I could lose you."

"I'll be fine," I insisted.

"Now, be mindful, I'm not supposed to leave you unescorted, but I know you'll respect my dilemma, not disappoint, and come straight home. We have important business to attend. Straight home, chile."

It sounded hopeful, and I could see the fight brewing in her eyes that said she'd put up a good one against the warden.

The extra two hours of being free were welcomed. I couldn't remember the last time I'd had even a minute alone after living under the watchful eyes of guards and tattling prisoners.

I'd lived so long feeling dead. To have this time to feel alive awakened my spirit, sent a burst of life tunneling through my bones. A joy lifted, and hope warmed my heart.

I was grateful. The ladies' earlier conversation had cheered me.

Mrs. Claxton would write the governor and find out more about the men's prison. Surely there would be a cure coming any day from Salk, and Jackson would be safe.

Maybe the following week, word would come from the governor granting my pardon. When the mayor read the article, he might assist Mrs. Claxton and contact him too. I perked. I had freedom for today and decided to use it to telephone Doc again.

Inside a drugstore, a clerk pointed to the back when I asked to use their telephone booth, still amazed the contraption could be found in every store and outside on most city blocks. The operator asked for the name, and I dug inside the change purse and dropped a coin into the slot.

Doc's telephone rang on the other end, and I sat down on the small wooden seat, hoping for news, anxious to share the pregnancy.

After several rings, the operator interrupted, "Miss, there's no answer. Would you like to try your party later?"

Later. That I could even try brought more hope. I'd telephone him again before I collected the suit. I pocketed the returned coin. Stepping out of the store, I smiled as the sun beat down on me, the freedom healing my burdensome troubles.

Giddy, I looked down the sidewalk and felt the heartbeat of this business district. It was alive.

To wander these streets among lively folks woke a happiness, stirring a soft flutter, awakening my growing babe.

Thirty-Eight

Inside a clothing store, I studied the pink box of necessaries that said DAYS OF THE WEEK PANTIES, admiring the cardboard that had been cleverly fashioned to look like a miniature chest of drawers. Gingerly, I opened each titled day's slot, searching inside.

I could hardly believe cityfolk clamored for such things. *Did they really need to be reminded to change into fresh necessaries every day?* I dared to touch the colorful nylon fabric, surprised by Saturday's devilish black pair. Clamping a hand over my mouth, I quieted a giggle.

Woman's necessaries back home were home-spun, made from flour, sugar, and nut feed sacks. All bleached, sunbaked, washed, and stitched out buttery soft, sewn by generations of women's gnarled hands. These drawers were embroidered in fancy cursive and marked for each day of the week.

A woman reached over my arm and picked up a box. "For my niece; she's been dying for a set."

If I bought Honey these, I know'd she would feel scolded, insulted. She'd been changing into fresh drawers daily since she was old enough to pull on socks. I moved on to a rack of hanging undergarments and scanned the racy lingerie, the sheer colorful fabrics.

A man sidled up beside me. "I'm needing a gift for my gal. It's our fifth anniversary. Which one do you favor, miss?" I stepped back.

A man right here in public asking about a woman's necessaries.

I stepped away, feeling my face warm, nearly tripping over a dolled-up mannequin as I made my way out the door. I passed Davis Brothers candy shop, the scents of taffy and fudge pulling in customers. EVERY DAY IS DERBY DAY, an advertising sign in the window proclaimed.

Inside another corner drugstore, I looked over all the goods, pausing at a bin full of children's books. Looking through the pile, I spied an old copy of *Poems of Childhood* by Eugene Field for twenty-five cents. I studied the cover of the giant sitting on a big stone and the small boy with the sword looking up and grabbed it, thinking of Odette in Forensics.

The girl loved the poetry I'd read to her, and Warden said her seizures had all but disappeared.

I would somehow mail it to her, hoping it would help keep the affliction away. Maybe Mrs. Claxton could take me back to the big letter box again. Though the thought made me wince to trust such a risky contraption.

At the cash register, I paid for the book with the money I'd earned. It had been years since my last paycheck from riding my library route with Junia, and I felt proud.

It was 4:12 when I spotted the big clock inside the ice cream and soda shop. I plunked down a nickel for a cold lemonade and took it outside to the bench, enjoying the stream of cheerful passersby.

Frankie and Otilia paused to wish me a good day as they toted brown sacks, their chattering tongues spinning the air. "It's good seeing you, Miss Cussy," Otilia said. "We're just picking up Miss Johnna's liquor for our Saturday-night guests." She wriggled mischievous brows.

Frankie exclaimed she'd written her very first letter to her mama. "I'm praying she'll write back, ma'am, and send me a bus ticket home."

I could see that the young woman was desperate to leave, and her smile never reached the homesickness pained in her eyes.

Otilia beamed, itching to tell me her news too. "Ma'am, the manager down at the print shop said he'd consider me. Last year, I stopped in twice, begging the old codger for a job. But now, I just filled out my first application, and he looked pleased." She bent over and cupped a hand and whispered in my ear, "That copper I helped with his lessons is taking me on a real honest-to-God date. Picking me up at the library and escorting me to a matinee at the movie house next week."

They talked a few more minutes before saying their goodbyes.

I watched the crowds of people passing as I sipped on my lemonade. Many had shopping bags in their hands. Up and down the streets, shop bells rang. I studied why the seamstress at the barber shop had fretted about the government destroying it all.

I shook my head at the absurd idea of such. Know'd that the government man wouldn't make the mistake of loosening their fat wallet to lose fatter tax dollars from these shops. But one never know'd the foolishness they might entertain.

The sun was warm, and I swatted away a thirsty bee as I finished my drink and placed it in the trash can beside me.

Turning back to the storefront window, I saw there was about twenty-five minutes before it was time to pick up the suit.

Exhausted from last night's restless sleep, and the new sights and sounds of the lively streets, I sat on the bench and pulled Odette's book out of the paper bag. Enjoying the rest, I opened the pages and began reading under the shade of the shop's awning.

I paused to admire the beautiful colored illustrations and stopped to read "Wynken, Blynken, and Nod." When I finished "Jest Fore Christmas," I looked up, ticking off numbers. *Why, the babe would be due around Christmas.*

My mind drifted to Jackson, Honey, and this new life tucked safe inside. I reread the pages, relishing the idea of a Christmas babe as I daydreamed about family.

Somewhere, a radio played: "*Goodnight, my love, the tired old moon is descending...*"

Thirty-Nine

I dropped the book when rowdy children whizzed past my bench, the hot breezes and playful shrieks stirring me back to the present.

The store's clock showed I had only fifteen minutes left to pick up the suit.

Pa's words of long ago crashed down on me: *A sneaky time thief is in them books.*

I jumped up and hurried toward the tailor's.

After walking several blocks, I stopped and silently cursed, remembering I'd left Odette's book on the bench.

The sidewalks were filling, and I paused to read the names of business signs, looking for the ice cream and soda shop. I passed several along the way, but they didn't look familiar. I turned and walked back, searching. Not finding the store, I spun around again, rushing through the crowds.

At last, I spotted the bench and snatched up the book.

When I glanced inside, it showed I had only nine minutes until Mr. Hamilton's closed.

Looking up and down the sidewalks, I grew more perplexed as panic splintered across my chest. *Which way was the building?* I prayed the tailor would keep his shop open a few minutes more.

I had to try.

Each step brought more terror.

If I was late, Reverend would not have the suit for his sermon tomorrow, and I hadn't kept my word to Mrs. Claxton.

Would the Claxtons sic the law on me?

I began to run down the blocks, weaving in and out of the growing foot traffic, my clunky prison shoes pinched and growing tighter with each stomp against the pavement.

Confused, I paused to stare up at the names of the buildings and twirled around. Once and then again. The business district filled quickly with folks getting off work, eager to spend weekly paychecks to shop and dine. Automobiles parked alongside curbs, and traffic was heavy as horns and engines sounded in the streets.

I could still make it.

Catching my breath, I turned to a man walking a small terrier. "Sir, please, I'm looking for the Mammoth Life, the tailor—"

"Darlin', why, you're headed the wrong way."

"Wrong way?"

He cupped a hand over his brow and pointed back in the direction from where I'd come. "Cross over here. You'll see it there on Sixth." He glanced at his wristwatch. "But Hamilton closes his shops at five thirty sharp, darlin'. Better hurry."

"Obliged." I turned and stepped off the curb, hurrying past the wide tail of a parked automobile.

A horn blasted, and tires raged against scorching concrete a split second before I felt the sickening thud against my flesh. The stink of rubber climbed into the heat.

A woman screamed, and the panic-stricken shouts laddered into the blinding sunshine before darkness descended upon me.

I awoke to the man with the dog kneeling over me, worry flashing across his face. "Darlin', just stay still. I'll go call for a policeman."

My eyelids shuttered against the bright sun. "*No.*" I tried to raise an arm. "What happened…"

"You've been hit by a vehicle."

"Miss Cussy? Miss Cussy." Someone shook my arm, and I could barely make out the face until I heard her voice call to me again. It was Frankie.

I tried to answer, the words a scratchy mewl.

"She's the librarian. Help me get her up and over to Johnna's," she cried to the crowd of onlookers.

"Is she a librarian or a whore?" someone else shouted.

"She's been working at the Western Branch while visiting Reverend Claxton!" Otilia rushed to my side.

"She was headed toward Hamilton's," the man with the dog said, his voice quaking. "In a big hurry, she was."

Another man dropped to his knees, his weak blue eyes glued to mine, the smell of whiskey and sweet pipe tobacco souring his breaths, gagging me. Then he stood and yelled to the crowd, "She just stepped righ' in front of my automobile. Without warning!" He flailed his arms. "None at t'all."

I pressed my elbows against the pitted asphalt, fighting to rise.

"I'm real sorry, miss," he said, frightened. "I didn't see you." He looked out to the crowd and declared again, "*I didn't see her.*"

"The girl looks like she'd be from Johnna's house," a woman mused.

"She sure does," one man clipped.

"She's a librarian, you dimwits. A real Book Woman!" Otilia shouted at them, her face heated and hovering over mine.

Someone else hollered, "Call the police. She took a bad tumble!"

Otilia hissed, "I ain't calling no coppers."

"No police." I struggled to move. "*No.*" It crossed my mind that the Claxtons might've telephoned the law and I could be listed as a fugitive.

"Miss Cussy, don't worry," Frankie said. "Johnna will take you to the hospital."

"*Not to Johnna's.*" The words scratched over my dry throat.

My mind muddled. Reverend would be furious if he found out. "I—I'm fine. Just help me up."

She raised my head. A slaw mix of sour lemons and sugar tickled my throat, then a flash of white-hot pain roiled across my eyes. I turned over and spewed my innards onto the concrete, my throat hot like crackles of glass had slid over it.

"Here, let me help. The name's Melvin." The man with the dog pressed a clean handkerchief into my hands, and I nodded my thanks.

"Let's get her to the hospital quick, Frankie. She lost her shoe, grab it," Otilia ordered.

I tried to sit but collapsed, the dizziness and headache colliding, eating across my head. "Where's my book? Odette's poems?" I scratched out.

"Here, let's get you up, Miss Cussy," Otilia urged.

I groaned. Pages were scattered across the pavement; its cover had been smashed and ripped.

"My vehicle is parked just across the street," Melvin offered, his deep-brown eyes wide with fright.

Several hands lifted me up, carrying me to the back seat of an automobile over my protesting cries. Otilia and Frankie followed us and climbed into the back with me.

Melvin turned the ignition in the automobile and said, "I'm taking you straight to the hospital, darlin'."

"I have to get to the tailor's and then home," I protested.

"We'll let the Claxtons know as soon as we get you to the hospital," he said.

"You've given us all a fright," Otilia whispered.

"But Reverend's suit is still at the shop."

"You need to get checked out by a doctor," Melvin said.

I could only hope they hadn't called the law. Frightened, I looked to the girls. Streaks of blackened mascara had dotted down Otilia's contorted face, and she held my hand in her cold one. Frankie sniffled into a handkerchief. "Scared the bejabbers outta me, Miss Cussy. Thought you were a goner for sure," she burst out.

"Mrs. Claxton's niece will take good care of you. She's seen to plenty of us girls over the years," Otilia said.

"Susan," I said, then cradled my belly, praying the babe was safe.

Forty

Inside the hospital, Johnna's girls went to find Susan while they left me in a wheelchair. She appeared in her white uniform and nurse's cap. "Oh, Cussy, don't worry. I'll take care of you now. You're in good hands."

Otilia turned to Frankie. "Hurry, get hold of the Claxtons."

"Thank you, ladies. Cussy, we're going to get you to a room where the doctor can examine you," Susan said.

Frightened of prying hands, more examinations, I shook my head. "I need to leave. Leave right now."

"You had an accident and could have serious injuries, hon. We need to make sure you're okay. Aunt Effie will be here soon."

Otilia appeared at my side. "I'll stay with you, Miss Cussy."

Susan started to protest, but Otilia said, "I better stay with the librarian. Mrs. Claxton would not be happy if I up and abandoned her." She laid her hand on my shoulder.

I was wheeled into a room. Susan helped me onto the bed. "Let me get you a gown. I see your skirt's been ripped. You've got yourself some nasty scratches on your legs."

I examined the ragged skirt with a torn pocket, alarmed. Patting both pockets, I realized the coin purse with my change, lipstick, and stamps was gone. Shaking my head, I clamped a hand over my mouth, stifling the moans. Ashamed I'd lost the librarian's generous gifts and that I couldn't complete her one simple task.

Susan retrieved a folded cotton shift from a white apothecary cabinet in the corner and tried to pass it to me.

"No, I'll not take off my necessaries for doctors again." I crossed my arms over my chest. "No, ma'am."

She looked at me, bewildered, as she pulled the long hospital curtain around us, sealing us off. "I'm going to take some blood work—"

"No more tests." I struggled to sit up. Otilia gently pushed me back onto the pillow. "It won't hurt, and it'll be over in an instant."

"It's just a small prick, and I promise I won't take a lot," Susan pressed. "Then we'll clean up your legs."

An hour later, Mrs. Claxton swept past the curtains. "Chile, oh my goodness, are you okay? I should've never left you on Walnut Street alone."

"I'm sorry I didn't get Reverend's suit. I lost track of the time."

The despair knotted in my belly, leaving me to cast my eyes away, afraid to witness the disappointment in hers.

She sat down on the bed and grasped my hand, tucking locks of hair behind my ears, fussing over me. "Such a fright you gave me."

Feeling her gentle touch, I sorely missed my mama, the heaviness landing, leaving me wrecked with homesickness. My shoulders quaked as I fought back tears.

"Shh," Mrs. Claxton soothed and drew me into her arms, stroking my hair.

I sobbed softly, unable to hold back the months of loneliness. Mounting heartbreak. The losses had piled on and were still being stacked, and I was toppling under the crushing weight.

When she finally eased us apart, she said, "How is she, Susan?"

"She won't allow us to do tests," her niece said as she passed tissues to me.

"Hear now, Cussy, it's only a pinch, and then as soon as we see the doctor, I can get you home," the librarian promised. "I know a certain pup that's been watching out the window, waiting for her friend."

"I've been poked all my life. Ever since I was a babe, doctors have been trying to snatch pieces of me, force examinations on me. Even holding me down and stripping off my necessaries in the big Lexington hospital!" I blurted, suddenly struck by a stabbing pain to my head.

Alarm flashed across Susan's eyes. "You need to stay calm. You're safe here." She rubbed my arm. "I won't hurt you or take away your undergarments, I promise."

"Cussy, Susan always keeps her word," Mrs. Claxton said. "She's smart and won't harm a hair on your pretty head."

Otilia echoed her words.

After a few more pleas and several more promises, I agreed and held up my arm. The nurse took blood; checked my temperature, eyes, and ears; cleaned and swabbed my banged-up legs with the stinging Mercurochrome antiseptic.

"Mrs. Claxton..." I looked down at my ripped skirt. "I lost your change purse. I'm sorry."

"It was yours once I gave it to you. Don't fuss it. We can always get another, but never another like you."

In between checking my limbs for any sprains or breaks, Susan wrote down notes on a clipboard. "How's your headache, hon?"

"It still hurts some, Susan."

"I'll bring you a Coca-Cola until the doctor can prescribe medication. That usually helps a headache." She pressed down on my belly and then placed her stethoscope against it, leaving me squirming and the baby suddenly awakening with a faint quiver. Susan turned away to scribble down more notes. I felt the child lightly stir.

The babe was alive. I squeezed back a tear.

Susan reached inside the apothecary cabinet and passed me a paper cup. "If you could go into the lavatory and give me a urine sample, we'll be done," she said cheerfully. "Likely, the doctor will send you home with pain medication, but he'll need to check your test results first."

I started to ask why, when Otilia grabbed my arm. She and

Mrs. Claxton helped me to the tiny washroom tucked on the other side of the room.

When I handed her back the sample, Susan said, "We'll get these tests, and then the doctor will stop by to see you." A few minutes later, she came back into the room and pulled out a tall tray at the end of the bed, rolled it over my lap, and left a glass of Coca-Cola with crushed ice. "Drink up. Doctor's orders."

Mrs. Claxton settled into a chair beside my bed, thanked Otilia, and sent her home.

"If you need anything, here's Miss Johnna's telephone number, Mrs. Claxton," Otilia said, slipping her a note. Mrs. Claxton firmly wagged her head as if she'd rather not pursue the acquaintance. Still, Otilia pushed it into her hand. "Get well, Miss Cussy."

A few hours before midnight, I bolted upright from the bed when the doctor and nurse entered the room. Mrs. Claxton slumped in the hospital chair beside me, softly snoring. Susan gently touched her aunt's shoulder, and she shot up from the chair, blinking her puffy lids.

The doctor listened to my heart and peered into my eyes with a light, lingering. "Pretty peepers—an unusual bluish gray," he said, then studied the chart. "It looks like you were extremely lucky."

"Yes, sir. I'm feeling much better."

"Any nausea or vomiting?"

"I got sick right after the accident. But I'd had too much lemonade."

"Hmm. You took a bad hit, but nothing that a little rest won't cure. We're going to keep you overnight so the nurses can observe you. You may have a mild concussion, and I want to make sure you're safe before I sign off on your release."

"The Coca Cola took care of my headache, and I feel pert,

sure enough. I'm ready to leave now." I swung my legs over the bed.

"All the same, I'm ordering hospital rest till tomorrow." He smiled kindly, but his words were firm as he adjusted his spectacles and peered over the chart again. "Get some rest. Your Hogben test says you *both* need it."

Mrs. Claxton straightened and gawked at the doctor, and then her eyes latched on to mine. Silently, she rolled the word *both* over her lips.

I tucked my head away from her quizzical stare.

The doctor turned to Susan. "The patient appears healthy. You've listed congenital methemoglobin in the notes. But as you know, we've only recently seen the color like hers in the one patient. And his color quickly returned after administering the drug. We've never had one like her." The doctor glanced over at me. "We have a responsibility to the safety of other patients and hospital staff. Best play it safe. Hang a quarantine sign on this door. No visitors." He stopped and adjusted his spectacles to peer at me.

"Yes, Doctor, right away. And I'll personally see to the patient's needs." Susan frowned behind his back.

Why, I was surprised the city doctor hadn't been schooled on methemoglobinemia, what my mountain doc know'd long ago.

I looked at his pale face and again repeated the words I'd been saying all my life. "You can't catch color, sir." I raised an arm to Mrs. Claxton and Susan's brown faces, then pointed at my own darkened blue.

Mrs. Claxton said, "An educated man such as yourself should know as much. I promise you, sir, her color's not contagious. Or contaminating. The same as mine and your nurse here. Though Lord knows, I've sometimes wished it were," she snapped to boldly deliver a stern admonishment.

Susan peered down, hiding a smirk that had sprang to her lips.

"Nurse, help the patient into a clean robe," he said curtly. "I'll be at home if you need me. Otherwise, you'll see me again in the morning at six. Until then, no visitors are allowed for this patient."

"I'm not leaving my charge," Mrs. Claxton huffed.

"I ain't staying!" I said as our sentences rose together in tangled quarrels.

The doctor stared at us for an uncomfortable moment, trying to decide whether his long night was about to get longer. "I'll allow the one visitor," he clipped and turned to the door, his white coattails dismissing any further discussion.

Mrs. Claxton stood and exhaled loudly when the doctor left. "What the devil is that doctor talking about?"

Forty-One

"*Suzannah Effie Landers*," Mrs. Claxton hissed, darting her eyes between me and her niece. "What is this *hogwash* test, chile?" She pulled her niece closer to her. "What does he mean by *both*?"

"Hogben, Aunt Effie. We always do one when we're unsure of injuries or before we prescribe medication. They use frogs now to test for pregnancy; it's faster and doesn't kill the creature." She grinned. "Congratulations, Cussy."

"*Law*. You don't use the rabbits anymore?" Mrs. Claxton whispered as her troubled eyes landed on me. "Did you know you were bellied, chile?"

"Mrs. Claxton, I'm sorry." The words came hot and fast. "Warden forbid me to tell you. The prison is going to abort the baby and sterilize me as soon as I return. They'll bury my babe in Chicken Hill just like the other babies," I blurted.

Both Mrs. Claxton's and Susan's hands flew to their mouths.

"Warden? You must have taken a bigger blow to your head than what I thought," Susan said. "It's best you're staying overnight so I can care for you."

"She's on community furlough, chile, from the women's prison out there in Pewee Valley. And I was only told she was their librarian and had not committed any acts of violence," Mrs. Claxton added.

The disgrace fevered my face.

"A prisoner?" Susan eyes rounded.

"I was found guilty of violating miscegenation laws. I'm a Blue who married a white man, imprisoned because I loved someone the law said I couldn't."

The room quieted, the sound of the ticking clock filling the soft pockets of my spent declaration.

Mrs. Claxton spoke first. "Susan, do you remember when they arrested that Negro doctor and his white lady friend from Texas. It was about a decade ago. The doctor treated whites and coloreds, you know, and was on his way to establish a practice up north when the police stopped him right here in downtown. They threw them both in jail and placed heavy fines on their heads. Colored folks were outraged. And when the couple appeared in court, it was packed with Negroes. Including my Jed. Remember?"

"Like yesterday, Auntie. The judge released them, and the crowd cheered."

"There were several more arrests that day." Mrs. Claxton nodded solemnly. "They dragged one couple out of their beds despite the woman insisting she was Negro. Forced a blood test on her. Later they found a teenage boy carrying around pictures of white girls. Took him directly to the can and tried to round up the girls who gave him the photographs to arrest them too."

"I'm dating a man who's of the Mongolian race," Susan whispered, her eyes growing frightened. "Though Eric and I have never gone out in public." She looked at her aunt.

Mrs. Claxton drew in a sharp breath, the surprise lifting across her brow. "*Susan*, you must keep safe, chile. You never know when the government's going to come knocking. We need to always keep our houses in order and protect ourselves from sharp tongues that utter hollow words and make nonsensical laws that burden the burdened."

I studied Susan and wondered if they were now tracking the unmarried, tricking the people to sign pledges so the government could keep a better eye on who was loving who. Who they thought shouldn't be loving.

Both women moved over to the bed. Susan sat down beside me and took my hand while Mrs. Claxton pulled her chair closer.

"How did this all happen, Cussy?" Susan's worried voice dropped lower.

I collared my tongue and looked to Mrs. Claxton, seeking permission.

"Go ahead, you're safe. Tell us everything," the librarian coaxed.

"We married in the fall of '36. When we left the courthouse with our marriage license, the law approached us and tried to arrest Jackson. Three months earlier, I'd adopted my patron's infant after she passed in childbirth. Before she died, I promised her mama, Angeline, I would raise her."

"Your Honey?" Mrs. Claxton said.

I nodded. "The law accused us of fornicating. Threatened to send my babe to the House of the Idiots in Frankfort. The sheriff ripped up our marriage license." I felt the words tremble on my lips.

Susan grabbed the cup by the bed and poured water from the small pitcher, passing it to me.

I took several sips before handing it back. "They beat my dear Jackson senseless and dragged his body over to the jail." I balled the anguish in my fist and swallowed the sadness knocking at my throat.

"And you?" Susan weakly asked, as if she was afraid to hear more.

"The law didn't arrest me. *That time.* The sheriff told the crowd how easy it was for Jackson to trick a simple-minded Blue." I worried my fingers over the sheet. "I took Honey and left. There weren't really nothing more to be said. The sheriff, God, and Kentucky had said it for me."

Mrs. Claxton hissed.

"When the law finally found us together again this past March, they arrested both of us. They broke my arm and just about killed Jackson. The judge sentenced us to prison and banned Jackson from living in Kentucky for twenty-five years after he's released. I was given a pregnancy test when I arrived at the prison, but it was too early to show anything. And then, when the warden found out I was childing, she made an appointment with the doctor for an abortion and to perform a sterilization."

Susan's eyes filled, and Mrs. Claxton shook her head, disgusted, and uttered, "They've been sterilizing young girls and women for years. *Law*, it's a crime if women have an abortion, yet the stuff-coats force eugenical sterilizing. Hmph."

The nurse dipped her head. "It's true. There's been so many who've been sterilized under the eugenics laws. Several were performed just a few weeks ago. Two on white girls the doctors declared imbeciles. One of those said to have fits of uncontrolled hysteria. The third had been declared an *idiot* and was a colored teen with bouts of disobedience reported by her father."

"They give lobotomies to the inmates who are struck with such illnesses and airs of defiance," I said.

"*Defiance*," Mrs. Claxton stole a glance at Susan and raised a brow before pulling a handkerchief from her pocketbook to dab at her forehead. "The wretched woman denied my request for another week. I'm sorry, Cussy."

Tears welled in the woman's eyes, but the gut-wrenching sob was mine, a cold terror like none other draping over me. "I would rather be dead than let them kill my babe," I spat before I could harness my anger.

Susan patted my shoulder. A buzzer sounded, and she sighed loudly. "That's my patient in 209. I'll be back shortly. You just rest." She left the room.

Mrs. Claxton fumbled for my hand, lacing her bony fingers into my cold ones. "Chile, you shouldn't speak such foolish words."

I rubbed my head, the ache getting worse. "My pa always said the fight never seems to rest—it's always there waiting for the next round."

A tiredness pinched her face.

"I've been foolish," I said quietly.

Mrs. Claxton took a deep breath. "We've got to believe that the baby will be spared and you'll soon be united with your family. I know a few important people. Good people in government, like our mayor. I'm going to use the telephone," she said.

"My baby won't make it in time for answers." I curled up on the bed as the truth gutted me.

"Rest now." She pulled the hospital cover over me and then shuffled her weary frame out the door. I knotted the scratchy fabric closer to my chin. Drowning in worry, I slipped out of bed.

Resting was for the dead, and what this baby would be if I didn't find a way to save us.

I stepped over to the window and stared out past the thick-paneled curtain at the empty streets below.

Kneading my temples, I tried desperately to think of a way to save us, each time coming up blank and feeling more foolish.

This was a hospital, not a jail. If I left, Susan and the doctor would report that I walked out without an official release, freeing Mrs. Claxton from any blame.

To the east, a crooked moon appeared, dusted in cinnamon. Again, I scanned the rooftops and twinkling city lights. Louisville must have a thousand streets in its mazes.

Who was I fooling. I dropped the curtain. *I couldn't even find my way back to the tailor's shop when it was just blocks down the street jutting up like a sore thumb.*

The city lights blurred, and I turned my back to the window, burying the quiet sobs into my hands.

When the women returned, Susan stared at me for the longest time before she sat down on the bed. Mrs. Claxton eased herself onto the other side. Then Susan huddled us together, and we talked in hushed tones, batting words between us, our whispers soaking the pale-green walls.

More pinched talk crawled around us, and several words climbed out before Susan held a shushing finger to her lips.

Governor.

Johnna.

Drug.

Defiance.

Rose.

Church.

Library.

When we'd filled our beggar's cup full of boldness, Susan stood, smoothed the seams of her uniform, and adjusted the sharp edges of her nurse's cap. "Cussy, if you have any misgivings, you need to let me know now."

"Are you sure you want to do this, chile?" Mrs. Claxton shifted tired bones, her eyes red-rimmed. "It could be risky, downright deadly," she reminded me again.

"Yes," I barely breathed.

The librarian stared at me like she needed to say more.

"Aunt Effie, let's visit the cafeteria. They just remodeled it, and I bet you could use a fresh cup of coffee about now. Let me check on two of my patients, and I'll meet you down there shortly."

Mrs. Claxton looked like she was ready to protest.

"Cussy needs her rest, Auntie." Susan patted my shoulder. "We'll be back, hon. Press the buzzer if you need anything, and the nurses will come get me." She walked her aunt to the door and lingered at the light switch before clicking it off, the bleached disinfectants and sterile odors suffocating the darkened room.

Mama had claimed the darkness brings doubt, just like the night brings fevers in young'uns.

But earlier I'd heard the feverish radio talk about the governor weakening his stance on Sassyann's second execution, claiming he was in discussions with the attorney general, despite doctors declaring the woman was living in a vegetative state.

Then the news had tumbled into more bad broadcasts. An announcer said, "It's taken quite a toll on the men's prison, and research is ongoing as we await Salk's latest trials..."

Jackson.

Pacing, I fought against the panic rising. Waited for my might to steal some courage.

Mrs. Claxton know'd a lot of important people.

Penniless promises from money-eyed politicians, the wise madam had insisted.

Searching my heart, I moaned. *Jackson could very well be dead.* I stilled, stricken by the thought, gnashed through the bones of harder ones crowding in.

The path ahead could very well be my undoing.

I clutched the tissue in my fist, watching my hand grieve to a dark azure blue.

Forty-Two

A syringe poked out of Susan's pocket.

Glancing at the clock, I kicked off the sheet. It would be dawn soon.

"Good morning, chile—" the librarian called out from behind her.

"Turn off the overhead light, Aunt Effie, and stay quiet," Susan said, setting down a stack of papers on the table next to me. "Cussy, again, if you have any misgivings…"

I looked from one anxious face to another, then shook my head before reaching for the package Mrs. Claxton held.

Inside the large paper bag were clothes, clean necessaries, my Yeats collection from Jackson, a large navy pocketbook, and Honey and Irene's letters. Underneath it all was Madam Johnna's red wig.

I held it up to the bedside lamp, inspecting the flexible cap the hairs were sewn into.

"Hurry and get dressed, Cussy. It won't be long before the doctor starts his morning rounds." Susan glanced down at her wristwatch, then opened the door to the tiny washroom, waiting.

A tremble took hold of my hands as I clumsily pulled on a pair of wide-legged women's britches and fumbled with the buttons on the long-sleeved flowery blouse.

I took a deep breath and opened the washroom door. Mrs.

Claxton grabbed my tattered clothes and Johnna's wig and then fastened the hair piece onto my head. Inspecting me, she took her lipstick and dabbed it onto my lips. Satisfied, she gave a solemn nod.

"After I told Johnna you would be *leaving* us, her girls wanted to give you something for your journey." Mrs. Claxton reached inside the pocketbook, opened a handsome women's wallet, and showed me the stuffed bills. "Thirty-nine dollars, to be exact." From another slotted compartment, she pulled out a card. Then, from the bottom of the purse, a booklet slightly bigger than my hand. "Your papers."

I looked at it under the lamp, its light dimmed. Running my fingers over the satin cover bound in gold thread, I examined the painted dove and pale-pink roses twined around a white cross. *Certificate of Baptism* was stamped at the top in gold letters.

Carefully, I turned the thin page to read the new identity I would take. *Angeline Mary Moffit.* A christening date for April 10, 1920, had been forged by the librarian.

As I turned to the older woman, I saw the answer in her eyes and know'd she had stolen the blank document from Reverend's church records. The certificate was considered legal identification, like gold, and would offer me safe passage.

"He's only been told you're being sent back, that the prison officials are picking you up from here," Mrs. Claxton confirmed.

I hugged her neck. "Ma'am, I promise I'll repay you one day."

"You already have, chile. In more ways than you'll ever know."

I studied Angeline's false records and realized no one cared about the life she and her husband had been rooted to, much less her sudden death after childbirth. Her grave lost, hidden in the hills of Troublesome Creek. Weren't but a three-year age difference between us, and I was grateful dear Angeline's name would live on.

"Here's your library card, Angeline," Mrs. Claxton said, smiling.

I pressed it to my chest, appreciative.

Mrs. Claxton noted the names were spelled correctly and the additional legal document would offer even more protection.

Stuffing Yeats and my new identifications into the pocketbook, I pulled out a fresh handkerchief that Mrs. Claxton had folded inside and clutched it to my chest.

Susan put my clothing in a bag and left them on the chair. "Ready?" She pulled the syringe from her pocket.

Forty-Three

Susan held up the sharp needle. "I just want to make sure you understand what I told you last night: Taking the drug is a risk. Methylene blue is not advised for pregnant women, and we don't know enough about its use in pregnancy. *You.* How it may affect the child or you. Sometimes not until after the birth…if the child survives."

I squeezed the handkerchief in my clammy hands.

"You'll see to Jackson, Mrs. Claxton?"

"I'll get word to him when it's safe, and to Honey also," she added. "Give her your arm."

"Mrs. Claxton, you would also be in danger if they find out."

The librarian shook her head. "We went over all that."

"But you could lose everything, and—"

"It's my decision to make," Mrs. Claxton said firmly.

The room quieted, lifting the loud ticks of the clock. My heart pounded, roared in my ears, almost deafening me to any other sounds.

"The doctor will be in soon," Susan urged, darting her eyes up to the clock. "We must not tarry a second longer."

The idea that my life could be wrapped up in a clock's tick stole the breath from me.

I held out an unsteady arm. Mrs. Claxton helped hold it still while Susan injected me with the methylene blue.

"I've been careful with the dose," Susan said, applying a tiny bandage over the injection. "Just enough to hopefully keep you safe. But I can't tell you for how long."

Instantly, my skin turned a soft robin's-egg blue, then white, leaving the two women gasping in disbelief.

"How do you feel?" Susan peered at me.

I'd parted my lips to utter a reply when, suddenly, a pain seized my scalp.

Susan grabbed her stethoscope and checked my heart.

"It's exactly like I remember when Doc gave it to me long ago. Though my belly had rebelled," I said, shaky. But just as quick, the ache went away. "It's easing some now. I expect the pain is left over from the accident but more from my lit nerves."

She held the glass thermometer up to my lips, then adjusted her stethoscope and listened to my heart again. Minutes later, she raised the thermometer to the dim bulb. "All good. Let me finish my notes, and then I'll go telephone the prison and give them the official news." Satisfied, she hovered over her paperwork.

Her hand shook a little and she grimaced and pressed down harder on the pen. "Stay in touch, Cussy, and write when you can."

Finished, Susan hugged me, and tears streamed down my cheek as I closed my eyes and whispered, "*Thank you. Thank you. Thank you…*"

"Godspeed. Go give your baby its rightful place in the world." She released her hold.

"I need to make my phone calls." Mrs. Claxton gripped my hand. She scrutinized me once more, and a small smile latched on to her lips. "It's working good. Real good, chile. Go have a look in the mirror."

Grabbing my pocketbook, I crossed to the tiny washroom, anxious to glimpse the color for myself.

The man walked in, nearly bumping into me, the breeze from his white flapping coat cutting the stagnant hospital air.

Puzzled, his eyes held mine for a brief second, searching,

before he pushed up the bridge of his glasses and looked back to his notes.

I spun to Mrs. Claxton to see her alarm mirroring mine.

"Okay, let's see how you're doing this morning, Mrs. Lovett." He scanned the room. "Where's our patient?" he asked, turning to the light switch.

I sucked in a small breath, know'd if the man could see in the faintly lit lamplight, he would've recognized the eyes he'd peered into earlier.

Would've found me in there.

Forty-Four

When the doctor brushed past me, he had mumbled an apology before reaching to flick on the overhead light.

I had raised the handkerchief up to my face.

At once, Susan grabbed the stack of paperwork from the stand next to the bed. Mrs. Claxton snatched my arm and hooked it into hers.

"Where's our mother-to-be, Nurse?" the doctor inquired again, perplexed by the empty bed. He signaled with a questioning brow toward the washroom door.

"No, Doctor, I'm sorry to say, the patient was found deceased at 3:11. There is no next of kin, and I've informed the proper authorities. The body's been transported to the Eastern Cemetery's crematory. You'll remember this is Mrs. Claxton, who's been here throughout the night, and another friend, Mrs. Moffit, we had down for a contact. I was just giving them directions to the crematory."

"Is there no Mr. Lovett?" he asked.

"Unwed," she said, barely above a whisper.

"I see." He wrinkled his nose in disapproval.

I squeezed the handkerchief, choking back the panic.

"Here are my nurse's notes, sir." Susan took the clipboard from the puzzled doctor and handed him a new one with papers. The doctor studied the chart, a grimace lengthening his face.

Susan turned and gave a curt nod, and I tucked my chin down lower. "I've bagged her clothing, ladies. It's there in the chair. Again, I'm so very sorry. I'll telephone the newspaper so they will properly record it." She touched Mrs. Claxton's arm in sympathy. "I know how difficult this news is. I hope you'll find comfort in the chapel at the crematory." To the doctor she said, "Sir, we have two patients who were just admitted an hour ago and are waiting. One appears to have a fractured tibia, and the other is complaining of stomach pains and nausea."

Silence.

I plucked at the dampening fabric of my blouse, the perspiration sticky on my chest. Terrified the blue would start oozing out, I folded my hands under my armpits.

"Dr. Samuels?" Susan's words rose, strained.

The doctor scratched his head and peered at the chart again. "Could be, given her genetic disorder, her brain was robbed of oxygen after the head trauma."

Susan pressed the stack of papers to her chest, brushed past us to the man's side.

Startled by her sudden moves, I squeezed my eyes shut. *Would my color burst through and betray me?*

Mrs. Claxton placed a steady hand on my shoulder, then pulled me into a hug, shielding my face from his view.

Had the color returned?

"Sir, if you'll step out to the nurses' station with me, I've got your morning paperwork ready for signature, including Mrs. Lovett's death certificate and the crematory papers. There's the other delicate matter. Mrs. Hancock in 209 has asked if you could take special care of her baby's birth certificate..."

She dropped the last words and left me straining to hear as I pressed my face into Mrs. Claxton's shoulder and then dared to peek out.

"Doctor, I know you've got a busy schedule ahead, but it shouldn't take more than a minute, and then I can get your paperwork filed."

He sighed as he read his clipboard. "Okay. My sincere condolences, ladies." He barely glanced at us but turned back, drawn to my one hand poking out from Mrs. Claxton's embrace.

My legs wobbled. Mrs. Claxton fumbled and clutched me tighter, squeezed once, twice, and then again, a warning to still.

But I couldn't calm the thoughts churning inside. The fear pummeled me, and I fought against the blackness that would surely swallow me any second.

I was certain the color would climb out screaming, denouncing my fakery and lies. Squeezing my eyes shut, I prayed for Pa to watch over me—begged for the strength needed to save the babe's life.

Susan said, "Ladies, we'll just give you a moment of privacy. Again, you have the hospital's sincere sympathies."

She moved closer to the doctor, gesturing to the door. "We released Mrs. Allen in 324. Mr. Faber in room 226 needs an X-ray, and Johnson in 221 is waiting for release," Susan chatted feverously, inching him toward the hall, the terror mounting with each shallow breath.

Then he cast his eyes to the nurse and tsked through clenched teeth. "I don't know what I'd do without you, Nurse Landers. You must be beat after working another twelve-hour shift." He adjusted the glasses on his nose, grunted, and followed her out to the nurses' station.

For a minute, we stood paralyzed on the threshold with our knees locked, watching while the doctor bent his head to Susan's paperwork and scribbled a signature, breezing through papers.

I dared to raise a hand. To my great relief, I found the drug working its magic.

Susan turned to us and gave a brisk nod before hovering back over him. When he was through, she picked up the stack. "I'll just get your coffee and then file these, sir." She shot a harried glance our way, her face tightening.

Mrs. Claxton jolted and gripped my arm.

We slipped out of the room, walked briskly down the hall to the exit and right past the hospital guard reading his morning paper over a steaming cup of coffee.

Forty-Five

Dawn summoned the slow-waking city, shedding its Sunday cloak of darkness.

Inside the vehicle, hot breezes tangled through my heavy wig, the smell of cigarette smoke and perfume clinging to the fake hair, raging a protest in my belly.

I stared out at the muddy Ohio River as Mrs. Claxton drove us across the bridge, the radio announcer's voice whirring as he delivered the morning news.

When the newsman said the governor was now prepared to execute Sassyann again, and as early as September, Mrs. Claxton moaned. "Ought to be law against that kind of savagery. *Law*, she's been living in a vegetative state and is as good as dead. Looking sickly, chile. Lean your head out and catch some more air," she advised.

I inhaled the fishy, earthen breaths of the dark river and could only imagine the horrors that awaited Sassyann.

Twisting around, I scanned for any signs of the law on our tail. I shuddered, suddenly jolted by the thought that if I made it, I would be looking over my shoulder for the rest of my life.

Mrs. Claxton turned off the radio and settled more comfortably in her seat.

When I saw the Indiana state sign a few minutes later, my breathing relaxed. A glance to my hands showed the drug was still working, the color a pale ruddy pink.

I placed fingers to my belly and softly tapped. There'd been nary a flutter since we left the hospital.

Mrs. Claxton reached awkwardly under her seat, fumbled, and pulled out a strange black cap and placed it on the dash. "How's that headache, chile?" she asked after crossing the Ohio River.

"It's back, ma'am. But—" I was getting ready to tell her I hadn't felt the baby but swallowed my grievance. Her face sagged under coal-bagged eyes. "Mrs. Claxton, I'm sorry I've put you through so much. You look spent."

"Ain't never felt more alive." She jutted her chin and pressed down on the pedal.

I lowered my gaze to my draped stomach, silently begging for a sign of life.

We pulled into a small Indiana town and parked on an empty gravel lot. "I need to call Jed at the church. Then the prison."

I waited outside the opened telephone booth as she fed coins into the machine.

"Jed, *Jed*. I'm glad I caught you. I have awful news." She glanced out at me. "It's our Cussy. I'm afraid we lost her."

A long pause. Then: "Yes, they did everything they could to save her. Uh-huh, Susan took care of the remains. It's all so heartbreaking. Yes, that would be real nice if you called for a quiet prayer circle tonight. Hmm. No. Yes, I'm calling the prison next… Whining? Uh-huh, I imagine Daisy's missing her about now. She'll be lost a bit. Take out one of my ham bones from the refrigerator and give it to her tonight. Uh-huh… I'm heartbroken."

She turned, and the muffled strings of conversation were lost. When she twirled around, the librarian stretched the telephone's chord and planted a shaking hand onto the booth's glass, resting her head atop the clawed palm. A passing truck cushioned her conversation for a moment.

Then her voice climbed outside. "Thank you, Jed. I knew you'd understand. A visit with Sister Rose will do good and right my nerves. Uh-huh. Yes, I'll be careful. No, I won't stop unless I absolutely have to. Yes, I have your cap on the dash. Phone Lillian for me and have her schedule Maureen to fill in. I'll see you in a few days. I'll call you at the church tomorrow. Uh-huh, I've got the books in the glove. Yes, I'll be extra careful. Talk to you tomorrow."

She placed the receiver in the cradle and pulled out a handkerchief and wiped her damp forehead. After a moment, the librarian took a deep breath and fed the machine again, the thunk of coins lifting.

I paced across the gravel lot, itching to get farther away from Kentucky.

When Mrs. Claxton finally connected with the next party, her words lit across the wires somber and measured, ending with several promises to send a letter of high praise to the governor about the generosity of the warden.

"Yes, ma'am, I've cast it to memory, exactly as you've said. Yes, word for word," she repeated. "Uh-huh... *Thank him for your prison's charitable donation of the inmate—declaring its services were a contribution to the city and adding a plea for the reinstatement of generous library funds.* I'll get that written to the mayor today, ma'am. Yes."

Its. The acknowledgment that I weren't nothing more than an *it* to the warden cut across my damning heart.

The librarian slammed down the telephone and muttered something I couldn't hear. She stepped out of the booth and looked up and down the street. "Let's get back on the road. We have a long drive." She took her handkerchief and blotted her forehead again and winced. "Law, we've got us another hot July day in store."

We climbed into her automobile, and I pulled off the sweaty wig, then glanced at the rearview mirror, relieved to see the drug was still working.

"Ma'am, you'll check on Jackson? Get word to him and Honey?" I asked again.

"I promised you. Now, put it out of your mind."

Turning to the window, I pressed a knuckle to my mouth. I didn't want to nag her. She'd already risked so much. *Her life.*

For several hours we drove without speaking, stopping only once to relieve ourselves in the tall grasses on an empty country road. The steady hum of tires slapped, grinding across our nettling thoughts.

Mrs. Claxton slowed as we passed a white bullet-ridden sign hitched to a tall oak post: STRANGER, DON'T LET THE SUN SET ON YOU.

I stole a peek at her and saw a fright rising.

At the next stop sign, Mrs. Claxton whipped the vehicle onto a dusty gravel road. She glanced into the rearview mirror then pulled her troubled eyes to the dashboard. Suddenly she groaned and parked the automobile off the road. "The needle is almost on empty. We'll have to find a filling station. Hand me that book in the glove compartment." Her voice shook.

I opened it and held up a small green book and scanned the cover. *The Negro Motorist Green Book.* Under the title was an outline of a scroll that had a long list stamped down it: hotels, taverns, garages, nightclubs, restaurants, service stations… At the bottom, it noted the book was *Prepared in cooperation with the United States Travel Bureau.*

"No, I need the latest, the '52 edition."

I dug into the glove and saw several and grabbed the newer one, *The Negro Travelers Green Book.* On the bottom left was printed CARRY YOUR GREEN BOOK WITH YOU. YOU MAY NEED IT.

Confused, I had never come across one while on my Pack Horse route. I passed the book to her. "What is this—"

She held up a shushing finger and flipped through the worn pages, a finger chewing down the lists of names, her face creasing with concern. Finally, Mrs. Claxton handed it back, and I placed it inside the glove box, wondering why it was so important.

The woman held a palm over her mouth and squeezed as if trying to think of what to do next.

"What is it, ma'am?"

She didn't answer.

"Are we lost?" I leaned my head out, searching browned fields. Beyond several dead trees, I spotted a farmhouse and pointed. "Maybe we can go ask for help?"

"Chile, get into the back seat. We need to stop and buy gasoline now." She darted her eyes to the mirror.

Puzzled, I stared at her.

"Go on. We're losing time, and that drug's not going to last much longer." Again, she glanced in the rearview mirror, like she was looking for someone or something.

I stepped out of the automobile and folded myself onto the back seat. "Is something wrong? Does it have anything to do with the sign we passed?"

She turned around and draped a bony arm across the top of her bench seat. "You're a white woman now, stopping in a hushpuppied town with your maid," she warned as a stiffness settled across her straightening shoulders.

I tucked my chin and picked through her haunting words.

"I have to protect myself, chile. And if that color of yours returns"—she stabbed a finger at me—"it'll make two easy pickings for the nightriders." As she turned her key in the ignition, the motor roared to life.

She scolded herself, "Law, I should've filled up in Louisville like Jedidiah always does before traveling." She thumped the big steering wheel. "Dammit, dammit." The curses rolled off her tongue. "Lord help me, I done landed us in a sundown town."

Numb, I stared at the back of her head, feeling helpless, the hairs lifting on my neck.

Minutes later, we pulled into the filling station, a rusted Shell sign blistered and peeling, her dashboard showing the fuel needle was below the red mark.

"Sooner we get out of here, the safer I'll feel," she said.

"Yes, ma'am." I looked over my shoulder out the back window, my own words winded and shaky.

"Don't use that salutation again," she snapped. "I'm your maid, you are the *ma'am*." She turned back to the windshield.

I pushed myself deeper into the back seat, her sudden anger befuddling me.

Mrs. Claxton righted herself with eyes locked statue-straight as we waited.

The sticky heat rolled inside, and I leaned my head toward the window, the sweat beading my brow, the fear crawling around us.

Films of oil and gasoline pooled on the ground. Fumes seeped into our opened windows, blanketing fresh air. My eyes watered, and I sneezed and swallowed back the sickening taste.

The man thumped the hood and peered inside to Mrs. Claxton, then parked his eyes to the backseat. "Fill 'er up, miss?" He stepped over to my window and leaned his head inside. "Miss?"

The librarian shifted uncomfortably, and I straightened. "I'll take a fill-up, sir."

I ran fingers across my belly, tapping. My insides didn't reply with so much as a stingy ripple.

When he was through, he knocked on the hood, peered into the back window. "Can I get your windshield, miss?"

I strained my neck and inspected the dusty, bug-smattered glass, and nodded.

After he'd finished, he poked his head back in and said, "That'll be two dollars and seventy cents."

Mrs. Claxton crooked her head slightly toward me.

Flustered, I dug into the pocketbook for my wallet and then twisted sideways so he couldn't see the contents. I dropped the bills on the floorboard, snatched them up and fumbled, passing him a five-dollar bill.

The attendant left with a muted *thank you*, then minutes later returned with the change.

Next door, a bell chimed from the diner. "We should grab

something to eat while it's still light, Cussy. I didn't have time to pack our dinner this morning. Get out of the automobile."

I climbed out and studied our surroundings as I waited beside her window. The air felt charged, and an uneasiness pushed up from my gut. "Let's leave. I can eat later."

"It'll help with the headaches, and the baby needs nourishment. Now, here's what you're going to do, chile." Mrs. Claxton jabbed a finger at the diner and went over her instructions. "Ask for *one* fried bologna sandwich, *one* bag of chips, and *one* Coke." She held up a knobbed finger and then rolled money into my palm. "Don't talk to a soul. Order, pay, collect the bags, and leave. If you see your color returning, you get out of there quick."

"You need to eat too."

"They will not cook their food for a Negro. Go on, be quick."

"It's burning up in the automobile. Just step outside and wait," I protested.

"You would be getting me killed!" She lifted her stubborn jaw and wouldn't budge.

"Do you at least have a cardboard fan in the glove?" I circled around to the passenger side, flipped open the compartment, and her old *Green Book* tumbled out onto the seat.

I glanced at the introduction page it landed on. The travel guide was published to keep the Negro from running into difficulties or embarrassments—*make his trip safer*, it read. I dropped the book as if I'd been stung. Mrs. Claxton leaned over and stuffed it back into the box.

Reaching across to the dashboard, I grabbed the odd cap and gave it to her. "Use this to fan yourself."

"Put that down! It's Jed's," she hissed.

I shrank back and tossed it onto the dash. "I'll hurry."

At the diner door, I read the white sign with red printing: ABSOLUTELY NO COLOREDS ALLOWED. I quickly checked the color of my hands.

When I pulled open the glass door, the bell announced me,

and cool breezes greeted my damp face. Curious eyes scrutinized me. Two farmers crowded at the counter, drinking coffee. Nearby, two more shared a small wooden table, while a couple in a booth chatted and lingered over dirty dishes. A jukebox in the corner played a low caterwauling tune.

I crossed to the counter, where an older woman was busy filling saltshakers.

She looked over my shoulder to the parking lot. "We don't cook for Negroes."

"It's for me." Studying the menu board on the wall, I ordered the double-decker fried bologna and cheese, offering her a friendly smile. It was returned with a cagey bother. I was an outsider and couldn't mistake the suspicion and unwelcoming that flitted across her piercing eyes.

Again, I inspected my hands.

"Would you like to add dessert to that?" She adjusted her ruffled waitress hat, pulled the pencil away from a grease-stained Guest Check notepad, and pointed to a cake stand with a glass dome. The four-layer caramel cake was missing several slices, its yellow cake dry, and the caramel icing had lost its luster and concreted.

"Made fresh today." Her eyes dared me to say otherwise as she scratched her auburn hair with the tip of her pencil.

"Just the sandwich, chips, and Coke." Whiffs of rancid oil, soured milk, and stale cigarette smoke wafted from her uniform.

She called out to the cook behind her, "Order, double-fried bologna an' cheese." A young boy popped his head up from a grill while she began emptying the welled-glass ashtrays along the counter. She stopped and refilled the farmers' cups, then rested an elbow in front of them and whispered. They glanced at me and looked over their shoulders toward the parking lot to our automobile. The towheaded farmer shrugged and hunched back over his drink. But his bearded friend continued to stare, his jaw twitching.

Growing uneasy, I turned to the automobile, the steamy

day rolling across the broken asphalt. Mrs. Claxton's head nodded to the steering wheel, and I know'd her ol' bones were exhausted.

"Mustard?" The waitress set down the Coke and held up greasy condiment packets beside the sack.

"Yes, please," I replied, peering back out the window, my eyes locked on her vehicle, more worriment nicking my thoughts.

"That'll be seventy-two cents."

Then the librarian's head dipped down, and she slumped over the steering wheel.

The waitress pushed the bag across. Dropping the five-dollar bill on the counter, I grabbed the sack and drink and ran outside.

"Mrs. Claxton?" I set the bag on the back seat and the drink beside it. The woman's eyelids drooped, and her face glowed with droplets stitched across the brow and down her cheek.

I snatched up the cup and dug out pieces of chipped ice. "Mrs. Claxton. *Mrs. Claxton*," I cried out, leaning over the steering wheel, rubbing the cold across her lips and brow.

"Miss. I'm Sonny Harris." The towheaded farmer crowded beside me, trying to glimpse inside the vehicle. "She's overheated." He tipped his ball cap and reached inside. "You need to get your help outta—"

"Take your hands off her." I stepped in front of him and glared, fearful of what he might do to Mrs. Claxton.

"I'm getting her outta that hot automobile *now*. Move aside, dammit." He pushed, and I stumbled back.

"Leave her be," I demanded, tugging on his sleeve.

He jerked away from my grip. "She needs to get outta there!"

Groaning, the librarian roused as the man eased her out, took hold of her arm, his face reddening from the heat.

"Let's get you inside the diner where the fans can cool you," I said, taking her other arm.

The man stopped and wagged his head.

She pointed a wobbly finger to the patch of concrete with a sliver of shade. "There," she rasped.

We helped her to the curb on the side of the diner. Drained, Mrs. Claxton rested her head on her knees.

"I'll get her some water," Sonny said and headed into the diner.

"Mrs. Claxton, what can I do?" I lightly shook her hot, dry arm, fearful of what was happening. "Please, sit up. Can I telephone a doctor?"

Someone had littered, and I picked up the diner bag and fanned her.

She grunted and slowly lifted her head, revealing reddened eyes and parched lips.

I fanned harder.

Sonny returned with a tall paper cup of ice water, an old metal bucket, and a dishrag, setting it down in front of us. Then he passed me Mrs. Claxton's change I'd left on the counter.

"Thank you," I said, grateful for his honesty.

I gave her the cup, and she drank slow. The water spilled out as I swished the cloth into the bucket and wrung it out. As I touched it to her face, she recoiled, then snapped to attention. "I'll tend to it…*ma'am.*" She snatched it from me and pressed it across her brow and neck.

"If you could let her cool off inside, sir. Just for a moment," I pleaded.

Mrs. Claxton looked up and shot me a warning.

Sonny tucked his thumbs into his overalls and stared off, rocking on the heels of his boots. He flattened his lips, then glanced at Mrs. Claxton and back to the road again.

"You seem like nice enough city folks. I hope your help feels better, ma'am. Wouldn't want ya'll to be stuck here so far from home."

Something in the man's weathered face showed a gentleness and a sincerity, but I suddenly got the allovers crawling around my neck when I followed his eyes to the diner's window. His bearded friend stared out at us, something cold and dangerous brewing in his eyes.

He pulled up ol' hauntings, reminded me of the preacher man who'd tried to drown those with odd markings. Me. His attack still fresh like yesterday and still after all these years. *The Devil's beastly slittail*, he'd called me before trying to force me off the trail while I was delivering books to my patrons. He'd beat on my sweet book mule and chased her off into the woodlands then lurched at me. I'd struggled against his muscled grip as the preacher proclaimed he'd put his *hot-white fire inside me to burn out my blue demons*.

My beloved Junia had screamed out and thundered back toward us, kicking up the forest's black earth and rot. Then the mule chased him through the woods with her big chomping teeth and maddening cries. When he came stalking again, she trampled him, rid me of the demon, and broke the devil man's ticker.

My hands shook as I hovered over Mrs. Claxton, the old disgrace lingering and still gnawing at me.

The diner's bell jingled. Curious, the waitress poked her head out, her face curdling as she looked on. The bearded man brushed past her and spat our way as he headed toward his truck.

The air suddenly felt dangerous, pricked, like an ugly evil had rooted in this town long before the first cornerstone had been laid.

Sonny took off his ball cap and wiped his brow. "Soon as you're rested, ya best move along. This ol' town can get a mite rowdy round these parts after dark. Hunters hunting them hushpuppies and all." His eyes rested on Mrs. Claxton. "Wouldn't want to see anything happen to you nice ladies."

Water dribbled down Mrs. Claxton's chin as she pulled the cup slowly away from her lips and looked up at him.

Hushpuppies. The word jelled as I realized I'd read it somewhere in an article or book. The fried cornmeal dumpling that escaping slaves tossed to distract and lead tracking dogs off their trail.

Mrs. Claxton flinched and said hoarsely, "Thank you, sir,

for your generous hospitality. We'll be leaving now." She took another greedy gulp and wiped her face, flailing as she stood up.

Sonny reached out to steady her at the same time I did.

"Obliged. I'll see to her, sir."

"I'm feeling better now, ma'am," she uttered low as she limped toward the automobile.

"Are you sure you can drive?" I settled her behind the steering wheel and glanced at all the knobs and dials. "I've never learned but I can try."

"That would be just as dangerous as staying." She took a couple of breaths and gripped the wheel. "Hurry and get into the back seat."

"Here, take a sip of your Coke." I passed it to her, and she dug out ice and rubbed it across her face and neck before swallowing several big gulps of the sugary drink. The ol' woman exhaled loudly, then vigorously shook her head to collect herself.

When she pulled out onto the road, the bearded man in the truck followed while Sonny knocked his boot on the curb, teeth tucked tight in a grimace.

"Mrs. Claxton, that other man's behind us. He's a'huntin'."

"Shh, let me concentrate." She kept darting her bulging eyes to the rearview mirror.

Forty-Six

The man tailed us for a mile down the road until Mrs. Claxton slowed, reached out the window, her arm turned upward to signal a turn. When she stopped at the crossroad, he revved the motor, then backed up and squealed his tires, speeding toward us.

"Mrs. Claxton, he's coming for us fast!"

Terrified, I watched as his growling truck flew closer, chewing through the road. Then he slammed on the brakes, barely missing the tail of our vehicle.

The librarian cried out.

Any minute now, he would ram into us and crush me in the back seat.

Again, he put his truck in reverse, gunned the engine, and sped toward us, his brakes screaming as it came within inches of stopping.

I reached forward and gripped the front seat, my knuckles a hot white. Mrs. Claxton sucked in a loud breath.

Then the truck sprayed up gravel and dust as the man put it in reverse again. I squeezed my eyes shut and heard the grinding of gears, the squeal of tires, as he drove straight toward us.

"*Go, go!*" I shrieked, slapping at the front seat.

Turning the big steering wheel, Mrs. Claxton pressed on the gas, and the automobile lurched forward just as the truck clipped the left side of our bumper.

Our screams rose.

A pain shot up from my neck, stabbing my head.

Cursing, the man leaned out the window and threw a beer bottle. We cried out again and ducked, the broken glass bouncing off the trunk.

The man laid on his horn before speeding off. We took a minute to catch our breath, then I dared to look back. "I think he's gone, ma'am."

"And that's just a warning given in daylight," she said, still breathless. "You can imagine the evil men like him do under the cover of darkness." Mrs. Claxton picked up speed, leaving a cloud of dust and pebbles trailing.

When we were several more miles away, she turned onto a red dirt road and stopped.

For a few minutes we said nothing. Somewhere across a field, dogs yapped and the quarrelsome chuk-chuk-chuk of blackbirds rose, splintering the silence. Then she banged her fist atop the dash and choked back a sob.

"Mrs. Claxton"—I placed an unsteady palm on her shoulder—"please drop me off at a bus or train depot, and go home. You need to keep yourself safe." But she just shrugged off my hand, climbed out of the car, and stood still, searching the skies.

I wouldn't blame her if she put me out and left me on the side of the road.

Straightening her backside, Mrs. Claxton hobbled around to the back of the automobile to examine the bumper. She groaned and then reached down to fiddle with it.

When I opened the door to help, she said, "Stay inside."

"You need to go home. I can walk."

"Hmph. Walk yourself right into bigger trouble. Imagine what them farmer-tan-browns would do with a Blue like *you.*"

"Mrs. Claxton, please go home—"

"That drug's armor is going to be leaving you exposed to his hateful kind soon enough." Mumbling, she settled back behind the steering wheel and stared straight ahead. "Now, you just keep an eye out from that back seat, chile."

In the distance I heard the unmistakable sound of a pickup truck's engine, its loud rumblings, a warning. "He's nearby, ma'am."

The librarian lifted her chin and fumbled for the key, and the automobile came to life.

Twisting around to watch out the rear, I rested a hand on the lip of the bench seat as the tires bounced along the rough road.

We hit several more ruts, and it weren't long before the metal bumper flew off, clanged as it tore away, pinging against rock.

I moaned. "Don't you need that?"

"I need us to live more." She pressed a heavy foot down on the gas pedal.

When it felt safe, I dug into the food sacks and leaned over the front seat and urged her to take part of the thick sandwich. "At least eat something. You'll feel better." Grabbing her waiting hand, I pressed half into it. She took a healthy bite.

I was relieved to see she had an appetite and with each mouthful looked more pert. More determined.

After swallowing a few bites of the other half, I opened the bag of chips, took a few, and passed the rest to her.

Hours later, we crossed the state line, and she whispered into the shadows of the day, "I told you that Jed would never allow us to go see Cab Calloway. What I didn't tell you, chile, was that my girlfriend, Sally Beth, and I snuck into one of his shows back in the thirties."

"Mrs. Claxton! Why you *rascal*, you," I teased, grateful to see she'd recovered.

"Yes, sir, we jived and jitterbugged all night long to Cab's songs. We were hep cats stepping live. Man, what a hummer he is." Her spirits had lifted, and she sang some of Cab's songs, scatting out his lively verses.

"Copper colored gal of mine
I love you 'cause you're so divine
Say you'll always be my clinging vine
Copper, copper, copper, copper colored gal of mine!

Just skeep-beep de bop-bop beep bop bo-dope
Skeetle-at-de-op-day."

Weren't long before the air cooled and her songs drifted into ol' church hymnals and grew woeful. She spotted a telephone booth on the side of the road near a small, boarded-up grocery store and pulled up beside it.

Digging for coins, she climbed out. "I need to make some calls. Check on my staff and make sure Jed got hold of them."

Mrs. Claxton leaned into the window. "The dark is coming. It's safe to sit up front now." I got out and slipped inside the passenger seat.

Lifting my hands, I winced as the blue stain crawled across them, then draped a palm over my belly, kneading.

No sign of life.

A few minutes later she came back to the automobile. "Get me that pouch of Yankee Girl 'bacco in the glove. I could use a chaw."

I found it buried beneath the books and papers, wrapped in tissue. She opened the lid and took a healthy pinch and stuffed it inside her jaw. "Underneath your seat is a small spit cup. Can you reach it, chile?"

I fumbled around and pulled out a tin cup.

She sighed deeply and settled comfortably in her seat. "My mother and Auntie Rhea always kept the chaw around to settle the female nerves." After a moment, she steered the automobile onto another state road. "Won't be too much longer till we get there."

She pointed to the dash at the odd hat resting there. "I'm sorry for my rude outburst back there. I forget you've never traveled much past our Kentucky mountains. Now, that cap is what every Negro motorist carries for survival. It's a chauffeur's hat. And if a Negro man is traveling, he best have one. *And* in full view."

I listened closely, heartbroken that the elderly couple had to dress in silly costumes out of fear for their lives.

She wagged her head. "Now, if you get stopped by the law in

a sundown town, you'll find yourself in a tricky situation. So, Jed would tell the sheriff that he's driving his white boss's automobile. If you're a Negro who happens to have your wife and child riding along, you can inform the lawman you're bringing your boss's maid to work, and that's her child. Now, in the trunk, I keep a small suitcase with a full maid's uniform. *My* armor. With everything happening so fast back at the hospital, I let my guard down and didn't put it on."

Horrified, I turned to the passing farmlands, haunted with a different anger—a helpless one that knocks late at night, leaving one to bury their anguish into a pillow.

Soon, the sun bedded, pulling on its blanket of darkness. From far away, lightning flashed across the skies as outside breezes curled over my drowsy lids, tossing my stringy hair. I rested my head against the seat, watching the headlights bounce over fog-soaked fields of sweet hay, the light chewing across the summer night.

Weren't long before I drifted into the tires' hum, and Mrs. Claxton's warbled singsongs lulled me to sleep.

I awoke when the automobile bounced across a deep rut in the road. As I straightened, I winced and kneaded my temples where another painful headache gripped and refused to let go.

Again, I poked at my belly, this time a little firmer. Twice. And once more.

The tiny butterfly child did not awaken.

In the darkness, I leaned over the floorboard and fought back the tears as a sharp pain stabbed deep into my gut.

"You awake, Cussy?"

Struggling to breathe, I pulled myself up as the effects from Saturday's automobile accident set more firmly in, my backside tender and pained. Despite the July night, my teeth chattered. "Wh-what's the name of that t-town a-gain?" I lifted the tail of my blouse and wiped the cold damp from my face.

"We're heading into Defiance, Ohio, right now, chile. Our secret's safe. You've been offered a sanctuary. And as Mad

Anthony up here once proclaimed to our old Kentucky general and governor, the Honorable Charles Scott, *I defy the English, Indians, and all the devils of hell to take it.*"

She reached over, fumbled for my palm, and clasped tight. "My folks always said the mothers of our mountains will watch over us. I've got the mantle now. When it passes to you, be ready to carry it for the baby. For now, just rest, Cussy."

In the darkness I squeezed back and suddenly felt the ol' woman's courage, and my dear Honey and Loretta's spirits. The mothers, daughters, and granddaughters of Kaintuck's vigilant mountains lifted from the librarian's fiery temperament and latched hold. A defiance strengthened her knotty grip, and I know'd somehow she'd fight all the devils in hell to protect her watch.

Forty-Seven

DEFIANCE, OHIO, 1953

Secrets were guarded.

Mrs. Claxton had kept her word when she dropped me off four months ago.

From inside the boardinghouse, I peered out the curtain, then ran into the boot room. "He's finally here, Miss Rose. Just in time for Thanksgiving!"

"Don't you *dare* be going out there in that snowstorm, Angeline Moffit." She used the name on my official baptismal and library records. "The walks are downright slippery! Get back in here. You could fall and break your neck—"

"I'll be careful," I promised Mrs. Claxton's sister, grateful for her generosity these past months. As soon as I had arrived in July, she'd given me a job cleaning the seven-room house and keeping her rental records in exchange for a clean room and a small weekly wage.

Only two blocks from the Carnegie Library and the confluence of the Auglaize and Maumee Rivers, the charming lodging she'd named the Rose & Shine was popular with motorists of all kinds. We'd welcomed weary businessmen traveling to and from Chicago, Detroit, and Toledo and parents visiting their young'uns at the local college.

For one week in October, the rooms had been packed with

families. I was surprised to learn they were Kentucky folks who visited every year to honor the three hundred soldiers buried at the Old Kentucky Burial Grounds in Defiance. Rose would spoil them with hearty meals using recipes from back home in Fishtrap while I'd marvel over the long trip they'd made to commemorate their fallen ancestors.

Like those in Louisville, most up here seemed to pay little attention to my peculiarity. Didn't feel the need to leave a room when I entered, nor give wide berth in passing on the street. A curious glance lasted only a moment before they cast their eyes back to the task at hand.

Miss Rose called out again, fussing.

Excited, I shoveled my feet into the boots.

She wagged her head. "It's dangerous out there in this weather. Put on your coat and mittens. Here, take this hat—Come back here, young lady, and put on these woolen mittens!"

I tugged and pulled on the hat and coat, and ran out into the falling snow, away from her scolding tongue.

Howling November winds curled around empty snowy streets as he made his way to me, hobbling up the walk with a crooked stick.

"I've tended to all my affairs and come to take care of my woman. *My bride*," the first words I'd heard from him since our last morning together in Thousandsticks.

"*Jackson*," I cried out, and flung my arms around his neck. "*You're finally here*."

"Cussy Mary." He stepped back to get a good look at me. Jackson's voice grew thick and gravelly. "*Finally*. Half of me has been missing for far too long."

He threw down the stick and pulled me close, dropping hungry kisses over my face and lips.

Opening my coat, he knelt onto the cold, snowy ground and brushed his lips across my belly, a low whirr hitched to his weary voice. "How much longer?"

"Near Christmas, the best we can tell." I reached for his hand and helped pull him up.

He latched hold of me, steadying us as he pulled out papers from his coat.

With trembling hands, I read his official release letter, which was dated over a month ago, and glanced at the city newspaper clipping from July 14. A single sentence had been cobbled for my obituary.

> On Saturday July 11th, a state inmate was struck by an automobile on Walnut Street and later succumbed to their injuries at Louisville General Hospital.

Jackson removed his hat and shook off the snow, puffs of cold breaths whisking into his words. "I visited Honey and told her you were safe, reminded our daughter she must not speak to anyone about you or where you're at—anything that's happened. She's smart and sends her love. Don't fret. And lastly, you'll be happy to hear I sold the Thousandsticks homestead for a fair price."

At this, an ache clouded our joyful reunion. I had longed for us to all be united and began to wonder if I would ever see Honey again.

Jackson sensed the change of mood and gathered my hands in his. "There's not a day that I don't ache for our daughter and home. We must be careful until I get us safely back one day."

Miss Rose called out from the door, "Welcome, sir. Happy Thanksgiving."

Jackson returned the greeting.

She hollered again, "I'm happy you've arrived safely, and I'll telephone Effie the news, but the doctor has ordered bed rest for your wife. Now, get her back inside 'fore she births that baby out in the snow." She huffed. "Foolish young people gonna catch your death of cold and mark that unborn an orphan!"

Jackson dropped his gaze to me, his eyes bright. "I'll make sure she stays warm, ma'am," he told her, then pulled me into a shameless, fiery kiss.

Forty-Eight

After supper, Rose retired early to her room. Jackson poured himself a cup of coffee and we sat at the kitchen table, where I pressed him for more news from home. *Honey.*

"Honey's healthy and growing up fast," he said. "Too fast, as a matter of fact. Going steady with a boy named Francis. Wears his ring, even. I had a mind to light your old courting candle when he came a'callin' one night too many."

I pictured Jackson adjusting the taper to burn for the shortest time to signal the beau's early departure and raised a disapproving brow. "My dear daughter," I whispered, relieved there was no mention of an engagement but alarmed at the thought of reviving Pa's ol' timekeeping ritual.

I'd suffered misery at the hands of Pa using it to screen his only daughter's potential suitors. Pa'd lit dozens of candles. A taper raised tall to burn meant a lengthy visit with a beau and the father's approval, but if the candle was tamped down, it would signal a shorter one was in order. Desperate to see me wed, growing sicker from the black lung, he'd eventually cranked up the ol' courting candle to burn for alarming lengths of time to lure a marriage proposal.

Many times, I'd sneak and reset the taper for a quick burn, or toss the spiral wrought-iron courting candle out into the yard after Pa left for the mine.

I rebelled at the idea that a mere candle could hold so much power over me, determine one's lifelong misery or joy. But growing increasingly worried for my safety, Pa lit it for what he thought was one last time for ol' squire Frazier, then immediately handed me over to the devil man, convinced he would protect me when Pa no longer could.

Jackson reached for my hand. "Junia was beside herself. The old apostle girl was fit to be tied when she saw me. Whimpering, hanging her head over my shoulder, carrying on something awful. Knocking that stubborn jaw against my back, sniffing my pockets like I was hiding something from her. Though I suspect the behavior was because I hadn't brought you." His solemn face opened with a wistful grin.

"Does Honey have everything she needs? Is Junia well?"

"Honey and Junia are thriving in the old Carter homestead. You'd be proud. They're taking care of each other just fine, so don't you fret another minute. Junia protects her young book mistress just like she did you. Honey's doing right nice by her new mule, Willa, as well."

We walked to our room, and Jackson spoke softly. "Now, about that courting candle: I needn't light it." A mischievous grin twitched on his lips. "Old Junia ran the pestering boy off for me."

I couldn't help but smile, thinking about Honey's letters of Junia's obstinance toward Francis, the mule taking over the duty of timekeeper. Protector.

For days, Jackson busied himself, tending to Rose's chores that had long been neglected. He replaced several busted window sashes and repaired the broken lock on the basement door. Making several trips, he limped out to the woodshed to fetch wood for the small fireplaces in the guest rooms. Then he went to town and purchased Miss Rose's supplies, hauling in bags full of toiletries, cleaning disinfectants, and food.

She was grateful for the needed repairs and extra help in the icy throes of winter. When Miss Rose tried to pay him, he balked and said our lodging was payment enough.

In between the work, Jackson worried for news of any labor pains I might be having. And as the birth neared, my own worrisome thoughts plagued me during most of my waking hours and into the late nights. *Would the child be healthy?*

The fear had taken on a life of its own. Just yesterday, I stored the feather pillow inside Miss Rose's closet that I'd been using. Instead, I set about taking clean rags to stuff a bed pillow for my own.

When Jackson looked at me puzzled, I didn't tell him about the angel crown left on our porch in Thousandsticks, just busied myself righting the new pillow on my side of the bed.

I couldn't take any chances.

On the eleventh of December, I felt the first spasms of labor strike at dusk. At once, Rose called the doctor, but the wires were silent. A raging snowstorm had gripped the town, knocking down telephone lines. Still, she tried to get hold of the switchboard operator to help connect her to the town midwife, and then again to the doctor when my pains grew unbearable. But it was useless.

Several hours later, Rose slammed the bulky receiver down in the cradle, then picked it up again and listened once more for a ringtone. Growing more frustrated, she gave up.

In bed, I gripped the mattress and moaned into the cotton sheets as the pains roiled over me.

Jackson put his hand over mine.

Miss Rose rounded the bed to my other side. "I've assisted our midwife here several times. And Mama with my two brothers and a sister before that. That'd be my sweet Effie." Her wise ol' eyes ballooned as she soothed me. "Don't you worry. Just four years ago, I delivered a healthy baby girl to a couple who took lodging for the night." She smacked her hands. "I'll just have to do."

The woman fretted a moment, then moved about the room barking orders to Jackson. "Get water and towels. Fill that washstand over there. More bedding is down the hall. In the green closet." She fluffed my homemade pillow. "And get her one of my nice feather pillows from a guest room."

"*No*," I said sharply, stopping her in her tracks. "No pillow, Miss Rose."

She frowned. "Put on the kettle, Jackson. Then bring in a stack of wood and get a fire going in here," Rose said.

Jackson flushed, his apprehension growing. "Should I go fetch the doctor?" He kissed my forehead.

"No. Stay with me."

"Just like a man getting foolish notions that'll get him killed. Sir, you won't get a block in this bitter weather. This child will need a father. Get the water on and bring me towels. Now!" Rose ordered.

Jackson looked torn and glanced over at Miss Rose, concerned if she was up to delivering a child.

"Don't go out there," I pleaded.

"You better get those towels right now 'fore I strip off your clothing and use them instead. Go on now, scat. Your woman's gonna be just fine," Rose ordered, wiping her tired eyes.

When morning broke on the twelfth of December, the babe still had not come, and Miss Rose's face took on a bigger worry as she sat in the chair in the corner of my room watching over me.

The labor pains intensified, stealing my breaths. Rose would rise and examine me several times, then slowly shake her head.

Close to noon, she peeked under the covers one last time and then checked the clock and smiled. "The babe is finally coming. Gonna be here in just a bit, Angeline."

My chin quivered as the memories of Susan's haunting words tumbled around my mind: *We won't truly know if the drug harmed the infant until the birth.*

Rose cut the umbilical cord, then placed the quiet infant on a towel atop the dresser instead of handing the babe to me. She rubbed a hand over the tiny back, patted and lifted the babe to her ear. Again, she repeated the steps.

But the child remained silent.

"What is it, Miss Rose?" I squinted, struggled to rise, straining my neck to get a better glimpse.

She clenched her jaw and rubbed the baby's back a little bit firmer.

Jackson dropped my hand and crossed over to her.

"Give me the baby. *Jackson, Miss Rose?*" I shrilled.

Jackson glanced at me, then turned back to the baby, but not before I saw the terror building in his eyes.

I pulled myself up on my elbows. Again, Rose rubbed the tiny bluish-gray back. Then she lifted the baby by the feet and smacked the child's bottom.

Panic grabbed hold and I couldn't stop shivering. "*Rose. No, Ro—*" My words knotted.

Jackson looked over his shoulder once more, something unfettered and desperate spreading across his face.

I swallowed hard, the words squeaking out, "*My babe, my babe.* Tell me my child is okay. *Tell me!*"

Then Rose did something I'd never seen before. She put her lips over the baby's mouth and nose and blew once and then again.

I pressed my hands over my ears. For a moment the silence was suffocating.

"*No—*" I screamed, just as the babe's lusty wail filled the room.

Then the baby sputtered out soft sneezes and squalled again.

Weeping, I collapsed onto the pillow, a fist pressed to my riotous heart.

"Okay, okay, you're safe." Rose sighed loudly and bobbed her head, rocking the infant in her arms, rubbing the back. "There you go, little one. There you go. Another breath. There you go.

You just needed some assistance, didn't you, sweetheart?" She closed her eyes and whispered a prayer of gratitude.

"You saved our baby's life, Miss Rose. We can never thank you enough," I sobbed.

"Rebecca, our granny woman back home in Fishtrap, did the exact same for a difficult delivery," Rose said, beaming.

Jackson's eyes filled and he placed a tender hand on Rose's small shoulder and murmured his gratitude.

"Such a tiresome journey, sweetheart," she cooed and carried the babe over to the bed. "Not to worry. The color's back now. And he's bald and blessed."

"*A healthy boy*," Jackson barely breathed.

He'd fought so hard to come into the world, to live, my greedy hands ached to hold him.

Rose passed the newborn to Jackson while she tended to the afterbirth. He tilted the baby down so I could see, then placed him into my arms.

I peered down at Elijah Jack Lovett, the names of both our fathers. Lifted his tiny fingers and toes, inspecting every inch of him. He had Pa's eyes. I was sure of it.

I wiped my own and examined him again. Our son had been spared the punishing side effects of the blue drug—and was safe from the blue-skinned misery that would have forever marked him as a target for hostile folks' mocking, cruel laughter, and taunts.

I pressed my lips onto the babe's cheeks and tip of his head, then drew my gaze to Jackson. "He's a handsome one," he said, dropping breezes of kisses to both our faces.

After a few minutes, Miss Rose washed the babe in the wooden stand's porcelain basin. When she had wrapped him in a towel, she handed the wide-eyed infant back.

Satisfied, Miss Rose pulled a celebratory cigar from her apron pocket and gave it to Jackson. "Been waiting a while to give this to you, *Papa*. It's one of the finest from Defiance Drugs & Liquors. Go on, take it downstairs to the parlor. This mother needs to nurse now." She shooed Jackson out. "Yes, sir, sweetheart, you're blessed for a healthy life." The woman ran a gnarled finger over his head.

I traced the boy's soft, wrinkled forehead and smiled at the ol' mountain wives' tale that foretold a child born with long hair is born old. Back home, granny woman Emma would insist such a babe would live sickly because all his might had been spent on growing hair.

Miss Rose squeezed my hand and I pressed a kiss to it, eternally grateful for her wisdom and quick actions.

"Well, now, let's try and feed little Elijah Jack. Nothing better than your milk to *keep* him healthy." The hungry babe rooted and latched on. Minutes later, he was asleep in my arms.

After she'd placed him in the bassinet, she took off her apron and draped it over an arm. "You should rest now. I'll just go check on the new papa. Maybe have ourselves a festive *drink* to celebrate Elijah Jack's birthday."

He was a content infant, and I couldn't stop marveling over our good fortune, despite Jackson's troubling glances I'd catch from time to time when he thought I weren't looking.

Occasionally, he'd bring up talk about moving to another city. Getting work. But I protested, insisting the babe was too young, or Rose still needed our help with one thing or another.

It was not enough; Jackson's unsettling spirit would not stay quiet.

Forty-Nine

Elijah Jack was almost two weeks old when Rose said, "It's nearly Christmas. Defiance will have on her finest holiday dress. It's a spectacle. Go see it and enjoy yourselves. Be sure and stop in at Bud's restaurant and have yourself some delicious lake perch." She rocked the baby in her arms and patted his bottom, shooing us toward the door after passing a small shopping list to me.

Eager to visit the hardware store, Jackson quickly accepted her offer.

In town, I bought diaper cloths, Oxydol washing powders, and a few candles Rose requested for the guest rooms while Jackson shopped over at the hardware store for a new latch for her busted gate and a rope cord and pulley for an upstairs window.

Although cold, it was an eye-scaldingly bright day, and the town carried the sparkles of Christmas finery. Lampposts were dressed in holly and evergreens. Shop windows displayed scenes of toys, dollies, sleds, skates, and wrapped presents with shiny bows that rested atop snowy blankets of sparkled cotton.

I slipped up beside a small boy who had his nose and face smashed to one of the windows, and I smiled at the child's wonderment. A mix of pine, gingerbread, Christmas oranges, and cinnamon wafted out of doors, and like the young'un, I marveled at all the regalia and drooled over the candied almonds, an invitation to step inside.

On a corner, a bundled vendor hawked his pine wreaths and cord-wrapped spruces as families waded through rows searching for the perfect tree. I walked the pathways a bit, then stopped.

Suddenly, the pine aromas pulled me back to the hills—to the crowning balsam paths Junia had ridden us on. I closed my eyes and inhaled the perfumes, thinking of the apostle gal who'd been my loyal protector for so long. Ol' Junia riding us through those rough, winding hills to get me safely home night after night. Through winter's snowy drifts and summer's prickly brambles. How I yearned for one more ride with her. Longed to be home for Christmas with Honey.

A giggling couple whisked past me, and I breathed in the fragrance one last time before moving along.

Later, I met up with Jackson in front of the drugstore. "I searched inside the hardware store but couldn't find you."

"I was rummaging through their supply room in the back to find the right-size pulley." He pulled the small bag from a pocket and inspected inside. "The house is so old; I should replace all the sash cords on those heavy double-hung windows for her safety. They only had the two at the hardware, but the clerk said he'd have more in next week. Rose can't risk a guest losing a finger if another rope breaks."

We stopped in to have dinner at Bud's restaurant, then strolled down the streets, pausing to admire the treasures inside shop windows. When we turned away from one display, Jackson stiffened and pulled me back to the glass. "Keep your eyes on the window dressing. Don't let him see you."

"Who, Jack—"

He lifted a finger to his lips.

I tucked the coat tighter to my chin, twisted slightly toward the sidewalk.

"Chester," Jackson called out, extending an arm and turning him away from the display.

"Well, Jackson Lovett, as I live and breathe." He shook

Jackson's hand. "Why, just in October, I met up with some other Kentucky folks. They were visiting the old soldiers' burial ground. Every year I see more of our people trekking this way to visit kinsmen lost in the battle." Chester pulled him into a hug and thumped his back.

"I heard they'd been in town." Jackson grinned, returning the friendly slap.

"It's always good to run into an old pal." Chester shared gossip about the Kentucky visitors for a few more minutes while Jackson smiled, enjoying the chatter. Then: "Hey, Jackson, a couple years back, a feller from your neck of the woods made the trip up here to the burial grounds looking for his kin. You might know him." He scratched his wool cap. "He was a tall, older feller named Davies, uh... Can't recall the full name right now, but maybe you'll know it." Chester rooted again in his mind. "Oh, yeah, I 'member something else. He said he'd been the sheriff of Troublesome for a bit and he'd be back soon enough. I looked for him this year, and I found out..."

The rest of his words were interrupted by noisy passersby. But I heard enough to realize it was Ken Davies, the very same sheriff who had torn up our marriage license and made it his moral duty to keep Jackson banned from Kentucky. That he had traveled here, walked these same streets, knocked the soft blue from my skin.

Jackson shifted his stance but remained quiet while Chester rambled on.

"Now, last I heard you were going to settle back down in Troublesome Creek? That must have been ten or more years ago. Myself, I haven't been back to Hyden for at least two decades."

"I stayed a while but had to move on," Jackson said.

"I sure do miss it sometimes," Chester said wistfully. "We had us a traveling Methodist preacher come through a few years back. I'll never forget when he found himself failing to describe heaven to the congregation, he simply exclaimed, *O my dear Honeys, Heaven is a Kentucky of a place.*"

The men grew somber, each seeming to reflect on home.

Then Chester asked, "Did you ever get hitched?"

"I did." Jackson dipped his head and said, "But I lost her not long ago."

Chester spilled kind condolences. Then he asked, "Are you here for a while?"

I tugged the coat down a bit, stretching an ear toward the men's conversation.

"Visiting, but heading to Toledo to see a man about a job," Jackson fibbed.

"I've been here now for seven years. There's plenty of good work in Defiance, pal. The town's been building on the canals and—"

"I've already set my sights on Toledo, but I'll keep it in mind should plans change." Jackson snuck a peek at me, jingled the coins in his pants pockets.

"It would be nice working together again. Better working conditions too. They got themselves some decent camp houses here." Chester quieted. "Say, what are they paying there in Toledo?"

"About to find out." He patted Chester's shoulder and moved away slightly. "I'm fixin' to head back to my room. I've got business to wrap up before I leave town. Merry Christmas."

When Chester crossed the street and turned a corner, Jackson stole over to me.

"Who was that, Jackson? What did he say he found out about the sheriff? Jackson?"

He stared after him, lost in thought. "Chester's just a Kentucky fella I worked with long ago on the Boulder Dam project. We had another buddy who was a high scaler, repelling down the giant canyon walls. We lost him after a rope broke. I was able to help Chester when the same thing happened to him a week later."

Jackson rarely talked about his work on Boulder Dam or, as most called it now, Hoover Dam. But I'd read that over one hundred men lost their lives building it and that the one job requirement called only for *men of strength, and cowards need not apply*.

I followed Jackson's eyes to where his friend had rounded the corner. "Are you concerned about the sheriff? Chester talking? Why did you tell him Toledo? I'm not ready to move Elijah Jack just yet."

"Don't you fret now. It's Christmas. Come on, let's have us a lil cheer." He pulled me under the shop's alcove and reached inside his coat and handed me a small box with a festive ribbon.

"But I didn't get you—"

He pressed a finger to my lips. "I have you. I don't need one more thing."

I untied the ribbon and held up an exquisite, gold-blushed hankie made of silk and the finest laces, embroidered with delicate flowers and sprigs.

"You never had yourself a proper bridal trousseau on our wedding day."

Jackson dug into another pocket. "When we were arrested, the law took away our rings." He pushed a gold band onto my finger. "Cussy Mary, I promise, I won't allow anyone, God or man, to thieve our time, take my bride from me ever again. I will not lose another minute of us together." A fire latched on to his promise.

My love and gratitude for him sprung to my eyes.

He nudged his chin to the mistletoe hanging above us, the wind tangling the festive red ribbon it was tethered to, then pressed his promise onto my lips, erasing my apprehension.

But with each passing day, he brooded, mulling over our safety, certain that word *would* get out. We might run into the Kentucky sheriff or Chester again. More Kentucky folks visiting their kin in the soldiers' graveyard. Fretted about the law, and what would happen to our son if we were caught. "We need to go where we can lose ourselves in a crowd of millions," he'd say.

Millions. Louisville had been big enough, but I couldn't imagine living in such a place. It sounded terrifying. Smothering. And it left me wondering how folks could breathe, packed in and stealing each other's air like that.

I'd been foolish, so busy with Elijah Jack and enjoying our newfound happiness, I'd pushed my cautions aside, stepped right into the shoes of a free dead woman, and learned how to breathe again.

The new baby had left me with bear teeth, a power I hadn't felt since the birth of Honey, but the mantle I carried to protect us grew heavier, the load more difficult.

The air had changed since we ran into Chester. Jackson had become more cautious and began looking over his shoulder. I found myself skittish at every strange noise, spending too much time sneaking peeks out Rose's windows.

For days our voices lingered in darkened hallways and crannies of the ol' boardinghouse as I clutched the baby close, an alarm pummeling my flesh.

Jackson reminded me that the child of an immoral blue heathen would be easy prey and quickly snatched into the law's cruel, iron grip, lost to the whims and misplaced paperwork of yawning officials in any one of many wrong states. Worse, he'd likely be locked away and experimented on.

"It's dangerous to stay any longer," he'd insisted yesterday as I placed Elijah Jack inside his bassinette. "That sheriff could show up in this town any day."

Exasperated, I held up a hand to tamp the discussion, collect my muddled thoughts. "Likely if he comes, it won't be until the Kentucky men make their fall pilgrimage."

"Cussy Mary." He fumbled a curse slipping off his tongue. "*Angeline*. I won't ever lose you again. I must keep you and our son safe." He kissed my forehead, the words fevered against my flesh. "I won't lose another child. *Us*."

But as Christmas came and went, I grew moody, plagued by thoughts of my daughter living alone. Agonized over the family she'd now lost and how I could give it back to her.

"It's too dangerous here," Jackson pressed again as I cleaned a guest room in the early morning.

Torn, I spun around. "What about Honey? It's dangerous leaving our daughter all alone! The hills are raising her, and it should be me," I lashed out, not sure what had gotten into me. "She needs her mama, Jackson." I anguished over the thought of not being there to protect her, help her through the rough patches a young girl faced. Listen to her hopes and dreams. Witness her growing into a woman.

He shook his head.

"Jackson, I don't want Devil John and Martha Hannah giving their blessing for any marriage proposal that might be coming. I need to be closer to Honey. The thought of moving farther from Kaintuck and to a bigger city feels like I'm losing her forever."

"You know that as a condition of my release, I had to agree to a banishment from home for twenty-five years. And if you're found alive, people like that meddling sheriff would like nothing better than to cause you grave harm. I would follow you to the ends of this tired old earth—back to our Kentucky and hide you in them hills again if I could keep you safe and be with our daughter. But we can't chance the law coming down on us and our son becoming an orphan."

"If only there was a way to be closer."

"Honey has been emancipated. She is safe and free. But we can never forget: We are not."

From the bed, two-month-old Elijah Jack kicked the knitted blanket off his legs. Patiently, Rose tucked it back around him, then lifted the babe up and kissed the top of his head. "You be a good boy for your mama, sweetheart. Grow up and be even a *finer* man for a good woman. Like your papa."

She gripped my hand, the scent of powdered roses wafting around her. "I sure will miss you around here." She fiddled with the angel brooch Jackson had given her for Christmas. "And my sweet Elijah. You did a good job cleaning and keeping the records. Jackson's been a blessing and the home's never looked better. It's been a big help for this old woman." She held up money. "Here's your last pay. Write to me, Angeline."

"I will as soon as we settle. But you keep it, Miss Rose." I pushed away her hand. "Jackson has work waiting for him in the masonry business, and his lawyers have wired our funds from the sale of our home. We'll be fine, ma'am." But my words were weighted with doubt.

"I know you'll be fine, young lady. Just *fine*." She lifted her stubborn chin bone, reminding me of Mrs. Claxton and my ol' Loretta. "Just the same, a smart lady should *always* have her some sneaky-Pete money set aside for emergencies. Pete being my grandfather and what Grandma taught me long ago after he went on one too many tears. Not that yours ever will, but... No need telling the menfolk now." She rolled the bills inside the baby's blanket and tucked tight.

From inside the pickup truck, I stared out, weary at having to put down roots again, anxious to one day be *fine*. Free of the laws that had shackled us to a nomad's life.

I pulled the bundled infant closer and nodded to Jackson.

The truck roared to life, and he shifted it into gear, the loudness awakening sleeping pigeons perched on snow-covered roofs.

On the porch, Rose stood squint-eyed in her thread-worn flowered duster, a lace shawl to her chest, her darkened frame frail against the blowing snow that bibbed her grayed cropped curls. She raised a gnarled hand, slowly waved, and I pressed my burning farewell onto the glass.

Fifty

We left Defiance for the noisy pockets of Detroit and settled into a small two-bedroom clapboard postage-stamped in between matching homes on Neff Avenue. There we folded ourselves in with the millions of other industrial working folks—a yearning for my dear Honey and Junia, the ol' grandmother mountains of our beloved Kaintuck always present and pulling.

Honey would give us a respite, visiting from time to time, but saying farewells opened old wounds and left us all gloomy for days.

Still, we could never go back with our past hitched so close, tempting the fates on such whims.

My kitchen calendar was a slow-ticking reminder that it was only 1964 and we still had fourteen more years to go until Jackson's banishment from Kentucky was lifted. My own, now infinite.

Today, under muted Detroit skies, I made my way home from the library where I worked as an assistant three days a week.

I'd parted ways with one of my patrons just a block from home. Looking over my shoulder, I quickened my steps, knowing Jackson would fuss.

Know'd I couldn't risk it happening again.

A few months ago, I'd left the library after dark when two boys snuck up behind me only a few blocks from home and demanded my pocketbook. They didn't look but maybe three or four years older than my eleven-year-old Elijah Jack.

I'd backed up to a streetlamp. The lanky one pulled out a knife and tried to snatch it from my hands.

But I yanked it away.

"Lady, gimme your purse," he'd demanded, wriggling the long knife.

The boy looked more frightened than me, and his hand shook as he swiped a dangling curl from his brow.

"I don't have money, young man."

"*Now*," he yelled as his friend nervously glanced around.

My backside brushed against the light pole. "I only have books." I breathed heavily, snugging the bulky pocketbook closer to my body, its contents full of dime paperbacks I'd borrowed from the library and the forged baptismal record and library card. More precious than gold, the documents had given me safe passage for years. And I'd kept them hidden in the inside compartment and always within arm's reach.

"Gimme the bag, or I'll slice you from gut to chin."

There was something in his eyes that said he'd do just that and I saw in his blackened soul that he might've done it before.

Pa's gravelly words had rose from the grave and nipped at my bone: *Daughter, like the bear or bobcat that makes itself bigger, never show fear, only your might.*

I puffed up as best I could and squared my shoulders. "I reckon you're gonna have to do some bloodletting to steal my pocketbook." I pressed it tighter to my chest. "But I have to warn you boys, I'm a Blue, and my blood carries the blue curse," I hissed, struck out my chin.

They both stared at me a moment, taken aback.

"A pox that you and your kin will carry for two hundred years!" I raised an ink-stained finger, warning.

"Let's go," the other boy said and slapped his arm. "She's a loco witch for sure. Just look at her. One of them gypsy freaks that'll curse our asses forever."

"Ain't leaving without it. Lady, gimme that damn purse, and hand over your jewelry." The boy pointed the knife at my wedding ring. "Grab her, Clancy." He motioned to his friend, then to me with the weapon. "Gimme it now!"

Clancy side-eyed me and shook his head. "Nuh-uh, I'm gonna beat feet. Ain't getting no blue cootie curse." He lit off.

The boy yelled after him, darting his bottle-brown eyes between his fleeing friend and me. Then he lunged with the knife. I jerked away but still felt it slash across my wrist, the flash of pain slowly fading as my anger climbed.

His cowardly eyes bore into mine, and an unspoken dare lifted from my jutted chin.

A porch light flicked on and a man bellowed from his door. "Hey, what's going on out there?"

I took a step closer, raised the bloody wrist, and then stretched out my neck like an ol' snapping turtle and hissed again, but louder this time, the spittle flying off my teeth.

The boy shrank back, and his eyes bugged as he glimpsed the dripping blood. Shifting from one foot to the other, he jiggled the knife against his pants, then cursed loudly and scrambled away.

"What are you punks up to?" the man yelled again, then ran out with a baseball bat and gave chase to the hooligans.

Clutching my pocketbook, I eased down onto the edge of the chipped sidewalk with my shoes in the gutter. I'd peered at my chocolate-colored blood and suddenly burst into nervous titters as the fright finally hit. Cackled like the blue witch I had them believe me to be.

In a few minutes, a nearby rail car rumbled into a factory's whistle, beckoning the evening shift.

Straightening, I wiped away an amused tear and lifted my gratitude to Pa.

The doctor had given me seven stitches, though he was more fascinated about the color of my blood and blue-darkened flesh.

I'd said little, only that I was under the care of my family doctor and then added to the fib, *in Georgia*."

After he'd sewed me up, he called two other doctors and a

nurse into the room to ogle me. Jackson snapped and removed the doctor's fingers off my face. "We'll be taking our leave now. C'mon, Angeline." He'd pulled me away from their befuddled gazes and prying hands.

Jackson had driven me straight home. "And they didn't get your purse or jewelry?" he'd asked again, sneaking a puzzled glance at my bandages. "Those thieving thugs just ran away and without the goods?"

"I reckon the man done scared them off." I rested my head against the truck window and realized my carelessness. Know'd I could've been toe-tagged in the crowded city morgue where other poor victims rested eternal.

Eternal. It had been years since I thought about my angel crown. Or what I imagined more, a death crown. I had finally convinced myself it had been a prophecy for a blank page waiting for a new chapter. A rebirth from a troubled past... Though recently, I'd discarded my handmade bed pillows and purchased the latest in bedding after I had read the advertisement for the new store-bought polyester-filled ones—insisting Jackson also mail a pillow to Honey for good measure.

After Jackson dropped me off from the hospital, he'd grabbed his hunting knife and went looking for the boys. But they'd disappeared, and from the fright on their faces, likely into another rat-crawling crevice of the city's dark alleyways.

When he'd returned home, we'd talked in whispers inside our dimly lit bedroom while Elijah Jack slept.

Jackson had plied off his boots and said, "There was a recent article about a new medical study going on over in Cleveland. It could be a chance to go home when my banishment is lifted."

I'd turned away from him and kneaded my temples, a dull ache rising. I'd finally resigned myself to a life in Detroit to keep us safe. And we'd been on the run so long, sometimes I forgot what we were running from.

But as the years passed, Jackson soured on the city, longed to be free of the shackles of its cage. He'd point out homes where more and more folks had barred up their windows because of rising crime. "I'd take a shack in our hills over any of these expensive houses. Having the biggest here like that, well, hell's bells, it wouldn't be enough," he'd remarked.

Until that moment it had never occurred to me that *I* might not be enough for him.

"It's been a day." I'd lifted my bandaged wrist, hampering the talk of medical news.

"Medicine is changing, Cussy Mary. It's the sixties," Jackson had pressed. "And the advances they're making are like none this world has seen. Why look at what they've done now. We've got vaccines for polio and measles. They're even transplanting kidneys, livers. Hell, even lungs." He thumped his chest. "Every day brings more medical news. More miracles. Just think, if they could cure you, it would no longer be a burden for us."

"*Jackson.*" My voice cracked as I remembered Pa saying almost the same thing long ago when he tried to get me cured. Fought to marry me off.

"I'm sorry I'm a burden to you, Jackson. I give you permission to leave me," I'd barely breathed.

He'd jerked as if the words scalded him.

"I love you, but I don't want to be a weight that anchors you here. You can divorce me." Tears sprung to my eyes as heartbreak and misery squeezed the breath out of me, my hands night-sky-colored and trembling.

"Cussy Mary"—he'd choked—"I've been trying to find a way out of here to get back home." Jackson bowed his head, searching inside himself. Slowly, the words came. "But I would never leave my bride." He rubbed his thumb across my cheek. "We are more than man and wife. We're knitted in bone."

Jackson clutched hold of me and we'd wept quietly.

As I stood in front of our home today, I could hear Jackson and Elijah Jack working out back.

I paused to watch the neighbor girl, her braids slashing through the spring winds as she played hopscotch on the chalk-drawn sidewalk.

In the backyard, music thinned across a heavy truck's gasping airbrakes as I slipped through the gate.

Our gray-muzzled pup, Yeats, pushed himself up from the grass, wobbled, then found his starched legs and ambled over to greet me. I bent over and pulled his snout to my face, gingerly rubbed his ears and dropped kisses atop his head.

Jackson had found the flea-infested mutt nine years ago at his construction site. He'd scooped him up from a pile of dirt and rubble, and the pup quickly wriggled his way into our hearts.

Yeats followed me to the patio as Lesley Gore cried out "It's My Party." The snappy tunes drifted across the yard. Elijah Jack was fond of the strange new sounds called rock and roll, especially a group named after what sounded like a hardshell bug that had swept the airwaves. He carried his pocket transistor radio everywhere, the leather case worn and curling.

I watched the two of them work the narrow stretch of grass. The city garden never amounted to much, often struggling to produce, its soil hesitant to latch root. Still, every year Jackson insisted. And I know'd working the land, as tiny as it was, helped ease his pain of missing home.

We were lucky if we reaped enough tomatoes, heads of cabbage, and peppers for me to do a little canning. Jackson and Elijah Jack craved the chowchow relish I'd make and always hoped we could put up enough jars for the winter. It was Mama's recipe and when I prepared it, I could almost feel her hands folded over my childlike pudgy fingers of yesteryear, steadying the spoon, helping me measure just so.

I looked over at Elijah Jack and remembered the stir-offs in the fall where I'd helped make the sorghum syrup and biscuits. Pa would cut the stalks, press, strain, and boil the sweetening.

Come daylight, Mama would clean off an old tree stump and dump her dough atop it and we'd take turns beating the tarnation out of it. At least three hundred whacks. If coal miners from Pa's mine were coming, it had to always be six hundred and fifty wallops exact, until the air in the dough was just right.

Later, she'd pull an apron over my sack dress and let me stir the syrupy juices in Pa's metal tub until it thickened. Then Pa would drain the rich sorghum into buckets, leaving me with a full mason jar to pour over Mama's hot, beaten biscuits in the iron skillet she'd set warming atop the woodstove.

Elijah Jack would never experience the traditions from his kin, and at times the guilt kept me awake at night with a helplessness known only to those who had no way out.

My son lifted his damp brow and called out a greeting from the yard before driving the hoe back into the dirt.

I waved a bag full of rhubarb and strawberries my supervisor had shared with the librarians. "Brought your favorite."

Jackson startled and twisted around. "You were supposed to stay put until I fetched you home."

"I tried to telephone and let you know I was getting off early, but I reckon you've been busy out here. A gentleman patron walked me partway."

Relieved, Jackson pointed to the small patio table. "Bought you a paper today. Of all the wonders, there's news of the president visiting back home."

Curious, I placed the sack on the table and plucked up the April newspaper. Lately the front page screamed volatile reports about the war in Vietnam. Growing concerns of organized crime bosses and rising tension and civil unrest in the big cities as black folks rallied for their rights, and ugly brute forces pushed back.

The beginning of the sixties was a difficult time for all folks, and 1964 was proving no different. But today's headline bolded news on a different story about another holler not far from Troublesome.

Surprised, I peered closer at the photograph of President

Johnson squatting on the porch of a man named Tom Fletcher. The front page read, "President Kicks Off His War on Poverty in Inez, Kentucky."

Jackson dropped his shovel and smacked his hands as he walked over to the table and pecked me on the cheek. "They done went and told those people they were poor. Called 'em hillbillies. When there's never been a more self-reliant person in this world than a Kentucky man." He gave a short laugh, his stance proud. "We were rich until coal kings and government came in and fattened themselves off our minerals, the land and our people. For decades, newsmen and presidents have sneered at us from a distance while guzzling down our fine Kentucky whiskeys from their fancy crystal glassware."

He sounded a lot more like Pa with each passing year, the news rising a rebellious spirit.

I scanned the article. They'd found a couple with *eight children living in a decrepit house*, the paper read. It reported that their living condition weren't nothing more than a tar paper shack, despite the photograph showed it was a shingled brick-patterned siding that looked neat and nearly new. The article stated Mr. Fletcher was unemployed, noted his bad teeth, and that the family was only given a few hours' notice to play host to the president.

The young'uns looked healthy and well fed, long past the ugly days when the Depression and pellagra bit at our backs.

Mr. Fletcher's daughters wore homespun play dresses, and the sons had trimmed haircuts and sported clean britches and sturdy shoes.

The family seemed robust and doing fine.

Jackson wiped his brow and muttered, "It's not our people who's poor; it's the miserable ones crammed inside this Motor City's hot tin box."

A lot of families had struck out from the South to cash in on better jobs, bigger pay. I looked out toward the smokestacks that soldiered the town. Most days the city belched its angry whistles signaling another factory shift change, folding into the wails of fire trucks and police vehicles.

"I reckon if the rich tell the small folk they're poor long enough, they'll start believing it," I said quietly.

Again, I glanced up toward the winter-baked Detroit skies, the color a constant dismal gray through the seasons. Pondering, I couldn't recall a single morning where I'd seen a children's moon since we'd arrived eleven years ago. The smoking factories had choked out the blue and robbed the cityfolk of the spectacle.

I sighed and steered the conversation to a lighter subject. "They're getting electricity up into the hills now; did you see it, Jackson?"

He hovered over my shoulder as I studied another photograph of the Kentucky family. It showed a long wooden porch with new plank boards, and I spied a meter where electricity was attached to the home. I lingered over Lady Bird's fashionable spring dress, coat, matching hat and shoes. "She's a right elegant First Lady," I told him. "They say she loves flowers and is planting them on highways, in cities and parks. Going to beautify America."

"We could use some of that beauty here. I'm headed down to the stockyards to get manure. Try to turn this sandy clay they call dirt." He motioned to Elijah Jack. "Come on, son, let's go get that load now."

The boy had his ear glued to the transistor radio. He'd lost interest in books this past year, drawn more to the *wilded music*, as Jackson called it, fretting. Sometimes he'd sneak books into Elijah Jack's room or purchase comics from the drugstore rack to coax him back into reading.

Instead, the boy snatched up the S&H Green Stamps we'd earn from grocery and gasoline purchases and paste them into the booklets. He had his eye on the wooden guitar on the S&H catalog cover he'd hung above his dresser. The inviting scene on the catalog showed two young'uns playing the guitar and record player, while two others pretended to fish from new poles inside a spiffed-up modern living room.

"Elijah Jack, put that radio away and let's get. We need to finish this garden today." Jackson dug into his pocket for the truck keys.

I reached for his arm. "Maybe we can go for a picnic this weekend instead of driving over to West Canfield? It'd be nice to go over to Bald Mountain and enjoy some fishing."

For all his fussing, Jackson spent many weekends looking at the older houses of the city, driving the fine neighborhoods with wide streets and welcoming bungalows. It was a sight to reckon with, and he'd marvel over the rich architecture and fascinating details of craftsmanship that graced Detroit. In the spring and fall, we'd walk West Canfield and admire the elegance of the stately mansions before heading back to our street with its rows of white homes that looked no bigger than dollhouses.

"I'll get your dinner basket down from the attic when I return if you'll promise to pack it with your fried rhubarb and berry pies. He planted a kiss on my forehead. "Let's get this sorry excuse for a garden fertilized," he told Elijah Jack.

Jackson was still miserable for home, and it folded into my own longing. The rumblings always seemed to arrive with the first buds of spring—his first turn of dirt.

And though we hadn't talked again of the long-ago evening when I told him he could leave, the offer was always sitting there like a small creek stone that had been smoothed by worrying fingers, scarred from battle-worn hairline cracks, waiting to shatter.

Often, Jackson would grumble on the back porch during the loud summers. "Hear that?" he'd say. "It's what's missing. What young Elijah Jack will never hear. The soft paws of forest critters and running brooks. Our singing pines. Remember it all? Why, you could even hear the acorns drop in autumn. Here, we are nothing but birds without song."

I'd studied and soon realized we'd lost so much of what made us.

Sometimes we'd both still to the grated cries of a dull catbird that mimicked the grinding charrs of the city, then search the smoky skies, pining for the cheered calls and slow trills of the colorful red cardinal back home.

Always he'd catch my eye, and together we were pulled back into our feral hearts inside the mist-kissed woodlands. There, I'd walk free alongside him on winding paths of moss and trillium, the murmurous forest floor my slippers.

As the years passed, we barely spoke of the mountains we call home.

Spoken even rarer these days, but always there, the longing could not stay silenced.

Fifty-One

On a misting June morning, I lifted my head to the screech of brakes and glanced up at the clock, then over to the hanging 1967 Ford automobile calendar that the filling station handed out to customers each Christmas.

I squinted and looked again.

Weren't nothing written down on its square today.

I knelt back over the kitchen floor and scrubbed the last patch of dull linoleum, then stopped to stretch before knee-walking over to the bucket, my bones tender and burning.

Jackson would always fuss and point to the cotton string mop that had hung untouched in our kitchen corner for years. But the city dirt always found its way back inside, wormed itself into cat-eyed cracks that a factory mop couldn't swipe away. Same as Troublesome's coal dust I used to sweep out as a child.

"Angeline. *Cussy, Cussy Mary!*" he hollered from outside.

Dropping the rag into the pail of water, I pulled myself up and arched my back, a question braided across my brow.

Jackson flung open the door, a newspaper in one hand and a small bouquet of flowers in the other.

"Leave your wet boots on the mat, I've just mopped. What's all this? Why are you home at this hour?"

Jackson's eyes glinted with a mixture of playfulness and something bold I couldn't put my finger on. He waved the newspaper then tossed it and the flowers onto the table.

I moved closer. "What's got into you? Did I forget—"

He swept me up in his arms. Twirled us around with a might I hadn't seen in years, almost losing his footing. Then his face pained when another hitch grabbed hold of his bad leg.

"*Jackson!*" I squealed. "Put me down 'fore you hurt your good leg." He planted me firmly on my feet, and I playfully batted him away. "There's nothing on my calendar today." I smoothed down my rumpled duster.

"Mark it now to pack our suitcases; I'm taking my bride home." He nudged his chin toward the newspaper.

Puzzled, I stepped over to the table and read the bolded headlines and inspected the photograph of an unusual-looking couple on the front page.

A breath collapsed in my chest, and I couldn't pull my gaze away from the woman or the man who'd brazenly draped a protective arm around her neck.

The newsprint blurred as Jackson slipped up behind me and buried a sob against my neck.

Fifty-Two

Sept. 25, '67

Dear Mrs. Claxton,

Thank you for your letter. Forgive me for taking so long to answer. I was delighted to learn you're offering the literacy program again this year. It seems like only yesterday when we walked your streets to solicit patrons!

We moved back to Troublesome in June after the Court's ruling, and finally got electricity up here! It's been a task fixing up the ol' Carter homestead. But Jackson and Elijah Jack built additions onto the cabin, and we are finally settling in.

My former supervisor, Eula Foster, retired from her library position, and in August, I was approached by the Committee to run the Troublesome Creek Free Public Library.

I'm pleased to write that our borrowing branch has just received, of all things, a motorized bookmobile! It appears a machine shop cut out the sides of the sturdy vehicle and then a cabinetmaker cleverly built shelves. Honey passed her Driving Exams and is licensed. She is smitten with her paneled library truck and its new-fangled pulls and knobs.

I was thrilled to hear your news of Susan's upcoming wedding to Eric. I, too, wish Reverend were alive to see it. We remain grateful to Mr. and Mrs. Loving, and for the Supreme Court's decision and our newfound freedoms and fortunes.

I pray the laws of the land will continue to change and favor all one day.

With a grateful heart, your friend,
Cussy

Fifty-Three

KENTUCKY, 1967

Woodsmoke drifted from the chimney of the Carter homestead, where I first drew breath fifty years earlier.

Under the ol' hickory out in the yard, October had dropped her golden skirt at its trunk. Leaves eddied and slapped against the furrowed bark.

Jackson left his cane and limped out the cabin door, then folded himself into the swing, pulling me close to him.

Moss-stitched woods and the whispering waters of Troublesome Creek greeted us from our candlelit porch. I rested my head in the hollow under his chin, the night choirs of warblers and brook-song awakening a hymnal across the coal-dusted hills, shielding us under a star-smattered Kentucky sky.

A breeze lifted across weathered boards, and a bright-yellow leaf landed on my shawl. I pressed it to my chest and know'd she was here.

She'd been gone now for years, but I could still feel the ol' girl's watchful eyes.

I stepped down and crossed to the hickory that Pa planted long ago.

Inhaling, I took a breath of mountain-raspered winds, the pine and earthen rot pleated, its perfumes tangling.

Sometimes, if I cocked my head just so, I could still hear her gentle whimpers, shivery whinny-haws, and quarrelsome snorts whistle through pine boughs, scraping down the ol' Kaintuck mountains.

I bent over Junia's small marker and brushed off her engraved stone, and laid the gold-jeweled leaf across it.

A Note from the Author

Dear Reader,

Thank you for allowing me to share my Kentucky stories with you. It's a privilege and one of my greatest honors, and always humbling. I promise I don't take it lightly.

Part of this work examines incarceration, criminalization and poverty, the effects on the poor and powerless, and the societal consequences of fractured family bonds. I hoped to wrap the testament of strength, survival, and the magic of the printed word into a vivid portrait of prison life and humanize the incarcerated.

In another section, it was important to introduce the nostalgic glimpses of a bustling multifaceted business district, soon-to-be lost community, and the sense of belonging and longing for home. I researched the devastating costs of "urban renewal" and the generational poverty it inflicted on millions across the United States. I wanted to showcase my hometown's eclectic community with its thriving businesses, restaurants, theaters, and mom-and-pop businesses before urban renewal.

Established by Congress in 1949, the controversial Urban Renewal federal program was implemented to revitalize declining urban areas. In the late sixties, Louisville, Kentucky, began the destruction of West Walnut Street, the multifaceted Black district where mostly Black-owned businesses worked alongside white-owned businesses and welcomed all religions and races due to the city's unique relationship with its powerful business leaders, who were both Black and white.

The denouement is a meditation of homecoming, a threshold for those who long and those still searching for place.

I am grateful to Louisville, Kentucky's world-renowned Black artist and sculptor, Ed Hamilton (Lil Biff), for graciously sharing many conversations with me and entrusting precious childhood memories, his West Walnut Street family and home, foods, traditions, and rich culture.

West Walnut Street was also part of my childhood. After spending my first ten years of life in a rural Kentucky orphanage, I was placed with six relatives, where I lived in a tiny three-room hovel within walking distance of West Walnut Street and the Western Colored Branch.

The Louisville Free Public Library Western Colored Branch was the first African American Public Library. This beautiful Carnegie-endowed library opened in 1908 under the leadership of pioneering librarian, reverend, educator, and civic leader Thomas Fountain Blue, the first African American to head a public library and a great servant and treasure to the community. The library was run by and for African Americans until 1948, when the doors were opened to welcome all.

As a child, I didn't realize or appreciate the wildly vast and diverse culture I was exposed to; I was simply trying to survive abject poverty and then homelessness as a young teen. Because I always insert Kentucky historical gems into all my works, it was critical to explore more of my history, including prisons, correctional education history, archaic case laws, the medical science behind lobotomies, the history of Defiance, Ohio, and Detroit's golden era—just a few of the many places where my research led me.

I was thrilled to connect with Cab Calloway's grandson Joshua Langsam, who graciously granted me permission to use Cab's music to introduce the legendary singer and movie star to my readers. Cab was an iconic jazz entertainer and King of the

Cotton Club. Before Sinatra, there was Cab Calloway creating an entirely different lingo. He was the first Black American to author a dictionary, the 1939 *Hepster's Dictionary*—a glossary of jive invented for him and his fellow musicians that inspired countless fans to learn the hepster language you witnessed Mrs. Claxton mimicking. Just one of the many, many venues Cab frequented, he also visited the Strand Theatre Record Shoppe on West Walnut Street, performed at the local Rialto Theatre in Louisville and in Eastern Kentucky in the coal-mining town of Lynch. It was an immense joy writing about Cab, and I know you'll adore exploring this beloved entertainer's legendary performances.

For prison research, I dug into official Kentucky State Reformatory records. I'm most appreciative to my husband, Joe, who recounted memories of working at the prison for three years after graduating from college. A lot of the stories and my findings were heartbreaking, especially discovering the history of Kentucky State Reformatory's cemetery, Chicken Hill, and reading old prison records.

Henry "Chicken" Montgomery (1901–1937) was sentenced many times for stealing chickens, receiving at one time a three-year sentence for the theft. The last incarceration resulted in a life sentence for his previous convictions of chicken theft, and new and final charges the courts recorded as assault and robbery. He died in the Kentucky State Reformatory in 1937 at the age of thirty-six. He was the first inmate to be buried in the official "Chicken Hill" graveyard, which the prison named after him and is reserved for inmates who have no family or the means for a proper burial outside the prison's razor wire. To date I have not received an explanation for why two babies, *Infant Nichols* and *Infant Richman*, and several women are also buried there. If you would like to explore more, please look into Find a Grave online or visit the KSR cemetery.

Kentucky has not executed a woman in more than 150 years, the last being in 1868 and that of a thirteen-year-old child known only as "Susan," accused of the murder of a toddler left in her charge according to newspapers. The history of flawed executions in the U.S. is alarming. But one that stood out to me in my research is one that took place in 1946, when teen Willie Francis of Louisiana was strapped into an electric chair called Gruesome Gertie and survived the violent electrocution. Many across the country called it *divine intervention and a miracle*, only for the state to execute the youth a year later.

One of the most shocking photographs taken in the U.S. and around the globe was in 1928 of Ruth Snyder, a homemaker from Queens, New York, who was convicted of murder and died by electrocution. During her execution at Sing Sing, and despite the prison's strict rules prohibiting cameras, a money-eyed journalist seeking salacious content strapped a camera to his ankle and captured the startling and gruesome moment between life and death. It was the only photo of a woman's electrocution in a U.S. prison.

At the hospital, Mrs. Claxton recounts to Cussy the arrest of a couple for violating miscegenation laws. In 1939, Dr. Joel P. Oliver, Jr., a Black physician, and his wife, Wilma, a white woman, were passing through Kentucky to their new home in Chicago, when they were arrested in Louisville, Kentucky, for violating the state statute that prohibited interracial marriage.

An annual guidebook, *The Green Book* for African American travelers was published by New York City mailman Hugo Green, from 1936 to 1967. In author Candacy Taylor's *OVERGROUND RAILROAD: The Green Book and the Roots of Black Travel in America*, Dino Thompsom recalls: "[it] didn't tell you if a place had a good steak, or good seafood, or had a soft bed... It told you where you would be safe; it told you where you'd be welcome..." Taylor has written a mesmerizing in-depth exploration of *The Green Book*'s history, and I highly recommend it.

For new readers: It's been an honor to meet relatives of the Kentucky Pack Horse librarians, their children and grandchildren, and a joy to recognize and lift up not only the people of my state, land, and rich history but the unique blue-skinned inhabitants of Kentucky, one of whom was an original Pack Horse librarian, and some who are librarians and dear friends today.

I'm overjoyed to report that after years of working on honoring these librarians, I was able to get the Kentucky State Historical Society to grant my application for a historical marker for the Pack Horse librarians now located in Hyden, Kentucky, the first outpost of the Pack Horse librarians. After ninety years, they will now be celebrated and honored in the state they served so bravely.

From my research and interviews with doctors, vascular surgeons, and hematologists, *congenital* methemoglobinemia is an extremely rare, often unreported, and non-life-threatening genetic defect that is inherited from parents. It stems from a deficiency of a certain enzyme or protein, leading to higher-than-normal levels of methemoglobin in the blood—a form of hemoglobin—that overwhelms the normal hemoglobin, which results in an inability to deliver oxygen to the body's tissues. Doctors can easily diagnose *congenital* methemoglobinemia because the color of the blood is chocolate-brown and provides the unique clue. People who have the gene disorder can live a long and healthy life. *Acquired* methemoglobinemia is more common and is life-threatening, and can derive from heart disease, airway obstruction, or interaction and/or overdosing from other drugs and toxins such as consumption of drinking water with high concentrates of nitrates, just to name a few. To learn more about methylene blue, the drug used to treat Methemoglobinemia, please visit my website.

Kentucky has always led in literacy, implementing and pioneering life-changing programs. There are more bookmobiles in Kentucky than in any other state, and it has a rich and unique history of getting books into the hands of those who had none.

In 1949, Mary Belknap Gray of Louisville, Kentucky, purchased her first surplus army ambulance and had it converted into a bookmobile and then donated the unusual vehicle to a library. Bookmobiles have made a big impact in areas where readers don't have access to libraries.

Kentucky's first motorized bookmobiles heralded the largest fleet in the U.S. in the 1950s, when brass bands and police escorts paraded over one hundred bookmobiles to the public. The organizers expected only a few books would be donated; instead it was over a million. Thanks to the tenacity and generosity of prominent Louisvillians such as Mary Belknap Gray, Mary Bingham, Harry Schacter, and Barry Lenihan, a statewide campaign for motorized bookmobiles was launched.

Currently, I'm leading a new initiative, *Courthouses Reading Across Kentucky & Beyond,* placing free little libraries in county courthouses across my state. With so many of the underserved walking through courthouse doors and unable to afford basic necessities, much less a book for themselves or a child, it is a way to honor the legacy of the Pack Horse librarians and spread literacy into book deserts. So far, I have twenty-six Kentucky courthouses with libraries, and the state of Indiana has adopted my program and is installing free little libraries in its county courthouses. California, Ohio, and other states have expressed interest, and I'm hoping they join in.

As a native-born Kentuckian and lifelong resident whose books are all set in Kentucky, I wanted to give a glimpse of adopted Kentucky sister Annie Fellows Johnston (1863–1931). Johnston was the beloved children's author who lived and died in Pewee Valley, Kentucky, a quaint, bucolic town filled with rich history. After purchasing her famous home, the Beeches, in Pewee Valley, she was inspired to write the Little Colonel series beginning in 1895. The books came to life in films in the 1930s with actors Shirley Temple, Bill "Bojangles" Robinson, and Hattie McDaniel and romanticized life in the South. It was also the first interracial dance coupling in film that depicted Temple and Robinson in their famous stairway dance and was banned in the South because of it.

I'd be remiss if I didn't introduce another prolific Kentucky pioneer. In 1911, educator Cora Wilson Stewart (1875–1958) of Farmers, Kentucky, founded the Moonlight Schools and was also the founder of the First Official Adult Literacy movement in the U.S., which impacted millions. In her later years, Cora went blind and died in a rented hotel room in Tryon, North Carolina, and was buried in a remote grave nearby with a stone the size of a brick that excised her full name.

I couldn't stop thinking about this woman's final resting place. If she had been a man, or perhaps a football player, a monument would have been erected. That a prolific educator who freed countless people—the Appalachians, Native Americans and Blacks, soldiers, prisoners, and more—from the bondage of illiteracy and crushing poverty around the country ended up with less than a final footnote of recognition in a cemetery, was crushing to me.

It was also a reminder of my Kentucky's Capitol and the all-male, bronze statues honored inside the stately Rotunda as in a lot of other state capitols. I think about the thousands of students, especially young girls who visit yearly and wonder what they must think when they don't see a statue like them in the Rotunda. If their echoes and footprints in history will be lost like Cora's. Currently, Governor Andy Beshear and Lt. Governor Jacqueline Coleman are trying to change this by reviving the long-neglected Kentucky's Women's Remembered Exhibit in the West Wing.

As in this novel and my new forthcoming children's picture book, *My Kentucky Moonlight School*, I felt moved to honor Cora and her unique program through the eyes of my characters.

To learn more about Cora's life and her worldly literacy impact, you can link to an article on my website, or more importantly if you are traveling around Polk Memorial Gardens in Columbus, North Carolina, please do drop in and leave a flower on her new marker with the permanent vase I've had erected for her.

I'm filled with immense gratitude to the dear readers for

following along on these journeys, your letters, personal stories, and praise, which I treasure always. Valued more than any award, prize, or moneys has been witnessing the great acts of kindness my works have inspired, from those who informed me they started bookmobiles during the height of the pandemic and others who wrote they were inspired to buy books for book deserts, and yet more who tell me they are now donating regularly to food banks or raising money for underserved libraries and more. I'm so grateful to today's librarians who work tirelessly to offer safe havens for the lonely and for those needing a voice. For sharing their invaluable resources to engage and build strong communities through the power of literacy. It is with great appreciation to indie booksellers for their dedication and passion to peddle my books and other writers' books waiting to be discovered and placing them into the hands and hearts of readers. You are cherished.

Again, it's been an honor of a lifetime and a privilege to share my Kentucky stories with you. And like the adage mentioned in the conversation between Chester and Jackson, and one often quoted by early frontier-traveling preachers: "*O my dear Honeys, Heaven is* indeed *a Kentucky of a place.*"

XO

Kim Michele

Read on for a look at

THE BOOK WOMAN OF TROUBLESOME CREEK

by Kim Michele Richardson

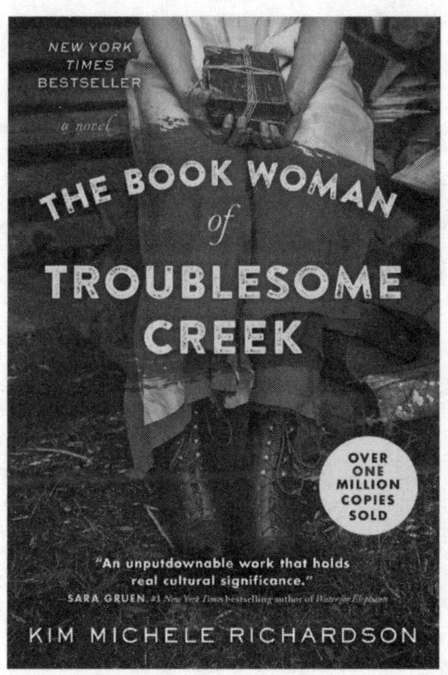

Available now from Sourcebooks Landmark

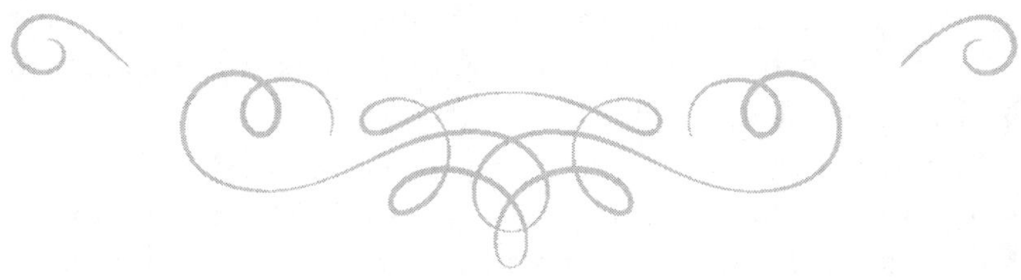

KENTUCKY, 1936

The librarian and her mule spotted it at the same time. The creature's ears shot up, and it came to a stop so sudden its front hooves skidded out, the pannier slipping off, spilling out the librarian's books. An eddy of dirt and debris lifted, stinging the woman's eyes. The mule struggled to look upward, backward, anywhere other than at the thing in front of it.

The book woman couldn't keep her eyes off the spectacle as she shortened the reins and clamped her legs against the mule's sides. Again, she prodded her mount. Baring tall, sassing teeth, the beast lifted its muzzle into the balsam-sweetened air, the quavering brays blistering the sleepy mountain.

The woman stiffened, drawing the reins in tighter. In front of her, a body swayed back and forth below the fat branch from which it hung. A rope, collared tight around the neck, creaked from the strain of its weight. A kettle of turkey buzzards circled above, dipping their ugly, naked heads toward the lifeless form, their tail-chasing shadows riddling the dying grass.

From the scorched earth rose strange cries, and the librarian pulled her stunned gaze away from the corpse and toward the ground.

Beside a large toppled can, a baby lay in the dirt, the tiny face pinched, scalded with fury.

Mountain breezes dipped lazily, shifting, carrying the stench of death and its soiling. The weighted branch crackled, groaning under its burden. A bloodied sock inched down from a limp, cerulean-blue foot. The librarian gawked at the striking blue flesh and cupped a hand over her mouth. The stocking slipped off, landing beside the squalling baby's head.

The wind rose higher, then plunged, skittering across the sock as if trying to lift it, but it stayed stubbornly put, rooted to the earth—too heavy to be sent off by a mere summer breeze.

The book woman looked up, lifted one darkening hand in front of her own blue-colored face as if comparing her color to that of the hanging corpse. She examined her cobalt-blue flesh, then dared to peek back up at the dead body, bound, eternally rooted like the black oak to the hard, everlasting Kentucky land so many tried so hard to escape.

One

The new year was barely fifteen hours old in Troublesome Creek, Kentucky, when my pa adjusted the courting candle, setting it to burn for an alarming length of time.

Satisfied, Pa carried it out of our one-room log house and onto the hand-hewn porch. He was hopeful. Hoping 1936 was the year his only daughter, nineteen-year-old Cussy Mary Carter, would get herself hitched and quit her job with the Pack Horse Library Project. Hoping for her latest suitor's proposal.

"Cussy," he called over his shoulder, "before your mama passed, I promised her I'd see to it you got yourself respectability, but I've nearly gone busted buying candles to get you some. Let this stick hold the fire, Daughter." He hoisted the old wrought-iron candleholder higher by its iron-forged rattail and once more played with the wooden slide, moving the taper up and down inside the spiral coil.

"I've got a respectable life," I said quietly, following him out to the porch, taking a seat on the wooden chair, and huddling under the patchwork eiderdown I'd dragged along. The first day of January had brought a skift of snow to our home in the cove. Pa set the candle down and struck a match to light a lantern hanging from the porch.

Two winter moths chased the light, circling, landing nearby. A clean wetting mingled into woodsmoke and umbrella'd the tiny cabin. Shivering, I buried my nose into the coverlet as a cutting wind scraped down mountains, dragging soft whistles through piney boughs and across bare black branches.

In a minute, Pa picked back up the courting candle, raised a finger above the wick, and jutted his chin, the approval cinched in his brow.

"Pa, I have me a good job making us twenty-eight dollars a month delivering books to folks who's needing the book learning in these hills."

"I'm back to work now that the mine is running full time." Pa pinched the wick.

"They still need me—"

"I need you safe. You could catch your death in this cold, same as your mama. You're all I have, Cussy, all that's left of our kind. The very last one, Daughter."

"*Pa, please.*"

He reached down and brushed a lock of hair away from my eyes. "I won't see you riding that ol' mount up and down them dangerous passes and into dark hollers and cold creeks just because the government wants to push their foolish book airs into our hills here."

"It's safe."

"You could be struck ill. Just look what happened to that book woman and her mount. Foolhardy, and the poor steed was punished for her temerity."

Snow gusted, swirled, eddying across the leaf-quilted yard.

"It was along in years, Pa. My rented mount is spry and surefooted enough. And I'm fine and fit as any." I glanced down at my darkening hands, a silent blue betrayal. Quickly, I slipped them under the folds of fabric, forcing myself to stay calm.

"Sound. *Please*. It's decent money—"

"Where's *your* decency? Some of the womenfolk are complaining you're carrying dirty books up them rocks."

"Weren't true. It's called literature, and proper enough," I tried to explain like so many times before. "*Robinson Crusoe*, and Dickens, and the likes, and lots of *Popular Mechanics* and *Woman's*

Home Companion even. Pamphlets with tips on fixing things busted. Patterns for sewing. Cooking and cleaning. Making a dollar stretch. Important things, Pa. Respectable—"

"*Airish*. It ain't respectable for a female to be riding these rough hills, behaving like a man," he said, a harshness rumbling his voice.

"It helps educate folks and their young'uns." I pointed to a small sack in the corner filled with magazines I'd be delivering in the next days. "Remember the *National Geographic* article about Great-Grandpa's birthplace over in Cussy, France, the one I'm named for? You liked it—"

"Dammit, you have earned your name and driven me to nothing but cussing with your willful mind. I don't need a damn book to tell me about our kin's birthplace or your given name. Me and your mama know'd it just fine." He raised a brow, worrying some more with the flame on the courting candle, resting the height of the taper to where he wanted. And as always and depending on the man who came calling, how long he wanted the old timekeeper to stay lit.

Pa looked off toward the creek, then back at the candle, and set his sights once more over to the banks, studying. He fought between raising the timekeeping candle and lowering it, mumbling a curse, and setting it somewhere in the middle. A taper would be cranked up tall to burn for a lengthy visit, or tamped down short for any beau Elijah Carter didn't favor as a good suitor.

"Pa, people want the books. It's my job to tend to the folks who are hungry for the learning."

He lifted the courting candle. "A woman ought to be near the home fires tending that."

"But if I marry, the WPA will fire me. Please, I'm a librarian now. Why, even Eleanor Roosevelt approves—"

"The First Lady ain't doing a man's job—ain't my unwed daughter—and ain't riding an ornery ass up a crooked mountain."

"People are learning up there." Again, I glimpsed my hands

and rubbed them under the quilt. "Books are the best way to do that—"

"The best thing they need is food on their tables. Folks here are hungry, Daughter. The babies are starving and sickly, the old folks are dying. We're gnawing on nothing but bone teeth here. Not two weeks ago, widow Caroline Barnes walked nine miles for naught to save her babies up there."

I had heard the poor woman staggered into town with the pellagra rash and died in the street. Many times I'd glimpsed the rash set in from starvation. And last month a woman up in a holler lost five of her twelve children from it, and farther up in the hills, a whole family had died the month before.

"But folks tell me the books eases their burdens, it's the best thing that could happen to them," I argued.

"They can't live off the chicken scratch in them books," Pa said, flicking the wick and hushing me. "And this"—he rapped the candleholder with a knuckle—"is what's best for you."

Jutted up high like that, the candle's nakedness seemed desperate, embarrassing. I caught the unsettling in Pa's gray eyes too.

It didn't matter that for a long time I'd shared Pa's fears about what might become of his only daughter, until the day I'd heard about Roosevelt creating his relief program called the New Deal to help folks around here during the Depression. We'd been depressed as long as I could remember, but now, all of a sudden, the government said we needed help and aimed to do just that. The president had added the Works Progress Administration last year to put females to work and bring literature and art into the Kaintuck man's life. For many mountainfolk, all of us around here, it was our first taste of what a library could give, a taste to be savored—one that left behind a craving for more.

I'd seen the flyers in town asking for womenfolk to apply for the job to tote books around these hills on a mount. I snuck an application and filled it out without Pa knowing, applying to be a Pack Horse librarian a month after Mama died.

"They gave *you* the job?" Pa had puzzled when I got it last summer.

I didn't tell him I'd bypassed the supervisors here by picking up my application at the post office. The job application said you could turn it in to the head librarian in your town or send it to the Pack Horse libraries' manager directly by mailing it to Frankfort. It didn't say anything about color, and certainly not mine. But I'd taken my chances with city folks I'd never meet instead of trusting it to the bosses here in Troublesome.

"Did no one else apply?" Pa had questioned me. "You can't work," he'd added just as quick.

"Pa, we need the money, and it's honorable work and—"

"A workin' woman will never knot."

"Who would marry a Blue? Who would want me?"

I was positive no one would wed one of the *Blue People of Kentucky*. Wouldn't hitch with a quiet woman whose lips and nails were blue-jay blue, with skin the color of the bluet patches growing around our woods.

I could barely meet someone's eyes for fear my color would betray my sensibilities. A mere blush, a burst of joy or anger, or sudden startle would crawl across my skin, deepening, changing my softer appearance to a ripened blueberry hue, sending the other person scurrying. There didn't seem to be much marriage prospect for the last female of blue mountainfolk who had befuddled the rest of the Commonwealth—folks around the country and doctors even. *A fit girl who could turn as blue as the familiar bluet damselfly skimming Kentucky creek beds*, the old mountain doctor had once puzzled and then promptly nicknamed me Bluet. As soon as the word fell out of his mouth, it stuck to me.

Whenever we'd talk about it, Pa would say, "Cussy, you have a chance to marry someone that's not the same as you, someone who can get you out of here. That's why I dig coal. Why I work for scratch."

And the disgrace would linger in the dead air to gnaw at me. Folks thought our clan was inbreeds, nothing but. Weren't true. My great-grandpa, a Blue from France, settled in these hills and wedded himself a full-blooded white Kentuckian. Despite that, they'd had several blue children among their regular white-looking ones. And a few of them married strangers, but the rest had to hitch with kin because they couldn't travel far, same as other mountain clans around all these parts.

Soon, we Blues pushed ourselves deeper into the hills to escape the ridicule. Into the blackest part of the land. Pa liked that just fine, saying it was best, safer for me, the last of our kind, *the last one*. But I'd read about those *kinds* in the magazines. The eastern elk, the passenger pigeon. *The extinctions*. Why, most of the critters had been hunted to *extinction*. The thought of being hunted, becoming extinct, being the last Blue, the very last of my kind on earth, left me so terror-struck and winded that I would race to the looking glass, claw at my throat, and knock my chest to steal the breath back.

A lot of people were leery of our looks. Though with Pa working the coal, his mostly pale-blue skin didn't bother folks much when all miners came out of the hole looking the same.

But I didn't have coal to disguise me in black or white Kentucky. Didn't have myself an escape until I'd gotten the precious book route. In those old dark-treed pockets, my young patrons would glimpse me riding my packhorse, toting a pannier full of books, and they'd light a smile and call out, "Yonder comes Book Woman… Book Woman's here!" And I'd forget all about my peculiarity, and why I had it, and what it meant for me.

Just recently, Eula Foster, the head librarian of the Pack Horse project, remarked about my smarts, saying the book job had given me an education as fine as any school could.

I was delighted to hear her words. Proud, I'd turned practically purple, despite the fact that she had said it to the other Pack Horse librarians in an air of astonishment: "*If a Blue can get that much learning from our books, imagine what the program can do for our normal folk… A light in these dark times, for sure…*"

And I'd basked in the warm light that had left me feeling like a book-read woman.

But when Pa heard about Agnes's frightening journey, how her packhorse up and quit her in the snow last month, his resolve to get me hitched deepened. And soon after, he'd shone a blinding light back on my color and offered up a generous five-dollar dowry plus ten acres of our woodland. Men, both long in the tooth and schooling young, sought my courtship, ignoring I was one of *them Blue people* when the prospect of land ownership presented itself. A few would boldly ask about my baby-making as if discussing a farm animal—seeking a surety that their Kentucky sons and daughters wouldn't have the blueness too.

Why, for all Pa cared, it could be the beastly troll in "The Three Billy Goats Gruff" who wanted my hand. Lately, he'd been setting the timekeeping candle uncomfortably long for *whoever* was keen on calling.

But I couldn't risk it. The WPA regulations said females with an employable husband wouldn't be eligible for a job because the husband is the logical head of the family.

Logical. I liked my sensibility just fine. I liked my freedom a lot—loved the solitude these last seven months had given me—and I lived for the joy of bringing books and reading materials to the hillfolk who were desperate for my visits, the printed word that brought a hopeful world into their dreary lives and dark hollers. It was necessary.

And for the first time in my life, I felt necessary.

"Right there'll do it." Pa fussed one last time with the slide on the courting candle, then finally placed the timekeeper on the table in front of my rocker and the empty seat beside me. He grabbed his carbide-lamp helmet off a peg and looked out to the dark woods across the creek that passed through our property.

The snow picked up, dropping fat flakes. "Reckon he'll be showing up any minute, Daughter."

Sometimes the suitor didn't. I hoped this would be one of those times.

"I'll be off." He dropped a matchbook into the timekeeper's drip tray, eyeing the candle one final time.

Frantic, I grabbed his sleeve and whispered, "Please, Pa, I don't want to marry."

"What's wrong with you, Daughter? It ain't natural to defy the Lord's *natural* order."

I took his palm in mine and pressed the silent plea into it.

Pa looked at my coloring hand and pulled his away. "I gave up my sleep to ride over to his holler and arrange this."

I opened my mouth to protest, but he held up a shushing hand.

"This harsh land ain't for a woman to bear alone. It's cruel enough on a man." Pa reached for his hand-carved bear poker with the razor-sharp arrowhead tip. "I've been digging my grave since the first day I dug coal. I'll not dig two." He tapped the poker against the boards. "You will take a husband so you'll have someone to care for you when I no longer can."

He buttoned his coat and grabbed his tin lunch bucket off the porch boards, ambling off to his night shift down at the coal mine. Hearing a horse's strangled whinny, I turned toward a rustling in the trees, straining to listen above the prattling song of creek waters. The courter would be here shortly.

I leaned over the wood railing and peered out. When I could no longer see the flicker of Pa's miner's lamp and was sure he'd disappeared into the woods, I reached over, adjusted the wooden slide on the timekeeping candle, and lowered the taper to where the wax would touch the old spiral holder's lip within a few minutes of being burnt—a signal to this latest suitor that a prompt and swift departure was in mind.

Raising my hands, I watched them quiet to a duck-egg blue.

Read on for a look at

THE BOOK WOMAN'S DAUGHTER

by Kim Michele Richardson

KENTUCKY

They still call her Book Woman, having long forgotten the epithet for her cobalt-blue flesh, though she's gone now from these hills and hollers, from her loving husband and daughter and endearing Junia, her patrons and their heartaches and yearnings for more. But you must know another story, really all the other important stories that swirled around and after her, before they are lost to winters of rotting foliage and sleeping trees, swallowed into the spring hymnals of birdsong rising above carpets of phlox, snakeroot, and foxglove. These stories beg to be unspooled from Kentucky's hardened old hands, to be bound and eternally rooted like the poplar and oak to the everlasting land.

One

THOUSANDSTICKS, KENTUCKY, 1953

The bitter howls of winter, uncertainty, and a soon-to-be-forgotten war rolled over the sleepy, dark hills of Thousandsticks, Kentucky, in early March, leaving behind an angry ache of despair. And though we'd practiced my escape many times, it still felt terrifying that this time was no longer a drill.

I remember when I was twelve, and the shrill air-raid alarm sounded in the schoolyard as we were dropping books off at the stone school over in Troublesome Creek. The teacher yelled out to Mama, "It's a duck-and-cover drill," and then rushed us all inside, instructing everyone to crawl under the desks and cover our heads. It had been scary, but I still felt safe under the thin, wooden lip of the school desk.

Today, at sixteen, I realized how foolish it was to think that a little desk could protect anyone from a bomb—how difficult it was now to believe that hiding would somehow save me from the bigger scatter bombs coming.

I shifted my feet on the stiff, frozen grass umbrella'd under the Cumberland Forest, breathing in the cold as Mama helped me into her heavy coat. In every direction, hoarfrost crowned the forest surrounding our cabin, its gray crystals shimmering through pines, hickories, and oaks, as the twining psalms of chickadees and warblers announced the morning. Overhead, a turkey buzzard glided low, scanning for dead flesh. I shivered as the ugly bird dipped lower and lower.

"You must hurry," Mama chided for the second time, a pull of the cold escaping her breath. "He'll be coming up here to escort us to court anytime now. Remember everything we told you. Everything we practiced."

From the side of our cabin, the hood of a lawman's parked automobile poked out behind a thicket of chokeberries, the first rays of sunlight flashing off headlights and polished chrome.

"I'm frightened, Mama."

"That's not a bad thing, darling daughter. It'll make you more cautious."

Two weeks ago, my parents hid me in the cellar when the law showed up to arrest them for violating miscegenation laws, after a peddler happened upon our family and remarked back in town about Mama's strange blue color. Papa hired counsel, bond was posted, and yesterday word came of a revocation hearing while I stayed hidden in the cellar. Today they would go in front of a judge because of Papa's parole violation on his 1936 banishment order and for daring to marry a woman of mixed color—a blue-skinned Kentuckian.

After Papa got out of prison, we'd moved over to Thousandsticks from Troublesome Creek, and our family had been living in secret here for the last twelve years.

I saw the fear in Mama's eyes as she reached for the scarf. Her hearing was also set for today.

Hiding inside after the lawman arrived last night, I peeked out the curtains and saw him watching from his automobile to make sure Mama and Papa didn't flee the county before the hearing. He'd stayed all night and was out there right now sleeping in his official vehicle.

"Mama, I don't want to leave you and Papa. *My home.*" I swiped at my eyes with the cuff of her scratchy wool coat.

"You're not safe here." She wrapped a knit scarf around my neck.

"I want to stay and wait for you and Papa to come back after the hearing. I'm nearly grown, almost seventeen—"

"It's too dangerous, Honey Mary-Angeline," she said, including my middle names she and Papa christened me with years ago when one of the saddlebag preachers stopped at our small cabin hidden near the forest. Mama asked what name I'd like to take and I had said *Mary*, for her middle name, *Cussy Mary Lovett*, the distinguished Book Woman of these ol' hills who'd worked for the Kentucky Pack Horse Library Project when I was little. Then I asked if I could have two and added Angeline for my first mama.

Angeline and my first papa, Willie Moffit, had been Blues, too, but neither of them knew it, Mama had told me later. Angeline died in '36, right after she birthed me. Mama never said much about my first papa, only that an accident caused his demise. By the time I turned six, I had lost most of the methemoglobinemia, the gene disorder that the ol' doc over in Troublesome Creek said me and Mama and the Moffits had.

Doc explained that Mama's parents, the Carters, like other clans 'round the country, were all kin to themselves, same as the royalty in Europe. Only difference, we didn't have us a family tree like most folk. Instead, we'd gotten twisty vines that knotted, wrapped, and wound around each other. And although my hands and feet still turned a bruising blue whenever I got scared or excited, only those parts of me took on the strange color.

I was grateful I could easily hide the affliction. *Affliction*. A hard word for me to swallow, but it wasn't nothing compared to hearing how Mama had been treated. How the law ripped her and Papa apart on their wedding day, calling them immoral and sinners and worse. Mama said I was only three months old when the Troublesome Creek sheriff had beaten and arrested Papa and threatened to lock Mama up, too, and throw me into the Home of the Idiots on that October day in '36.

Lifting my palms, I watched the tint of a robin's-egg blue rise and spread with a darker tinge outlining them. Nothing as dark as Mama's color that covered every inch of her. I thought of the fright, scorn, and horror that would appear in others' eyes when they glimpsed Mama's ink-blue skin. The embarrassment, shame, and sadness leaching into Mama's.

Once, when I was six years old, we were buying apples inside a store in Tennessee when the man behind the counter called Mama an ugly name and ordered us out. When I saw the hurt pooling in Mama's eyes, a blinding fury like no other rose inside me. Unable to tamp it down, I threw my apple at the shopkeeper. He snatched up a thick wooden broom. Mama apologized to the angry man and scolded me as she rushed us out the door, shielding my small frame while taking the brunt of the shopkeeper's battering strikes and raging curses.

Mama received eight stitches on her scalp. After that, I learned to keep quiet and lower my head—learned what a Blue had to do to stay safe.

I looked over at the lawman's automobile, my stomach stitched in knots. Mama's hands trembled as she reached into my coat pocket, pulled out a pair of gloves, and handed them to me. She'd been knitting these to hide my blue skin and to keep me, the last of our kind, hidden from the rest of the world. Papa, wanting to contribute, had stitched me black leather ones to switch out. They were my armor, a shield against folk who hunted the Blues.

"Can I go to Tennessee and visit Papa's kin instead?"

"Great-Uncle Emmet's place is bursting at the seams. There's fourteen in the home and they can't squeeze in another soul. I'm sorry, Honey, there's no one else."

She flipped down the thick collar on the coat and straightened it. "I packed your brown journal. You be sure to keep writing those pretty poems of yours."

I nodded, feeling the tremble on my chin. The journal was my favorite and what I wrote down all my poetry in.

"Papa's packed your .22 for the journey," Mama went on, fussing with the bulky leather-wrapped coat buttons, pausing to wipe away a tear.

I glanced at our mule, standing to the side and out of sight from the law, and spotted my rifle poking out of the rawhide scabbard.

"Take Junia and ride straight to Troublesome, and don't stop till you reach Miss Loretta's," Mama said, her voice thickening.

The next county over was thirty-some miles away, but with all the rough terrain, narrow mountain trails, and countless switchbacks, it might as well have been three hundred.

"Straight to Loretta's," she said again. "If you meet any trouble, find Devil John."

Moonshiner Devil John was one of Mama's old library patrons who also lived over in Troublesome Creek. He'd been visiting us here in the Cumberland for years.

"Mama, I love Retta, but she's got to be one hundred years old. How will she care for me?"

"Ninety-one, and you'll help out Miss Loretta, and she'll keep you safe till we can all be together again." Her words were swollen in grief, pained.

"Yes, ma'am, I will," I whispered.

"Listen to your mama, lil Book Woman." Papa stepped outside, his bright eyes now troubled and dark. He raked his fingers through thick brown hair, peeked at the law's automobile, and dropped his voice to a whisper. "You need to hurry. He'll be waking up any time now, and we dare not let him see you here. Remember, your mama has sewn a little emergency money into the lining of your coat. Be gentle with old Junia, and she'll see you safely there."

"Ol' Junia never minds me like she does Mama," I said, stalling. "Can't I stay just a bit longer—"

"We talked about this, Honey. Your mama and I have been accused of breaking the law. If the judge finds us guilty"—he stole a glance to Mama—"there will be a punishment."

I tugged on Papa's coat and squinted up at him. "But won't your lawyer fight it? What—"

"Shh. We have to be prepared. Slip on those gloves now,"

he said more sternly, more slowly, making me latch on to his every word.

If my folks were found guilty and taken away, the court could send me to the orphans' home until I turned eighteen or, worse, to the House of Reform where the children wear chains and toil from sunup to sundown on the farms till they're twenty-one.

"C'mon, Honey," Papa said. "Let's put the pannier on Junia and get you home to Loretta."

"Papa, what should I say if the law comes after me?" I glanced out at the automobile and pulled my gloves on.

"Right now they only know we have a daughter, but they don't know where you are, Honey, or what you look like. And they won't find you where you're going. Mr. Morgan shares the same office as our attorney, Mr. Faust. He's signed up with the courts to represent you and is working on the legal papers to get you a guardian. You remember Bob Morgan, don't you?"

"Yes, sir."

"Just don't say anything except that you want to talk to Mr. Morgan if anyone asks. He'll help you."

I clung to Mama, afraid. That I could lose them both because men would punish my parents for loving each other was terrifying. And I knew somehow that going back to Troublesome was going to be *troublesome* for me.

"*Mama.*"

"My darling daughter, you'll be safer there." Mama wrapped me in a hug. A moment later, she said quietly, "When we went back to your grandparents' cabin last fall to visit and clean the cemeteries, you'll remember we stocked the root cellar with food."

"Yes, ma'am, I remember."

"Your papa took some more victuals over last month. Key's in your pocket. Don't lose it. And you be sure and share everything with Miss Loretta." She gave one last hug, then kissed my cheek. "I'll send word when it's safe. If all goes well, you might be able to come home tomorrow at first light." She drew back and gave me a small, reassuring smile. "I'll come straight to you. I promise."

But there was no promise to be had in her worried eyes, the darkening blue flesh of her face betraying the words. "Mama," I said, chasing down the ghosts of childhood to return to a safer place—any place other than where they were going and where I was being sent. I searched their faces. "Mama, Papa, I love you."

Mama laid her head against mine. "I love you, darling daughter."

Papa pulled us into his embrace and spoke softly: "I love you. Ride safe, lil Book Woman." He drew back, kissed my forehead, then pulled us close once again. When he released his hold, he turned back toward the automobile. But not before I saw a small tear fall from the corner of his eye.

"*Papa*," I whispered, my heart breaking, the ache deep, my love and the pain of losing them cutting even deeper.

"Be quick, Honey," he said hoarsely, keeping his back to me. "You'll return when we come for you, or when we send word it's safe." Once more he peeked out at the automobile, then snuck quietly over to Junia.

There was a sober finality in our brief goodbye, and we all felt it. Our future together was about to be erased, the same as in 1936 when the sheriff over in Troublesome erased my papa and mama's marriage and then the courts banished him from entering Kentucky again for twenty-five years. What was coming loomed bigger, bolder, and the fear seized hold, punching hard at my bones.

I hugged him once more and climbed atop Junia, then rode her out on the narrower trail on the other side of the yard, away from the lawman and his automobile, the cold winds lashing at my stinging wet cheeks, the pounding of the beast's hooves raging in my chest, stoking the anger and sorrow inside.

When I was at a safe distance but could still make them out, I climbed down. From behind a grove of trees, I stood beside

Junia, peeking over her withers, waiting, and then watched as the lawman sauntered up to the cabin. In a minute my parents stepped out the door.

Mama stood helpless, clasping her hands while Papa talked to the official, their conversation lost to the wilderness. Several times, the lawman shook his head, his face darkening to a mottled red. With each shake it felt like a knife piercing, and I held my breath, watching until Junia swished her tail and a rumble threatened to leap from her chest.

"*Shh*," I hissed. But it was too late. The ol' girl pinned back her ears as the man took a step toward them. Mama cowed, raised an arm protectively over her face, and tried to back away. But the lawman latched hold and twisted her arm up behind her back, pinning her tight against the automobile. Mama tilted back her head and, with deep, guttural anguish, howled into Junia's startled whinny, drowning the beast's fury.

I didn't need to hear the crushing snap to know he'd broken her arm.

Again, cries pulled from the mule's chest, and I quickly put my hand on her muzzle. "Quiet, Junia," I warned, not taking my eye off my parents.

Papa grabbed the lawman by the shoulders, pulling him off Mama, but the man spun around, whipped out his billy club, and struck Papa hard upside the head. He crashed to the ground on both knees, cradling his face with both palms. Shouts lifted as the lawman handcuffed him and knocked him over onto the cold ground. He gave a swift kick to Papa's side and turned back to Mama.

Junia pawed the earth when she saw the man shove Mama into the back seat of his automobile.

Calling out for Papa, Mama banged on the window with her fist.

I wanted to scream and curse the man. Instead I clamped my hand over my mouth, watching in horror as tears streamed from my eyes.

Junia lifted her muzzle and bawled into the sleeping woods, and I ducked lower, barely peeking over her withers.

The lawman stopped and turned our way. My gaze dropped to my .22, then fell back on the man, and my breathing hitched as I shifted toward the scabbard.

He took a few steps forward and cupped a hand over his brows, searching. My gloved palm slid over the shoulder stock. Seconds later, he dropped his arm and turned away.

Quickly, I tugged Junia deeper into the trees, climbed atop, and rode the mule hard toward Troublesome Creek.

Old West Walnut Street Chili with Tamales

INGREDIENTS

- 1 lb ground beef
- 1 medium onion, diced
- 1 tbsp olive oil
- 1 ½ tsp garlic powder
- Salt to taste
- 2 tsp paprika
- 1 tsp black pepper
- 2 tsp ground cumin
- 1 cup water
- 2 beef bouillon cubes
- 8 oz canned tomato sauce
- 28 oz canned crushed tomatoes
- 15 oz canned red kidney beans (drained)
- Chili powder to taste
- 1 jar prepared tamales (Derby Beef Tamales originally used but is no longer made)
- 16 oz spaghetti
- 8 oz block of cheddar cheese from deli

INSTRUCTIONS

Lightly brown ground beef, drain, and set aside. Sauté diced onion with olive oil, garlic powder, salt, paprika, black pepper, cumin, and add to ground beef. Add water, beef bouillon cubes, tomato sauce, and crushed tomatoes. Stir kidney beans and chili powder into pan. Bring to a slight boil, then reduce heat for 10 minutes, cover and simmer on low for 30 to 45 minutes. Heat tamales in a separate pan on the stove. Cook spaghetti and drain. Shred cheddar cheese. To serve, layer spaghetti in a bowl or on a plate and top with meat sauce, 1 tamale, and a ladle of chili juice and shredded cheese. Serves 4.

Reading Group Guide

1. If we think of Rosemary Kennedy and look back throughout history, more women than men were lobotomized. Discuss what feminine "traits" were deemed so undesirable or embarrassing as to justify lobotomy. Anxiety? Depression? Hysteria? How amorphous is the definition of "undesirable traits?" Could it have also included the excise of free will in opposition to the male?

2. According to studies, U.S. Correctional Education is traced back to 1789 and was named "Sabbath School" so that inmates would learn to read the Bible. It was designed to encourage inmates to ask for forgiveness for their sins and to change one's moral compass to be virtuous. Today, educational degrees and various studies are offered in U.S. prisons. Can you think of other ways to help reduce recidivism?

3. What happens when others and/or the government decide what books you or your loved ones can or can't read?

4. When the bustling West Walnut Street district fell to "urban renewal," it devastated families, inflicted generational poverty on thousands, and destroyed a thriving, diverse culture. What do you think those in power hoped

to achieve? Why was the land that was "renewed" allowed to go to seed? What was the government's intention? Discuss the impact the inherited businesses would have had on future children and grandchildren and great-grandchildren. What changes, if any, have been made to revitalize these vacant areas?

5. In light of the Supreme Court case *Loving v. Virginia*, what legacy was left by laws in place before the landmark decision, and how did it change lives? What would banishment from towns, communities, and churches mean to those who long for belonging?

6. As you look back to 1936 in *The Book Woman of Troublesome Creek* with the local sheriff destroying the marriage license, and on to Daniel, who was incarcerated for being a homosexual in the 1950s, and then to the former Kentucky county clerk who denied same-sex couples a marriage license as recently as 2015, what do you think has changed? And what role, if any, should government or any powers that be play in private lives?

7. Mrs. Claxton and Cussy run out of gas and land in a hostile town. Published annually from 1936 to 1966, *The Negro Motorist Green Book* enabled Blacks to safely navigate roads and avoid discrimination and danger. Discuss the value of the annual book and the possible risks of not having one.

8. In consideration of inequities in the justice system like mass incarceration, what are the pros and cons of prison for drug addiction and/or relatively minor offenses versus serious and violent crimes?

9. Cussy was born in 1917. Babies were generally delivered at home during this time, and births were often recorded in

Bibles, baptismals, and cradle roll certificates that were later used for identification. The first Social Security cards in the U.S. were issued in 1936. It wasn't until the 1980s that parents of newborns could request Social Security cards for an infant. In 1934, Kentucky started issuing driver's licenses. How has personal identification evolved in the United States? Can you think of other ways the government could record births over one hundred years ago and track citizens?

10. Prison wine, or jailhouse hooch, has always been part of the culture for the incarcerated. Today, jails and prisons limit fresh fruit/produce and rarely provide it to inmates for fear of it being fermented into alcohol. This results in the incarcerated having weakened immune systems.

    In a few states, free telephone calls are allowed for the incarcerated. Yet in most, inmates and loved ones are charged excessive fees that are controlled and run by wealthy outside companies, making it extremely difficult for loved ones and friends to connect, leaving inmates lost and forgotten. Can you think of ways the U.S. could improve the mental and physical health of the incarcerated?

11. Women are rarely sentenced to death. Do gender stereotypes work against or in favor of women in the justice system? Does that influence differ depending on the crime? Has that changed as women have gained more autonomy?

12. Think about rural versus urban living and Cussy's shock when she sees so much waste, spending, and frivolity in the city but also how much more opportunity the city offers. What are the advantages and disadvantages of living in a rural location or in a city? Do you see bigger wastes and frivolity of lifestyles in either one?

13. The majority of those who received forced sterilization under eugenics' laws were women. The eugenics movement and forced abortions existed at the same time that abortions were criminalized. Discuss how people might have accepted these contradictory ideas.

14. Superstitions are often passed down from generation to generation. For example, the phenomenon of angel crowns, or death crowns, introduced in this book is unique to Appalachia, and they often become heirlooms if found. Shotgun houses were known to hold superstitions, which is why some homeowners insisted the entry or back door be built unaligned. In the book, the governor appears as both a God-fearing and superstitious man when confronted by reporters about a second execution for Sassyann. Discuss any superstitions that were passed down to you and whether you adhere to them.

15. Mrs. Claxton risks her life to help Cussy escape. Would you have done the same? Is it right for Cussy to run away, or should she serve out her sentence?

16. The Free Library of Philadelphia uses unique "Book Bikes" pedaled by library staff to provide mobile outreach services. To reach readers, Melanie Moore of Cincy Book Bus Depot refurbished an antique VW book bus she named Tilly. Did you have a bookmobile growing up? What kind of bookmobile would you design today?

Images

First Bookmobile, The Clay County Public Library in Manchester, Kentucky

Old Kentucky Bookmobile

Public Information Collection, Archives and Records Management Division, Kentucky Department for Libraries and Archives

Gov. Combs visiting the Kentucky Correctional Institution for Women Pewee Valley, Kentucky

Dr. Thomas Fountain Blue with his librarians at the first free public library in the nation for African Americans staffed entirely by African Americans. On October 29, 1908, the newly constructed Carnegie Library opened at its current location.

Photos courtesy of Louisville Free Public Library (Louisville, Kentucky), Western Library Archives

Photos courtesy of Louisville Free Public Library (Louisville, Kentucky), Western Library Archives

Children's room in the library

Photos courtesy of Louisville Free Public Library (Louisville, Kentucky), Western Library Archives

Exterior of the Western Colored Branch Library

Morehead State University, Stuart S. Sprague Photo Collection

Moonlight school students

Photo courtesy of Kim Michele Richardson Collection

Illustrations found within children's picture book *Junia, The Book Mule of Troublesome Creek,* written by Kim Michele Richardson and illustrated by David C. Gardner. Painting on loan and display at Frazier Museum, Louisville, Kentucky, beginning summer 2026.

Cab Calloway, American jazz singer and band leader

Van Vechten, Carl. (1933) Portrait of Cab Calloway, January 12, 1933, used with permission of the Van Vechten Trust

Morehead State University, Stuart S. Sprague Photo Collection

Pack Horse librarians begin their daily route.

Historic American Buildings Survey (Library of Congress)

Shotgun houses, Louisville, Kentucky: A typical "shotgun" house, having three rooms back-to-back perpendicular to the street with a fourth over the rear third room, forming a "camelback" configuration. According to legend, it is called a shotgun house because when all doors on the first floor are open, one can shoot a bullet through the house without striking anything.

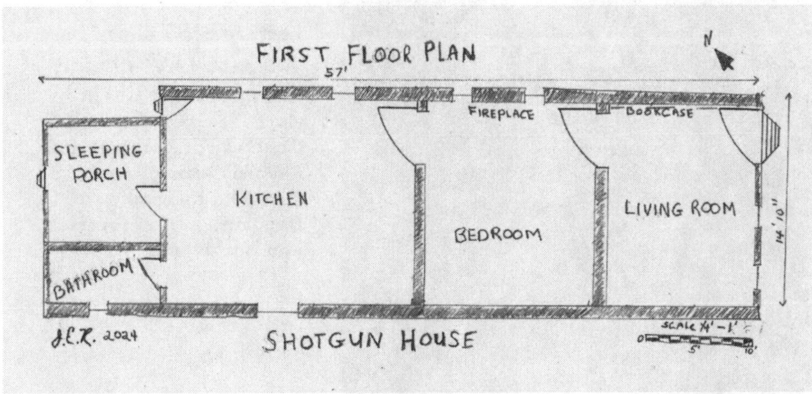

Photo part of the Kim Michele Richardson Collection, Drawing by Joseph Richardson

Floor plan of shotgun homes

Above: West Walnut Street, 1942

Caufield & Shook 1887–88, Archives and Special Collections University of Louisville

Left: Annie Fellows Johnston 1904 with Little Colonel Hattie Cochran

Courtesy of Archives and Records Management Division, Kentucky Department for Libraries and Archives

Used with permission from Melanie Moore

The Book Bus Mobile (named Tilly) is Melanie Moore's creation. Moore is the owner of The Book Bus Depot bookstore located in Cincinnati, Ohio.

Photo courtesy of Tom Bickel—KET/PBS Producer and Director

1930s Original crate of books sent by rail for donation to the Pack Horse library. The crate along with other historical Pack Horse librarian artifacts were acquired by Kim Michele Richardson and will be on loan and on display at the Frazier Museum, Louisville, Kentucky, beginning the summer of 2026.

The Negro Travelers
Green Book
Carry Your Green Book With You You May Need it.
Regular Edition
1952
PRICE
$1.25

Schomburg Center for Research in Black Culture, Manuscripts, Archives and Rare Books Division, The New York Public Library: "The Negro Travelers Green Book: 1952" New York Public Library Digital Collections, accessed June 15, 2024

1952 edition of the Green Book

Angel or Death crowns

Angel or Death Crowns from Mike Shaw, Shaw's Antiques, Hot Springs, Arkansas

Packhorse Library Lists Local Route

Books, Magazines Available To All People In Rowan County

The Packhorse Library has 35 centers scattered over Rowan County. Following is a list of each carriers' centers:

Zelda Fugate—Clearfield, Pettits Store, Dry Creek, Paragon, Lower Lick Fork.

Bessie Cornett — McKenzie, Mt. Hope, Bangor, Charity.

Martha Sparkman—Vale, Elliottville, Minor, and at the four last stores between Elliottville and the Elliot County line.

Lurline Alfrey—Bluestone, Brady, and one on the ridge above Rockville.

Lillian Tolliver — Sharkey, Bull Fork, Blue Banks, and at her home.

Jess Eldridge — Christy, Perkins, and Old Town Creek.

Leslie Hilderbrand—Triplet, Clark, Hardeman, Adams, Elk Lick.

Lee Reed—Clear Fork, Cranston, Pond Lick, and at his home.

Mary Smith — Haldeman, Gates, Glenwood, and the two last stores near the Carter County line.

Pearl DeHart—Her home, Cooper Black's Store, Hilda, Big Brushy.

Clara Cragg—Carey School, Lewis Pond, Farmers, Moore.

Clinton Mann—A new carrier who plans to make several centers in his district.

The Library plans an open house day for May 6, everyone is invited to visit the library this day.

Pack-Horse Library Plans Book Shower

The Packhorse Library is giving a book shower and Ice-Cream Party June 8, at 1:30 p. m. Every one is invited. Refreshments will be serv-

W. P. A.

STATE EXHIBIT

June 10 and 11

at

Pack Horse Library

Opposite Sandy Valley Grocery Co.

Main St. PAINTSVILLE, KY.

Handicrafts, Weaving, Basketry

and Other Salable Articles

Puppet Show - Drum and Bugle

Morehead State University, Stuart S. Sprague Photo Collection

Acknowledgments

I'm indebted to WHAS news anchor Doug Proffitt for his enlightening production of "Louisville's West Walnut Street: A Black History Perspective," which inspired some of the scenes in book two. And love and gratitude to former news anchor and dear friend Rachel Platt for your always-generous support over the years—and for dropping everything to drive a *very* long, six-hour trip to pick up a one-hundred-year-old musty, worm-eaten crate for me.

Once again, thank you to G. J. Berger, a wise critiquer and longtime friend, whom I often turn to for insight. A special thank-you to horror author and friend Alice Loweecey for a generous heart and vast knowledge of everything biblical. I'm truly grateful to Susan Gibson for the exhaustive research of archaic Kentucky laws, thought-provoking discussions, and for lending wise edits for part of the discussion guide.

It's been a privilege to have brilliant editors who will shape your work to make it the best. Endless appreciation to Shana and my TV *Survivor* watch buddy MJ. Huge thanks to copy editor Rachel Norfleet and proofreader Sara Walker for their keen attention to detail and making *The Mountains We Call Home* shine. Mad appreciation to the wonderful Sourcebooks team: Cristina Arreola, Margaret Coffee, Valerie Pierce, Beth Sochacki, Molly Waxman, Patience Bramlett, Diane Cunningham, Jackie Barba, Liv Turner, cover artist Ploy Siripant, and the many,

many folks behind the scenes—all of whom are a power team of fierce bookwomen who have worked tirelessly over the years to champion the Book Woman series. Sourcebooks has been a dedicated and excellent partner for almost nine years, handling me, my works, and the Kentucky people with great sensitivity and respect, and I'm thrilled and deeply grateful to them for this new journey. With their unstinting support, I have been able to continue my community work and contributions to help libraries as well as the people of Kentucky.

I'm deeply honored and eternally grateful to Dolly Parton, who fell in love with *The Book Woman of Troublesome Creek*—for her support and the incredibly jaw-dropping and generous gift she surprised me with. Thank you seems small, but thank you, thank you bunches and buckets, dear Book Lady! *I cannot wait to share it with the world.*

I'm so appreciative to Sydnee Harlan for your dedication and thoughtful help, always. I'm deeply grateful to dear friend and colleague Stacy for your steadfast belief when I vowed to you and Susan Ginsburg thirteen years ago (and now eight books later) *you'll only be getting one book from me.*

Love, love to my dear readers for your always-generous hearts and my heartfelt gratitude to Writers House, Sourcebooks, Barnes & Noble, author and kindred spirit Jeannette Walls, and all the bookwomen and book men who answered my call during the devastating 2022 Kentucky floods, and who donated money and books to help rebuild flooded eastern Kentucky libraries. With your generosity, nearly two hundred thousand books were delivered, and over thirty-three thousand dollars was raised for libraries.

I'm eternally grateful to the book angels who donate books to my Courthouses Reading Across Kentucky & Beyond initiative: Anne Federlein, Melanie Moore, Janlyn Weintraub and her Troublesome Book Women group, and book warrior Leslie Zemeckis, along with the indie booksellers Carmichael's, Poor Richard's Bookstore, and so many others. Sincere gratitude to the judges and clerks across Kentucky and Indiana who have adopted my program to place Little Free Libraries in their counties and have pledged to make books accessible to those individuals and families facing hardships and uncertainties as they pass through scary courthouse doors.

I'm forever beholden to my husband, Joe. *Always my first reader, always my always for everything and all.*

About the Author

A native-born Kentuckian, Kim Michele Richardson is a *New York Times*, *Los Angeles Times*, and *USA Today* bestselling author who has written six novels, including *The Book Woman's Daughter* and *The Mountains We Call Home*, along with a memoir and, most recently, two children's picture books. Her works have been published in more than fifteen languages. Her novel *The Book Woman of Troublesome Creek* is taught widely in high schools and college classrooms and has been adopted as a Common Read selection by states, cities, and colleges across the country and abroad. Kim Michele lives with her family in Kentucky and is the founder of Shy Rabbit, a writers' residency, and a literacy initiative, Courthouses Reading Across Kentucky & Beyond.

THE BOOK WOMAN OF TROUBLESOME CREEK

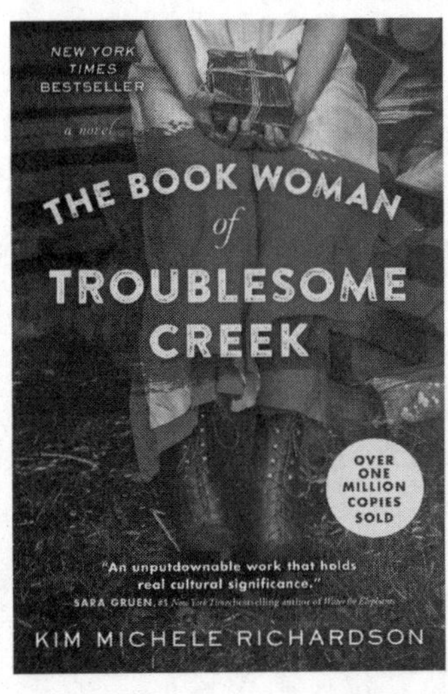

The folks of Troublesome Creek have to scrap for everything—everything except books, that is. Thanks to Roosevelt's Kentucky Pack Horse Library Project, Troublesome's got its very own traveling librarian, Cussy Mary Carter.

Cussy's not only a book woman, however; she's also the last of her kind, her skin a shade of blue unlike that of most anyone else. Not everyone is keen on Cussy's family or the government's new book program, and along her treacherous route, Cussy faces doubters at every turn. If Cussy wants to bring the joy of books to the complex and hardscrabble Kentuckians, she's going to have to confront dangers and prejudice as old as the Appalachias, and suspicion as deep as the holler.

Inspired by the true blue-skinned people of Kentucky and the brave and dedicated Kentucky Pack Horse library service of the 1930s, *The Book Woman of Troublesome Creek* is a story of raw courage, fierce strength, and one woman's belief that books can carry us anywhere—even back home.

"A lush love letter to the redemptive power of books."

—Joshilyn Jackson, *New York Times* and *USA Today* bestselling author of *The Almost Sisters*

For more Kim Michele Richardson, visit sourcebooks.com.

THE BOOK WOMAN'S DAUGHTER

In the ruggedness of the beautiful Kentucky mountains, Honey Lovett has always known that the old ways can make a hard life harder. As the daughter of the famed blue-skinned Troublesome Creek Pack Horse librarian, Honey and her family have been hiding from the law all her life. But when her mother and father are imprisoned, Honey realizes she must fight to stay free or risk being sent away for good.

Picking up her mother's old Pack Horse library route, Honey begins to deliver books to the remote hollers of Appalachia. Honey is looking to prove that she doesn't need anyone telling her how to survive. But the route can be treacherous, and some folks aren't as keen to let a woman pave her own way.

If Honey wants to bring the freedom books provide to the families who need it most, she's going to have to fight for her place and, along the way, learn that the extraordinary women who run the hills and hollers can make all the difference in the world.

"A brilliant and compelling narrative—a powerful portrait of the courageous women who fought against ignorance, misogyny, and racial prejudice."

—William Kent Krueger, *New York Times* bestselling author of *This Tender Land* and *Ordinary Grace*

For more Kim Michele Richardson, visit sourcebooks.com.